EDGAR ALLAN POE
and the Empire of the Dead

Also by Karen Lee Street

Edgar Allan Poe and the London Monster

Edgar Allan Poe and the Jewel of Peru

EDGAR ALLAN POE

and the
Empire of the Dead

———

Karen Lee Street

PEGASUS CRIME

NEW YORK LONDON

Edgar Allan Poe and the Empire of the Dead

Pegasus Books, Ltd.
West 37th Street, 13th Floor
New York, NY 10018

ISBN: 978-1-64313-422-2

10 9 8 7 6 5 4 3 2 1

Printed in the United States of America
Distributed by Simon & Schuster

Para Santiago
Te extraño

Ye who read are still among the living, but I who write shall
have long since gone my way into the region of shadows.
For indeed strange things shall happen, and many secret things
be known, and many centuries shall pass away, ere these
memorials be seen of men. And, when seen, there will be
some to disbelieve, and some to doubt, and yet a few who will
find much to ponder upon in the characters here graven with
a stylus of iron.
(Edgar Allan Poe, "Shadow: A Parable")

Books always speak of other books.

(Umberto Eco, *Postscript to The Name of the Rose*)

WEDNESDAY, 3 OCTOBER 1849

It began with a cat. I was walking along the High Street in Baltimore and a brisk wind stirred up the street's detritus, which whirled around my ankles, sent grit into my eyes. Despite the leaden sky, the foliage gleamed with unnatural color, and beams of light jumped from one pane of window glass to another until the street echoed with their harsh brightness.

As I wandered, the glare made my head ache and my legs were unsteady. My throat felt strangely tight and I tugged at my neckcloth, tipped down the brim of my hat to shade my eyes. First, I heard her, a mewling call, then she appeared from nowhere and crossed in front of me so that I almost stumbled. She was a tortoiseshell, a common enough breed, but there was something in the shape of her, in that gentle but insistent cry, that recalled my own cat, who was hundreds of miles away, safely at home in New York. I watched as the tortoiseshell trotted daintily along the footpath, then paused to look back over her shoulder, entreating me to trail after her. This continued for a time, the little cat weaving along, disappearing into shadow and coming forth again. I simply followed. Reason told me it could not be our Catterina, but the more I studied the creature, the more I felt in my heart that it could not be any other.

And then she was gone. I surveyed the street intently, searching for her, and my gaze was captured by a woman approaching
from a side street. Catterina was prancing along next to her.
Immediately my head began to pound. I squeezed my eyes shut
and opened them again—she was still in plain view. When I
tried to run to her my legs buckled.

"Virginia!" I called out, but the silence remained undisturbed.
"Sissy, my darling," I tried again, and my voice was turned to
dust, by joy mixed with fear and disbelief. Even so, my wife—
my darling Sissy—looked up from Catterina, where her attention had been fixed, and gazed directly into my eyes. Rather
than run to me and enfold me in her embrace, she turned away
and commenced walking, with Catterina at her heels. A wave
of biliousness roared over me and the sunlight blazed in my
eyes. When the glare finally diminished, she had vanished.

I dashed to the end of the road, thinking she could not have
gone far. The street was curiously empty and I was distracted
by the glint of golden letters painted across a window:
Apothecary. Displayed in the window were two sizable carboys,
one filled with a violet-colored liquid, the other with a citrine
fluid. The dimly lit shop was fitted out with elegant wooden
counters and cabinets upon the walls, each drawer neatly
labeled in Latin: *Artemisia absinthium, Chininum hydrobromicum,
Oxymel scillae, Oleum pini pumilionis, Opio en polvo, Calomel,
Syrupus sennae, Papaver* and *Tolu*. A cabinet of gruesome curiosi-
ties was on display, with large glass jars holding malformed
creatures preserved in brine and oddities of nature, all presided
over by a small stuffed crocodile with razor teeth. It was a
strange place, yet oddly familiar. My skin prickled.

The apothecary, a man with thin gray hair and pale blue eyes,
was busy at his counter, decanting medicines into vials and
packets. A woman came into view and I pressed my face closer
to the glass, for it was Sissy. She stood there quietly, watching

the apothecary work, yet he did not seem to notice her presence at all. His concentration was focused on a sheet of paper that he consulted as he prepared his concoctions. I observed his eyes narrow as he reread the script, brows knitted, then he turned and selected the apothecary jar labeled *Atropa belladonna.*

The apothecary mixed a tincture from the belladonna and as I watched I was certain that I had seen him do this very thing before—had it been in a dream or was I within one now? He poured the medicine—the *poison*—into a small, cobalt blue bottle and slid it across the counter.

At that moment, I was overcome once more with nausea and my breath fogged the window. When the discomfort subsided, I rubbed at the glass with my coat sleeve and peered through, only to meet the frightened gaze of a young woman stationed behind the counter of quite a different shop. I stepped back, bewildered—I was on Lombard Street, somewhere else entirely, very near the tavern I had been in earlier, a suffocating place so fraught with menace I had escaped to the street.

Filled with confusion, I struggled to breathe as the air became warmer and thicker, as the light sizzled and shadows darted all around me, until I crouched down to alleviate the dizziness. There was a nudge against my leg and Catterina tiptoed about my feet and sat down, her green eyes fixed on mine as if she were a mesmerist. As my vision began to ebb away, I realized where I had seen the apothecary shop before and when I had witnessed the very same scenario that had just played before me. And I prayed that I would find a way to tell my most honorable friend, the Chevalier C. Auguste Dupin, the truth about how I had finally been murdered and by whom.

SUNDAY, 17 JUNE 1849

The dénouement has been decided and cannot, I think, be undone. Let me start at the beginning, or what I know of it, and give all the facts regarding my delivery to this grim place.

It was June of 1849—the seventeenth, I believe. I had spent the morning writing, or trying to, but the weight of the silence stilled my pen and, finally, the prison of my chair become intolerable. I unfurled a gently purring Catterina from about my neck, left her curled up on the table and escaped my study for the sanctuary of the garden.

The cherry and apple blossoms had flurried down weeks previously and there were nubs of fruit on the boughs as spring ambled into summer. The foliage was still a tender green and rain in the night had scented the air with the richness of loam. I examined the wildflower garden I had planted in the shade under my wife Virginia's guidance; the violets which formed a border were in bloom, peeping out from heart-shaped leaves, their cheerful faces deep purple, lavender and white with blue embellishments. Stern jack-in-the-pulpits, some fully green and others striped deep purple and emerald, watched over a bevy of gossiping lady's-slipper orchids. Sissy had marveled over those peculiar deep pink blooms. In the sunny patch away from the fruit trees, the earth was covered with a crazy quilt of flowers, all sent as a gift by Mrs. Carr of Bartram's Gardens in Philadelphia. She and Sissy had become fast friends just prior to our move from the Quaker city to New York in April of 1844. It was two years before we found our perfect home in the village of Fordham, fourteen miles from the city, and Sissy immediately wrote to Mrs. Carr, describing the little cottage set on two acres of land that we rented from Mr. John Valentine, whose name my wife found perfectly delightful. We moved into the cottage in May 1846, and two weeks later a crate from Bartram's Gardens was delivered by coach. The cleverly constructed transport box was filled to the brim with bulbs, seeds and potted plants. Included were detailed instructions of how to plant and care for each specimen.

"You will soon have a hummingbird and butterfly garden," Mrs. Carr had written, "for these plants attract both."

My wife was thrilled with this notion, and Mrs. Carr's promise was quickly fulfilled. The young plants took to the good earth, and later that year produced drifts of ebullient color that had butterflies gliding around them like sailing ships encircling tropical islands. My wife was most pleased by the arrival of what appeared at first glance to be an enormous insect.

"What a comely gentleman he is, with his emerald cap and coat and ruby-colored neckcloth," she said fondly.

The hummingbird visited the garden most days and did not seem to mind our presence as he darted from flower to flower, watched suspiciously by Catterina, who seemed to fear him—perhaps with good reason, as he was a pugnacious little creature. To my surprise, my wife would not name the bird; she said to do so would tether him, and his true beauty was to dart and wheel and dip amongst the blossoms before disappearing into the wind itself. But when she spoke to the creature, thinking herself alone in the garden sun, she conversed with her "little

Seraph" and the dazzling creature would hover, listening, then flit back to the blossoms as if depositing her secrets there.

When the weather turned in mid-September, bringing a sharpness to the morning air, my wife waited patiently on the front porch for the hummingbird's morning tour, but he did not appear. Sissy refused to leave her station until the sun dropped to the western horizon and the sky was stained to match the fading blooms that shivered near the porch.

"He's flown south," I told her, "to winter in Mexico. Wouldn't that be glorious? To migrate with the hummingbirds and return to our garden for spring?"

But Sissy would not turn her mind to my fanciful notion. "I hope he is safe. I could not bear it if something happened to him."

"He is sipping exotic nectar, I am sure of it. Be pleased for the little fellow. He was clever to escape before the first frost."

"You're right, my dear. He is obeying the law of Nature." She was silent for a moment, her face pensive, then she murmured, "It is selfish, I know, but I had hoped to see him again. Summer left us sooner than I thought it might."

"You'll have to wait until spring, I fear, but I promise he will return, for undoubtedly he has made our garden his summer home."

Taking pity on me, she mustered a smile and joined my wishful reverie. "I'll be glad to see him when he does, for truly you have made a garden that is perfect for hummingbirds and for us." She clasped my hand in hers and we said nothing more as twilight gathered in around us.

On the day in question, the seventeenth of June, I worked in the garden for an hour before lunch. Three years had passed since I'd first planted it and the borders were thriving. Dahlias, mignonette and heliotrope had joined the showy parade assembled by Mrs. Carr. Each morning I would drag my fingers through dirt, assisting the industrious earthworms; I pulled out weeds and doused the thirsty greenery with rainwater from the barrel. The air was scented with jasmine and sweet honeysuckle; our hummingbird had returned again and he was not alone this year. A female had arrived in our garden soon after he did and crouched in the cup of a nest attached to a dogwood tree branch, warming a pair of tiny eggs. He was a neglectful husband, though, and sped from flower to flower, greedy to partake of them all, but he brought no nectar back for his mate to sip, nor did he take his turn upon the nest, an intricate assembly of twigs, leaves, lichen, bound up with spider webs. She sat there alone, a fierce little warrior of the air.

When Muddy, my mother-in-law, opened the door and announced that she'd baked a fresh loaf that was ready for eating, I made my way inside, quickly washed up and sat down at the kitchen table. The scent of bread was thick in the air and hunger seized my belly. Muddy poured coffee for the two of us and set down a plate with two thick slices spread with melting butter. We wolfed down the warm bread, swigged coffee and did not speak a word to each other.

"That was delicious," I finally said.

The hard angles of Muddy's honest face were eased by a smile.

"The garden is coming along well," I continued. "And the hummingbirds—there are two eggs in the nest. I'm looking forward to the little ones. I don't believe I've ever seen a bird as small as they will be." I sipped some coffee, waiting for a response, but none was offered. "Have you?" I prodded.

Muddy thought for a moment. "No, I don't believe I have."

"Well, it should be quite something to have a family of hummingbirds living in our garden. It will be enjoyable to watch them."

Muddy gave a nod of her head, then briskly reached for my plate. Her large, capable hands seemed to scoop up all the dishes at once and deliver them to the sink, then she refilled my coffee cup. "I thought we would finish yesterday's stew for supper." She looked to me for an opinion.

"Perfect," I murmured.

Muddy turned away and began to wash the dishes. If Sissy had been at the table with us, we would have talked about the excitement of the hummingbirds, how beautiful the garden looked, and all the other blooms we might grow in our little sanctuary. But Muddy would not be engaged in fanciful talk of the garden, and I had tired of trying to find some nicety to offer up, so the silence gathered until the air grew thick with our loneliness.

I returned to my study that afternoon, but did not manage to write anything I much cared for. After supper I went upstairs to read, but I lost my place several times when my eyes slipped closed and the pages of my book whirred shut. Catterina leapt onto the bed, caught my sleepy gaze with her peridot eyes, then gracefully curled into herself. Hypnos had defeated me so I set the book aside and blew out the candle.

Later—how much later I do not know—I came awake. It was utterly quiet and I could not think what had caused me to leave my dreams, but as I stared at the surrounding shadow, there was a quivering over my skin. Then a glimmer of moonlight seeped through the curtains, and I saw that Catterina was sitting up, the triangles of her ears alert. She did not move and nor did I. Moments later, there was a stutter in the darkness, like the faintest ripple in very deep, very still water when something lurks beneath the surface. Then there was a smudge of soft white in the black and it grew and spread as if someone were drawing onto night itself with an unearthly phosphorescence.

My unease grew, but I was unable to avert my gaze as a shape slowly formed, *her* shape. And there, moments or perhaps hours later, seated in the chair by the window, hands folded in her lap, her face turned toward mine, was my wife. I whispered her name, then said it louder still, but she did not reply and I did not know what I should do.

Death is never simple. It may be sudden and a shock or so protracted it comes as a relief. Many fear it, others fight it, some welcome it. The mourner weeps over what might have been—a future thwarted, a promise lost, the legacy of a family curtailed. I had dreamt so many times that Sissy had come home again, that a diabolical error had been reversed and she was revived. I had dreamt that our life together would resume, even more perfectly, for she was alive and fully well again.

How cruel it was to awaken afterwards.

So I sat in my bed and simply gazed at my darling wife while she smiled gently back at me. I thought I heard her say my name once, but the birds called up the dawn and Catterina and I watched as she dissolved, silently, into the pink morning light.

3

MONDAY, 18 JUNE 1849

My morning began like any other but something had changed. There was a peculiar hum in the air and invisible sparks seemed to dance around me. Catterina followed me from room to room, her tail held high in the air, her eyes constantly seeking mine. When we adjourned to the porch, the colors outside seemed more vivid, the garden's perfume intoxicating. I wondered if the veil between this world and the next had torn when Sissy came back to us in the night and whether she was watching us as she had promised she would. When Muddy appeared on the path home, clutching a basket of pigweed, garlic mustard and spring onions, she was startled that I hurried to meet her, Catterina at my heels.

"Here, let me help." I pulled the basket from her arm and fell into step beside her. "How did you sleep last night?"

"Very well, thank you." Muddy looked at me warily, perhaps anticipating complaints that insomnia had returned to trouble me and that I might resort to various calmatives to quiet my restless mind.

"Did you see anything? Or feel a . . . *presence?*"

Muddy frowned and shook her head, her discomfort growing.

"Sissy came. We saw her." I nodded to Catterina. "Just before dawn. She sat in her chair near the window. It was almost as if she never left us." The details of the scene flooded my mind. "She did not speak," I added. "But she smiled."

"You poor boy."

My fearful joy dissipated when I saw the pity on my mother-in-law's face, and I was left feeling wounded.

"I was happy to see her. *We* were happy to see her, to know she is all right. It was not a dream," I insisted. "And I had nothing to drink if that is what you are thinking. I have made a pledge, and I will keep it."

"I know you will." Muddy patted my arm, but her attempt to soothe me had the opposite effect, and I was thoroughly disgruntled by her lack of faith. We had both suffered enormously during Sissy's final decline, but I had done my best not to add to my mother-in-law's hurt, and when I could not help myself, endeavored to make amends. When one loves acutely, the pain of loss is correspondingly acute. At my lowest, it seems that love is not worth the agony, then later I feel nothing but shame at my morose thoughts, for it is necessary to swim on through the murkiest waters, knowing that pain will slowly ebb away.

I decided a tramp through the countryside would be a good tonic and fetched a letter I had written to Annie Richmond—I would take it to the post office in West-Farms, which was a few miles away. Annie had proved to be a sympathetic friend in the time since my wife's passing, and I was grateful, but had been a poor correspondent.

As I struck out for West-Farms, Catterina followed me down the front path and onto Kingsbridge Road, which was odd in itself as normally she was content to loll on the porch or curl up on my chair when I went for a ramble. As I walked down the road, she paced back and forth on the verge, her tail twitching in agitation. When last I looked back, she had settled on her haunches like a sentry guarding the boundaries of our little homestead, the early morning sun seeping through the trees. I paused to admire our cottage of Dutch shingles; it was rustic and plain and very beautiful—a place of incomparable joy and sadness.

I walked for a short time along Kingsbridge Road, then left the track to vagabond through the woods and fully immerse myself in the natural world, in part to enjoy its wonders, but mostly to see if the feeling that Sissy had returned to me would persist, or if Nature would chase away the specters of my dreams. As soon as I entered the woodland, the rules of our world fell away like a discarded cloak. A deep silence enveloped me; then there was birdsong and the rustling of the invisible. A tangle of scent rose up around me: chocolatey loam, sweet rainwater, blossoms and new leaves, distant pine. Brightness glistened on the green, dripped onto the forest floor like morning dew, and I knew absolutely that my wife *was* with me, could almost feel her hand slip into mine.

I followed a natural path that meandered through the undulating terrain, perhaps the secret avenue of the deer and wild turkey that roamed by day or the foxes and raccoons by night. The leafy canopy of chestnut, hickory and black walnut intermingled with oaks, and sassafras trees swayed and chattered. Perfume spilled from the last of the yellow-green tulip tree blossoms. As I walked, squirrels tracked my movements, scurrying up and down tree trunks or leaping above me from bough to bough. A blood-red cardinal soared overhead and joined its mate. When I passed a glade filled with grass as lush as Genoese velvet and speckled with wildflowers, a doe turned her eyes to mine as if to greet me, then resumed her grazing. That moment alone made me fully certain that Virginia was with me, her gentle spirit soothing the shy creatures that lived amongst the trees—and, so too, my own anxious spirit was calmed.

When I emerged from the forest into the pleasant little town of West-Farms, I was momentarily disconcerted by the bustling activity. Two farm wagons rattled past me and an old man smoking a meerschaum on his front porch wished me a good morning, as did a harried young woman trying to herd a gaggle of boisterous young children somewhere they did not wish to go. A dog sleeping in a puddle of sunlight gave one lazy bark, then immediately fell back to sleep, and a blackbird hidden in a tree overlooking the carriage track filled the air with a glorious melody. When I opened the door to the post office, which was also a general store, its bells jangled.

"'Tis some visitor tapping at my chamber door. Only this and nothing more," intoned a deep voice. Moments later, a smiling fellow with black curling hair, luxurious mustachios and a well-cultivated belly emerged from a back room to take up his station at the large polished wooden counter that smelled of lemon oil. "Always a pleasure to see you, Mr. Poe."

The postmaster enjoyed quoting lines from my own verse to me, a habit I found irksome, but as he had taken the trouble to commit the poem to memory and ever commented on how it enchanted him, it would have been churlish to diminish his pleasure.

"How are you, Mr. Quinn? It's a fine morning for a ramble."

"You say that every time I see you, my friend, but you will never persuade me. After my day is done, I enjoy putting my feet up after a nice dinner." He cheerfully patted his belly with both hands. Mr. Quinn then reached under the counter and brought out a basket full of neatly organized post. "Must be an important letter," he said as he deftly sifted through the folded pages. "I only just wrote up the list of names with post to collect."

"In fact, I came to send this." I slid the envelope over the counter to him.

But Mr. Quinn was focused on a letter he had retrieved from the basket, carefully examining the front of it. "Well, you've saved us both some effort, then. This was brought up from the city yesterday. Posted less than two weeks ago. Doesn't seem that long since the days we'd be waiting more than a month— sometimes two—for news from the family back home," he reminisced. "And much could change in life while waiting for a letter to cross the Atlantic," he added sagely. He stared at the missive in his hand a moment longer, then, seemingly satisfied that it was for me, handed it over.

My name and address were inscribed on the front in small precise letters without an ounce of showy flair or embellishments. It was handwriting that I immediately recognized.

"Steamships will change the world, mark my words," Mr. Quinn observed.

"Indeed," I murmured to be polite, but in truth I had stopped absorbing the postmaster's chitchat. Unable to contain myself, I broke the seal and opened the letter.

No. 33 rue Dunôt,

Faubourg St-Germain, Paris

1 June 1849

Dear Poe,

I was pleased to receive your letter dated the nineteenth of April and am glad a lift in the weather has eased your melancholy and contributed to an improvement in your health. After making the acquaintance of your wife in Philadelphia, it is not difficult to imagine your continued grief in losing her and its ill effects upon you. As your true friend, might I respectfully suggest that a change of environment might prove a mild tonic?

Enclosed you will find a ticket to sail on the twenty-seventh of June, from Philadelphia to Le Havre. I have made some discoveries that I believe will enable me to receive justice for all I have endured. With your assistance, I will at last prevail against my nemesis.

May I also suggest that you bring the letters. You know the ones of which I speak—your legacy. I have information regarding the whereabouts of the man who wishes you ill and believe the letters will prove useful.

I hope you will journey to Paris and assist me in my mission. Of course, I insist on taking care of all your expenses during your journeys and your stay here.

Your obedient servant,

C. Auguste Dupin

Dupin's message left my mind a-swarm with questions. Had my friend at last located his enemy Ernest Valdemar? Or had he merely an idea of his location and some kind of plan to draw him out? And what would happen when he finally cornered the man who had destroyed his family? I knew from experience that Dupin would not hesitate to murder the villain—I could not envisage him taking any other action as he would fear that Valdemar would find a way to escape prison. While I did not fully support my friend's desire to end the life of his foe, it was not difficult to understand why he so despised him, for Valdemar had sent Dupin's paternal grandparents to the guillotine, had murdered his mother and provoked the death of his father. He had appropriated their money and valuable accouterments, then had taunted Dupin by selling those prized family heirlooms at auctions. Given Dupin's renown in Paris for solving the most complex mysteries, it was all the more humiliating that the infamous Valdemar had eluded him for so many years. I had no doubt that Dupin would eventually find a way to destroy his nemesis, but I was not certain he would have the good sense to make it appear an accident.

"Not bad news, I hope."

Mr. Quinn's voice made me jump and his look of genuine concern increased.

"I'm sorry. The letter is just . . . unexpected. I may need to make a journey to visit a friend," I added.

"In Paris?" Enthusiasm replaced the look of worry on his face.

I was startled by the postmaster's mind-reading capabilities until I realized he had seen the stamp of origin on the envelope.

"Indeed."

"My wife has long dreamt of going there. She speaks the language, you see, and is very taken with *The Mysteries of Paris*. I think she has read the confounded thing several times now." He shook his head. "All those miscreants and murderers—she revels in their awful deeds." He shivered dramatically. "I like a cheerful romance when reading for pleasure, and one with fewer pages than that never-ending tome."

I smiled at the thought of the postmaster's equally plump and very pretty wife devouring Eugène Sue's novels. She seemed such a light-hearted, frivolous creature with her enormous blue eyes brimming perpetual innocence and her pastel dresses over-decorated with bows and lace.

"I have not been to Paris in many years, indeed not since I first met my friend there. It may very well do me good to visit him—and Paris—again," I said. But in truth I was remembering the words Dupin had so often said to me: *Amicis semper fidelis*— "Always faithful to friends"—and he had ever been true to his word when I most needed him. With that recollection, I made up my mind. The Chevalier C. Auguste Dupin had asked for my help and of course I would go to Paris to do what I could to assist him.

That evening Muddy served up chicken with cooked greens, spring onions and bread, and I revealed my news.

"I'll be leaving for Philadelphia this Wednesday and then will make my way to Paris. Monsieur Dupin has sent me a ticket. He needs my assistance in a matter."

"Helena has not gone missing again, has she?" Muddy asked anxiously.

Five years previously Dupin stayed with us in Philadelphia and helped to rescue an abducted heiress from London, Miss Helena Loddiges. I had edited an ornithology book for the eccentric Miss Loddiges, who was also an expert taxidermist, and Sissy and she had become good friends. My mother-in-law was also fond of the lady, but was far less sure what to make of Dupin. Sissy grew to like him by the end of his visit and the feeling was reciprocated, though few would easily perceive that Dupin considered my wife a friend. And perhaps truly he did not, perhaps his only friend was me, but there was no doubt that if Sissy had been in any danger, Dupin would have sacrificed his own life to save hers. Unfortunately, he could not vanquish Death himself and nor could I.

"I'm quite sure Miss Loddiges is safe," I told Muddy. "This concerns a Dupin family matter and I must assist, given all that he has done for me."

"Well, he would not ask for help if he was not in dire need of it," Muddy observed. "Virginia would certainly want you to go."

Her words took me by surprise. "Quite right. Virginia would insist."

We were both silent for a moment, imagining that scenario, which I knew to be true once I had voiced it.

"I don't know how long I will be in Paris, but I'll let Mr. Valentine know I'll be gone for a while and will ask him to stop by as often as he can. Mr. Quinn over in West-Farms knows my plans and will have my letters brought over, for I will write to you regularly."

"So long as I know you're safe and when you will be home again, Eddy. I will worry until I hear from you."

"Please don't. I will be home as soon as I can and I promise I will write."

Muddy nodded solemnly, taking my vow to heart.

I tried to read for a while in the parlor but could not concentrate, so I made my way upstairs, Catterina following. I went over Dupin's letter. There was no question but that I should assist him in his efforts to avenge his family. I was uncertain, however, about his suggestion that I attempt to locate the man who wished me ill. George Reynolds had caused me much grief, yet had vanished from my life since our move to New York. But to ignore Dupin's suggestion to bring the letters would be to ignore an *instruction*. I knew my friend well enough to understand that.

I knelt down and levered up the planks in the floor that kept my legacy safe. There was the mahogany box that held my worst secrets—a Pandora's box, but without hope hidden within its depths. Reynolds had sent it to me, claiming it was my inheritance, and the letters inside it suggested that my maternal grandparents had been notorious criminals acting as the "London Monster", who half a century ago had assaulted more than fifty young women in the city of London, slashing their dresses with a blade. Worse still, an innocent man had been imprisoned for their misdeeds and that man was Reynolds's own father. I had traveled to London nine years previously in hopes of proving the letters false with Dupin's assistance. Our investigation achieved exactly the opposite.

I opened the mahogany box and took out the bundle of letters tied up with an antique green ribbon and the violet eye brooch that had saved me from death. Reynolds had lost the love token—a painted miniature of his wife's eye—and in reaching to pick it up I narrowly escaped being murdered by him. I felt terrible sorrow as I gazed into it, for Rowena Reynolds had fallen to her death like a broken-winged angel and I had failed to prevent her murder. George Reynolds blamed me for that too.

Catterina padded into the room and sniffed at the gap in the floor, contemplating whether to creep inside. I forestalled her whim by replacing the planks, then dropped the letters and brooch back into the mahogany box, locked it and put it on the dresser, determined to hide it in the bottom of my trunk when morning came.

The house was silent but for the usual night rustlings indoors and out, and yet I could not fall asleep. Catterina remained awake also, head resting on her paws, eyes fixed straight ahead. Moonlight pushed through the curtains, leaving mysterious trails of silver, and the warm night was disrupted by a blanket of cold air that fell down around me. There was the same rippling in the shadows, and a smudge of chalk appeared that grew and spread until I saw that Sissy was before me, standing at the end of my bed, looking down upon me and Catterina, who stared back at my glimmering wife and was as immobile as a statue.

"Sissy," I whispered. "Sissy, my dear."

As I said her name, the atmosphere grew even more chill and a stream of air flowed from the window and around the room. The papers on my night table rose up like a swarm of eerie butterflies, then flurried down, and as they did my wife, my darling, melted into the night.

Catterina slipped off the bed and disappeared through the gap in the door to search the house for her mistress, and I wanted to follow, but a strange fear held me back—the joy I had felt in Sissy's first appearance was somehow tainted. I lay there, hoping sleep would find me, but the darkness was so heavy I struggled with the weight of it, shifting this way and that, every muscle aching, my skin tormented by the touch of the bedclothes, the hours until morning stretching endlessly before me. Then sunlight washed into the room, and I opened my eyes to find Catterina back in her spot at the end of the bed. My papers were scattered wildly about the room and my letter from Dupin was torn into four neat pieces and deposited on my bedside table.

4

PHILADELPHIA TO LE HAVRE,
27 JUNE TO 8 JULY 1849

The signs were not auspicious the day I sailed from Philadelphia. Those versed in the language of the stars would surely have spoken of their ill aspects and advised against crossing the sea while Saturn's gaze afflicted the moon. Gulls shrieked overhead like demons and the mood of the passengers was fraught as we stood in a pelting rain, waiting to embark. If Dupin had not asked for my assistance and if he had not sent me the ticket for my passage—a drain on his ever-scarce resources—I would have abandoned the journey.

When I at last stepped onto the *Independence,* there was no one to wave me farewell, so I made my way to my stateroom feeling shaken. I dreaded the thought of almost two weeks at sea, even if I had endured considerably longer journeys in the past, and that foreboding only increased once we were out in the Atlantic, surrounded by gray seawater, the constant rise and fall of the waves threatening to drown me in melancholy. I stayed hidden away in my room, taking my meals in private and reading to pass the time. Dreams I refused to remember visited me each night, and I was certain on one occasion I heard my wife calling out: "Go home, Eddy, go home." But I stuck to my pledge of abstinence and did not partake of a drop of solace, knowing that it would only make the horror worse. When I awoke from my tortured sleep unable to breathe, panic coursing through my veins, I opened another book or put pen to paper, determined not to let fear conquer me.

When I did venture out onto the deck, I could not shake the feeling that someone was following me. The other passengers were rather odd, which did not inspire a sense that all was well. There was a woman dressed all in black, swathed in a heavy veil of the same shade. Mourning gloves covered her ungainly hands and the quantity of memento mori adornments she wore gave her the appearance of Death's morbid sister. I felt sympathy for her great loss, but the polite greetings I offered were always met with stony silence. At first her apparent rudeness unsettled me, but eventually I gathered that she was traveling alone and presumed she was guarding her reputation; thereafter, I simply nodded or tipped my hat and avoided the dour widow, as I had labeled her in my own mind.

Two completely different characters—convivial and rather noisy—were also sailing on the *Independence*. The younger, who was in his fourth decade, was from the upper classes in Germany, or so I guessed from his accent and expensive, showy attire. He was tall, slender, with chestnut hair and a small mustache, both of which had a fiery red gleam in the sunlight. His companion was a brawny Englishman of perhaps fifty years of age who seemed to be in his employ, but also a true friend. His head was bald as an egg but for a mousy fringe of hair and his face was ruddy as were his whiskers. There was something familiar about the two fellows and I wondered if I had met them previously, but they seemed not to know me so I concluded they were merely of a type I had been acquainted with during my army days, due to their irritating habit of practicing various martial arts on deck: fencing, shooting at invisible things in the sea and wrestling with a ferocity that entertained the ship's crew but must have frightened the ladies on board. Their antics became tiresome very quickly, adding to my desire to hide myself away.

The voyage seemed interminable, but I gave earnest thanks to God and the inventor of the steamship that the trip did not take twice as long. As we neared Le Havre, it was that magical hour when the sky is cerulean, just before it lapses into black. I stood on deck, scanning the crowd for Dupin. Five years had passed since he had stayed with us in Philadelphia, and while we had exchanged numerous letters, I was anxious to enjoy his company again, for his discourse was always surprising and one never knew what adventure might take place if joining C. Auguste Dupin on a walk through the city at night.

By the time we docked, I still had not spotted my friend and disembarked to wait for him. A porter delivered my trunk to me and I settled down on it, watching the throng of people milling about the docks as I reaccustomed my ear to the French language. Eventually the crowd thinned to what appeared to be locals who made their living at the busy port.

"It appears you've been forgotten, sir."

The voice was male and cultured, the words in English. I leapt to my feet and turned to face the speaker. It was the German nobleman and his companion, which left me feeling uneasy given their boorish behavior and love of a fight.

"Not at all. My friend is merely delayed," I said.

The German raised his eyebrows, unconvinced. "We were on the *Independence* with you, but did not have the pleasure of making your acquaintance," he said. "I am Rodolph Durand and this is Walter Murphy. We hail from the grand duchy of Gerolstein, but have been on an adventure in the Americas. At your service." He bowed elegantly, despite his overly casual introduction, and his valet, or whatever he was, did the same. "We are traveling to Paris by coach and would be pleased to assist if that is your destination also."

"Thank you most kindly, but I am certain my friend will be here shortly."

The German leaned in closer and said in a low voice. "It would not be wise to tarry here, sir. Several eyes are upon you, and if we leave you alone it will not matter if your friend arrives to collect you a mere ten minutes from now, for you will be gutted like a fish by the man who has you in his sights." He nodded, his eyes flicking to my right, and I followed his glance. At first, I could discern no one, but then perceived a rough, red-faced man with a brutish brow, dressed all in gray so that he blended in with the gloom that had descended around us. "We have arrived at this port many times and there seems an unspoken agreement between the police and the criminal fraternity that any who tarry here after sundown are fair game for the hunters, if you understand me."

I did, but traveling with the two combative fellows did not seem an entirely safe option either.

"You are right to be wary of Mr. Durand," Murphy said, who must have sensed my trepidation, "for he is indeed more trouble than he is worth at times, but I can assure you that his advice is good and the offer well meant. Besides, there was ample opportunity to murder you on the journey over if that were our aim," he added with a smile.

I furtively examined the area again and espied more than one brute lingering. Mr. Durand's invitation suddenly seemed very attractive.

"Thank you, sirs," I said. "I appreciate your kind offer. I am Edgar Poe and am indeed traveling to Paris."

"Very good, Mr. Poe," Durand said, extending his hand and shaking mine so firmly my entire body rattled. "We are at your service. Where does your friend reside?"

"Rue Dunôt, in Faubourg Saint-Germain," I said.

"We shall get you there alive. Have no fear."

"Rue Dunôt, did you say?" Murphy frowned.

"Yes. I'm visiting the Chevalier Dupin. Perhaps you've heard of him?" I asked, not a little proud of the reputation my friend enjoyed in Paris.

Durand shrugged slightly, but Murphy nodded.

"We have not met him," he said. "Not yet. I believe he is admired as a . . . ratiocinator?" He said the word hesitantly, as if it were unfamiliar to him.

"That is correct. The Chevalier Dupin is accomplished in the art of ratiocination—his skills of deductive reasoning are unparalleled and he is able to unravel the most baffling puzzles. The prefect of police regularly calls on his skills," I added.

"You see," Murphy said to his employer. "It is true."

Durand shook his head dismissively. "And so it might be, but we have no need of his services. Not to belittle the abilities of your friend," he said, turning to me. "No doubt his skills of deduction are admirable."

"Indeed they are. I know of no one better equipped to solve a mystery or deduce who is the perpetrator of a crime than the Chevalier Dupin." For some reason, I felt compelled to defend him, which would not have pleased Dupin in the least.

"I will remember your recommendation, sir. Mr. Durand does not always know when he requires assistance," Murphy said tartly, as he heaved up my trunk, despite its considerable weight.

"Nor do you, old man," the German retorted, grabbing the other end of trunk. The two had shifted it over to a handsome carriage before the driver could assist them and stowed my belongings away with their own luggage. Durand opened the carriage door and leapt in. Murphy indicated that I should precede him so I caught my breath and followed, hoping my assessment of their characters was correct. Seconds later, the carriage rattled into the night.

5

Sissy's cough had deepened until it shook her bones and, finally, she remained in bed, overcome by a chill that a layer of blankets topped with my overcoat and Catterina could not diminish. For months, I had done my best to conquer the need to sleep, so fearful was I to wake and find Sissy gone. But after a time, my nerves were utterly frayed. Muddy made up a cot in the room and demanded that I sleep while she kept watch in my stead, knitting to pass the hours. And yet, my wife maintained the demeanor of a saint and grew ever more beautiful—if that were possible—even as her life force faded.

True to her own premonition, Sissy was not with us to greet spring or say hello to our little hummingbird when he returned from residing amidst the rich blooms of Mexico. She left us on January's thirtieth day in that cruel winter of 1847.

"My girl, my dear, sweet girl," Muddy whispered as she stroked her daughter's face. "Farewell. Blessed release at last."

Blessed release? Her words filleted through me. How could my darling's own mother say such a thing? Surely she should feel only pure sorrow and the knife of grief, for I knew that if the positions had been reversed, if I or Muddy had been felled by ill health of any sort, Sissy would have been faithfully at our sides, ready to do anything she could to alleviate our pain, soothe any regrets and ease our journey to whatever awaits us on the other side of the veil. And when we had finally breathed our last, she would have wept with pure sorrow, wishing that she could have done more to hold Death away.

But then I saw the tears tracing the lines of my mother-in-law's face, gleaming on the backs of her hands after she pressed them to her eyes, and I saw her shoulders quivering with the stoical weeping of a mother who, finally, loses her only child. I realized in that moment that my anger at dear Muddy's words sprang from my own remorse—my shame at the rush of relief that had surged through me when Sissy left us. Relief! Instantly, I had suppressed that ignoble emotion and had locked it up inside me, for how could I be so *small* as to feel relief when I had lost the person dearest to me in this world? And I wondered yet again why my darling wife had loved a man as imperfect as me. *Blessed release*—that declaration had, at first, filled me with self-righteous anger, a symptom of my own guilt. But I soon understood the unselfish devotion in my mother-in-law's words and they have sustained me thereafter.

"Mr. Poe, are you with us?"

Someone jostled my shoulder. When I opened my eyes, two strangers were peering down at me. As my disorientation faded away, I remembered Durand and his companion who had, according to them, rescued me from the villains of Le Havre.

"Not much of a conversationalist, is he, Murphy?" Durand said.

"Unless what we took for snoring was some foreign tongue we are not acquainted with," Murphy offered.

"Well, Mr. Poe? Is Murphy correct?"

"I'm terribly sorry," I said, sitting upright, for I had been sprawled in sleep on the carriage seat across from my two companions. "I did not mean to be so impolite."

Durand shooed away my apologies. "Many do not sleep well when traveling by ship, and I was pleased to see that this carriage, which *some* believed cost more than it should,"—he directed a pointed glance at his companion—"made the journey comfortable enough for you to slumber. I therefore conclude that my money was well spent. Thank you, Mr. Poe."

"And I conclude that Mr. Poe's ability to fall unconscious for several hours on the road is little indication of the fairness of the price paid for a carriage. Further, if this is a display of your powers of deduction, sir, then *I* conclude that there is no denying your need of Mr. Poe's friend the ratiocinator."

Durand snorted rudely in response. Moments later, the coach stopped abruptly. "I believe we have arrived, Mr. Poe. Have you been here before?"

"Yes, but close to two decades ago."

I had first made Dupin's acquaintance in 1832, when staying in Paris. We had met at a library on rue Montmartre when looking for the same book and our subsequent conversation revealed that we had the same interests, including a shared passion for enigmas, conundrums and hieroglyphics. Dupin had offered me accommodation at his residence so that I might conserve my rapidly depleting funds and I accepted with gratitude. Both rue Dunôt and Dupin's apartment had an air of severely diminished gentility at that time, but now, as I looked out, the dwelling's façade glowed white as the moon in the night sky, suggesting it had recently been painted. The heavy black door was also immaculate, and the brass door furniture gleamed under the street's gaslights. Two large numbers affixed above the door knocker proclaimed "33".

"This is it," I said.

"Very good." Durand threw open the carriage door and leapt out. Murphy followed and they disappeared to the back of the coach, then reappeared moments later carrying my trunk and placed it just outside the front door before I could fully exit the coach. I was glad to see that a window was open at the top of the building, where Dupin's apartment was located, and light glowed behind the curtains of his parlor.

"Thank you very much for your delivering me here," I said. "If ever I can—"

Durand raised his hand to halt my words. "It is my mission to assist those in need and so it was my great pleasure."

"Would you care to meet the Chevalier Dupin?" I offered.

"No, thank you," Durand said firmly. "I would not wish to disturb him at this hour and we must be on our way."

"Very good." We all shook hands and I made my way up the stairs to the front door as Durand and Murphy retreated to the carriage and quickly drove away. The German was clearly being stubborn in his resistance to hiring Dupin for some task, much to the irritation of Mr. Murphy, but it was none of my business in the end and, in retrospect, my offer had been ill-considered, for Dupin would not welcome an intrusion from strangers at his home. When I reached the door I found another change since my previous visit: four brass mechanical doorbells. I reached up to the top bell that was engraved with "*Troisième étage*" and turned the key. Just as I was beginning to worry that no one was in the apartment after all, the parlor curtain twitched.

"Dupin!" I called up. "'Tis I, Poe. I was given a seat in a carriage from Le Havre."

A woman's voice emanated from the open window. "Who is it?" she said in French. "What do you want at this hour?"

"Is this the Chevalier Dupin's home?" I asked, wrong-footed.

The curtain was pulled back and a woman stared down at me.

"I am Edgar Poe, his friend. He is expecting me. I sailed from Philadelphia. He sent me a ticket on the *Independence*. I thought he might meet me at Le Havre," I babbled with a touch of desperation, feeling ridiculous shouting up at her from the street in my less than perfect French.

"Wait," the lady instructed and she disappeared from the window. I was beginning to doubt the facts I had just presented, so odd was the situation I found myself in, and looked around me with unease. The street was utterly deserted, and I had no idea where I might find a carriage, much less a hotel.

Then the curtains in the window to the right of the front door parted as someone peered out. Moments later the door flew open. "Poe! It is you!" And there was Dupin before me, a look of disbelief on his face, gripping his cobra-headed walking stick with the rapier concealed within it. He stared at me and I at him.

"It is me, of course," I said.

"I see that, but you have surprised me. Come in. Ah, a trunk," he said, a note of discomposure in his voice.

"It is rather heavy, I'm afraid. I packed a number of books in hopes of shortening the trip."

"A small inconvenience for a wise use of time at sea," he said as he grasped one handle of the trunk. I took the other and we heaved it inside, then Dupin closed the front door. "Come upstairs. I'll have someone bring up your trunk in the morning." We made our way up to the third floor and into Dupin's apartment, where we were met by the woman who had peered at me through the window. She was about forty years old, with brunette hair, large gray eyes and even features made less attractive by her scowl. She wore a blue dressing gown, nightcap and house slippers.

"A guest? You did not mention it," she said, annoyance sharpening her voice.

"I am sorry to arrive at such a late hour," I said apologetically. She did not offer a nicety in return.

"Perhaps you were expecting to meet me at Le Havre in the morning?" I asked Dupin. "It should have occurred to me to find lodgings there, but when two gentlemen who were also on the *Independence* invited me to travel with them to Paris, I took the opportunity."

"I see," Dupin said, knitting his brows. "But if you had alerted me to your arrival, I would certainly have taken the train to meet you."

"I admit, I was expecting you there and was planning to wait, but was advised it was dangerous and, hence, accepted the offer of the coach journey."

"There seems to be some confusion," the lady interrupted. "From this conversation, I gather that the Chevalier Dupin was not expecting your arrival, but you, sir, believed that he was. Am I correct?" She spoke in English, which took me by surprise, for I had perhaps unfairly supposed she did not speak the language. Furthermore, she had fathomed the situation completely.

"Madame, you are correct that I presumed the Chevalier Dupin was expecting me, for he sent me the ticket to sail upon the *Independence*, with a letter stating that he needed my assistance in a matter." I retrieved the envelope from my pocket and turned to Dupin. "Perhaps it slipped your memory?" This would be very unlike my friend, but it was the only explanation I could think of. I pulled out my steamship ticket and the torn letter, which I had stored with it. "Written on the first of June," I said, handing him the four pieces of the note. "I will explain why it is torn later," I added with an inadvertent glance at the lady, who noticed my look, as did Dupin.

But he turned his gaze to the pieces of the note, which he examined with great curiosity that shifted to wariness. "It is a very good likeness of my handwriting," he said. "If unversed in the art of autography, one might think that I wrote this letter."

"But you did not?"

Truly, my question was rhetorical, for my mind was racing. The letter a forgery? Why would anyone but Dupin wish me to come to Paris?

"Obviously he did not write it," the lady said impatiently. "May I suggest you sit in the parlor, and I will make some tea. We are all in need of a restorative."

"Yes, good idea," Dupin murmured, still staring at the letter.

"That would be pleasant," I said. "Thank you."

My words seemed to bring Dupin back from the letter. "Apologies. This is Madame Morel, my housekeeper. And this is my friend Edgar Poe. You will remember that I've spoken of him," he said to her.

"Yes," she said curtly.

Before I could offer any polite words of greeting, she turned on her heel and strode to the kitchen.

"Come, Poe," Dupin instructed as he walked into the parlor, eyes fixed back upon the letter. I followed and immediately came to a halt, such was my surprise at what I saw. The parlor was immaculately furnished. When I had visited previously, the room had offered antique armchairs in need of reupholstering, moth-eaten carpets and draperies, and light was provided solely by candles. Now there was an elegant little sofa of vermilion velvet positioned to face the fireplace, with two matching armchairs on either side, all of which formed a semicircle around a rosewood coffee table. Glowing Argand lamps were centered on occasional tables and a crystal chandelier filled the chamber with glittering light. A painting was situated to the right of the fireplace: an enormous human foot *d'or* in a field of azure. The golden foot was in the act of crushing a rampant serpent with fangs embedded in its heel. This was the Dupin coat of arms and it fully represented how Dupin reacted when attacked by an adversary.

"Please sit," he directed as he eased himself into his armchair. "In my last letter, I wrote that it would be far better to express all I had to tell you in person and now, it seems, my wish has come about in a mysterious way. Did you receive the letter that I sent in early May?"

"No, I'm afraid not. Just the letter you hold in your hand." Now that we were seated, I could see that it was not just Dupin's apartment that had changed, however; while the place had clearly undergone immense improvements, its owner looked tired, thin, sallow-skinned and haunted—circles beneath his gray eyes, a deep furrow between his brows and lines across his high forehead that were not there when we had last met. I did not think it was age overtaking him, though, for I could not discern a wisp of silver in his hair. My mother-in-law had claimed that Dupin might be my twin when she met him—I wondered if she would still perceive such a close resemblance.

Dupin glanced again at the letter, then handed the four pieces back to me. "If you look closely at the writing, you will notice that the text drifts down slightly and the words slant a little to the right—they are not precisely vertical. Furthermore, I underscore my name from right to left, whereas this line was drawn from left to right and the forger put only one small vertical mark through the middle of the underscore, not two as I always do. Do you see?"

I examined the signature more closely. "Yes, when you point it out I do. In my defense, the aberrations are so minor I doubt if anyone but you would ever notice them."

"Perhaps," he said dismissively. "More importantly, this missive copies the first paragraph of my own letter, but the rest is fabrication. I did not ask you to travel to Paris, nor did I send you a steamship ticket. I did mention that I'd had a change in circumstances, but said that I would reveal more once I had pursued some promising information regarding Valdemar's whereabouts. In any case," he continued, "we must conclude that someone intercepted the letter I sent to you and forged the one you hold. Someone who wanted you to travel to Paris and meet with me. It could only be Valdemar."

"Valdemar? Why would he want me in Paris?"

Dupin shrugged. "No doubt we shall find out. But let us not forget that Valdemar, as my nemesis, operates under the principle that if you are my friend, then you are his enemy."

"But my grandparents' letters—why would Valdemar ask me to bring them? And how could he know anything about them?"

Dupin looked unsettled for a moment, then said, "Never underestimate what Valdemar knows, what he can persuade people to tell him willingly or otherwise. And remember that he was in London during our investigation," he added more confidently. "The instruction to bring your grandparents' letters convinced you that this forgery was genuinely from me. Correct?" He rattled the letter in his hand.

"Yes, of course." But I could not dispel a sense of anxiety at the thought that a man as evil as Valdemar was cognizant of my forebears' crimes.

"Keep the letters locked in your trunk," Dupin advised. "Presumably you brought them with you?"

"Of course. Do you believe that Valdemar has something terrible planned? Something involving the two of us?"

"Yes, now that you've arrived in such a peculiar manner. Clearly, Valdemar did not want to risk the possibility that you might refuse to come to my aid given the length of the journey, so he sent you a ticket."

Or more to the point, he sent me the ticket as he did not want the cost of traveling from the United States to France to be a deterrent. Dupin had obviously thought the same, but was too polite to raise the issue of my limited funds.

"You mentioned that the *Independence* sailed from Philadelphia rather than New York," he continued. "Was there anyone suspicious on the ship with you?"

I knew that he was remembering my voyage from Philadelphia to London nine years previously and how my own nemesis and his lover had near succeeded in unraveling me through secretly tormenting me as we crossed the Atlantic.

"I rarely left my stateroom, so did not come into much contact with the other passengers. The two gentlemen who invited me to accompany them in their coach were unusual fellows—Durand and Murphy. They amused themselves by fighting with a variety of weapons during most of the trip. They were tiresome, but did come to my aid in Le Havre."

"Or so they would wish you to think," Dupin observed.

I had not detected anything malicious about the two, dismissing them as buffoons when on board the ship, then feeling grateful for their assistance at the port.

"They had every opportunity to murder me during the journey to Paris. Or while we were at sea."

"True. But then you would serve no purpose. If these fellows, Durand and Murphy, are in the hire of Valdemar, they would be traveling on the *Independence* to ensure you arrived in

Paris—that you arrived *here*," Dupin pointed out. "For is that not exactly what George Reynolds and his wife did when they played the role of doctor and nurse on the ship during your voyage to London? Didn't they ensure they knew exactly which hotel you would be staying in?"

The rattling of china diverted us from our conversation. Madame Morel had appeared, as if by magic, carrying a tray with a teapot and three cups. "Who is in the hire of Valdemar?"

Dupin frowned slightly at her question, but merely said, "Just put the tray there." He indicated the coffee table. She put the tray down and immediately poured out three cups of tea. "You're joining us?" he asked.

"Yes."

She handed Dupin a cup and settled down on the sofa with her own, leaving me to reach for my cup. She was surely the worst housekeeper I had ever come across, yet Dupin hardly seemed to notice.

"Shall I repeat my question?" she asked.

"The two men who brought Poe here," Dupin answered. "Who vanished before I arrived at the door." He turned back to me. "Did you not think it odd that Durand and Murphy abandoned you so quickly?"

"Not entirely. Durand was very keen to avoid you whereas the opposite was true of Murphy. Not only did he wish to make your acquaintance, he wanted to engage your services."

"Did they mention what they needed assistance with?"

"No, but they were aware of your skills of deduction."

Dupin waved his hand dismissively. "That is not uncommon knowledge. We must remain suspicious of them until we find out more about them."

"I should, perhaps, mention that Durand is German and appears from his manner, dress and accent to be an aristocrat.

Murphy is employed by him, but they seem to be true friends. I believe they said they are from Gerolstein."

Madame Morel frowned for a moment, then said, "Gerolstein is the name of a grand duchy of Germany, but I do not think Valdemar has any connection to the grand duke or duchess."

"That does not negate the possibility that he is in league with them," Dupin countered.

Madame Morel shrugged. "We must consider Durand and Murphy enemies until we discover otherwise." She abruptly rose to her feet. "I am very tired. The bed in the guest chamber is made up. Good night, Monsieur Dupin, Mr. Poe." She nodded to us each in turn. "Breakfast will be at eight o'clock." And with that, Dupin's peculiar servant left the room.

Silence reigned for a time while I poured us each another cup of tea and settled back to wait for Dupin to explain. He did not oblige my overt curiosity, however, but filled the time by preparing his meerschaum and lighting it.

When the silence became too frustrating, I said: "You told me earlier that you'd mentioned a change in circumstances in the letter I never received. Now that I'm here, it's obvious—new furniture and decorations, the carpet, draperies, gas lighting." I gave a little wave at the room. "You said nothing about improvements in your letters. It is quite the transformation. And you've hired a servant. Extraordinary."

Dupin emitted a sound of mirth as he puffed on his meerschaum. "Very true. Forgive me, Poe. I was unaware that you had an interest in furnishings. Or housekeepers."

"I have an interest in how we choose to design our environment and how it affects our state of mind, which you would know if you had read my essay on the subject. Certainly, if I had greater resources, there are changes I would make to my home. *Improvements*," I said.

Dupin gave another bark of amusement. "The reason I did not write of the improvements to my apartment is that they are directly related to Valdemar. Do you remember when I told you that I found my grandparents' locket in the shop on rue d'Enfer—the locket that had been up for auction in London? And the man in the shop had given it to me?"

"Yes, of course."

"Suffice to say that the shop led me to a far greater cache of items stolen from the Dupin family and to resources that have enabled me to make the improvements you see." Dupin puffed on his meerschaum and exhaled a cloud of smoke. "Fear not, Poe. I will reveal more to the tale in the morning, for it is better for you to witness it than merely to hear about it."

I knew from experience that it would do no good to push Dupin to divulge more, for he would only play the goat and dig his heels in.

"Very well. I look forward to seeing with my own eyes the origin of your secret, but perhaps you will answer me this. Why have you hired such a disagreeable and, dare I say, incompetent housekeeper?"

"Madame Morel fulfills her tasks very effectively. She saves me an enormous amount of time by taking care of my accounts, the shopping and the cooking, which, unfortunately, is the least of her skills. She does, however, know the best vintage wines and is surprisingly informed about art, music and literature. It is true that she does not bother with certain niceties and is, on occasion, overly to the point."

"She is *frequently* overly to the point, as you put it. And she works for you as a servant, yet invites herself to have tea with us and involves herself in our conversation. I am surprised you tolerate it."

Dupin shrugged. "She is more interesting than you might think. Her theories on a number of subjects are very advanced."

"And where did you find this scholar disguised as a housekeeper? Are there agencies for such advanced ladies in Paris?"

"She found me," Dupin said. "She came to the door with a letter of introduction from my mother's cousin, and she knew details about my mother's family that an imposter could not be aware of. Obviously, I questioned her thoroughly," he added.

"She is down on her luck, I suppose? Her husband dead? She would be left to beg on the street if you did not employ her?"

"She did not describe her situation in that way, nor did she beg for a position. Indeed, she advised me that I needed her assistance and as her arguments were convincing, I employed her. Therefore, I am not comfortable treating her like a servant. Perhaps the arrangement is rather like that of you and your mother-in-law."

"Pardon?" I could not keep the astonishment from my voice. "I think not."

A look of amusement crept onto Dupin's face. "There would seem to be similarities—or perhaps meeting your very capable mother-in-law persuaded me that I might find a housekeeper's skills advantageous. However one views the situation, the experiment has proved a success, for after just five weeks, Madame Morel has made herself indispensable."

"She has only been here for five weeks?"

"Correct. And now shall we retire? I have somewhere very important to show you in the morning."

"Of course," I said.

I did not bother to ask Dupin if he was concerned that Madame Morel was truly an emissary of his enemy Valdemar, for I knew that he would not reveal any such suspicions while we were inside the apartment and might be overheard. But I would ask in the morning when we were making our way to the mysterious destination that had brought such change to Dupin's life.

6

MONDAY, 9 JULY 1849

I feared I would not sleep well given the strangeness of all that had occurred since my arrival in France, but I was wrong—my slumber was absolute and rejuvenating. This was in part due to the fact that Dupin's improvements to his apartment had extended to his large guest bedchamber, which was simply but beautifully furnished. I was just reaching for my pocket watch when there was a rap upon the door.

"Poe? Are you awake? It is ten o'clock and we have much to do."

"I'll be with you in a moment. I slept far too well, I'm afraid."

"Very good. Use the dressing gown provided and come to the breakfast room. Two men are waiting to bring up your trunk and Madame Morel will see to it that your clothes are laundered."

I quickly did as Dupin instructed and went to find him. The breakfast room was on the other side of the apartment and had a very large east-facing window, which filled the room with morning light, making it a delightful place to begin one's day. The smell of coffee enriched the air and made my stomach pinch with hunger.

"Allow me." Dupin immediately filled my cup and refilled his own as I sat down. There was a basket of bread, butter and jam on the table. "Would you care for a cooked breakfast?" he continued. "You did not eat anything last night. Eggs, perhaps, or the porridge of which your mother-in-law is so fond?"

"Eggs would be wonderful."

"How should I prepare them?" Madame Morel's voice came from behind me and I turned to see her in the doorway that led to the kitchen. I had hoped her temper would improve after a night's sleep, but the same sour expression puckered her face.

"Fried or boiled, whichever causes less trouble."

Madame Morel gazed fleetingly at the heavens as if bemoaning my idiocy to the Lord himself. "I will make you two fried eggs with bread if I must decide for you." And she turned on her heel and disappeared again. I directed my gaze and exasperation to Dupin, who merely grunted his amusement, but I was determined not to allow her impertinence to be ignored.

"Did we visit the Beehive Tavern when you were in Philadelphia?"

Dupin shook his head.

"It has a reputation, still unparalleled, for employing the most surly and intractable barmaid in that fair city. So ill-tempered is she, the tavern is known as the 'Wasp's Nest'. Men dare each other to risk her wrath by attempting to engage her in conversation."

Dupin stared at me quizzically for a moment, then said, "It sounds as though the barmaid's sharp tongue brings custom to the tavern. I am not certain what I am meant to take from your little tale?"

"Perhaps that was not the best comparison, but surely breakfast would be more pleasant with a cheerful housekeeper?"

Dupin shrugged. "I find that too much cheerfulness is tiresome in the morning, but I will ask her to try if you wish."

"No, no. Forget I said anything."

If Madame Morel's ill-tempered rudeness was irksome, I was certain that being told to be cheerful by her employer would make the lady even more irascible. Moments later my two fried eggs with bread arrived and I wondered if she had overheard me and taken her revenge through the cooking of my breakfast. Both eggs and bread were scorched and heavy with grease.

"Thank you, madame. It looks . . . delicious," I said disingenuously.

Madame Morel nodded once, wiped her hands on her apron and returned to the kitchen.

I glanced at Dupin to see his reaction to the state of my breakfast, but he was engrossed in the map of Paris that was spread out on the table.

"I have some important things to show you today." He tapped the map, which was annotated with his own obscure code. "I hope your shoes are comfortable for walking and not overly slippery on wet surfaces. If not, I have some you may like to borrow. I believe we wear the same size shoe?"

"I think so." Dupin and I were almost identical in height and build and had discovered in the past that we were able to wear the same clothing. "Where are we going today?"

"To the Bibliothèque Mazarine. It has certain similarities to the library that was at St. Augustine."

"How so?"

"In the seventeenth century, its books were in the care of a priest—it was originally the personal library of Cardinal Mazarin. He collected rare books, manuscripts and art and had amassed the largest library in France, but it was almost destroyed in early 1652 when Mazarin and Louis the Fourteenth were in exile. Thousands of books were burned or sold."

"There are similarities," I agreed.

The church of St. Augustine in Philadelphia had possessed an enviable library that was the joy of scholars, full of rare tomes and exquisite treasure books bound with precious metals and jewels, with wondrous illustrations inside. Unfortunately, the library was lost when the church was burned to the ground by rioters just a month after Dupin's visit there.

"Mazarin's librarian at that time, Gabriel Naudé, had the good sense to conceal the most valuable books at the abbey of Sainte-Geneviève. What a pity that did not happen at St. Augustine," he added.

"It is heartbreaking to think of the treasures lost there."

"When Mazarin returned to Paris and to power in 1653, Naudé was able to reclaim many of the books that had been stolen or sold, and so Mazarin built up a second great library. I should say that from 1643 Mazarin had opened his library one day a week to scholars and it was in demand as one of the largest libraries in Europe. To ensure it remained intact, Mazarin bequeathed it to the Collège des Quatre-Nations, part of the University of Paris. The library continued to grow even during the Terror due to the efforts of the librarian during that time: Monsieur Gaspard Michel."

"Were the books in the Bibliothèque Mazarine obtained by nefarious means?"

"Part of the collection was, many would say. Monsieur Michel bought books that were confiscated from monasteries and also from noble families forced into exile. He collected valuable artworks too, from the same sources."

"Including items from the Dupin family?"

"A few items, but they were returned to me without argument."

I wondered if this was because Dupin simply took them, as he had when he came across a stolen Dupin family heirloom in Philadelphia.

"But we are not going in search of rare books this time. I have something extremely interesting to show you."

"And what is that?"

"You will see in due course. Do not forget what I have said about footwear. When you finish your breakfast, we will begin our little journey."

I looked at the unappetizing eggs and greasy bread. If finishing my breakfast was some sort of test devised by Dupin, my stomach did not care if I failed it. I excised the cooked egg's blackened frill, but the white still tasted charred, so I made do with slicing through the egg yolk and dipping pieces of fresh bread into it. Once I'd washed that down with coffee, I felt sated enough for the journey Dupin had in mind. A simpleton would instantly understand that I had not cared much for my breakfast, but I doubted that this fact would bother Madame Morel very much. It certainly did not bother Dupin. He glanced at my plate, raised his brows fleetingly and said, "Shall we go in five minutes?"

We made our way to Avenue de la Bourdonnaye then turned right onto rue Saint-Dominique, Dupin leading the way yet refusing to fully divulge his plans for the day and why he had fitted us out like frontiersmen for a walk through the streets of Paris on a very fine Monday morning. Dupin wore a small canvas haversack on his back with surprising aplomb, and I had a ditty bag slung by its strap across my chest, which chafed and looked quite ridiculous.

"Are we vagabonding to another city to visit the library you wish to show me? For surely we cannot need these accouterments to examine rare books," I had complained when he presented me with the ditty bag and all it contained: a small water-skin, smoked beef, bread, an apple, a pen knife, a metal box filled with phosphorus matches, a collapsible lantern and several candles. Dupin had the same items in his haversack along with a rolled-up length of rope, a ball of twine, a compass and a small oil lantern.

"We will not be leaving Paris, but you will be glad to have the bag, I give you my word." Despite my best efforts, Dupin would reveal no more than that. He merely led the way forward, tapping along with his cobra-headed cane as if hiking through alpine terrain with a rustic walking stick.

Finally we came to quai Malaquais. Dupin stopped in front of a stately building composed of fawn-colored stone with three arched doorways and three rectangular windows directly above them. The words "BIBLIOTHECA A FUNDATORE MAZARINEA" were displayed in large letters on the entablature. Its impressive façade looked out across the Seine toward the Louvre on the opposite bank, and a metal bridge with nine arches—Pont des Arts—struck a path across the water as if to connect those two important sanctuaries for art and learning.

"That is Cardinal Mazarin's coat of arms," Dupin said, indicating the decoration on the tympanum, which was framed by two elegant figures situated on either side of it. "You will see it throughout the library as all the bookcases installed once belonged to Cardinal Mazarin."

We made our way inside and the man positioned behind the desk near the library's entrance gave Dupin a solemn nod of acknowledgment and did not, to my surprise, query his haversack or my ditty bag. Instead he merely raised his index finger to his lips and waved us through. The interior did not disappoint. The wooden bookcases were elegant, decorated with carved Corinthian columns and the cardinal's coat of arms held aloft by a pair of cherubs. The shelves were lined up seamlessly in rows along the walls and completely filled with a cornucopia of literature, an enviable collection of tomes that emitted the scent of old paper and print so admired by those who love books. Gilded bronze chandeliers were anchored overhead and spilled golden light, which gave warmth to the deep hush of the place.

Dupin strode along, oblivious through familiarity with all that surrounded us, while I looked this way and that, trying to absorb the library's treasures. Eventually we reached a quiet corner with shelves of ancient books that shimmered with dust.

"See here?" Dupin asked, waving at a bookshelf. "Do you see it?"

I looked at the spines of the leather-bound volumes and tried to discern the titles, but they were either too cracked and worn to read or simply blank.

"What am I looking for, Dupin?"

He stepped closer and indicated the frame of the bookcase, which had a leafy design carved into it.

"Do you see it?" he repeated, pointing at one of the friezes.

I leaned in to examine it more closely and just when I was about to admit defeat, I noticed the carving extended into the interior of the bookcase and there, just above eye level, camouflaged by leaves, was a bird sitting on a branch.

"Is it an owl?" I wondered.

Dupin nodded. "Precisely."

"It's difficult to spot."

"That is the point. Now take out your lantern and fit it with a candle," he instructed, his eyes scanning the room for any observers to our transgressions. Apparently reassured, he retrieved his own collapsible lantern from his haversack and deftly pulled it into shape, then inserted a candle.

"But—"

"Please, Poe. We must be quick." He retrieved a match and lit his candle with practiced speed, then did the same with mine. We closed the glass doors to the small lanterns, which emitted a gentle glow, and before I could say a word, Dupin put his hand on the edge of the bookcase, next to the image of the carved owl, and pushed hard. The bookcase pivoted inward and revealed a narrow opening in the wall behind, leading to a wooden staircase that curved down into the heart of the build-ing. "Come," he said and stepped over the threshold. I followed and he pushed the bookcase door back into place, sealing us in darkness.

7

Our footsteps pattered softly on the stairs as we descended, lantern lights moving like giant fireflies across the wood-paneled walls. The scent of ancient tomes stayed with us until we reached another door, which Dupin pushed open. Cold air and the faint smell of damp confronted us, but Dupin advanced, lantern held before him, revealing a stone tunnel.

"Close the door behind you," he instructed as he strode forward.

"Where are we going?" I demanded. "This is no cellar beneath the library, is it?"

"No." Dupin did not pause in his progress.

I momentarily considered ascending the steps again and retreating through the library, but curiosity conquered me. I pushed the door shut and scurried after Dupin, my shoes gathering purchase on the gravel that was scattered on the stone floor. My candle flame glimmered warily but clung to the wick, and I was grateful for the folding lantern as I pressed on in pursuit. So inky was it that I stumbled into Dupin before I saw him.

"You did not tell me our true destination as you knew I would resist coming here," I said angrily.

"Nonsense," he lied. "You are not the coward you sometimes believe yourself to be."

I did my best to imitate one of Dupin's huffs of derision, as I could neither agree nor disagree with his pronouncement without making myself seem a fool. As we moved forward, our lanterns revealed little but the arched walls above us that glowed softly and eerily in the candlelight.

"Limestone." It was as if he had read my thoughts, a trick of Dupin's that oft made him seem to have supernatural powers. "These tunnels are the remnants of mining operations that produced the stone from which the city was constructed. The Romans began the work, using limestone to build the place they called Lutetia. From the thirteenth century onward, my countrymen tunneled underground in order to retrieve enough stone to construct masterpieces like Notre-Dame, the Louvre." His pride in his city was clear in his voice. "The tunnels from mining limestone weave beneath the Left Bank of the Seine for approximately two hundred miles. And there are gypsum quarries over on the right-hand side of the river." Dupin stopped for a moment and turned to face me. "A subterranean city exists beneath Paris, tunnels mirroring the streets above, mysterious chambers carved out beneath our most noble buildings."

"Fascinating," I muttered, but in truth I immediately pictured those tunnels and chambers swallowing up Paris, the hungry depths erasing all above it and returning "la Ville Lumière" back to solid stone once more. Dupin resumed his confident progress through the tunnel, his words echoing back to me.

"I have old maps of the tunnels that note entryways constructed by the quarry workers, but I found the secret entrance at Bibliothèque Mazarine by chance when exploring this tunnel. Imagine my surprise when I climbed the stairs, opened the door and saw where I was."

"I would imagine that the attendant who guards the way into the library was equally surprised when you exited without ever entering."

Dupin grunted his amusement. "The trick is to leave confidently and courteously, but without offering explanation."

"Indeed," I muttered. "You are quite the master of avoiding explanation when it suits you. For example, why we are in this place." I lifted my lantern higher and shuddered as the candle flame quivered and did nothing at all to dispel the gloom around me.

"Fear not, Poe. You will learn everything soon enough. Suffice to say that I have discovered incredible things down here, some of which you will be familiar with from your reading, but there are other mysteries that I will show you. In truth, words cannot adequately describe what you will *see*."

"The catacombs?"

"The catacombs cannot fail to surprise you. But there is more. This place is a kingdom unto itself, in part a tomb for the dead but also a vault for treasure and strange artifacts. Smugglers, thieves, the homeless, refugees from prosecution— all have made use of these tunnels. As have practitioners of esoteric arts. You shall see."

Dupin's refrain did not fill me with scholarly enthusiasm as he seemed to think it would. Scrabbling through the tunnel with nothing but two candle flames to guide us made my heart gallop and my palms as clammy as the walls that wrapped around us. When my friend was fully immersed in the realm of the intellect, he often neglected the corporeal world, forgetting to eat properly and take enough care of himself and his home— or that is what I had experienced when I first met him. It also made him less conscious of physical dangers. Exploring underground tunnels alone might seem to many the activity of a desperate or mad man; Dupin was neither except for when it came to a quest for knowledge. Then he was relentless and, at times, lacking in good sense. As was I, truly, in following him.

"I assume, since you've explored this tunnel previously, you know where we are," I asked, "in relation to the city above?"

Dupin stopped abruptly and turned to me again, his lantern twisting his features into quite the ghoulish mask. "As I've said, I consulted maps of the tunnels before I began my explorations. Not only do I possess a copy of a detailed map made by the Quarry Inspection Department, I also have drawings by Carthusian monks and a highly useful map I found in the shop on rue d'Enfer, which I believe was made by smugglers."

"And, of course, you have committed them all to memory," I said.

"I amalgamated them all to make my own version to study for patterns. Indeed, you saw it at breakfast. And I committed that more detailed map to memory. Of course," he added.

"And did you find patterns?"

"I think so. But first, to allay your fears, see here." He moved forward a few paces and held out his lantern to reveal a tunnel creeping off to our left. "Do you see?" He moved the light nearer to the stone wall. At about eye level and scratched into the wall, then colored black with charcoal, was a string of numbers and a letter. "A marker, put here by the Quarry Inspection Department, which indicates the number of the retaining pillar installed by the department, the year of installation and the initial of the quarry inspector during that time. This inscription mirrors what is recorded on the Quarry Inspection Department's map." He held his lamp in the entrance to the other tunnel and the candle flame shuddered and nearly failed. "But we wish to continue straight ahead," he said and moved forward with confidence. I scurried after, having utterly lost any notion of whether we were moving north, south, east or west.

"We are walking away from the Seine," Dupin said, reading my mind again. "In a southwesterly direction."

"I will take your word for it, for I am utterly disoriented."

"That is very common. There are tales of those who became lost here and never returned to the surface."

"Apocryphal tales, I suppose—warnings for those without a proper sense of caution?"

A huff of laughter echoed around us. "Quite sensible warnings, actually. About fifty years ago, a porter for the Val-de Grâce hospital made his way into the catacombs via a staircase in the hospital courtyard, much like the one we just descended. They found his bones over a decade later, quite near the place he had entered. The porter became so disoriented, one must presume, that he failed to find his way out and starved."

"How very reassuring, Dupin."

"On the contrary. The tale has acted as a deterrent. Most are too terrified to set foot in the tunnels for fear they will suffer the same fate as the unlucky porter."

"Quite a sensible fear," I muttered. "But what is—or was— the Quarry Inspection Department?" I asked.

"It is exactly what it would seem to be. Excavations were so intensive, there were numerous unmapped tunnels and voids left behind, which created a disaster-in-waiting as more and ever-higher buildings were constructed in Paris. In the late eighteenth century, houses began to collapse, and then an entire street was swallowed up by a void." Dupin kept moving forward as he talked, the light of his lantern guiding us further into the depths until I felt the stone roof pressing down on us. "In the year of your country's birth—1776—King Louis the Sixteenth ordered that a service be created to remedy this problem. Quarry inspectors explored these underground passages in teams and wrote down all they saw in detail, including the names of streets and important monuments that were situated above each location underground. These extensive drawings were gathered together to create the *Paris Underground Quarry Atlas*."

"I'm relieved your prodigious memory of the atlas means you know where we are, but what of the structure itself? Your tales of collapsing buildings and entire streets descending into Hell are hardly reassuring." My words rang off the stone that surrounded us, as though we were in the interior of a bell.

"Fear not, Poe. The quarrymen were also charged with adding in new ceilings and pillars to strengthen the underground galleries and prevent any further collapses. Better still, these men took it upon themselves to create works of art—exquisite subterranean architecture that you will have the privilege of examining."

I was not convinced it was a privilege, nor was I pleased that Dupin had tricked me into our subterranean expedition. We continued to trudge onward, Dupin holding up his light to indicate a symbol carved into the rock, explaining again and again where we were. Truly I did not much care after we had walked for what seemed like an hour.

"We are almost at our destination," Dupin offered reassuringly.

"What *is* our destination?" I countered, though I knew he wouldn't answer.

"Here we are," he said at last and seemed to disappear into the tunnel wall itself. Terror enveloped me—had Dupin been spirited away and was my fate the same as the unlucky hospital porter?

"Poe? Follow my voice."

I shuffled up to the wall and held my lantern to its surface. The gentle glow revealed an outcropping of rock that gave the

illusion of being part of the tunnel wall, but that concealed, I
soon discovered, a wooden door. I stepped through it and
found myself in a large chamber, where Dupin was waiting for
me.

"We are below the Théâtre-Français, near the Palais du
Luxembourg. Both locations have hidden passages that lead to
this chamber."

I digested this notion for a moment, trying to imagine why
such glorious buildings had entrances leading to this tomb-like
space.

"Is the chamber for protection? A place to hide if under
attack?" I asked.

"Perhaps that was its primary purpose, but let me show you
what it is used for now." He reached into his haversack and took
out the small oil lamp, which he lit. Then he carried it and the
lantern further into the chamber, chasing away the shadows as
he moved forward. I followed and moments later saw that the
far wall had perhaps two dozen wooden chests propped up
against it in stacks of three or four. "They were locked, but that
was simple to remedy. Lift the lid from that one," he said,
nodding at a chest to his left. "I'll direct the light so you can see
the contents."

I did as he instructed and caught my breath as the lamplight
glinted on a trove of silver and gold and faceted gems. I reached
toward the glittering objects but instinctively stopped before
touching the treasure.

"It is not a trap if that is what you fear. There is no venom-
ous creature or smuggler's ghost hidden in the chest to take
revenge on any looter," Dupin said, the amusement clear in his
voice.

"Are you certain of that? For surely this resembles a pirate's
chest of booty," I retorted, trying to make light of my jangled
nerves. "If a thief were clever enough to steal such a quantity of

valuable objects, would he not find a better way of protecting his bounty than a lock that anyone might easily pick?"

"The locks would present a challenge to most, just not to me," Dupin said with a touch of irritation, for he was rather proud of his lock-picking skills. "And obviously I survived dipping into the chest so it is likely that you will also."

I tentatively reached in and removed a golden statue of the Virgin Mary, and then a chalice, also of gold, which was decorated with precious stones. The chest was filled with similar objects.

"Is this the source for your refurbished apartment? You've sold objects from this trove?"

"Correct."

"And you presume that everything stored here is stolen—that it does not belong to the Théâtre-Français or the Palais du Luxembourg?"

Dupin responded with a snort of derision. "Certainly none of it belongs to the theater—that's a ridiculous notion. And if the chamber was a storage room for the Palais du Luxembourg, then what does it matter, for then surely all here was ill-gotten. But look." He held the lamps closer to the chests. "See the carvings and the metalwork."

Some of the wooden chests had ornate carvings. All had decorative metalwork—the hinges, around the lock, on the edges. "Spanish?" I asked. "Or perhaps Portuguese?"

Dupin nodded. "That is what I believe. The chests all contain jewels, religious statues, bars of gold and silver."

"What do you know, then, of its provenance? Surely there must be records of such an incredible treasure going missing."

"I have a theory, of course. From my research, it is possible that it is part of the Lima treasury which was sent to Mexico in 1820 when the viceroy feared revolt, but was lost when the captain of the ship turned pirate. All the items here match those on the Lima treasury inventory: golden religious statues, chalices, crowns, bars of silver and gold, two hundred chests of jewels, over one thousand diamonds, and a number of other precious items. I believe the captain and his fellow pirates divided up the spoils and this is a portion of them."

I looked at the stack of chests—even if just a part of that lost treasure, there were enough riches stored in this chamber to allow any man to live comfortably for the rest of his life.

"You feel no remorse in profiting from stolen treasure?"

Dupin turned and held the lantern so that it illuminated both our faces rather than the treasures within the chest. "Why would I? If my theory is correct, these artifacts were originally stolen from the peoples of Peru long before Captain Thompson claimed them. Is it possible for me to return all that is here to the rightful owners? I think not. Do I feel remorse in taking treasure from a thief? Absolutely not." Dupin set the small oil lamp and his lantern on the stone floor and rifled through the chest as I watched, still holding my own lantern over the glittering treasure. He extracted a small bar of gold and a dagger sheathed in the same material, decorated with what appeared to be rubies. He admired the beautiful weapon for a moment, then placed both items into his haversack.

"Poe?" He waved at the jumble of precious objects. When I shook my head, he laughed. "Surely the sale of any item within this chest would improve the quality of your life immensely? It would buy you time to work on your tales without worrying how to secure the practicalities of life." Seeing that his comment did not move me, he added: "And you would be free to purchase anything your mother-in-law might need or desire. Some item to make her daily tasks less onerous—a maid perhaps," he suggested with a saturnine grin. "Or some pretty trifle to bring her a moment of joy without the worry of an empty purse."

He was right and my hand dipped toward the box, but as I reached for a golden figurine, a fog of malaise pressed down on me and my skin crawled as if pinched and prodded by dead men's fingers. I shivered and withdrew.

My face must have betrayed my discomfort even in that dim, quavering light, for Dupin exhaled in exasperation. "Do you fear that these articles are cursed or some such nonsense? For if there are any such tales connected to this stolen trove, they were concocted by the thieves who put it here."

Dupin's argument was logical, but I had the strong feeling I had come to the right decision. "It is not a curse I fear, but truly the location does not agree with me. I am sure you understand why."

Dupin nodded once and said, "I have spent so many hours exploring the tunnels that I forget that others do not share my enthusiasm for such adventures." He replaced the lid on the box. "Follow me." He walked further into the chamber and the darkness swallowed him. My heart immediately began to race. I hurried after and at the back of the chamber, I found an open door that led to another set of steps. I closed the door after me and dashed up a staircase that spiraled like a corkscrew. Dupin was waiting for me by a door at the top. When we exited, I saw that we were behind the stage of the Théâtre-Français. Dupin closed the secret door, and so entirely did it disappear into the wall that I did not think I would ever locate it again—until I noted a decorative sconce in the shape of an owl.

"Does this—" I began.

But Dupin held his finger to his lips and merely nodded. He then led us through the back of the theater to a door that opened on to the street. I regretted that we could not stop to examine the building properly as I remembered it being quite magnificent. Instead, we stepped out into fresh air, blue sky and sunlight that made me blink. I fear I stared at the pedestrians who hurried past us, astonished that they were oblivious to the mysterious world that existed beneath their very feet.

8

Madame Morel met us at the door, her face stiff with annoyance that she made no effort to conceal.

"You are late," she said to Dupin.

"Oh?"

She glanced at me and lowered her voice slightly. "Your appointment."

Dupin appeared baffled for a brief moment, then said, "Ah, Froissart."

"Yes," she said. "He is waiting in your study."

"Very good. Tell him I won't be long. And if you would make tea for Monsieur Poe after that."

Madame Morel nodded—reluctantly, I thought—to the second request and made her way to Dupin's study.

"Dr. Froissart is here?" I asked.

He had treated me in London after I had suffered a horrible ordeal trapped in a cellar, and his presence for an appointment with Dupin at his apartment made me focus on how gaunt Dupin's face had become, the circles under his eyes, the furrows in his brow. In short, he did not look well, yet had confided nothing in his letters about any problems with his health.

Dupin shrugged. "With the odd events connected to your unexpected arrival, I forgot Froissart was coming today, but our meeting should not take long. I will bring him to say hello afterwards," he answered, neatly sidestepping my unspoken question. "Have a look at the library in the parlor. There are many new acquisitions you will find of interest." And Dupin went off to his study, leaving me with no option but to do as he suggested.

I entered the parlor and approached the bookshelves. Dupin had acquired many new tomes; the shelves had been half-filled when last I visited, but now there was little space left. The library was organized into five sections: belles-lettres, history, jurisprudence, sciences and arts, theology, then further divided into categories meaningful to Dupin. These were written out on labels in his precise writing and affixed to the shelves. The books within each category were arranged alphabetically by the author's name and again alphabetically by title if the author had written a number of works. I made my way to the poetry shelves and, after a short search, confess to being perhaps too pleased that all my collections were there, including *Tamerlane and Other Poems* (despite the attributed author being "A Bostonian"). There was also a leather-bound box with a hinged lid labeled with my name, in which I discovered a large selection of my poems published in magazines and newspapers, along with an index key written out by Dupin. I then browsed the fiction shelves and found two identical leather-bound boxes also labeled with my name, which were filled with my tales published within periodicals. As I was leafing through that box, Madame Morel came into the room, carrying a tray with a pot of tea, a cup and a bowl of sugar. She raised her brows slightly, but said nothing, and I returned the box to its place on the shelf, certain she was judging the fact that I was perusing a collection of my own work.

But all she said was: "Your tea, Monsieur Poe." In truth, it was highly unlikely she could possibly be aware of what I had been looking at unless she had eyes keener than an eagle on the hunt for prey or a mind as acute as Dupin's and had memorized the placement of each volume in the library as she dusted its shelves. I took a seat in the armchair next to which she had placed the tray of tea things.

"Thank you, Madame Morel. Much appreciated."

She nodded regally, but rather than return to the kitchen, she stood there, openly staring at me.

"Won't you have a seat?" It had become too awkward to ignore her presence, and I indicated the sofa on which she had stationed herself the previous night. She did not need to be asked twice. She shut the parlor door and settled down, her eyes still fixed upon me. "Have you been employed by the Chevalier Dupin for long?" I asked.

"As I believe he told you last night, I have been here for five weeks."

This was true, but I had no recollection of the lady being in the room when he had revealed that fact. Had she been eavesdropping or had Dupin relayed that information? Before I could think of another polite question, the lady asked her own more direct one.

"Where did you and Auguste go today?"

I was taken aback by the familiarity of the housekeeper; it was more than inappropriate. Yet in my chagrin, I somehow was moved to answer her impertinent question.

"Bibliothèque Mazarine—which proved to be as impressive a library as the Chevalier Dupin described."

"And the catacombs?" she demanded.

This time I instinctively held back. "The catacombs?" I echoed.

"Yes. You know what they are, I suppose?" Sarcasm laced her words and her expression was impatient.

"I've heard they're underneath us," I said, refusing to give her the answer she craved. "That there's a whole subterranean city beneath Paris that mirrors it."

"Not true at all."

"Oh?"

"No. It is a ridiculous notion. Catacombs, yes, but there is no fantastical kingdom hidden beneath Paris for gentlemen explorers to discover." She gestured at my attire.

"Well, that is good to know." I took a deep drink of my tea, turning my eyes away from hers. A more sensitive person would have understood such an obvious dismissal, but not Madame Morel. She huffed and raised her voice slightly.

"Let me be direct. Auguste must stop exploring the catacombs. It is highly dangerous. He has enemies there who will not hesitate to murder him."

"Enemies lurking in the catacombs? That sounds overly dramatic," I said, without quite believing my own words. "I'm sure there are ruffians that know some of the tunnels and use that to their advantage, but the Chevalier Dupin always carries his walking stick with him, and as you must know, it has a quick and vicious bite when in his hands."

"You know of whom I speak," Madame Morel declared, her eyes fastened on mine. "Ernest Valdemar has explored the catacombs for years and has committed a detailed map of them up here." She tapped at her head. "Please dissuade Auguste from going into them anymore or he will not leave that necropolis. And nor will you," she added. Her words sounded like a threat, but her anxiety was not feigned.

"How is it you know so much about Ernest Valdemar?"

Madame Morel opened her mouth to answer, but promptly shut it again when the parlor door flew open. Dupin strode in, followed by a gentleman of perhaps seventy years of age who resembled an immense stork, with very long legs, a large pointed nose and a shock of white hair that seemed to stand on end. The tall fellow's clothing was somber and elegant, but rather too short in the arms and legs. He was carrying the same huge alligator bag full of medical paraphernalia he had brought to my sick room in London.

"Dr. Froissart, it is a pleasure to see you again." I rose to my feet and offered my hand. The doctor had a strong grip and enthusiastic handshake.

"Mr. Poe. It has been too many years since we last met, but the occasion is vividly implanted in my mind," the doctor replied in his sonorous voice. "What a pleasure it is to see you so fully recovered. One can never tell what maladies one might suffer after being exposed to rats in such an unpleasant way."

A shiver scurried up my spine at the memory of that abhorrent experience, and I noticed that Madame Morel could not suppress a grimace. I wondered if his allusion repelled her or if she had had her own repugnant experience with the sharp-toothed creatures.

"Would you like some tea now, Dr. Froissart?" she asked.

"Madame, that would be much appreciated."

The housekeeper immediately picked up the tea tray she had reluctantly brought me and left the room with it.

"Do sit," Dupin instructed, indicating the sofa Madame Morel had been perched upon. "It isn't often Mr. Poe visits our fine city and it is only slightly more frequent that Madame Morel offers anyone tea before they ask for it." Dupin smiled.

"Truly? I am very flattered then, for she always offers me tea when I am obliged to wait for you," Froissart replied.

Dupin looked to the heavens and sighed. "I am a busy man, sir. You do choose the most inopportune times to arrive."

"No, I come precisely on time for appointments we have made and you try to avoid them."

Dupin waved his hand in the air as if to dispel Dr. Froissart's words, and we lapsed into silence for a time as Dupin sulked like a child. This amused the doctor as much as it did me and I liked the fellow all the more. He and I exchanged a few more pleasantries until our conversation was broken by the clacking of wooden wheels on the floor mixed with the rattle of china. Madame Morel rolled a trolley of tea accouterments into the room. She poured for everyone, including herself, and after distributing the steaming beverages, settled down next to Dr. Froissart on the sofa.

"Many thanks. This is exactly what I am in need of," the doctor said.

She smiled graciously and sipped at her tea, as did we all. When Dr. Froissart finished and put his cup down on the table to be refilled, he reached into his capacious medical bag and pulled out an amber-colored glass bottle.

"I am giving this to you, Madame Morel, as Auguste has proved an exceedingly difficult patient, far more interested in discussing what is in this *elixir vitae* I have prepared than in dosing himself with it. Perhaps you will be able to ensure that he takes ten drops twice a day?"

"Of course," the lady said confidently, taking the flask. "Is it acceptable to mix this elixir into another drink or would that diminish its effects?"

"It is perfectly acceptable to do so."

"Very good." Her glance at Dupin made me think she was more versed in slipping *elixir de mort* into the drinks of others.

"I suspect that you are both conspiring against me," Dupin said. "Do not put any potions into my food or drink without my express permission," he told Madame Morel.

It was an order he certainly should not need to give, but her response was to purse her lips stubbornly and Dr. Froissart could barely suppress a smile of amusement. I saw my opportunity to fish for information about Dupin's malady since he had stead-fastly repelled my efforts to broach the subject.

"Is the *elixir vitae* a general tonic or does it cure a specific ailment?" I asked Dr. Froissart.

"In small doses it is a general restorative, but I believe it may assist in countering the progress of a number of maladies for which we do not yet have a cure."

"Such as?"

Dr. Froissart looked at me and then at Dupin, but said nothing.

"It is a minor complaint over which too much fuss is made," Dupin finally said. "I see this elixir as a useless and unpleasant tonic."

"And I believe the 'useless tonic' is effective against your complaint," Madame Morel countered.

"Quite," Dr. Froissart agreed.

"You may believe what you like. There is, however, no proof of what you claim. And no scientific way to test it. Now, enough on the subject." Dupin waved his hand petulantly.

"Certainly, the elixir has not improved your temper," I joked, trying to lighten the mood.

"There is no scientific way to test that either," Dr. Froissart observed. "But I am in agreement with you, Mr. Poe."

"Auguste has a perfectly acceptable temper," Madame Morel said staunchly, but both Dr. Froissart and Dupin looked some-what bemused by her lukewarm compliment.

It was clear that no one was going to illuminate me regarding Dupin's "complaint", so I changed tack. "If I remember rightly, Dr. Froissart, you were employed by the French ambassador to England when Dupin and I were there nine years ago. Given all that has occurred in France politically since then, might I presume that you have a new situation?"

"You have an excellent memory, Mr. Poe. I was Ambassador Guizot's personal physician in London, but when he took up the role of minister of foreign affairs, I returned to Paris with him in the autumn of 1840. I remained in his employ until he was forced to return to London in March of last year."

I nodded. "He was prime minister during the February Revolution, wasn't he? There were some accounts of it in American newspapers last year, but Dupin's letters were far more informative. Monsieur Guizot's move must have been disadvantageous for you," I said as delicately as I could.

"It might have been more difficult," Dupin observed. "For we believe Valdemar was one of the instigators of the revolution—but his goal would not have been to improve the life of the working man and woman, but rather to take power himself. Thankfully that did not happen."

"He wanted to be in the position of Napoleon the Third?" I asked.

"Through force, not election," Dr. Froissart said.

"He wishes to be emperor of France and if he ever achieves that position, he will undoubtedly turn his back on those who put the crown upon his head."

Dupin's words made me think back to the little I knew about Valdemar. He had done his best to destroy the Dupin family, first by sending my friend's grandparents to the guillotine during the Terror. I had never come face to face with the man, bar a startling meeting with a wax replica of him at Madame Tussaud's almost ten years previously, and that facsimile presented a man well past his prime.

"Valdemar has left it quite late in life to grasp for such power. He must be over eighty years old. Surely no one would put their faith in such an ancient fellow?"

Dr. Froissart's bushy eyebrows descended. "Think of the years of knowledge we ancient fellows accumulate. Have you no faith in me, Mr. Poe?" And then he laughed at my mortified expression. "I am jesting. You make a valid point, sir. I am not quite the age of Ernest Valdemar, but my ambitions are rather less grandiose. He is said to be a peculiar character, but in truth I do not know anyone who has met him in the flesh in recent years. He evidently favors the shadows more than the sunlight's glare, but that does not diminish his ever-expanding ambitions, or so it seems."

"Enough talk of that devil," Madame Morel said with such vehemence one might think she too had a grudge against the man.

"Quite," Dr. Froissart nodded. "For if we speak too much of the devil we may well conjure him up, and I for one wish to spend the remainder of my days without Monsieur Ernest Valdemar in them. And in belated answer to your earlier question, Mr. Poe, Monsieur Guizot's hasty move to London might have been highly disadvantageous for me if Auguste had not intervened. He has kindly ensured that my old age will be very comfortable." Dr. Froissart smiled and bowed his head gratefully to Dupin, who waved away his friend's thanks. "I have retired from practice except for one very difficult patient and have the luxury of devoting most of my time to my studies, experimenting with remedies from ancient texts and discussing my theories and findings with like-minded colleagues at the Isis Society."

"That sounds very rewarding," I said.

"I believe so, even if some deem my elixirs useless," he added with a pointed glance at our mutual friend.

"You will prove him wrong," Madame Morel said so firmly that it sounded like a command rather than a platitude.

"I will do my best, madame."

"I trust that you do not discuss your patients at this society of yours," Dupin said fiercely.

The doctor's face twitched slightly with guilt, or so it seemed to me, and I could tell Dupin thought the same as his glower intensified.

"Of course not, Auguste. We never speak of any patients by name," Froissart declared, a slight flush creeping up his neck. "We discuss maladies and their possible cures. Nothing more than that. It is an excellent way to advance our studies, pooling the experience and thoughts of other men of science. In fact, I wanted to tell you about one immensely interesting doctor I met when the society last convened. His name is David Willis and he was once a slave in Florida, but now acts as the physician to a princeling of a grand duchy in Germany when called upon—quite the reversal of fortunes. A most impressive man and a deep thinker. Dr. Willis's employer is a gentleman adventurer who has made a pledge to assist good people in need. This lofty goal has inspired him to track missing persons like a sleuthhound and Dr. Willis believes the fellow's impetuosity and recklessness will be the death of him. Truly he needs an expert ratiocinator for his current adventure and naturally I recommended you."

Dupin grimaced at this, no doubt coming to the same conclusion that I did.

"Is his name Durand?" I asked. "And does he have an English companion called Murphy?"

Dr. Froissart frowned slightly. "He is Gustavus Rodolph, Grand Duke of Gerolstein. But his companion is indeed called Sir Walter Murphy. Perhaps he is incognito. You know the fellow?"

"I made his acquaintance on the journey over and they invited me to travel with them from Le Havre to Paris. Mr. Murphy was insistent that Herr Durand—as he introduced himself to me—was in need of Dupin's skills, whereas Durand was equally insistent that he did not need any help from Dupin or anyone else. They did not divulge any details about the nature of the crime or mystery, however."

"Theft or blackmail or an assassination attempt, perhaps," Dupin said. "Something tedious. Thankfully I have no need to take on cases like that anymore. Unless as a favor to the prefect of police," he added.

"Perhaps the situation is not quite so tedious as you think," Dr. Froissart said. "The grand duke is investigating a theft, it is true, on behalf of a family friend. What the lady has lost is of immense value and utterly irreplaceable. And a villain you well know is implicated." The doctor chose that moment to slowly finish the tea in his cup.

Dupin's interest was piqued, though he tried his best to conceal it. "Well?" he finally demanded.

"The lady lost her only child—a son—years ago and feared him dead. But the grand duke has learned that the boy survived and is now a young man in hiding from his own father somewhere in Paris. Dr. Willis fears that both the young man and the grand duke are in grave danger, as Valdemar had a hand in the boy's abduction."

Dupin's mind was immediately engaged but Madame Morel interjected. "A very sad tale, Dr. Froissart. It is terrible when a parent loses a child through abduction. Truly terrible. But if the German adventurer is not interested in receiving assistance from Auguste, then this conversation is pointless, is it not? One cannot force the man to accept help, even if he is in dire need of it. Perhaps you might secretly assist in some way, but to interfere directly would be detrimental."

I could not help but think that the lady was referring to the obstinate Dupin and his reluctance to take medical assistance. It seemed, from Dr. Froissart's expression, that he did also.

"Wise words, madame." The doctor smiled. "Perhaps I might arrange a meeting between you and Dr. Willis, Auguste? I guarantee you will find him a fascinating person."

Dupin shrugged. "Arrange something through Madame Morel. I have promised to give Monsieur Gondureau assistance with a case of theft tomorrow, which I suspect is a more complicated matter than he presumes, so I may be preoccupied for a time."

The doctor unfurled his long limbs and rose up from the small sofa. "Very good. Perhaps I will bring him along to our next appointment. Farewell, Mr. Poe. I hope to see you again before you return to your country." We shook hands and Dr. Froissart went on his way, leaving me none the wiser as to the nature of Dupin's secret ailments.

9

TUESDAY, 10 JULY 1849

Marriages may be contracts of convenience, alliances based on money, the promise of comfortable living and a good place in society. And there is love like a bonfire, all spark and heat and dancing flame that blazes hot then turns to ash—that is what my mother's parents suffered. And they put it all into letters that traced their love's journey, beginning with ungovernable passion and ending in ignominy. My great fortune was to find a love that was more than mere love with a woman who gave her heart fully despite the lack of niceties I could offer, despite our precarious living arrangements. She was clever and brave and beautiful in every way. Our happiness was brought to ruins by her illness, the agony of her slow death. When my mood turns despondent, I feel certain that it is better never to find such perfect love if one is destined to lose it so quickly.

Perhaps it was our reminiscences of the investigation in London that tainted my dreams with a haze of gloom and resurrected the anxiety I had suffered when I feared losing my wife's affection if she learned of my ignoble heritage, of my bad blood.

"You would never have lost my love had you shown me the letters, had you told me your fears. Surely you know that in your heart?"

I dreamt my wife's voice and the reassurances I wished she had truly said, for it was my great regret that I had withheld the truth from her, had lied through omission and thus broken a pledge never to bring falsehoods between us.

"*It matters not. I knew enough, sensed enough.*" Her gentle voice came to me again, and I woke with a start, shivering in the warm night, my head squeezed tight as if in a vice. I sat up and reached for the cup of water I'd left on the bedside table, gulped down its coolness and near dropped the cup when I heard her voice again.

"*Eddy, you must stay safe. He won't stop until he ends you.*"

Moonlight trickled into the air and coalesced into her form—she was sitting in the chair near the fireplace, glimmering and pale.

"Virginia?"

"*Stay safe.*"

And her form faded to quavering spectral light, then dissipated, drifting away like the seeds of a dandelion clock.

When morning first touched the window glass I left my bed, for sleep had evaded me since the visitation from Sissy. While I had believed in my heart that the spirit of my wife had come to me on those previous occasions, they were so fleeting, so dream-like, that in my head I had half-dismissed what I saw as the force of my memories combined with a powerful wish to see my love again. This was different. We had told each other that our bond was so strong that it would survive death, and surely this was proof of that?

I dressed quickly and crept downstairs to the parlor, thinking I would look through Dupin's library and find some ancient tome to read until breakfast. When I entered the room, I was startled to find Madame Morel, attired in her dressing gown and nightcap, curled up on the sofa, reading a book by the light of an Argand lamp. She too jumped and her book fluttered closed, transforming her expression of surprise to one of annoyance.

"Good morning, Madame Morel. Did you have trouble sleeping?"

"No. It is my routine to rise at this time and read before my morning duties."

I noticed that a cup of chocolate was on the table next to the lamp.

"What is it you're reading?"

Her frown deepened, but she turned the book toward me. "*L'ombre de la damoiselle de Gournay* by Marie de Gournay." She looked to see if the title meant anything to me.

"Certainly I know of Madame de Gournay, but I've not read her work."

"She is a very important French scholar, writer and translator of the early sixteenth century. She translated Sallust, Ovid, Virgil and Tacitus into French, and Montaigne, for one, admired her greatly. Marie de Gournay was an autodidact who strongly supported education for women. She believed—quite correctly—that men and women are intellectual equals." She glared, waiting perhaps for me to scoff at Marie de Gournay's beliefs.

"How very interesting. You will know, if you've read the publications I have edited, that I am acquainted with a number of female writers and intellectuals and, in fact, have published them."

Madame Morel's brows flicked up as she nodded her head slightly, and it seemed to me that her gaze became infinitesimally kinder. Probably I was fooling myself with that notion.

"Very good," she said.

"I will make sure to obtain her books." I was not sure why I felt the need to placate Dupin's irascible housekeeper—she had an attitude that seemed to demand respect. We stared at each other in awkward silence for a time. "I thought I might find something to read." I indicated the bookcase, for I had the sense that Madame Morel was suspicious regarding my presence in Dupin's parlor at such an early hour.

"There are many books there." Madame Morel's voice held a large dollop of sarcasm. "Auguste is very particular about how they are arranged," she added.

"Alphabetically by author."

"You should wait for permission before examining the more ancient works."

"Of course." I did not succeed in keeping the annoyance from my voice and quickly made my way to the bookcase before my impatience became too obvious. I scanned the titles on the shelves and found works by renowned philosophers, celebrated authors and highly regarded historians through the centuries. Despite Madame Morel's command—or perhaps because of it—I was most drawn to the esoterica, artistically bound books that had been in the Dupin family for generations or that he had sourced himself in obscure bookshops or from private collectors. I came across a beautiful treasure book I recognized from its silver spine inlaid with a cross formed from amethysts and rubies. I gently slid it from the shelf and reacquainted myself with the cover—a checkerboard pattern of gold and silver squares, set with precious gems. I undid the jeweled hinges to admire the frontispiece, which was illuminated with glorious illustrations of birds around the book's title: *La Langue des Oiseaux*. Underneath the title was the Dupin coat of arms. My reverie was interrupted by Madame Morel noisily clearing her throat; when I turned to her she was staring at me with a look of cold anger.

"It is a very rare volume. A Dupin family treasure."

"I am aware of that," I said as evenly as I could. "It was stolen by an enemy of the Dupin family and was sold to the library at St. Augustine Church in Philadelphia, which is where my friend found it again. I was very pleased that his journey to Philadelphia resulted in the return of such a precious family heirloom."

"Then you understand that it would be best to ask Auguste's permission before perusing it," she countered.

"I do not think he would mind. Indeed, he offered it to my wife to read when he was visiting us and I simply did not have the time to look at it properly."

Before our standoff could escalate further, there was the sound of the apartment door opening and we both jumped. Dupin strode in moments later, fully dressed, carrying his haversack and spattered in mud.

"Good morning," he said with some surprise.

"You have been in the tunnels?" Madame Morel's anger deepened.

"That would seem obvious." Dupin gestured at his clothing.

"You should not go there alone. You should not go there at all," she snapped.

"Madame Morel, I appreciate your concern, but that is enough on the subject," Dupin said with great formality. "More than enough," he added sharply as she opened her mouth to respond.

The lady turned her gaze to me as if hoping I would support her complaint, but she had done little to win my allegiance. I held up the treasure book instead.

"Madame Morel and I were just discussing how you recovered this family heirloom in Philadelphia. I hope you don't mind that I took the liberty of examining it again. It is such a glorious work and there was no time for me to read it in Philadelphia."

"Please take advantage of my library while you are here, particularly the rarest volumes."

I could not help but turn a rather triumphant gaze to Madame Morel, then immediately felt like an ill-mannered child when she rose to her feet, gathering up her book and her dignity.

"I suppose you will want breakfast shortly. I will get to work," she said.

"There is no hurry." Dupin glanced from Madame Morel to me and back again. "Why don't you read in your room? I am perfectly capable of making coffee for us and I have much to tell Mr. Poe."

Madame Morel looked torn. She was being given a rest from her duties but dismissed to her room, thus being denied the chance to learn what Dupin might have discovered in the tunnels. Dupin stared at her silently until she turned and made for the doorway.

"As you wish." And she was gone.

Soon we were settled at the table with bowls of coffee and Dupin's map spread before us. He made another mark on it before he spoke.

"These points circled in red are the places where I have discovered hidden entrances into the tunnels: rue des Saints-Pères, rue de la Sorbonne, rue de l'École de Médecine, Place du Pantheon, rue Clovis, rue des Deux-Moulins. Make no mistake, there are numerous entrances to the tunnels, but these ones are marked with a discreet symbol of an owl."

"Like the one at the Bibliothèque Mazarine?"

"Each owl is presented differently, designed to fit in with its surroundings. Some are of wood, some stone, others are painted or constructed of metal. But I believe the choice of symbol is relevant."

"The owl hunts at night and is a carnivore," I said. "It is associated with Athena, goddess of wisdom—but the screech owl is sacred to Hades, god of the underworld."

Dupin nodded. "Death and darkness, wisdom and, we might add, magic and mystery. So a cogent symbol for an entrance to the underworld. But it must be more than that."

"Perhaps the owl is a heraldic symbol for some sort of society, guild or family," I suggested.

"That seems plausible. Or a religious order, perhaps."

"Nothing to do with Valdemar?"

Dupin shrugged slightly. "The carvings are not recent, as you will have noted at the Bibliothèque Mazarine. Some of those rendered in stone seem as old as the tunnels. But I do believe that Valdemar is aware of them and uses them. Hence his ability to disappear as if by magic when I have pursued him."

"He went into the tunnels through a secret doorway?"

"I am quite certain that is the case. I also believe he has used the tunnels for his smuggling operations. Objects he stole from other families were hidden down there and then sold or auctioned later. And if he has found troves of precious objects like the one I showed you, it would explain his wealth. Consider the expense to hold a ball as extravagant as the one we attended at Madame Tussaud's in London."

It was an event I would never forget. Valdemar had hosted an astonishing masquerade in Madame Tussaud's exhibition halls, with seven elaborately designed chambers and quantities of performers, food and drink. It was the sort of spectacle that might be held at a palace by a king or a queen.

"One would indeed need unusual resources to finance such pageantry."

"Quite. And it is the type of pomp and pageantry a man who wished to be emperor of France might put on display in a show of self-aggrandizement. Valdemar grows ever more dangerous. He is not content merely to ruin his enemies, he wishes to *rule* them. And, therefore, I have made it my mission to construct a new map of the quarry tunnels that includes all the concealed entrances from the city above so that I might fathom who made them and why—and how best to use them to finally capture Valdemar."

My heart sank at his words. Exploring the quarry tunnels seemed dangerous enough given the physical challenges, but facing Dupin's enemy in such a place—terrain Valdemar may have reconnoitered for quite some time—made Dupin's plan even less attractive.

Dupin glanced at his pocket watch, then stood up. "I must change my clothing and attend to a few things. Help yourself to more coffee and do not hesitate to ask Madame Morel for whatever you'd like for breakfast. We have a meeting with the prefect of police later today. He has asked for my assistance with a case of theft. I think you will find the victim of interest."

"Why is that, may I ask?"

"She is a champion of the arts, of literature in particular, and a poetess—or that is how the lady describes herself."

"And others do not?"

Dupin smiled slightly. "I will let you form your own opinion."

And he was gone.

10

A thin male servant wearing alarming orange livery and a sour expression guided us to the salon. Crossing the threshold into the room was like stepping into a confectionary shop filled with glazed cakes, sugared candies and marzipan sweetmeats, all glistening with a surfeit of sugar. The walls were pale pink and the cornices and moldings pure white, giving the effect of piped icing on a petit four glacé. The space was large, formed by two adjoining drawing-rooms, and it was crowded with a collection of armchairs and sofas, upholstered in competing floral patterns, a disconcerting mix of lemon, lavender, coral and mint. There was a gigantic chandelier overhead—certainly Venetian—that resembled a translucent pink octopus and was, bizarrely, decorated with a quantity of glass fruits hanging from its limbs. All this gave an air of expensive chaos to the room, which was amplified by a crowd of guests chatting as they queued to present themselves to Madame Legrand, who was draped across a violet divan, her face obscured by a fluttering ostrich feather fan. Monsieur Gondureau, the prefect of police, waited with Dupin and I near the ornate white marble fireplace with quite another crowd—the collection of porcelain figures that was arranged there.

"Extraordinary," Gondureau muttered, eyes fastened on the figurines.

"Quite," Dupin said wryly. "Madame Legrand is famous for her willingness to play the muse. She poses for a variety of artists—all for posterity, of course—and was the model for this collection, which inspired her *nom de guerre* 'Undine'."

I looked more closely at the little figures and saw that they were indeed replicas of the same woman, whose hair flowed around her like a fairy-tale princess or, perhaps, a water sprite. The miniature ladies were posed theatrically and dressed in highly revealing costumes or wore nothing but a very proud smile. These were the figures that the prefect of police was examining with great interest badly disguised as consternation.

"Do you like them, Monsieur Gondureau?" A low mellifluous voice made us all jump and turn like guilty schoolboys to its source.

"Ah, Madame Legrand," he stuttered. "What a great pleasure to see you." He immediately reddened at his words as the lady's eyes shifted to the figurines and her brows shot up.

"How kind of you to say so." The purr in her voice undermined her contrived sincerity.

The artist had done an admirable job of capturing Madame Legrand in porcelain. The lady before us had bright golden locks, partly pinned up with jewels, with the remainder of her long tresses tumbling down her back. Her pale blue silk dress was in defiance of the early hour, with her shoulders bared and a foam of lace drawing attention to rather than concealing a daring décolletage. The numerous strands of pearls at her neck did not succeed in bringing any modesty to her costume.

"Madame Legrand, thank you for your kind invitation." Dupin bowed neatly to the lady.

"Thank you for attending my salon, Monsieur Dupin. I hope you will be able to assist me."

"I will do my best. May I introduce Mr. Edgar Poe, a friend visiting from New York. He is a well-known author in his country."

"Truly?" She directed her gaze to me. Her eyes were a vivid turquoise and her skin had a similar luster to the pearls at her throat, adding to the perception that she might in truth be a water nymph. "How very interesting," she said in English. "Will I find your novels in French or will I be forced to read them in your language?"

"I am better known for my poetry and tales than my novel, but fear that if you wish to read them, it must be in English, as they have not been translated to my knowledge."

"Pity." She immediately turned her attention back to the prefect of police and Dupin. "Let me come directly to the point," she said, switching again to French and flicking her fan open to hide what she was saying from the others in the room. "An important letter was stolen during my salon last week. I need this letter, as the thief well knows, to preserve my reputation."

I could not help but glance at Dupin, remembering the stolen letters that had threatened my own reputation. Dupin's eyes met mine briefly, then returned to those of our hostess.

"All in this room, except for ourselves, attended your last salon?"

"Yes. There were other guests too. Perhaps five or six more who sent their regrets today."

Dupin nodded. "A list of names would be useful."

"I will draw one up. And the letter was inside my writing desk—I am certain of it as I put it there just before the first guest was shown into the room. Shall I show you?"

"Yes. And I will observe your visitors for any traces of guilt as you do so," he said in a low voice.

We moved as a group to Madame's writing desk, a delicate piece of painted furniture decorated with pink roses and gilt. She retrieved a small key from her pocket and unlocked the desk. The opened lid was covered in leather and inside there were shelves for paper, pots of ink and pounce, a collection of writing instruments and a slotted area where letters might be stored.

"I placed it here." She indicated one of the slots. "The desk was locked and I always carry the key with me."

"It is not a difficult lock to persuade open without the key," Dupin said, as he scrutinized the other guests. I looked at the literary coterie and could not see anyone exhibiting signs of nervousness or guilt.

Dupin turned his attention back to Madame Legrand and said, "May I ask how it will destroy your reputation? You are widowed and may do as you please in carnal matters. You own your home, do not want for possessions and have property that brings you an income."

"You sum up my position quite well, sir. But despite my efforts to retain my independence, a thief wishes to manipulate and threaten me. I myself have done nothing wrong, but the thief of my letter claims that one of my forebears was involved in activities that some important people might misconstrue."

"And you are being blackmailed?" Dupin asked.

"Yes." Madame Legrand's voice was steeped in annoyance. "I believed that I had secured the safety of my reputation through the written confession of an aged Englishman and that letter has vanished. Worse still, the elderly gentleman has inconveniently died, which I fear is no coincidence, so a replacement confession is impossible."

Dupin immediately entered the throes of ratiocination, then announced: "The Englishman resided in a place called Herne

Bay, I presume, and owned several ships that frequently traversed the channel during the Terror?"

Madame Legrand could not hide her shock at his words. "How did you know?"

Dupin's demeanor became slightly more formal. "I follow the activities of a number of English auction houses as items that belonged to my own forebears are often sold there. I met the Englishman of whom you speak nine years ago on a trip to Herne Bay." Dupin glanced at me, a subtle reminder of the day he had left me in Margate at the mercy of George Reynolds to pursue information about Valdemar. "The Englishman of whom I speak reluctantly confessed his involvement in a smuggling operation instigated by certain individuals here in Paris." Dupin paused to stare at Madame Legrand for a moment. His expression made it clear to me that he thought she knew much more about the smuggling than she had confessed. It seemed that Madame Legrand understood Dupin's insinuation, as she narrowed her eyes and tightened her lips, but admitted nothing. "Suffice to say," Dupin continued, "I know who has your letter—it is the operation's organizer, a man who has profited greatly from exporting stolen artifacts to England and continues to profit from such theft still."

Madame Legrand frowned slightly at the last part of Dupin's declaration. "You speak as if the man is still an active member of the criminal fraternity."

"That is correct. One might ask why he has decided to black-mail you now rather than years previously." Dupin glanced at Madame Legrand in a way that made me think he suspected she was hiding something. It seemed, from her fleeting look of discomfort, that she thought that too. "But truly our task is to retrieve the letter for you."

"Yes, that is a point of urgency. I must first have that letter back in my possession, then you may throw the criminal into

prison as he deserves," she said with a glance to the prefect of
police.

"I give you my word I will do precisely that, madame,"
Monsieur Gondureau said, tearing his eyes back from the figurines that had cast a terrible spell over him.

The astute Madame Legrand replied, "And I give you my
word that if you and Monsieur Dupin succeed in this mission, I
will be delighted to present you a gift from my porcelain collection—they are very valuable, I assure you. You may choose the
figurine that most pleases you." She waved her fan regally at the
army of miniature females on the mantelpiece and gave a tiny
smile as Monsieur Gondureau's face reddened.

"I could not accept such a valuable gift," he stuttered.

"You can and you will, dear sir. And now I must begin the
salon or my guests will become suspicious. I trust none of the
horde knows you by sight, Monsieur Gondureau?"

The prefect of police scanned the group and shrugged. "I do
not know any of your guests by sight, so can only surmise the
lack of recognition is mutual."

"Well, let us hope your deduction is more accurate than it
sounds." Madame Legrand sugared the acid of her words with
a smile. "And you, Monsieur Dupin? Is there any need to conceal
your identity or Mr. Poe's?"

"I think not," Dupin answered. "I am known for my scholarly writings, so my attendance at your salon should not cause
undue suspicion, and Mr. Poe is an author your friends should
be acquainted with."

"Very well, then." Madame Legrand turned abruptly to her
other guests, who were chattering away and helping themselves
to wine and a remarkable array of hors d'oeuvres laid out on a
sideboard. "Shall we begin?" she demanded, immediately
capturing the attention of all in the room.

There was a murmur of assent and a scrabble for seats. The cicada-like chatter of moments earlier turned to eerie silence as the *grande dame salonnière* made her way to her violet divan. When she was settled and a glass of wine was placed in her hand by an attentive fellow to her right, she spoke again.

"I believe those who are regulars of my salon are acquainted, so I will merely introduce three new participants: Monsieur Vidocq, an ardent admirer of the arts." She gave a casual wave toward the mantelpiece. "And the Chevalier C. Auguste Dupin, who is one of Paris's most formidable scholars. Perhaps he is a relation, Aurore?" she asked with a sly smile, turning her gaze to a striking woman with jet curls framing her face and large dark eyes that widened at Madame Legrand's words.

The lady quickly recovered herself and said to Dupin, "It seems we have a coincidence, sir. My brother's name was Auguste Dupin, the son of Maurice Dupin. It was our terrible misfortune to lose him when he was a mere babe. I suppose he would be your age now," she added with a wan smile.

"Your family *lost* your brother?" Madame Legrand asked with mock horror. "How very careless. Or are you suggesting that he was stolen away?" As the dark-eyed woman fixed her with a glare, Undine pretended great wonderment. "Might the Chevalier Dupin be your lost brother, returned to you after all these years?"

She cast a look around the room, her eyes resting on a jovial-looking fellow, who chuckled and said, "My dear Undine, I believe you are insinuating that my plots are laughingly incredible? And yet you have the bad manners to borrow from them."

My face must have revealed my surprise when I realized that the gentleman was the famed writer Eugène Sue, for our hostess did not bother to conceal an ungracious smile at my expense. I was beginning to dislike her more and more—how could I possibly know who was in the room without proper introduction? It was very likely that I had read and possibly reviewed the works of those around me if Madame Legrand habitually invited the crème de la crème of France's authors to her salons, but the physical looks of the country's most prestigious living writers were a mystery to me.

"And my brother was not mislaid or stolen, Undine," the dark-eyed lady said with a bite in her voice. "He died an infant and I recall the day very well, despite my tender age." She promptly turned from our hostess to Dupin. "But perhaps there is a connection between us—is your family from the province of Berri?"

"I am afraid not, Madame Dudevant, or perhaps you would prefer *Monsieur Sand*?" His words set some of the guests chuckling and delighted our hostess.

"She is not dressed for that role today." Undine waved her fan at the lady's rather dowdy frock. "I have forbidden it."

The authoress known as George Sand rolled her eyes at this remark, then turned her attention back to Dupin. "My preference is Aurore, dear sir. Please call me that. All here do, even our wretched *Undine*. And we are, after all, kin in name."

"But not by blood, I fear," Dupin said smoothly. "My father was François. I am unaware of any connection to Berri, though I understand it to be a very pleasant place from your novels," he added graciously.

"I should add," Undine said to the other guests, "that the Chevalier Dupin is highly gifted in the art of ratiocination, so be careful what you say, as he will find the flaw in any unworthy arguments you may advance."

"Then he will be mightily busy with much of what you offer," Madame Dudevant retorted waspishly.

"Oh, pish, Aurore. You are ever more without humor and far better suited to one of Madame d'Espard's dull salons. I need to find a livelier person to replace you—perhaps Monsieur Poe." She flicked her fan in my direction. "He is from America and is a writer of poetry, stories and one novel. Some of you may be acquainted with his work?"

"I have read Monsieur Poe's work," came a voice in English.

I looked around the crowd and met the piercing gaze of a pale man with thinning hair draped over the high forehead of an intellectual. He wore somewhat dandified attire and his mouth turned down at its corners as if perpetually disgruntled.

"Very fine it is too. I urge you all to read his entire canon," he said.

I was about to thank the fellow, but Madame Legrand immediately cut in. "I disagree most completely, Charles. A small sample of Monsieur Poe's verse would suffice, for much of it deals with the same morbid theme ad infinitum. A beautiful woman dies or is on the verge of death or is interred as if she were dead and a man suffers terribly and interminably. It is repetitious and maudlin," she complained in a torrent of French.

I fear my mouth dropped open slightly at the lady's attack. She had pretended to be unfamiliar with my writing, but now it appeared that had merely been a ploy to humiliate me in front of her guests. Before I could gather and defend myself, the fellow who knew my work charged in, reverting to French. His defense of my "genius", as he put it, was littered with vulgarities but most articulate, even when it devolved into an attack on "Undine" for being an illiterate creature of the sea who would not know the difference between the sublime or the derivative in Art, as her own tepid verse demonstrated.

"Enough vapid eulogizing, Charles," the *salonnière* interjected, her glacial tone bringing an immediate chill to the room.

"The only course of action, as I see it, is for Monsieur Poe and I each to recite one of our poems and then to debate which has more merit."

"Excellent idea," a young man effused. From his unctuous expression, there was no doubt whose poem he would prefer.

"Do you agree, Mr. Poe?" the lady asked, fixing me with her turquoise eyes.

"Of course, madame," I said with as much confidence as I could muster. "Will I recite in English?"

Madame Legrand gave me a look that would curdle milk. "We are in Paris, but if you must." She flicked her fan open and then closed it again in a gesture that was perfectly disdainful.

"I would be proud to translate, Mr. Poe," the man called Charles cried out.

"Ridiculous," Madame Legrand growled. "Let him present in English. Those who understand—fine. And those who do not? Well." She shrugged and flicked her fan again. If nothing else, the lady deserved accolades for her theatrical use of an elegant prop.

She took a large gulp of wine, handed her glass to her young admirer and stood up, assuming a dramatic pose like one of her figurines.

"I shall recite my new poem 'The Evening Star'," she continued in her own language, then threw a tiny smile at her acolyte, who would have wagged his tail if he had one.

"Brava!" he chirped before retreating into red-faced silence from the acid gazes he received from the other guests.

Our hostess began her recitation in a hushed, theatrical voice:

"When from my darkened window fades the light,
And shadows dance upon the wall,
I hear the trailing garments of the Night,
Rustling through the marble halls,

All silently, the little silver moon,
Peers down from Heaven up above,
My friend the Night has come and none too soon,
For I await the one I love."

She closed her eyes and pressed her hand to her heart while the young man almost squealed in pleasure. I noticed that the fellow she called "Charles" made no effort to conceal an exasperated sigh.

"The evening star, that messenger divine,
A beacon in tenebrous skies,
Casts off her radiant garments and reclines,
When my true-hearted love arrives."

Undine pretended to throw some article of clothing to the winds and froze in another odd position. I was baffled momentarily, then realized that she was mimicking the poses au naturel that were captured in porcelain upon her mantelpiece.

"With gentle sighs and cooings of the dove,
We ascend in rapturous flight . . ."

As the lady elegantly flapped her arms like a bird, the authoress George Sand openly chuckled, as did Eugène Sue, who was more successful in disguising it as a cough. Undine paused to fix each with a gimlet eye and angrily clawed her fingers, which gave them the look of talons as she drew them back to her sides.

"My morning and my evening star of love—
Come set aglow the chamber of the Night!"

The anger in her voice turned the invitation into an unfortunate demand. Even so, her paramour, who clearly perceived
himself to be the subject of her verse, clattered his hands
together ferociously as he leapt to his feet. And then, to my utter
astonishment, all the others in the crowd applauded sedately
and murmured words of appreciation. Undine nodded her head
coyly at their apparent admiration, then lowered herself into her
chair like a queen and took a goodly gulp of wine.

"Comments? Points for discussion?" she asked.

"Such exquisite rhymings," the young man said. "A poignant
subject beautifully rendered."

"Anyone else?" Undine stared imperiously at the group, but
she was met with shakes of the head. When her eyes met mine,
I was about to speak, for it was inconceivable to me that no one
should comment on the monster she had cobbled together
from several badly translated Longfellow poems, but Dupin
nudged me and, when I glanced at him, his warning was obvious, so I cleared my throat instead.

"I am so happy that you enjoyed it," the *salonnière* smiled. "And
now if Monsieur Poe would do us the honor of a recitation.
Something new, if you please." She presented a malignant smile.

"Of course." I stood and faced the group. "This is a recently
completed piece and my first recitation of it. Apologies for
presenting it in English. Perhaps some day I will translate it into
your beautiful language."

Faint applause greeted my words, but I would not let their
lack of enthusiasm deter me, for truly it would not be difficult
to surpass the ridiculous rhyme the beautiful but talentless
Undine had offered up.

> "It was many and many a year ago,
> In a kingdom by the sea,
> That a maiden there lived whom you may know

By the name of Annabel Lee.
And this maiden she lived with no other thought
Than to love and be loved by me."

Undine grimaced and huffed at those words, but I carried on
with the poem, encouraged by the nods of others around me.
And as I went on, I was pleased that most in the room seemed
transfixed by my words. When I reached the last stanza, I recited
it slowly, with all the feeling I could muster.

"For the moon never beams without bringing me
dreams
Of the beautiful Annabel Lee;
And the stars never rise but I feel the bright eyes
Of the beautiful Annabel Lee;
And so, all the night-tide, I lie down by the side
Of my darling—my darling—my life and my bride,
In her sepulcher there by the sea,
In her tomb by the side of the sea."

I inclined my head to emphasize that it was the end of the
poem. The subsequent applause gave me some comfort that I
had performed with adequate expression and most in the room
had grasped my words. I sank back into my chair.

"Bravo, sir," the excitable dandy called Charles cried out in
English. "It is profound. It shimmers like a dream. It—"

"Oh, enough. It is the same theme yet again!" Undine
snapped in French. "Another woman sent to her grave while the
supposed lover—according to his description of events—
mourns her relentlessly, going so far as to break into her tomb
and sleep there at night, with her *corpse*. Truly, Monsieur Poe?
Tales of the macabre and now poetry too? Why such ghoulish-
ness in matters of love?"

I was stunned momentarily by the ferocity and ridiculous nature of her attack, but again my defender leapt in. His retaliation was as vicious as Undine's, but without the thin veneer of *politesse*. I failed to absorb the entirety of his barrage, but he called her a bumpkin, illiterate and stupidly verbose but without any depth of judgment or delicacy of feeling. And while I was initially pleased with the fellow's defense of my poem, his furious outburst became so much a personal attack it was an embarrassment.

"Monsieur Baudelaire is quite the supporter of your work," Dupin murmured. "He is an interesting critic and promising poet, but his lack of restraint makes enemies."

Undine's expression indicated she was fast becoming one of them.

"Thank you, sir," I intervened. "I am appreciative that you think well of my poem, but am afraid that my French is limited and I cannot comprehend all that you are saying."

Dupin took the opportunity to rise to his feet. "And I am afraid that I have a pressing engagement and must spirit Mr. Poe and Monsieur Vidocq away. Many thanks, Madame Legrand, for such an informative afternoon. Ladies, gentlemen." Dupin gave a half-bow to the coterie of guests.

"As you wish, sirs." Madame Legrand's voice was sharp with anger. I rose to my feet and the prefect of police followed suit. She waved dismissively to the door.

"Thank you, Madame Legrand," I said. "I must echo the Chevalier Dupin's sentiments. I hope we will meet again." This was not true, as the lady was well aware, but it seemed rather unavoidable if Dupin was to locate her letter and return it to her.

"Farewell, Monsieur Poe. I hope some day to read a happier poem from your pen." As she turned back to her guests, Charles Baudelaire leapt to his feet and followed us to the door.

"Mr. Poe, allow me to shake your hand," he said fervently, then shook it overly rigorously. "I am a great admirer of your work and feel that you are my . . ." He released my hand to wave his in the air as if hoping to capture the correct word there. "You are my *semblable*," he announced. "And my inspiration. And it is my mission to make all of France acquainted with your genius."

From another person one might suspect a sarcastic attack, but Mr. Baudelaire's expression was earnest and genuine.

"I am extremely flattered, Mr. Baudelaire. And thank you for defending my new poem, for it is one that means a great deal to me."

"It is magnificent," Mr. Baudelaire said. "I am honored to have heard it from you in the flesh."

"I am pleased." I was beginning to become uncomfortable with such extreme adulation.

"Charles!" Undine's imperious voice seemed to echo through the room. "You are being tedious. Come present something so we may judge if your genius, as you declare it, will save the intellectual spirit of France from our buffoonery."

"Of course, madame. Though I fear there are many who are immune to the redemptive qualities of true Art, as we have already witnessed today," he yelled back.

"Farewell, Monsieur Baudelaire. We really must hurry." Dupin grasped my arm and ushered me and Gondureau toward the front door. I would have liked to have heard Mr. Baudelaire's performance, even if I'd had more than my fill of Undine's flowery verse and evil temper.

11

Gondureau exhaled a gust of pure relief when we escaped
Madame Legrand's apartments, then dabbed at his brow with a
handkerchief. I felt equally uncomfortable and turned to the
direction of the Seine, hoping a breeze would make its way
from the river to where we were standing on rue de la Bûcherie.
My hopes were in vain.

"Are you quite all right, my friend?" Dupin asked the prefect
of police with contrived concern. "Did Mr. Poe's morbid verse
unsettle you too?"

"No, no, not at all!" Gondureau chirped. "Your verse was
most impressive, sir. Very heartfelt. It was Madame Legrand—
she is unsettling, for one never knows when she will pull out the
stiletto and aim for the heart."

Dupin smiled openly this time. "As Mr. Poe experienced. We
will go now and console ourselves with an early supper. Would
you care to join us?"

"Thank you kindly, but I must make my way home. My wife
began cooking *tête de veau* this morning—it is a work of art, my
wife's cooking. Those tidbits in there," he said, waving his hand
at Undine's door. "No comparison with proper French food.
My wife cooks the cow's head with carrots, celery, leeks,

potatoes—delicious! And for seasoning: thyme, parsley, bay leaves . . ." Gondureau was lost in wonderment at the deliciousness he was describing. "Then the head meat is put with the tongue and vegetables in a dish with the cow's brain and cooked some more, then served with *gribiche*—a sauce from boiled eggs, mustard, capers." He kissed his fingers. "Unbeatable!"

"You are making my stomach protest its emptiness," I said truthfully.

"Come as my guests," Gondureau said. "You will see how perfect my wife's food is," he beamed. "But no discussion of the investigation. That is forbidden at dinner."

"That is very gracious of you," Dupin said. "But perhaps another time. Mr. Poe and I must discuss the investigation, I'm afraid, or details might be forgotten."

"And I'm sure your wife would like you all to herself," I added.

"You are missing a treat, but all the more for me," he said, grinning. "It was a pleasure, Monsieur Poe. And thank you, Monsieur Dupin. You will be in touch, yes?"

"Certainly," he replied.

The prefect of police shot off down the road, anxious to get home for his supper.

The aroma of cooked food garnishing the air made my belly grumble, and I was very glad when Dupin opened the door to the establishment from which it was emanating. The building's exterior did not reveal that it was a restaurant, but it was obviously a well-known fact in Paris as a lively crowd was inside. The smoke-hazed windows and flickering candlelight did little to brighten the wood-paneled room with its jumbled maze of ancient dining furniture. We weaved our way through it in search of an empty table. Conversation hummed around us and I had the sense of wandering deep into an enormous beehive.

"Table for two, sirs?" A dapper fellow appeared before us. He had a shiny pate, stood straight as a soldier and wore an immaculate apron.

"Please," Dupin replied.

The waiter led the way through the crowded dining area to what seemed to be the last remaining empty table. Dupin took the seat that placed his back to the wall and gave him a good view of the entire restaurant. I would have preferred that same position, but was accustomed to giving Dupin this privilege— he never allowed himself to be seated anywhere with his back exposed.

"I would recommend the quail and the *civet de lièvre*," the waiter said.

I expected Dupin to demand more choices, but he shrugged. "Fine."

The fellow bustled away and a serving girl arrived, poured us each a glass of wine and left the pitcher with us.

Dupin raised his glass and his mouth twitched toward a smile. "To the talented Undine."

"If rudeness is a talent, the woman is truly a genius." I took a goodly sip of wine, despite the vow of temperance I had made. If there were ever an excuse for a drink it was in feeling the claws of the monstrous Undine.

"It is true that few can compete with her in that area. Monsieur Baudelaire, perhaps, but he is not so cool-headed and descends into shouting insults."

"Rather than speaking them quietly?" I retorted. "Madame Legrand is the most unpleasant person I have come across in quite a while. The Devil himself will surely welcome her into his fold. Furthermore, she is a plagiarist. I am mightily surprised that no one at her ridiculous salon challenged her and cannot understand why you cautioned me against doing so. It was my impression that the purpose of a salon is to debate literature rather than 'brava' a woman who recites mixed-up scraps of Longfellow as an ode to the fledgling she has seduced." I took another sip of wine and waited for Dupin's explanation.

"It is my understanding that Madame Legrand performs a similar piece at each of her salons and those who regularly attend have learned not to challenge her, for she is skilled at talking in circles for hours to avoid conceding an argument. If she were challenged, her guests would not have time to perform and discuss their own work."

"It was hardly a discussion of my poem. She immediately dismissed it after a cursory denunciation of its theme."

"The hatchet man does not enjoy the hatchet," Dupin noted slyly.

"That is not true," I retorted, bridling at his reference to an unwarranted nickname I'd been given as a magazine editor. "There was no dissection of my work. The other guests were denied the opportunity to analyze the piece in any way. Madame Legrand is like her apartments—full of glittering surface, but with little deep complexity of thought."

"Unfortunately, your defender, Baudelaire, did not help your cause. He admires your work so much that it seems no one can critique it without an irrational attack from him in response."

"Again, that is not true. Monsieur Baudelaire's arguments about the quality of the poem were perfectly sound even if his attack of the *salonnière* lacked gallantry. If he and I were permitted the chance to critique Madame Legrand's ridiculous rhyme, a far livelier discussion would have ensued."

Dupin laughed. "Believe me when I tell you that I saved you from yourself. Do you know why Madame Legrand is called Undine?"

"A sobriquet borrowed from Friedrich de la Motte Fouqué's tale, I presume. She is undoubtedly beautiful, with the hair, eyes and grace often attributed to a water nymph."

Dupin shook his head. "Not quite, though that is perhaps what the *salonnière* thinks. She is called Undine because it is said that she was born without a soul and has an inhuman heart."

I could not help but laugh. "A very clever appellation."

"It is also said that Undine kills with a kiss. When she is attentive or kind, all the more reason to be wary. She has, in jest, declared the Marquise de Merteuil her spiritual mother, but most take the notion literally and believe that Pierre Choderlos de Laclos wrote *Les Liaisons dangereuses* as a true account of Madame Legrand's equally notorious grandmother."

"That seems highly possible from what I observed today. Why is it, then, that the literati of Paris venture to her salons with such regularity? They might simply meet in a drinking establishment and save themselves the horror of hearing her verse."

"The answer requires little analysis, Poe. Did you taste the wine? Or the hors d'oeuvres? Incomparable. It is common knowledge that the lady spares no expense on such niceties."

"As it happens, I did not have the chance to try either. And so the truth is that the most prestigious writers in Paris are led by their stomachs rather than their intellects?"

Dupin barked another laugh. "Perhaps we can agree that the French are a very practical people who value food for the body as much as sustenance for the intellect or soul."

"If you say so," I replied. "But what I truly wonder is why you are assisting such an odious person. It is difficult to believe that her forebears were innocent of anything, given how steeped the lady is in malice."

At that moment, our food arrived. Dupin signaled that I should receive the quail and the *civet de lièvre* was placed before him. Both my spirit and my stomach leapt with joy at the sight and smell of the feast before us. Carrots and roasted potatoes accompanied the two small roasted quails and there was a basket of freshly baked bread. I discovered that the *civet de lièvre* was a hare stew with carrots, onion, mushrooms, a profusion of herbs and a thick sauce made from wine, the hare's blood, and flavored with juniper berries, or so Dupin explained. It smelled marvelous and Dupin ladled some into one of the empty bowls we had been provided with. We were both lost in the delicious flavors for a time.

Eventually, Dupin rested his fork and knife and said, "As it happens, I do not believe that Madame Legrand's forebears are innocent. I think both her grandmother and grandfather were in collusion with Valdemar, who conceived the smuggling operation that was run with Mr. Hart, the man I went to see in Herne Bay. Valuable articles stolen from families such as mine were spirited away by Valdemar and others in his employ, who pretended to support whoever was in power at the time. They smuggled the bounty to England on boats owned by Mr. Hart or Monsieur Legrand, then hid the treasure in caves until Mr. Hart's men could transport their plunder safely to London. Madame Legrand was clever enough to demand a confession from a dying man to exonerate her family, for she is aware that even her sizable fortune cannot save the Legrand family reputation if her forebears are revealed as thieves who stole valuable family heirlooms from the French aristocracy to sell at English auction houses."

"Not even her excellent wine and hors d'oeuvres would save her?" I asked, slicing at my quail.

"Touché." Dupin took a long drink of wine and poured himself more. I stopped him from refilling my glass and he raised his brows slightly, but merely pulled the pitcher closer to himself. "As I have pointed out, enmity runs deep and if Undine shows any sign of weakness regarding her less than salubrious reputation, the mob will pounce as she well knows. The lady would not survive for long in prison, even with all the garnishes her money might buy."

"This letter written by Mr. Hart that exonerates the Legrand family must presumably denounce Valdemar. Am I correct in understanding that you hope to find him by assisting Madame Legrand?"

"Yes. She may well know where he is or have information that will lead me to him." Dupin gave a little smile. "And if Valdemar knows that I am assisting the lady, he will not be able to resist challenging me somehow, even if it might lead to his own destruction."

From what I had learned about Valdemar during the years I had been acquainted with Dupin, he seemed to have an unnatural desire to bring misery upon my friend.

"And what is your plan if your assumption proves true? Will you turn him over to the prefect of police?"

Dupin fixed me with his gray eyes and shook his head gently in amusement. "I will not do you the disservice of answering that query, as you undoubtedly know what I will do when I finally corner Valdemar." He drained his glass of wine and immediately refilled it.

When we left the restaurant, I felt far merrier than when we had entered the premises, for the delicious food had successfully diminished my anger at the awful *salonnière*. But while my mood had lifted, the weather had changed. Heavy storm clouds made it appear that dusk had fallen and growls of thunder and flashes of heat lightning greeted us as the first fat raindrops bounced off the cobbles.

"An unfortunate end to a very fine meal when one does not have an umbrella," I said.

"Very true. This way," Dupin instructed.

The rain began to pelt down. As we jogged along the lonely street, holding on to our hats, a burst of lightning suddenly revealed the pockmarked face of a heavy-set man in shabby clothes who loomed before us. The fellow made a grab for me, but Dupin pulled me from harm's way and with a fluid movement thrashed my attacker with his walking stick.

"Run," he hissed as the cutpurse roared in pain and anger. It was then that the heavens fully opened up and rain crashed down upon us in a torrent. The cobbles were treacherous, but Dupin and I sprinted through the deserted streets. Even so, the sound of footsteps followed us. We ran on and on, both drenched to the skin. Dupin's breath became terribly labored, and I began to fear he would be unable to go any further, but thankfully we reached rue Dunôt and his apartment came into view. I jogged ahead of Dupin, whose pace was rapidly diminishing, in hopes of alerting Madame Morel to let us inside. But as I passed a narrow street, a figure crashed toward me and grabbed my arm. It was the cutpurse.

"I have something for you, Monsieur Dupin," he growled. I tried to twist away, expecting the slash of a blade.

"I am Dupin—you have the wrong man." Dupin's words were fractured by his ragged breathing and he staggered toward us on unsteady legs.

The cutpurse turned and leapt back as Dupin swatted at him with his walking stick, but before he could reveal the secret blade, the cutpurse waved a piece of paper.

"None of that! I've chased you far enough and won't suffer another whack on the knuckles. Take this and good riddance." He thrust the letter at me and backed away, keeping his eyes on Dupin's weapon.

"Who sent you?" Dupin asked.

"The Great Berith." The man's voice was steeped in awe.

"I am not familiar with any such person," Dupin replied.

"Everyone in la Cité knows him. And all of Paris will soon," the ruffian declared.

"Truly," Dupin said sardonically.

"Truly indeed," the ruffian averred. "You'll see."

Dupin threw a coin at the fellow's feet. It bounced off the cobbles with a metallic chime and disappeared into the ruffian's large paw before he melted into the night as quickly as he had appeared.

"Let us see what this mysterious Berith wants from me." Dupin made his way up the steps to his apartment door, unlocked it and stepped inside.

12

We were settled in our armchairs, having changed out of our wet clothes, and Dupin was puffing away on his meerschaum as Madame Morel carried in tea, poured us each a cup and settled down on the little sofa she seemed to favor.

"So, was Madame Legrand's salon of interest?" she asked. "It is said that the most important authors attend it."

"That is true, though Madame Legrand herself offers little original in her poetry. She is far more creative in her mischief-making," Dupin observed with ill-disguised amusement.

"You insinuate that the lady follows in the footsteps of her grandmother. She was a dragon who was at her most inventive when delivering insults. A terrible woman and utterly without scruples," Madame Morel added.

"You're aware of the smuggling operation her husband was involved in?" Dupin asked with surprise.

"Believe me when I say that Charlotte Legrand was the mastermind behind it. Her husband was merely a pawn. It was said that Charlotte made certain that if her husband were caught with stolen contraband in his boat, he would die before he could implicate her."

I wondered how the villainous Charlotte had arranged that and, more importantly, how Madame Morel was party to such tales. She had not struck me as the gossiping type, especially as she was recounting tattle of half a century ago. Dupin did not advance the same queries, however, which surprised me.

"The lady is the stuff of legend," he said. "Her wit and cruelty were meant to outstrip her granddaughter's and that, as Mr. Poe will tell you, is not said lightly."

"Let us hope her literary talent did also—but that would not be difficult," I retorted.

Madame Morel frowned slightly. "I can assure you that Charlotte Legrand had no literary talent. Nor did she much admire it."

Again, a strange comment from Dupin's housekeeper. I truly could not understand why my friend was so patient with the odd woman, for he rarely exhibited patience with anyone else.

"Will you open the mysterious message, Dupin?"

He nodded and broke the plain red seal, then unfolded the paper. He stared at it for a moment, then huffed a laugh. "The Great Berith is a magician and mesmerist," he said. "He possesses 'uncanny powers that will astound and terrify'. There is to be an exhibition of his 'extraordinary skills' on the twelfth of July at seven o'clock in Montparnasse, at the theater on rue de la Gaîté."

"An illusionist? That devil who chased us made me think the Great Berith was the leader of a criminal gang."

"And perhaps he is, for surely this is Valdemar," Dupin said, rattling the paper. "Why else would that cutpurse follow us so doggedly?"

As soon as Dupin made his pronouncement, I knew he was correct. An illusionist trying to entice an audience would not employ such an unsavory character to pursue people with his advertising leaflets.

"If Valdemar is luring you to this show, then naturally it is a trap," I noted.

"Yes, but as we are aware of that, it will not be a problem."

I was not sure that Dupin was right, and neither was Madame Morel.

"You must not go," she said vehemently. "It is more than a trick and you will most likely meet your death." The lady stared intently at Dupin, her face pinched with fear. "It is true that the Great Berith is much admired in Île de la Cité, but he has won their hearts through fear. Please do not attend."

The lady's knowledge of the insalubrious citizens of la Cité added to my mistrust of her intentions, whereas her comment merely irritated Dupin.

"I am afraid that I must attend, madame," he said formally.

"Then you must be armed."

"I always am." He nodded at his walking stick, then turned from Madame Morel's gaze. "Have you come across the name 'Berith' before?" Dupin asked me.

"Other than the illusionist advertised on the paper just delivered to you? No, I don't believe I have."

"The name has been borrowed from a far more powerful entity—Berith is a great duke of Hell," he declared. "I will show you."

After that extraordinary pronouncement, he walked over to his library and collected a very large, hammered silver case from the bottom shelf. He set the case, which was about thirty inches in length and twenty inches in width, on the table. What appeared to be a sizable slice of agate was embedded in the case's center and it was held closed on the side by a small lock shaped like a human skull. Dupin removed the stickpin from his neckcloth and inserted the tip into one of the eye sockets, thus releasing the lock. He opened the case and lifted out a tome that was sheltered snugly inside; it had a black leather cover embossed in gold with strange sigils. Dupin opened it and carefully leafed through the highly decorated pages until he came to a wondrous illustration of a glowering soldier dressed in red clothes and wearing a golden crown. The figure was astride a fierce red horse that billowed smoke from its nostrils, and an elaborate border composed of strange vegetation was drawn around them and painted vibrant colors. The text was equally beautiful—all was done by an artist of exceptional skill in the manner of a medieval illuminated manuscript.

"The Duke Berith is a very powerful character with twenty-six legions of demons under his command. He is a liar who only tells the truth when asked a direct question. When conjuring him up, one must wear a silver ring on the middle finger of the left hand and hold that hand before one's face for protection. His adversary is St. Barnabas," Dupin said, his finger lightly tracing along the lines of text. "But the most interesting thing about Berith," he explained, looking up, "is that he is the demon of alchemy and controls the element with which all metals can be transmuted into gold."

"I see. Perhaps the illusionist will transform some objects into gold to astound his audience," I suggested.

"It seems very likely," Dupin said. "For it is not a name one would choose without knowing its origin."

"But what is this volume, Dupin? It looks quite ancient and the artwork is magnificent."

Dupin closed the book gently and ran his hand across the embossed leather. "I purchased it from a dealer in antiquities for a very modest sum. It is a grimoire—quite ancient as you have observed. The seller claimed that it was studied by a gallery of scholars: Albertus Magnus, Johannes Trithemius, Heinrich Cornelius Agrippa and Paracelsus. He believed it to be cursed, however, and was happy to rid himself of it." Dupin raised his brows and smiled at this notion, then carefully turned to the frontispiece, which was illuminated with fantastical beasts from some other world. "The book has no title and no author is attributed. There is only this." He indicated roman numerals written within the flames emitted by a cheerful-looking dragon: *MCCXXIV*. "This grimoire is purported to be the basis of Agrippa's books on occult philosophy."

"It was produced in twelve twenty-four? How extraordinary. I suppose the claim is possible if the date is true."

Dupin nodded. "I have devoted much time to its study these past few years and can assure you that it is not merely a capti-vating work of art—it contains impressive scientific observa-tions, including recipes for medicines, various poisons and their remedies, esoteric philosophy and more. It is a treasure."

This book was the sort of treasure Dupin valued far more than gold, silver or precious gems—in fact, I had first met him while he was on the hunt for precisely that sort of tome.

"But what of this demon, the Duke Berith? I am surprised that Valdemar knows anything about occult entities. I myself have read a number of esoteric works, but was not aware of such a demon."

"I expect he made a perfunctory study of Johann Weyer's *Pseudomonarchia Daemonum* and selected the name of a demon whose character might bring most appreciation from his intended audience. What better than an entity with the ability to change base metals into gold or silver? The promise of that alone would win him many friends. The suggestion that the Great Berith has infernal powers is very useful if Valdemar is trying to win the allegiance of those who live in la Cité, most of whom are criminals with their own violent sense of justice."

"And that is who you will be surrounded by should you be foolish enough to attend that magic show," Madame Morel snapped. She stood up, teacup rattling in hand. "Goodnight, Monsieur Dupin, goodnight, Monsieur Poe." She fixed her piercing gray eyes on me. "Please talk him out of this folly. I fear you will both die if you do not." And with those ominous words, Madame Morel flounced from the room.

Dupin watched her leave, an odd look on his face—one of *admiration*. "She is most stubborn," he said.

"Though not perhaps as mulish as you, my friend."

Dupin smiled. "If you had been here longer, you would change your opinion. Madame Morel is intractable and opinionated, but also, thankfully, knowledgeable enough that I can normally forgive those deficits."

"You forgot to mention that she is unmanageable, at least as a housekeeper. I am beginning to think that you feel a certain affection for the lady." And while I joked, I meant it, despite the fact that I hadn't a clue whether Dupin had ever courted a lady.

"Affection is a strong word. Respect is more accurate. And there would be no point in me hiring a housekeeper who lacked intelligence and interesting ideas, for she would quickly irritate me."

That I knew to be utterly true. Dupin placed the grimoire back into its case and returned it to its shelf.

"By the way, there is another reason for my interest in Madame Legrand's missing letter," he said, as he settled back into his armchair. "Madame Legrand's apartments were previously occupied by her grandparents."

"The grandmother who was the inspiration for the Marquise de Merteuil and the smuggler grandfather?"

"Correct."

And then a puzzle piece slipped into place. "You believe the thief found a more subtle way to steal into Madame Legrand's apartments and abscond with the letter?"

"Exactly. A smuggler such as Grand-père Legrand would have required an obscure way to spirit his plunder to the Seine before transporting it to England. I suspect there is a secret entrance to the tunnels somewhere in the apartments."

"And that is how Valdemar stole into Undine's parlor and took the missing letter?"

"Precisely." Dupin picked up the scroll lying on the occasional table next to his chair and unfurled it on the larger table in front of us, then weighed down its corners with small paperweights. "Here is Madame Legrand's apartment and I believe there is a tunnel that leads to the Seine here." He indicated what would be quite a short, direct route. "Perfect for taking contraband to and from a boat."

"Very true. Do you think Madame Legrand is aware of the tunnel?"

Dupin considered this for a moment. "No, I think not. She would have sealed off any such entrance into her apartments, for the lady trusts no one."

"For good reason. She must have a number of enemies."

Dupin looked amused. "Perhaps. Let's investigate whether my theory is correct tomorrow." He tapped the spot on the Seine where he believed the tunnel to be.

"Very well, though I can't say I relish the notion of spending hours in the empire of the dead, especially to assist a person as unpleasant as the infamous Undine. I have no desire to make Death my master too soon."

Dupin presented me with one of his saturnine smiles. "Fear not, Poe. I give you my word that I will keep the grim reaper at bay during your stay in Paris."

It was a promise that was pleasant to hear, but far too difficult to keep.

13

WEDNESDAY, 11 JULY 1849

The smell of burning bacon and bread woke me from a pleasant, dreamless slumber. I had yet to discern the qualities in Madame Morel that Dupin found so attractive; it could not be her culinary skills as she scorched most everything she cooked. To make it all the more baffling, Dupin was very skillful in the kitchen himself, yet suffered through her dreadful offerings— something one might do for their beloved, but for a servant? I quickly dressed and made my way to the breakfast room, as we had planned to leave his apartment at nine o'clock for our walk to the Seine in search of the entrance to the tunnel Dupin believed led to Madame Legrand's house.

"Ah, Poe. I was about to come and wake you." Dupin poured a cup of coffee and handed it to me. "Are you hungry?"

I looked at his plate, which was filled with blackened bread, burned bacon and charred fried egg glistening with grease.

"Coffee is perfect," I said as I took a sip, hoping it hadn't been boiled. It had. I drank it despite that.

Dupin expertly dissected his own food, removing the charred pieces and putting them on a side plate. Then he lifted the lid from a covered dish and dipped in a large spoon. He ladled two large scoops of perfectly sautéed mushrooms onto his plate and onto a side dish, which he pushed toward me.

"Eat," he instructed. "You will not regret it."

I inhaled the aroma and suddenly felt ravenous. "I presume you cooked these?"

Dupin smiled. "I will not allow Madame Morel to attempt it. Despite her name, the lady has no affinity for *champignons de Paris* and these are the very best."

The mushrooms were as good as Dupin claimed. We savored them in silence and I did not demur when offered more. There was no sign of Madame Morel. Perhaps she was in hiding after her disastrous attempts to cook breakfast and even the clanging of bells announcing a morning caller did not bring her forth.

"Unusual," Dupin muttered as he rose from the table. A few minutes later, he returned with Monsieur Gondureau in tow.

"Good morning, Mr. Poe. I am sorry to intrude on your breakfast." The prefect of police stared at the scorched offerings that were left on the table and frowned, but did not comment.

"Would you care for coffee?" Dupin asked.

"Thank you, I would. My own breakfast was interrupted— my wife was up at dawn baking bread and there is nothing like it fresh from the oven." He looked deeply regretful at the memory of his curtailed feast and took a hearty drink of coffee. I had to smother a laugh at the grimace that contorted his features upon tasting it. "How . . . bracing," he muttered, push- ing the cup away from him.

"You said you had received important news of another crime? Something to do with Madame Legrand?"

"Yes. The lady has vanished."

"Vanished? How do you mean?" Dupin asked.

"According to the officer who brought me the message, when Madame Legrand's maid arose to begin her duties, she noticed that her mistress's bedroom door was ajar and went to see if she required anything, but the lady was nowhere to be seen. The maid found this very unusual as Madame Legrand had retired just before midnight with her assistance, and it is the lady's custom to be roused at nine o'clock to enjoy a cup of chocolate in bed."

"Perhaps she has risen early and gone for a walk?" I suggested.

"Her servants declared that impossible. Madame Legrand always requires assistance dressing and the servants were adamant she would not leave the house without them knowing unless she were abducted." The prefect of the police shrugged slightly and said: "The story has the ring of truth. Madame Legrand demands much from her staff."

"She certainly expects to be waited on hand and foot," I agreed.

"But it would not be the first time a servant had a hand in his or her employer's disappearance," Gondureau added.

"François Benjamin Courvoisier, if you recall," Dupin said to me.

I shuddered. Nine years previously we had witnessed the hanging of Courvoisier, the valet who murdered his employer then summoned the police, pretending that a housebreaker must be the perpetrator. It was good police work, in Dupin's opinion, that sent Courvoisier to the gallows.

"I presume that you have yet to interview the servants yourself?" Dupin asked Gondureau.

"I am on my way there now," he replied. "Given that you were engaged by Madame Legrand to recover her stolen letter, I thought perhaps you would like to accompany me. The two disappearances may be connected."

"We shall see." Dupin rose from the table. "If we question her servants and examine the premises we should quickly ascertain if something prompted Madame Legrand to abandon her usual routine or if in truth she has been abducted against her will as her maid claims. Are you ready, Poe?"

* * *

A gleaming lion's head of brass decorated the front door of number thirty-seven. The prefect of police let the ring clenched in its jaws fall against the door several times until it was finally opened by the servant in the orange livery.

"Ah, Monsieur Gondureau. Thank you for coming. We are very worried about Madame," the fellow said.

"Yes, I understand," the prefect of police replied. "It's Monsieur Poiret, isn't it? And you recall the Chevalier Dupin and Monsieur Poe? They will assist in our search for your mistress."

"Very good," the servant said, looking at us nervously.

"Perhaps you might let us inside, Monsieur Poiret," Gondureau suggested. "We have questions for you and Mademoiselle Michonneau."

"Yes, yes, certainly." The servant stepped back and waved us past him. He smelled heavily of tobacco smoke and unwashed flesh doused with bad cologne. Poiret led us to the rooms where Madame Legrand held her salons. Seated at a card table there was a lady's maid, small and bony, with a plain, shriveled face that had seen sixty years or more. She was puffing anxiously on a clay pipe and exhaling plumes of smoke that gave her the look of a half-starved dragon.

"Monsieur Gondureau!" She leapt to her feet, hiding the pipe behind her back. She peered at Dupin, then me, then behind us. "She is not with you? Your men did not find Madame?"

"Sit, please, Mademoiselle Michonneau, Monsieur Poiret," Gondureau instructed.

The two servants retreated back into their chairs. Mademoiselle Michonneau took a last puff on her pipe, then left it on a saucer. Poiret picked it up, inhaled deeply, then released smoke in a deep sigh.

"I take it that you are Madame Legrand's personal maid?" Dupin asked the woman.

She nodded as she anxiously crumpled her apron in her claw-like fingers.

"When did you last see her?" he asked.

"When she retired for the evening. I helped her to undress and brought her a small cognac to drink as she normally does of a night-time."

"And when did you discover that she was missing?"

"In the morning at seven o'clock. I pass her chamber on the way to the kitchen. Normally her door is closed but this morning it was ajar. I looked in to see if she needed assistance, for usually she does not wake up until I bring her a cup of chocolate at nine o'clock. To my surprise, Madame Legrand was not in her chamber. When I looked in the breakfast room, she was not there either. So I went to fetch Monsieur Poiret."

"We searched the entire house, every single corner, but we found no trace of her," Poiret added. "There was only one possibility—Madame Legrand was abducted, for she could not simply vanish."

Mademoiselle Michonneau nodded vigorously.

"So I ran all the way to the prefecture of police," Poiret explained, "to ask that Monsieur Gondureau be alerted."

"Why did you assume that Madame Legrand was abducted?" Dupin asked. "Perhaps she has merely gone for a morning walk?"

An incredulous laugh escaped Mademoiselle Michonneau. "But that is ridiculous. Madame never rises before nine o'clock, and she is incapable of dressing herself."

"And, of course she would not willingly leave the house in her nightdress. There is no other possibility—Madame Legrand was abducted," Monsieur Poiret asserted.

"There are always many possibilities. It is when they are overlooked through misdirection or one's own carelessness that a mystery remains unsolved." Dupin stared coolly at Poiret and

Mademoiselle Michonneau, which increased their nervousness. "Did either of you hear any unusual noises in the night?" he continued. "Did Madame Legrand call for help? Were there sounds of a struggle?"

"No, nothing," Poiret said. "And it is very unusual not to be awakened at night by Madame. She always rings the bell at unreasonable hours and demands that we fetch something for her. Rarely does one get a full night's sleep when working for Madame Legrand."

"I *never* do," Mademoiselle Michonneau sighed.

Dupin nodded slightly, as if he believed their tale. "Now we must search Madame Legrand's chamber," he told the servants. "It may hold clues that will reveal who spirited away your mistress. If that is what truly happened," he added, giving them a hard stare.

Mademoiselle Michonneau rose unsteadily to her feet, clutching her chair for support, then took a deep breath as if to muster courage. "I will take you there," she said, her voice trembling.

We trooped upstairs to Madame Legrand's bedchamber, which proved to be as overwhelming as her salon. The color scheme was of various shades of pink with splashes of gold and the reigning motif was roses and cupids; indeed the place was swarming them. It was not surprising the lady had trouble slumbering, as the leering cherubs were armed with bows and arrows.

"Bloodthirsty little fellows," a wide-eyed Monsieur Gondureau muttered. "I wouldn't sleep a wink in this room." He turned toward the fireplace, and where one might expect to see a large mirror over the mantelpiece, there was instead an enormous oil painting derived from Botticelli's *The Birth of Venus*, but with Madame Legrand in the leading role, standing in a large scallop shell that floated in a turquoise sea, her long blonde hair flowing around her body in an ineffectual attempt to preserve her modesty. Pink roses rained down from the heavens and a flock of armed cupids fluttered around her, perhaps on the hunt for some fish for her supper.

"Do you prefer the statuettes or the painting, Monsieur Gondureau?" Dupin asked, a smile twitching at his lips as he observed the flustered prefect of police.

"They are both very . . . *artistic*. I really could not choose between them," the fellow muttered.

The servant in orange livery shook his head and rolled his eyes, perhaps overly acquainted with such words of admiration.

"It certainly appears that Madame Legrand was in her bed last night," Dupin said, indicating the rumpled covers and the drawn window curtains. "The smell of her perfume lingers—roses, naturally." He nodded at the pink blooms that infested the room. Dupin threw open the curtains to let in more light and continued his inspection. Something in the bed immediately captured his attention and he pulled back the coverlet to reveal a cobalt blue bottle and a letter. He picked up the bottle first, which was shaped like a skull. "*Atropa belladonna*," he said, reading the label pasted on the back.

"Was it used to subdue her?" Gondureau asked.

"It seems unlikely, for how would any assailant make Madame Legrand drink it?" I wondered.

"A good question." Dupin picked up the letter and began to read it. "Interesting," he said, directing his gaze at me. "Are you aware that you are deeply in love with Madame Legrand and if she refuses you again, you will make certain that no one else will have her?"

"Let me see that," I demanded, and Dupin handed the letter to me. I read the protestation of unrequited love written in my own hand, or, more accurately, in a hand that perfectly mimicked mine. There was no doubt who the true author was. The lurid tale was remarkably similar to one of the fellow's damnably awful theater plays and I realized that the belladonna was a reference to the drug that was used to murder my grandfather, a terrible fact that he, my nemesis, had revealed to me. "Has a man by the name of George Reynolds or George Williams ever called on Madame Legrand?" I asked Monsieur Poiret.

His eyes scanned the ether as he considered my question for a time before he answered with an abrupt, "No."

"An Englishman of about fifty-five years, five and a half feet tall, slight in build, brown hair with some gray through it, long side-whiskers, ordinary features and deep-set brown eyes?" I could not think of any unusual physical characteristic that Monsieur Poiret might remember. The thing that most stood out to me when regarding Reynolds was his intense air of malevolence, but he was hardly likely to display that to Madame Legrand or her servants. He had, to an extent, learned from his unfortunate wife the skill of projecting charm.

Poiret stared at me as if I were especially stupid for a moment, then said, "Madame Legrand has many guests and a number of them could be said to look like that."

"What is the letter?" Gondureau asked, and I handed it to him without thinking. As the prefect of police read the note, his brows crept ever higher up toward his hairline. "I was under the impression," he finally said, "that you didn't much care for the lady's sharp wit."

"I do not."

"But . . ."

"The letter is a forgery, Monsieur Gondureau. Poe's enemy, a man called George Reynolds, is likely to have written it. He is an experienced scrivener and, it seems, an excellent forger. Poe has already received a letter that mimicked my hand. So you must not immediately presume that a letter implicating Poe in some crime is genuine."

Monsieur Gondureau nodded but clearly thought the entire situation more than odd.

"We also think it likely that George Reynolds is being employed by Ernest Valdemar, to use his forgery skills."

"I see," the prefect of police said.

I was certain he didn't, though, because I myself hadn't a clue why Valdemar might join forces with Reynolds, in spite of Dupin's assumption that we shared this conclusion.

Just then, something captured Dupin's attention and he was immediately focused as he picked up a candleholder that was perched on a small table situated beneath the window and next to the bed. He sniffed the candle, which was pale lavender in color.

"Did Madame Legrand recently receive this taper as a gift?" Dupin asked the lady's maid. "From an admirer perhaps?"

Mademoiselle Michonneau shook her head. "From an admirer? No, I don't recall so."

"You have noted that Madame Legrand is very particular. Given the consistency in the tone of her décor, surely she would demand pink candles throughout her bedchamber?" Dupin persisted. With his eyes fixed on the maid's face, he indicated the pink tapers in the wall sconces and on the mantel, then held the lilac candle aloft.

"Yes, the candles are usually pink," Mademoiselle Michonneau admitted, flustered. "I did not notice it was changed."

I did not fully believe her and nor did Dupin. He took a small silver box from his pocket, extracted a match and lit the partially burned candle. We all waited patiently, wondering what his experiment was, then the thick, sweet scent of violets snaked through the room. Monsieur Poiret and Mademoiselle Michonneau soon became unsteady on their feet, and the perfume quickly made me feel sleepy too. As I struggled to keep my eyes open, I noticed that Monsieur Gondureau's had drifted closed. Dupin blew out the little flame and opened the window.

"If you remember, Poe, it was a gift of violet-scented candles that caused the death of my mother. A gift from Monsieur Ernest Valdemar. I believe this taper was used to send Madame Legrand into a deep sleep. Then Valdemar, perhaps with George Reynolds's assistance, spirited the lady out of the house. Reynolds left behind the letter and this curious belladonna bottle in hopes of implicating you or simply to taunt us."

Dupin's theory made sense in light of what we had experienced from our two enemies in the past. Reynolds had delighted in delivering letters to me that were written by my grandparents and showed they were guilty of attacking a number of women in London. And he watched as I desperately tried, with Dupin's assistance, to prove that the letters were false, that my grandparents were not common criminals. Unfortunately, the more we uncovered about my forebears, the clearer it became that they were guilty, and oh, how Reynolds had enjoyed my dismay.

"But how did the men of whom you speak remove Madame Legrand from the house?" the prefect of police asked. "I know this area very well and the houses on rue de la Bûcherie normally have but one point of entry and that is the front door. Monsieur Poiret?"

"There is a kitchen door," the servant explained. "It leads to a small walled garden, but there is no exit from it to the street."

"And I assume you keep both doors locked and bolted?" Gondureau asked, staring hard at the servant.

"Yes, of course! They are bolted from the inside every night and locked. I keep the keys to both locks, and I swear on my liberty that I did not leave the doors unlocked or let anyone in or out of the house last night." The fellow's protestations were so genuine I believed him, and so it seemed did Dupin.

"I have an idea." He strode from Undine's rosy bower and we all hurried after as he led us back to the salon. Dupin stood in its middle and turned slowly in a circle, scrutinizing all aspects of the room, his brow furrowed in thought. He walked over to the desk where Undine's letter had been hidden and pushed it to one side, then proceeded to examine the wall behind it, rapping on various parts of the decorative panel and running his fingers over it.

"There's a void behind this panel," he announced. Dupin shifted his attention to the nearby fireplace and its surrounds. Two matching rosewood panels ran down either side of the mantelpiece and they were carved with plants and creatures of the forest. "See here on the right panel, Poe," he said, beckoning me over.

I looked more closely at the carving and, as usual, Dupin's keen perception had spotted a well-hidden clue: an owl peered from a tree cavity. "You think there is a door?" I asked.

Dupin nodded. "May I?" I moved away from the panel to give him space, and Dupin ran his hand across the owl—but at that very moment the door knocker clanged out. We froze as if caught in a nefarious act. Dupin turned to Monsieur Poiret. "Perhaps you should see who has arrived?"

The servant dithered, torn between his duty and wanting to see what Dupin might reveal.

"Please go," the prefect of police instructed.

We heard the door open, followed by a tense exchange of words, in which Monsieur Poiret explained that his mistress was ill-disposed and could meet with no one, but there was a yelp and a thump and moments later a voice rang out in English: "Ah, Mr. Poe. What an unexpected pleasure." Two fellows strode into the room. I stared at them and they stared at me.

"Herr Durand. And Mr. Murphy. What a surprise to see you here."

"A strange coincidence indeed," the Englishman said. "Where is Madame Legrand?"

"Missing," Dupin said.

"Missing?" Durand frowned.

"Abducted, to be precise." Dupin stared hard at the two fellows, as if viewing them as possible suspects.

Durand and Murphy exchanged a glance. "Incredible," Durand growled.

"Quite," Murphy agreed.

Dupin turned his attention to me. "It appears you are acquainted with these gentlemen, Poe?"

"My apologies. May I present Herr Durand and Mr. Murphy, who were on the *Independence* with me and were kind enough to drive me to your apartment the night I arrived in France. And this, good sirs, is the Chevalier C. Auguste Dupin and the prefect of police, Monsieur Gondureau."

"Ah! Monsieur Dupin. We have been hoping to make your acquaintance," Murphy exclaimed in French.

"Yes? Why?" Dupin responded in English, clearly vexed by the interlopers' presence.

"We wish to engage your services."

"We do not," Durand cut in before switching to French. "Do you know who abducted Madame Legrand?" he asked Monsieur Gondureau.

"Not yet."

"We will assist and bring the devil to justice," Durand declared.

"Not necessary," Dupin said.

"It is for us. I believe the lady has information we need regarding a Monsieur Valdemar who is involved in a crime against a dear friend I am assisting."

This caught Dupin's attention. "Valdemar? What sort of crime?"

"You know Valdemar?" Durand countered.

"I know who he is, of course."

"Interesting. Many believe he has died, but I have found no proof of his demise. Yet, if he is still alive, he is like a ghost. Do you know his whereabouts?" Durand asked.

Dupin shrugged. "What is his crime against your friend?" he asked again.

"He assisted with an abduction."

"Two abductions, in fact," Murphy interjected. "They took place over a decade ago and both victims were believed dead, but we have learned that our friend's son is alive, and it gives us hope. That is why we wished to engage your skills, sir—"

"We have no such desire," Durand rudely cut in. "I am sure you are more than capable, sir, but Mr. Murphy presumes to speak for me when he should not."

"I speak up when you are too stubborn to ask for the assistance you require," Murphy retaliated. "We have followed many false leads about Valdemar's whereabouts, including a smuggling operation in America, which led us back to Paris, for we learned that Madame Legrand's father was in Valdemar's employ. It is strange she has vanished just before our visit."

Dupin pondered this for a moment. "We are as eager to find the lady as you are. And when she is found, I am sure Monsieur Gondureau will relay that fact to you." Dupin bowed slightly. "It was a pleasure to meet you." He returned to studying the panel, curtly dismissing them.

"You've discovered something, haven't you?" Durand asked, following Dupin's gaze. "Is there an entrance to the tunnels there?"

Dupin was visibly surprised by Durand's words.

"Yes, we think so," I said, determined to stop any more cat-and-mouse games between Dupin and a potential ally. "What prompted such a supposition from you?"

"Let us say we gently persuaded a thief we are acquainted with in la Cité to take us to a smugglers' tunnel, which led to a secret entrance in a grand house. It was a house that had a reputation for being haunted as so many valuable objects had mysteriously disappeared from it, despite the doors being fitted with every type of lock invented. The crimes baffled the police." Durand shrugged apologetically to Monsieur Gondureau.

The prefect of police thought for a moment, then realization dawned. "The scoundrel! We'll fix that," he muttered. "Come, let's see if Monsieur Dupin's theory of Madame Legrand's abduction is correct."

Dupin was not happy about sharing what we had discovered with the two strangers, but reluctantly bowed to the majority. He returned to the owl decoration on the panel, running his fingers over it carefully. Then he pressed on its carved eyes and there was a distinct clicking sound as they retreated under his pressure. Dupin then pushed on the panel and it floated inward. The servants cried out so spontaneously that their innocence regarding knowledge of the hidden door could not have been feigned.

"She was taken in there?" Mademoiselle Michonneau spluttered.

"I fear so." Dupin pulled two collapsible lanterns from his pocket and handed them to me. "Would you do the honors, Poe?"

I quickly lit them and handed one to Dupin, keeping the other for myself.

"The secret tunnel of Madame Legrand's father the smuggler," Dupin said with satisfaction.

"You think it leads to the river?" Gondureau asked.

"That seems most likely." Dupin took a step toward the threshold, as did Durand, and Dupin's eyes narrowed. "It would be prudent if you stayed here. There is no telling who or what might be down there."

"We are acquainted with the tunnels," Durand said and he gestured casually at Murphy, who was lighting two lanterns he had retrieved from his own pockets. "And surely it would be best if the prefect of police remained with the servants, for if the lady was abducted, perhaps a demand for ransom will be delivered."

"A good point," Gondureau said, eyeing the murky portal with trepidation. "And I will need to visit the morgue to see if Madame Legrand has been delivered there."

Mademoiselle Michonneau gasped at his words and collapsed into a chair. There was something inconsistent in the reactions of Undine's servants. They appeared to heartily dislike her, which was not surprising to me, but they also seemed genuinely fearful that she might have been harmed, which made me doubt they were accomplices in her abduction.

"Shall I lead the way?" Durand held a glowing lantern aloft and, without waiting for an answer, plunged ahead of us into the void. Murphy hastily followed.

"Come, Poe, before your friends commit some reckless folly." Dupin stepped over the threshold and entered the tunnel. Holding the dainty candle flame before me, I followed him into the ravening darkness.

14

Golden light shimmered along the bleak walls, but our four lanterns did little to dispel the malevolent atmosphere. Sounds were amplified: pattering feet, the flutter of wings, chatters and squeaks—sounds that might fill one with the joy of nature in a woodland or some attractive city park, but evoked nothing but dread in this tomb-like space.

"How far to the river?" I asked Dupin.

"Approximately a quarter of a mile," Durand answered. "As the crow flies."

"I believe you mean, as the *bat* flies or the *rat* runs," Murphy said grimly.

"Indeed I do not," Durand said cheerfully, "since they do not travel in a straight line. If this tunnel mimics the movements of a bat or a rat, it might be very twisty indeed and far longer than a quarter of a mile."

Murphy groaned. He did not seem to relish our journey through these Plutonian depths any more than I did.

"I believe the tunnel will continue to be quite straight and spacious if it was used to smuggle their spoils to the river," Dupin said. "But there may be hidden chambers along the way where stolen goods were stored, so be vigilant."

Good advice that did nothing to ameliorate my unease.

"Look here." Dupin stopped and held his lantern up to the wall. There in its glimmer, just below shoulder level, was a number "37" etched into the limestone and traced with charcoal. Next to it was a carved arrow that pointed in the direction we had come from. "A useful marker for smugglers," he added.

"And there," I said, holding my own lantern up higher. Niches were cut into the tunnel walls and from the sooty marks and dribbles of wax it looked as if candles had been burned there.

We walked forward silently for a few minutes until Dupin observed: "Notice we are moving up an incline."

It was subtle, but Dupin was right. "You think the path will lead directly to the riverbank—no stairs?"

"Correct."

"A chamber," Durand announced.

On the left-hand side of the tunnel there was a fissure in the wall that would be difficult to see if approaching from the other direction. Durand turned to go in, but Murphy grabbed his arm. "Wait." He shone his lantern into the entrance, as did Dupin and I. It was a cave of about six feet long and six feet wide, tall enough to stand up in, and it was empty.

"Large enough to store a goodly amount of plunder," Dupin observed.

"Or a body," I added.

"Very true," Murphy agreed.

And then I saw a glint on the floor where my lantern light fell. I stepped inside the chamber and stooped to pick it up. It was a jeweled hairpin.

"Madame Legrand's?"

"Very possible. We will ask her maid later," Dupin said, pocketing the hairpin. "Let's continue."

We returned to the tunnel and trooped along until Durand called out, "There is a passageway to the right which would appear to turn away from the river and run south."

The four of us clustered at the opening, holding up our lanterns so they beamed their thin light into the tunnel, but they did little to dispel the deep gloom. Dupin suddenly darted further in, his lantern held at shoulder level. He stopped to scrutinize something on the wall.

"Strange. There's a complex glyph here on the wall, gilded with silver so it catches the lantern light. It is some kind of marker for those who know the tunnels well."

"I'm sure you're right, Monsieur Dupin, but our mission is to see if the main tunnel leads to the Seine. Perhaps you will come back to study that route at another time."

"Our mission, sir, is to fathom where Madame Legrand's abductors took her. It may have been to the river or it may have been in another direction," Dupin snapped.

But Durand was already on his way, moving at speed through the main tunnel, Murphy at his heels.

"Puffed-up imbecile," Dupin muttered, but he quickly followed after them, as did I.

Eventually Murphy said, "I see light."

There were indeed faint glimmers, like cracks in the darkness. Moments later we came to a large wooden double door at the end of the tunnel. It was secured shut with a flat metal bar that slotted into a sturdy bracket affixed to one door and a large bolt on the other.

"Locked against entry from the outside," I observed. "Controlled, it seems, by the inhabitant of thirty-seven rue de la Bûcherie."

"And anyone familiar with the passageway that branches off from this tunnel," Dupin added.

"Let's see where we are," Durand said. He lifted up the bar, moving it as though he was reversing the hand of a large clock. Murphy cautiously pushed one of the doors open and Durand peered out. "There's an overgrown track perpendicular to the entrance, screened by thick shrubbery. It's wide enough to get a wagon down it." He and Murphy exited and we followed cautiously. I pushed the door closed behind us.

"Let us hope no adventurous soul comes across this entrance," I said to Dupin. The other two were already out of sight. "Or Madame Legrand's home may have some unexpected visitors."

"Unlikely, I think," Dupin replied. "It's well hidden and most fear the tunnels, including the police. Come, let's see what the German and the Englishman are meddling in now."

Dupin hurried along the track and I followed. We came to a gap in the shrubbery and found we were on a footpath that ran along the Seine. Herr Durand was striding along a good hundred yards ahead of us with Murphy in tow. When we caught them up, he pointed at the single-arch masonry bridge that spanned the Seine just ahead of us.

"Pont au Double. Interesting."

"How so?" Dupin and Murphy said simultaneously, the first with an edge of sarcasm, the second with pure curiosity.

"It leads to the Île de la Cité, of course," Durand said.

Both Dupin and Murphy nodded, as if Durand's meaning were obvious.

"And that is relevant . . . why?" I asked.

"It makes this the perfect smuggling route. The tunnel to the river and then either along the Seine by boat or across Pont au Double to the light-fingered citizens of la Cité," Herr Durand said as he made for the bridge. Murphy immediately hurried after, with Dupin hard on his heels.

"Are we going somewhere specific?" I called after Durand.

"Le Lapin Blanc—'The White Rabbit'."

I reached Dupin's side and gave him a questioning look. "Do you know it?"

"No," Dupin responded. "But he is correct about it being the perfect smuggling route. I am curious to learn more."

"Why the Lapin Blanc?" I called again to Durand.

"It is a den of thieves. We will have lunch and find some answers. When one has heavy pockets, much can be learned from Mother Ponisse."

"If her food does not kill us first," Murphy grumbled.

Durand laughed. "Do not worry so much about the food. It is her customers who are more likely to fatally disagree with you."

Dupin looked unfazed by Durand's comment and seemed confident we would discover something useful at the Lapin Blanc. I was far less convinced. It wasn't the first time I wished I had a pistol with me and I feared it would not be the last.

15

"Nightly Lodgings Here" was written in red letters on the glass of the lamp suspended above the front door.

"For rats, fleas, bed bugs and worse," Murphy muttered.

It felt as though the smaller of those pests were scurrying up my back as we prepared to enter the Lapin Blanc, a dilapidated building situated in the middle of rue aux Fèves, its windows covered in a coat of whitewash that obscured the view of whatever awaited us inside.

The interior was even less salubrious, dimly lit, smoky, with an oppressively low ceiling. The plaster on the walls was cracked and sooty, the floor was made of packed earth scattered with old straw. Most of the tables were occupied. Two men sat huddled over a pitcher of wine, whispering and casting furtive glances around the room. They looked to be beggars, their clothes in tatters, beards untidy, faces an unhealthy shade, but they'd consumed quite a feast by the stack of plates, bowls and pitchers on their table. There was a young fellow—barely more than a child—sitting alone, staring into his large jar of wine. Further away, near the hearth, six brutes tore into a scorched carcass like wolves and swigged at jugs of some powerful liquor. At a table in a secluded alcove, a young girl sat by herself, sipping at a watered-down glass of wine, and near her were two unoccupied tables in need of a good clean. Durand sat on a bench stationed at the least filthy one and we gathered round him.

"Mother Ponisse!" he called out as a matron took her place on the other side of the lead-covered counter. She was very fat and florid, with her hair tucked up in a cap and wearing a shabby rabbit-skin shawl draped over a plain woolen frock. Sitting on the counter next to Mother Ponisse was her familiar, an ugly brute of a black cat with an ungainly physique and vicious yellow eyes that missed nothing—or so I imagined.

"Ah, sir. Very good to see you." The matron's eyes—and her cat's—gleamed at the sight of Durand. She bustled over, wooden shoes clattering. "You'll be wanting a nice spread. May I suggest four quarts of the best wine, a basket of bread and two harlequins to start with?"

"Whatever you think best, madame," Durand said, emanating charm.

"Of course, of course," she said with a grin, returning to her counter. "For you, an excellent price. We have missed your company. Wine first, eh?" And she vanished through a door that led to the kitchen.

"Excellent price?" Murphy scoffed. "More like triple the price."

"A small amount to pay for the information we require," Durand retorted.

"We shall see. You might have insisted on something better than a harlequin," Murphy grumbled.

"What is a harlequin?" I asked with some trepidation.

Dupin shrugged slightly at my query, but Murphy obliged. "A hodgepodge, a bit of this, a bit of that—meat, fish, cheese, poultry. In truth it's the scraps servants collect from the homes of the wealthy and sell on to Mother Ponisse."

My expression must have reflected the lurching of my stomach, for Murphy gave me a sympathetic nod. The normally fastidious Dupin seemed less concerned about the origins of our fare, for he was scanning the room, examining our fellow guests, who had gone silent when Mother Ponisse greeted us. I wondered if they were more or less suspicious of us after her display of favor. My eyes kept returning to the young girl sipping her wine, for she looked incongruous in such a vile and dangerous place. Her features were pretty—she had sorrowful blue eyes and lovely auburn ringlets, but was too thin and alarmingly pale. Her overlarge brown dress and worn-out orange-colored shawl did not diminish her melancholy charm. Her only ornament was a necklace of coral beads that her fingers anxiously touched.

"Here you are, my friends." Mother Ponisse deposited four quarts of wine on the table along with four cups. "Your feast will be ready shortly. Enjoy." She bared her ochre teeth in what was meant to be a smile and waddled back to the kitchen door, where she shouted instructions to someone unseen. Returning to her station behind the counter, she said with false jollity to the young girl seated near her, "Come, my little princess, sing for your supper."

The girl glanced nervously over at us, but did as she was told and began to sing a sorrowful song with a clear and lovely voice. Durand had taken it upon himself to pour us each a cup of wine, but he paused in his duties to listen to the songstress. There was a pattering of applause and a number of ungentlemanly declarations of appreciation from the wolves near the fireplace. The girl was rewarded with a bowl of soup and bread, which she immediately began to devour.

Durand leaned toward Dupin and murmured: "I am sorry, but it is best if we speak to each other in English while we are in here."

"It is not a problem," Dupin responded. "My English is perfectly adequate." From his tone, I understood that he was insulted Durand might think otherwise.

"Very good," Durand smiled, oblivious to Dupin's irritation. "The Lapin Blanc is a place of rendezvous for those with little regard for the law and Mother Ponisse knows a great deal about what goes on in the criminal fraternity, for men deep in their cups seldom remember to guard their tongues. She herself is an 'ogress'—a returned convict—though I'm not certain what her crime was."

"Crime? I promise you there was more than one. Calling the inedibles she sells for supper 'food' is a crime in itself," Murphy declared.

I glanced over at Mother Ponisse. If she understood English and overheard what was being said, she was quite the actress. Certainly, "ogress" was the perfect sobriquet for the woman, given her countenance and physique; she looked exactly like the sort of creature that might grind human bones to make bread.

"Ogresses with a good mind for business such as Mother Ponisse," Durand continued, "provide services that cater to the dregs of Paris: thieves, assassins, returned convicts and other criminals. She plies three trades: she keeps the Lapin Blanc, she provides furnished rooms and she lends clothing—at a price— to the poorest on the streets of la Cité."

Murphy was about to make a comment, but snapped his mouth closed when Mother Ponisse arrived at our table, ushering in the smell of sizzling fowl and fish.

"Your harlequins." She set down two trays laden with pieces of chicken, biscuit, sausage, tarts, mutton bones, pastry crust, fried fish, vegetables, cheese and woodcock's heads, the last of which turned my stomach.

"Thank you." Durand handed over some coins before she revealed the price. The widening of her eyes made it clear that he had paid an even more extortionate amount than Murphy had expected she would demand. She immediately stashed the coins in her bodice for safekeeping.

"Much obliged, sir. If you need anything at all I'll be right where I always am." She made her way back to her station, where the cat stood guard.

"Tuck in," Durand said, helping himself to a tart, which he quickly gulped down, then launching into one of the odious woodcock heads. He grinned at our reluctance to follow suit. "It is much better than you presume."

I took some cheese and bread while Dupin sampled a tart. The wine was close to vinegar but undoubtedly safer than water to drink.

We ate for a time, Dupin, Murphy and I tentatively, while Durand consumed the food before us with such gusto it did not seem feigned. As we picked at our dubious feast, a strange character moved past us to approach Mother Ponisse. She was an old woman, neatly dressed in a brown gown, a red and black checked shawl and a white bonnet, but with a very ugly face and only one round green eye. When she directed that glaring orb in our direction, her evil expression made me shiver. I noticed that Dupin also watched surreptitiously as she had a muted conversation with the ogress. I could not hear what was said, but Mother Ponisse handed the one-eyed woman a pouch that jingled when she bounced it in her hand before secreting it in her gown.

"Thank you, dearie," she rasped, then bestowed a horrible grin on Mother Ponisse, who scowled at her in return. The one-eyed harridan tottered past us again and out the door.

Durand leaned in, took the chicken leg he was chewing out of his mouth and said in a low voice, "*La Chouette*—the screech owl."

"More a harpy than an owl," I muttered.

"Perhaps," Durand nodded. "She will maim or murder for a fee and is said to enjoy her work—an evil creature both hated and feared in la Cité."

I glanced over at the sorrowful nightingale of a girl, but there was just a half-empty bowl and glass at her table.

"Perhaps it is best if I present our questions to Mother Ponisse," Durand continued, taking a break from his meal and sitting back. "What is it you wish to know?" He looked first at Dupin, then me, and back again at my friend. I expected Dupin to debate Durand's offer, but I was wrong.

"We must find out if she knows anything about our mutual enemy, Ernest Valdemar, and his accomplice George Reynolds, along with any smuggling operations in the area connected to Madame Legrand," Dupin said.

Durand nodded. "Presumably you wish to conceal your true names from the lady?"

"Of course," Dupin said.

Durand immediately waved at the ogress. "Mother Ponisse, will you have a glass with us?"

She immediately bustled our way, a drinking jug in her hand. "Thank you, sir. Your company is always a pleasure." She pulled up a chair. Durand poured her a liberal measure of wine and she helped herself to various delights from the harlequin, licking her fingers and smacking her lips.

"These are my fellow tradesmen," Durand said. "Monsieur Dubois who constructs fans," he said, pointing at Dupin, "and Monsieur Petit, who is a fan painter like me."

It had not occurred to me up until that point that Durand would have concocted an alternative life for himself while rubbing elbows with criminals. Fan painter? Presumably he chose the occupation to explain the fact that he did not have the rough hands of a manual laborer. I hoped the canny ogress would not grill me on the subject of fan painting as I knew nothing about it.

"Ah, what a lovely trade. You are artists, unlike this charcoal seller," she said, sneering at Murphy.

"It is an *honest* if dirty job," Murphy retorted, then barely suppressed a yelp as Durand kicked him under the table, presumably to halt further insulting repartee that might jeopardize his interrogation.

"My dear Mother Ponisse. It's common knowledge you're aware of all that goes on in la Cité."

The ogress gave a queenly nod at the perceived compliment. "Perhaps not everything," she demurred. "But I am very respected and many do confide in me."

"That is obvious." Durand nodded. "We"—he indicated Dupin, me and himself—"have been given the opportunity to make some fans for a lady named Madame Legrand. I wonder if you have heard of her? I ask, as there is talk that she is not quite the fine lady she pretends to be."

"I have heard of Madame Legrand," the ogress replied. "'Undine', they call her, but she is sly as a fox. Perhaps she should be called 'Reynard'." She grinned as if she had delivered a wonderful witticism and Durand, to his credit, slapped his thigh and roared with laughter, which made her more confiding. "Her servants come here on occasion—a pinched, skinny woman, very plain, and her fiancé, who is also thin, short in stature, ill-tempered and ungenerous. If you have heard rumors that they steal from her, the rumors are true," she said vehemently. "They have tried to sell their spoils in my tavern and always demand double of what an item is worth. Though they never get it," she added.

Not from Mother Ponisse, I imagined, guessing she was in the market for stolen goods. It would not be surprising to find that she was involved in smuggling also. I looked to Dupin, who gave a subtle shrug, which was not lost on the ogress.

"I have had no dealings with them, of course. I have merely heard rumors."

"I understand," Durand nodded. "And what of Madame Legrand herself? You suggest that she is unscrupulous and this worries me."

"Oh, she is sly, it is true. Without doubt. But why does that worry you, my dear sir?" Mother Ponisse took a deep drink of her wine, eyes locked on Durand, eyelids fluttering as if flirting with the fellow.

"Is there something in your eye, Mother Ponisse?" Murphy asked with mock concern. "Would you like me to look for you? Hold the candle up and I will gladly help."

She scowled back at him, then grabbed a woodcock head in her large fist and delivered it to her mouth. There was a horrible crunching of bone as she devoured the thing and Murphy flinched, much to her amusement.

"Such a dainty eater for a charcoal seller," Mother Ponisse said. "Perhaps you believe yourself above your station in life. If so, you are very mistaken." The ogress delicately licked the tip of each finger on her right hand to emphasize her point.

"Madame, I know my station and do not imagine myself above it," Murphy began. The wince on his face suggested he had suffered another boot delivered to his shin.

"Let us forget my friend the charcoal seller for a moment, Mother Ponisse, and return to your comments about Madame Legrand—sly like a fox, you said. I do not mind revealing to you—and you alone, my dear friend—that your description of the lady makes me very nervous. For Madame Legrand has ordered quite a number of fans from us. I fear if she is as unscrupulous as you so delicately suggest, we may never be paid." Durand fixed his large eyes on the ogress and waited. She returned his stare, but in a much more calculating manner. It was clear to me and to Dupin, but not the man himself, that the ogress was utterly aware of his efforts to charm her.

"Tell me more," she leered.

Durand sighed deeply then admitted: "The subject causes me great pain. We four have all accumulated terrible debts. If Madame Legrand sells the fans for us as promised, we are saved. If not . . ."

Mother Ponisse threw back a gulp of wine, then patted Durand's hand in a manner that was meant to be reassuring. "My poor dear fellow," she soothed. "What a terrible spot you have yourself in, for Madame Legrand is not to be trusted. If she promised to ship your painted fans to England where they might fetch a large price, believe me when I tell you that I'd find you a better price and would take a smaller commission. Do not allow yourself to be duped, my boy."

Durand stared at the ogress in awe. "How did you know that Madame Legrand said she had a buyer for our fans in England? It's a secret I've told no one."

The ogress laughed. "It's common knowledge amongst the leaders of la Cité that Madame Legrand's family smuggled goods to England to sustain their fortune. Her forebears were criminals, no matter how much they sought to hide it with fine clothes and fine manners. And she follows in their footsteps. Perhaps they duped the high and mighty citizens of the Left Bank, but not those of la Cité," she said proudly.

Durand shook his head as if stunned. "You have saved us much misfortune. Let me ask you another question then, my friend." He filled her jug and pushed a tray of food toward her. Mother Ponisse immediately consumed several mouthfuls, which she washed back with wine.

"Ask away, sir, ask away," she finally said.

"Madame Legrand mentioned two men that she had dealings with—I believe they had something to do with selling the fans. I worry that if we refuse to do business with Madame Legrand as agreed, we may have trouble from her associates."

"You are right to worry," she agreed.

"I feared so. Now tell me, do you know Monsieur Ernest Valdemar or a fellow who works for him called George Reynolds?"

Mother Ponisse's small eyes immediately narrowed and she examined Durand as a cat might an insect.

"Valdemar, you say?" she asked lightly.

"And George Reynolds," he added.

The ogress took a long draft of wine until her jug was drained, then stood up and made her way back to her counter.

"Mother Ponisse?" Durand asked.

She began to polish her counter with an old rag that was probably doing more harm than good. The cuckoo clock on the wall behind her suddenly whirred into action, the bird launching itself from its home to sing its name twice.

"You are welcome to come here for the wine and for the food, but leave your questions behind next time," the ogress said in a brutal tone. "Do not assume I am a spy who sells her secrets like Madame Legrand's servants have been known to do. Now I think it is time for you and your friends to leave." She nodded her head at the door.

"As you wish, Mother Ponisse. I did not mean to offend you," Durand said contritely. "For your good health." He laid several more coins on the table and led us from the tavern.

When we were outside, following Durand down a narrow, winding street, he said, "She obviously knows them, but that helps us little."

"She fears Valdemar," Dupin said. "Or is in business with him, or both."

"Yes, it seems so," Durand agreed.

"And she will be telling Valdemar that the four of us were in the Lapin Blanc and asking questions," Murphy added.

As we followed Durand, who seemed very familiar with the area, the houses became murkier in color, more dilapidated and closer together. The stench increased when we went by alleys the sun failed to illuminate even at its zenith. We passed houses with food stalls on the ground floor, where men and women were selling wilted vegetables, worm-eaten fruit and meat populated by colonies of flies. Despite this, there were bars on the windows to protect those paltry wares from la Cité's inhabitants at night.

I was disoriented and confused by the rabbit warren we were in, for it seemed that we were walking further into the heart of the Île de la Cité rather than making our way to Pont Neuf or another bridge that would take us to the safety of the Left Bank.

"Herr Durand, is this the right direction? We seem to be moving away from the river."

"You are correct, Mr. Poe," he said in a low voice. "Someone is trailing us and I wish to remedy that. Don't turn to look," he added.

"Short fellow with a limp?" Dupin asked.

"Correct. A child, actually, but a devil just the same. A spy and worse. The ogress may have sent him, or perhaps his father, who is a bigger criminal than Mother Ponisse. This way."

Durand led us down one narrow street, then quickly turned into another and pressed himself up against a wall, directing us to follow suit. Moments later, the fellow tracking us came into view, looking this way and that. Durand leapt out and grabbed the wretch by the coat, lifting him up.

"I have warned you about skulking after me, Tortillard," Durand said.

A boy of about ten wriggled in Durand's clutches. He had a weasel's face, small, black restless eyes, no chin to speak of, a yellow complexion and a wild thatch of hair that matched it.

The fact that he was pinned to the wall, legs dangling, did not faze the brat.

"I was not following you, sir. I was going to visit my grandmother," he said in a wheedling voice.

"Well, she shall have to wait a few hours for your company," Durand declared. He nodded at Murphy, who took a length of rope from his coat pocket and trussed the boy's hands to his feet so he could not move. He then removed a kerchief from his pocket and tied it around the boy's eyes.

"Help me! Help!" the boy yelped.

But no one came out into the street to see what the commotion was. Perhaps the neighborhood was accustomed to such disturbances. Durand stuffed his own handkerchief into the boy's mouth, thus transmuting his words to muffled grunts and growls.

"This way," Durand said, striding away from the trussed-up boy. "Someone will come along and release him and it's best to put some distance between us before then."

And he led us at pace back through the winding narrow streets to Pont Neuf. Once we had crossed the river to the Left Bank, the air seemed suddenly much sweeter.

16

After our adventures in la Cité, we separated from Herr Durand and Mr. Murphy, who promised to relay any information they uncovered about Madame Legrand's disappearance or our mutual enemy through the prefect of police. Durand and Dupin seemed eager to escape each other's company while Murphy and I were equally keen to join forces.

"He is very stubborn," Murphy observed.

"Very," I agreed. "He is not intentionally rude."

"I was referring to Durand," he laughed. "But the two have certain qualities in common—or perhaps I should say 'faults'. Here, this is where you will find me." He removed a small notebook from his pocket, scribbled down his address with a mechanical pencil and handed me the page. "Durand prefers to keep his lodgings as a hard-working fan painter secret, but my accommodation is near to his on the rue du Temple."

"Thank you. And you know where I am staying, of course."

We went on to relay what we had discovered to Monsieur Gondureau, who insisted on buying us a decent supper to chase away the taste of Mother Ponisse's food. He said that he had visited the morgue, but there was no sign of Madame Legrand there, which was reassuring. The prefect of police was deeply concerned, however, when Dupin informed him that the tunnel from the lady's house did lead to the river and that whoever had abducted Madame Legrand might have smuggled her onto a boat or across Pont au Double into la Cité.

"I fear for the lady's virtue if that is the case," he said. "It is true that Mother Ponisse makes her living as a tavern-keeper and landlady and that she lends clothes for a price. But she is also a purveyor of lady's charms, if you understand me, and not all the ladies work willingly for her."

"Mother Ponisse is formidable, but if she hopes to press Madame Legrand into service, I doubt even she will have much success," I said. The young songstress with auburn curls was another matter entirely, though, and it pained me to think she might be a victim of the tavern-keeper.

"The ogress is more ruthless than you think," Dupin told me. "However, I observed Mother Ponisse during the German's interrogation and am certain that Madame Legrand is not held captive by her. Her dislike of the lady is so extreme, it is doubtful she would be able to contain her glee at having the upper hand over Undine."

"But if the ogress is as ruthless as you say, she will not hesitate if she has a chance to *indenture* her, for want of a better term," I observed.

Dupin nodded. "True. You may wish to have your men watch the activities at the Lapin Blanc with extra vigilance," Dupin suggested to the prefect of police.

"I will make sure of it," Gondureau said gravely.

It was almost ten o'clock at night before we arrived back at number thirty-three rue Dunôt.

"How peculiar," Dupin muttered, staring up at his parlor windows, which were glowing with light.

"Is something wrong?"

"The curtains are not drawn. Madame Morel is very rigorous about drawing the curtains when she lights the rooms. She dislikes the notion of voyeurs." He hurried up the steps and unlocked the door, then pulled the rapier from his walking stick and warily stepped inside. I followed as Dupin led the way upstairs. The door to his apartment was closed, but unlocked.

"Madame Morel?" Dupin called. There was no response. "Madame Morel?"

He advanced, rapier still at the ready. Silence was so heavy in the air not even our footsteps could disturb it. I vowed that I would find somewhere to purchase a weapon the following morning. Dupin continued through the hall toward the parlor, and when we reached the doorway it was evident that something had happened to Madame Morel, for the room was empty but in disarray.

"Let us look in the other rooms."

We made our way to the kitchen, breakfast room, Madame Morel's bedchamber and my own room, but his housekeeper was nowhere to be found. We went to Dupin's bedchamber next, which was modestly furnished with a plain suite of walnut furniture. The only luxury was displayed on the mantelpiece: a marvelous golden Belanger clock, decorated with two sphinxes.

"It was closed, I am certain of it," Dupin said, making his way to the window, which faced the back garden.

"Surely no one could enter the apartment from that window? Three floors up?"

"Let's see." He leaned out of the window and twisted to look up, then pulled himself back inside. "There is a rope," he announced. "Attached to the chimney. It appears that someone came from the roof and lowered himself to the sill, opened the window and climbed inside." My face must have expressed my disbelief, for Dupin said: "Look for yourself."

I leaned out and twisted round to stare up at the roof. A rope did dangle from above, near enough to the window for a highly agile criminal to make his way inside. I looked at the considerable drop—surely a fall to one's death—and pulled myself back inside.

"A dangerous way to gain access," I said.

"A method of entry Madame Morel would not expect, making it far easier to take her by surprise."

"If Madame Morel were attacked, especially if taken by surprise, she would scream as loudly as she could, would she not? And surely someone would take notice of the cries of a woman in peril? We should speak with your neighbors."

"Now that we are certain Madame Morel has been abducted, that is sensible," Dupin agreed.

We went to interview Dupin's neighbors on the lower floors. The elderly couple who lived below Dupin thought perhaps they heard a thump but nothing more, and they saw nothing suspicious. No one answered the door when we called at the other apartment. We approached the occupants of the buildings on either side of Dupin's also, but again nothing suspicious was noticed.

"Very odd," I said when we re-entered Dupin's apartment. "Madame Morel is undeniably bold and clever. It is surprising she did not make enough noise to alert someone to her situation."

In truth, I was beginning to wonder if Madame Morel had been abducted at all. Perhaps she had colluded with her supposed attackers.

"There are ways to subdue people quickly and quietly," Dupin said. "And as you are aware, many who directly witness a crime give conflicting accounts of what occurred. It does not surprise me at all that my neighbors do not recall hearing anything unusual."

Dupin led the way to the parlor and stared intently at the disruption. The sofa Madame Morel favored was overturned, as was the occasional table next to it. Her copy of *L'ombre de la damoiselle de Gournay* lay on the floor next to a glass that had held red wine, which had splashed the carpet. He then paced around the overturned furniture, occasionally squatting down to look more closely.

"If Madame Morel was sitting here on the sofa, book in hand, glass of wine on the occasional table, it would not be difficult for an assailant to creep up on her from behind and either put a cord around her neck or perhaps a bag over her head so that her cries were muffled. She would drop the book, which by my calculations would fall just there," Dupin said, indicating the volume on the floor. "As she struggled, it is likely that she or her attacker would upset the glass of wine. Pulling the sofa over backward would make it more difficult for her to fight back and put her in the perfect position to be trussed up. For she would need to be unconscious or tied up to remove her from the apartment." Dupin looked to me for a reaction.

"You are presuming that what we see before us is the aftermath of a struggle," I said, giving voice to the doubts that were growing in my mind. "But might all this merely be staged to seem so?"

Dupin immediately shook his head at my suggestion. "You mean staged by Madame Morel or an accomplice? Of course not."

"I am merely raising the sort of question you yourself would normally ask if brought to the scene of a crime by the prefect of police."

"You seem to have an unreasonable dislike of the woman," Dupin said with annoyance.

"And Madame Morel knows that you lose all sense of objectivity where her actions are concerned. She also knows that you would immediately believe she was abducted when faced with this." I waved my hand at the disruption before us. "But it is hardly a difficult scene to create."

Dupin frowned. "Why on earth would Madame Morel stage her own abduction?"

"What better way to purloin something of value, yet appear entirely innocent?"

Dupin laughed with disbelief. "So, in your opinion, Madame Morel has just absconded with some valuable artifacts. Why tonight, dare I ask? If theft was her objective when asking for employment in this house, why wait for weeks when she has had ample opportunity before now?" He laughed again and strode over to the bookshelves. "We had better test your theory." He scanned the meticulously arranged shelves then turned to face me, mock surprise on his face. "How peculiar, the books are all in place, even the priceless treasure books—surprising, given they would not be difficult for the lady to carry off." He pivoted in a circle and silently pointed at various items. "Silver candlesticks, a small Dürer, a jeweled snuffbox—all possible to steal away on one's person." He raised his eyebrows at me.

"We must be thorough in our investigation—facts not presumptions, as you always insist. I think the better strategy is to look in Madame Morel's room and see if any of her possessions are missing. If they are, we must be suspicious, for an abductor would not allow her to bring anything with her. If nothing is missing, it lends some credence to the presumption that she was carried off against her will."

"Fine. Let us test your suspicions," Dupin said with a baleful look, then turned heel and led me to Madame Morel's bedchamber. It was small, sparsely furnished and utterly lacking in decoration. It could have been a room within an institution. There was a chest of drawers, a small armoire, a bed, an empty bedside table.

"Investigate," Dupin said, gesturing at the room. "Find proof that Madame Morel is a thief or a spy, or whatever duplicitous creature you think her to be."

He was obviously offended by my insistence that we examine the evidence rather than work from presumptions, but I felt I had to protect him from himself, for hadn't he done the same for me in the past? We had already looked under the bed when searching for Madame Morel, so I began with the chest of four drawers. It was an uncomfortable task under Dupin's judging gaze, but to acquiesce to his determined belief that Madame Morel had nothing to hide would be a dangerous disservice to my friend, for the best dissemblers were the most convincing. The drawers proved to be filled with the lady's garments, but nothing else. I felt like a criminal rifling through her delicate things, which were of surprisingly good quality—excellent silk, lace, the finest cotton, beribboned and beautifully stitched. I had expected the plainest fabric, unadorned, highly starched.

I looked to the armoire next. On top of it was a large carpet bag, which was empty. According to Dupin it was the bag she had arrived with and he believed that if she were a thief, she would have filled it with valuables and spirited it away with her. I thought that was too obvious. The armoire itself contained several very plain ladies' garments and a worn pair of boots. I could not accept that Madame Morel kept nothing more personal than unexceptional clothing, so I pulled out the garments and inspected the interior of the armoire more closely, rapping on the wood, testing for signs of anything hidden, but again found nothing. I returned the clothing to the armoire and as I picked up the boots, felt something solid lodged in the toe of the right one. I unbuttoned the boot and reached in to extract a very small, hinged box, which I held out to Dupin triumphantly.

But he merely shrugged. "Open it, then. Reveal all the terrible secrets of Madame Morel's past."

"Very well." But my attempt to dramatically reveal the box's contents was thwarted, for it was locked. "You see? Madame Morel has something to conceal."

"It's a jewel box, Poe. They often have a lock and key, though I grant you that putting a lock on a box this small seems pointless given how easily it might be carried off. But allow me." He took the diamond-topped pin from his neckcloth and undid the lock in seconds. He handed the jewel box back to me. "Please. Astound me."

I lifted the lid and found a wedding band and a golden locket set with a small diamond. I looked to Dupin for a reaction, but he merely shook his head.

"Do you find it surprising that the lady was married? She told me as much when she first arrived. She is a widow."

I ignored him and prized open the locket with my fingernail, hoping to find a portrait or an inscription. I was disappointed. It contained a small lock of dark hair, but nothing more.

"And what have you proved with your investigation, Poe? Let me see," he said sardonically. "The items are attractive enough but of no great value beyond the sentiment associated with them, so perhaps we might rule out the notion that Madame Morel stole them from some previous employer. You may have learned that Madame Morel is more sentimental than you presumed and if she is as fond of these two pieces of jewelry as concealing them suggests, then it is unlikely she would abscond without them. Correct?"

I had sorely wished to prove that Dupin was foolish to trust a woman he knew so little about, but his argument had a ring of truth to it.

"You may be correct, but I am only following the principles you have instilled in me—look at the evidence, do not rely on mere presumptions."

"I am glad I have taught you something, Poe, but we are wasting time that might be more profitably used to fathom who abducted Madame Morel and where she might be."

I put the little jewel box back into the boot and the boot back in the armoire. "What are you thinking—that Madame Morel, if she were abducted, found a way to leave a clue?"

"Possibly, though if taken by surprise that is unlikely. Her abductors might have been careless, though."

We returned to the parlor and Dupin collected from the library shelf an ornate magnifying glass that he used to look at fine detail in his precious books. He got down on his hands and knees and examined the carpet with the glass. I prepared to crouch down too, but he held up a cautionary hand.

"Better if I do this alone as I am looking for a hair or something from her attacker's clothing."

I watched as Dupin conducted his inspection, but to his disappointment, he found nothing.

"Help me with the sofa, please," he asked.

We righted it together and as we did, a small notebook with a mechanical pencil attached by a chain was revealed on the floor.

"Madame Morel's?" I said, passing it to Dupin.

"Yes. She often writes down observations as she reads and transfers her thoughts to a larger journal later." Dupin opened the notebook and flicked through it. "Look, Poe." It was open to a page with a pencil drawing, a complex symbol with an arrow and crosses and curling lines that meant nothing to me. Under it was scribbled: *Follow beneath Undine's.*

"It's the glyph highlighted with silver that I saw in the smugglers' tunnel," Dupin announced.

"You believe it's a clue regarding Madame Morel's abductors? From her?"

"Possibly," Dupin said.

That notion made my skin prickle unpleasantly, for if Dupin were correct, the clue had something to do with the tunnels, and Madame Morel had firmly warned us about the dangers there. She knew something she had not fully revealed—had that danger come to claim her?

"But unlikely," he added, still staring at the note. "The handwriting looks like Madame Morel's, but an expert forger like your enemy George Reynolds could easily produce this. Furthermore, if Madame Morel were taken by surprise, as it appears, she would have had little opportunity to scribble a note, especially given the intricacy of the symbol."

"Perhaps she wrote it under duress? Her abductor or abductors forced her to write it?" I did not like to think that Reynolds was so closely involved in these nefarious activities.

"That is possible." Dupin looked again at the message then closed the little notebook with a decisive snap. "In the unlikely event that Madame Morel found a way to write this note quickly in hopes we would find it, then it is a clue as to who abducted her and where she might be. But if her abductors wrote it or forced her to, then it is very likely to be a trap."

"Quite," I said, as I picked up the occasional table and returned it to its proper place. "And I hope we will do our best to avoid delivering ourselves into it." Then I retrieved the housekeeper's copy of Madame de Gournay's book. Inside the tome was a paper marker, and I could not resist turning to that page. The marker was, in fact, two tickets.

"Dupin," I said. "There's something else." I handed him the tickets, even though every fiber in my body wished to tear them up into small pieces.

Dupin examined them. "Tickets to see the Great Berith perform. Our second invitation."

"I suspect they arrived earlier and Madame Morel was reluctant to give them to you."

Dupin looked more closely at the tickets, which had our names written on them, specific seat numbers, the theater address and date of the show—the same one advertised on the leaflet the cutpurse gave us.

"And here, the same sigil," Dupin murmured. He showed me a delicate border on the tickets and I saw that it was composed of a series of the same glyph drawn inside Madame Morel's notebook. Then he batted at his head and exclaimed: "My memory is failing me!" He charged over to the bookcase and pulled out the silver-cased grimoire he had shown me, then brought it to the table near the armchairs. He quickly opened the skull lock with his diamond stickpin and lifted out the tome inside, then leafed through the beautiful book until he came to the illustration of the Duke Berith, the glowering soldier dressed in red clothes astride a fierce red horse.

"Look, Poe. Do you see?" He tapped at the page and I saw that same peculiar symbol drawn next to the demon's name. "I don't know why I failed to recognize this sigil in the tunnels."

I took a deep breath. "Tell me that we are going to heed Madame Morel's advice—that we will not attend the Great Berith's show."

Dupin stared at me, a look of incredulity on his face. "Don't be ridiculous, Poe."

17

THURSDAY, 12 JULY 1849

Mornings or evenings, afternoons or the depths of night—I cannot say which makes me feel most alone, but when darkness falls, the region of shadows seems so very near, more tangible than the waking world. It was a Saturday when my wife left me and her funeral was three days later on the second day of February 1847. Words of consolation were an appreciated kindness but could not truly lift my spirit. I would have been lost without Muddy's stoic presence, her practical ministrations that ticked through the day like a reliable clock, or Catterina's warmth and solemn gaze of affection. The nightmare that continues to cause me most pain is one in which I dream my wife has returned, as if from a holiday, and we discover that her demise has been a terrible mistake. I feel confusion and relief— and fear that she might learn we had, in error, presumed her dead. So persistent is this reverie that it leaves me disoriented for hours with the pain of hope. It is the dream I had that night and which left me uneasy in the morning, expecting to find Sissy at the breakfast table. But neither she nor Madame Morel were there.

Dupin was awake, however, and immersed in planning our day. He handed me a soft-boiled egg with toast, sautéed mushrooms and a cup of coffee, as if he had known precisely when I would arrive at the table.

"When we finish breakfasting, we will go back to the place where we saw the sigil on the tunnel wall and see if there are further clues that might help us to locate Madame Morel. It may be that she is being held captive somewhere that is accessible through the tunnels."

I was not pleased with the idea but knew Dupin's intuition was likely to be correct, and, needless to say, I had to assist.

It was the perfect morning for walking so we made our way down rue de la Vierge and turned right onto quai d'Orsay so we might follow the river to our destination. Sunlight danced on the ripples of the Seine and the air had a surprisingly fresh smell. Birds performed acrobatics near the water and called out to each other while Dupin and I strolled along in companionable silence. When we arrived at the hidden door that led to the smugglers' tunnel, I wondered if it might be locked shut again, but it yielded when Dupin pulled it toward him. Once we were both inside, Dupin slid the bolt in place.

"Do you fear we've been followed?" I asked.

"I don't fear it," Dupin said. "But it is wise to guard against the possibility." He lifted his pocket lantern and I followed suit. Gold light danced over the walls, in eerie contrast to the morning sun on the river. We walked for a time, Dupin directing his lantern light to the wall on our left while I used mine to illuminate the track before us. When we came to the turning the gloom seemed to thicken. Dupin held his lantern up to the wall.

"Here it is," he said. There was a silvery glimmer as the gilt on the curious sigil captured the light.

We continued on down that passageway, our footsteps echoing around us, our lantern lights quavering.

"We are moving south," Dupin said. "Away from the river and toward the catacombs."

"Wonderful," I said with gritted teeth.

Our journey felt long and slow, most of it made in silence as we examined the walls for clues and listened for any sign that others were nearby. Eventually Dupin held his light up to the wall and revealed another quarry marker.

"We are getting closer to the catacombs," he said. "Visitors are taken in through the Barrière d'Enfer, but there are many other ways to enter the ossuary."

"By dying, for example?" I asked grimly.

"Yes, but that is not our plan."

We continued down the tunnel until Dupin caught sight of another mark on the wall: the sigil of Berith.

"This way," he said.

I merely followed as I had lost my sense of direction long before. Then the surface under my feet seemed to change—I lowered my light toward it and saw with horror that crumbled bones were mixed with the gravel that covered the floor. Moments later, we rounded a curved wall and my gasp of fear echoed around us. There, illuminated by our quivering lights, was a wall composed of bones, thousands of them, and these were interspersed with skulls that appeared to be grinning at my discomposure. The display of long-dead bodies was completely hideous, yet elegantly arranged—as if the demons of Hell had been gifted with an artist's sensibility.

"It may seem a morbid notion," Dupin said, reading my unspoken thoughts, "but to leave the bones where they were would have been far worse. Louis-Sebastien Mercier made a number of pertinent observations in his twelve-volume master-work, *Tableau de Paris*. He noted that whenever a new grave was dug at the Cimetière des Saint-Innocents, older human remains had to be exhumed and these were stacked in the charnel

houses, where the rats lived amongst them. Many were frightened by witnessing the disturbing animation of the bones,
which in truth was merely the vermin moving beneath them,"
Dupin explained.

"I see." Unfortunately, I did, instantly envisioning the shifting
and rattling of bones until they reassembled into their human
forms and began a macabre dance of the dead.

But Dupin kept walking calmly along the path, leading me
on a tour with all the composure of a guide describing the
history of a museum's treasures. "Worse still, the newly buried
corpses polluted the air as they decayed, bringing such a stench
to the area and inside the very churches that quantities of
incense could not obscure it. The unwholesome air also brought
pestilence to the living. An injunction was carried out to stop
the use of the cemetery when the walls of a basement that
bordered it collapsed under the weight of the cadavers, and it
was decided that the old quarries might be a useful place to
rehouse all the bones. It was a very practical solution," Dupin
added.

"But gruesome. And it's an egregious thing to remove the
dead from their place of burial and use their bones to construct
a decorative wall in this morbid necropolis." I indicated the
cross formed from skulls in the wall before us. "How did families feel about their ancestors, their loved ones, being shifted
from a cemetery to the remains of a *quarry*?" As I said the
words, I thought for the briefest of moments that I saw my
wife, pale as ivory, in the eternal night of that terrible grave-
yard, and then she was gone. "And what of the dead themselves?" I muttered. "What do they think of it all?"

"It was done in a very ritualized and respectful fashion, Poe.
On the seventh of April, 1786, the ground of the quarry tunnels
beneath rue de la Tombe-Issoire was sanctified and the inhabitants of the Cimetière des Saint-Innocents were transferred after

nightfall in funerary carts draped in black sheets. Priests walked with the carts, chanting the Office of the Dead." Dupin waved at the wall of skulls and bones stacked before us. "Over two million were exhumed from the Cimetière des Saint-Innocents. By 1814, sixteen other cemeteries were also exhumed and their dead brought here."

A veritable march of the dead—the stuff of nightmares, like the one I was caught up in at that very moment. On one wall, amidst the skulls and bones, I noticed a plaque that declared the remains in that area were from the Cimetière de Saint-Laurent, moved to the ossuary in 1804. Then I saw something more chilling.

I grabbed Dupin's arm. "Look—is there someone up ahead?" There was a light shimmering and for a moment I wondered— no, *feared*—that it might be Sissy. Why, I do not truly know.

Dupin began to tread more carefully, but as we neared we saw it was a stone urn on a pedestal with a flame burning within it.

"The sepulchral lamp," Dupin said with what sounded like relief. "To assist with the quality of the air."

His words directed my fears away from the supernatural and back to more tangible threats.

"But is it always lit or has it been ignited in anticipation of our arrival?"

There was silence for a moment, then Dupin admitted: "I don't know for certain."

This was unusual and added to my worry that Dupin would charge in recklessly if he believed he could ensnare Valdemar. My senses were overly heightened as we continued along the pathway that was bordered by walls constructed with pleasingly arranged osseous matter. We kept walking and at every possible turning, Dupin checked for the sigil of Berith. I felt someone was watching us, but we met with no other surprises

until we came to a turning and held up our lanterns to see a
curving passageway heaped full of scattered bones more than
six feet deep.

"It's like the lair of some mythical beast that has devoured
thousands of humans," I murmured.

"One might imagine that," Dupin said softly. Surprisingly, he
did not offer an explanation for that awful mountain.

After what seemed an endless sojourn through that necropolis, we came to a steep flight of stairs, and as we ascended, faint
daylight began to drift down to us. A door with dusty windows
was before us, and as we pushed through it, we found ourselves
in a mausoleum where red, yellow, blue and green light cascaded
onto the stone floor from a stained-glass window above the
outer door. The room we were in was large enough to hold a
very plain but sizable casket, which looked to be newly placed
there. Above the casket, affixed to the tomb wall, was a white
wooden plaque, with an inscription painted in elegant black
letters. Dupin and I stared at the words written there:

> Edgar Allan Poe
> 1809–1849
> Writer of Tales, Poet, Critic
> After life's fitful fever, he sleeps well.

Dupin read the words aloud and they seemed to reverberate in
the chamber and inside my own head. An eerie calm fell over
me—was it truly so? Had life receded away from me so quickly?
And then Dupin strode over to the casket and heaved up the lid.

18

I had expected to see a body, neatly dressed in somber attire, hands clasped across the breast, chalky skin, a rictus mouth, lifeless, staring eyes. I had expected to see my own self lying there.

But inside the casket was a woman attired in a white lacy dress, a veil falling from dried orange blossoms that crowned her chestnut hair. Her gloved hands clutched a bouquet of the same flowers to her bosom. Tied around her neck with a ribbon was a locket in the shape of a heart. Her face was chalky white and she had a rictus grin—true enough—for all that remained of her youthful form was a gleaming skeleton. There was a white satin pillow next to the bride's head and on it was a red rose, placed in the indentation left by someone's head. It was as if her husband had joined her in death, but rose up again and abandoned her there.

I emitted a sound like a wounded animal, then my breath wheezed in, smothering my anguished voice.

"Poe . . ."

I reached for the locket with trembling fingers and after some effort managed to prize open the jewel with my nail. It fanned into a pair of hearts. A film of tears blurred my vision for a moment and I blotted my eyes with my cuff.

"It was your wife's locket?" Dupin asked.

I shook my head. "She did not own such a jewel." I steeled myself to examine the portraits inside more closely. On the left was a miniature of Virginia and on the right was one of me. It was a likeness I detested, a tiny replica of the portrait my wife had insisted on hanging in our parlor. Few knew of its existence but my family and some friends. Dupin had seen it when at our house in Philadelphia. So had George Reynolds.

My friend waited quietly as I composed myself. When I felt that my voice would no longer quaver, I said, "The locket was not Virginia's, nor were the miniatures. This painting of me is a replica of the one that was in our parlor—perhaps you remember it?"

"Yes, of course."

"When George Reynolds came to our home on the pretext of inviting us to his wife's memorial, he took notice of the portrait. You will recall that he also met Virginia at Professor Renelle's magic lantern show and he saw her again at the theater the night his wife was murdered. Either someone under his guidance painted the miniatures or Reynolds is able to forge paintings as well as documents."

Dupin contemplated this briefly. "Yes, I see. That Reynolds was involved in the abductions of both Undine and Madame Morel seems certain now. Furthermore, to direct us on this circuitous and futile expedition he must have known we went into the tunnel at Undine's, for the message left in the notebook would mean nothing to us without that knowledge—information gleaned from Madame Legrand's servants perhaps or possibly from Durand and Murphy."

"But what reason would Reynolds have to abduct these two ladies?"

"Aside from the opportunity to torment you? Money. For I am confident that the sigils of Berith were put in place by

Valdemar over many years as part of his smuggling operations, and given Reynolds's knowledge of this navigation system, it seems very likely that he was tasked with the abductions of both ladies by my enemy for some foul scheme we have yet to discover. Whether or not this particular odious little game of Reynolds's was with Valdemar's permission, however, we can only guess." He gave a resigned sigh as he lowered the casket lid. "I am sorry you were subjected to this grotesquery, Poe, but if there was any doubt before, it is now clear that Reynolds is in league with Valdemar."

His words rang with truth and yet as my fingers gripped the polished wood of the casket, I again felt the agony of watching my wife's coffin descend into the earth.

"Do not let these theatricals unsettle you, Poe. Your pain will merely gratify Reynolds."

"I'm fine," I lied. I ran my fingers once more across the casket, then stepped back and focused my gaze on the glowing stained-glass window above the mausoleum door until my urge to weep subsided.

Dupin pushed the door open and stepped outside. I followed. The sky was utterly blue and sunlight made the tombs and headstones gleam so brightly I felt dizzy.

"Where are we?" I asked.

"The Cimetière du Sud in the Montparnasse quarter. It is but twenty-five years old." Dupin led the way along the footpath that followed the cemetery wall. "Valdemar must have had the tomb constructed, either to conceal an entrance to the catacombs that already existed or to hide the creation of a new entrance."

"For what purpose?"

Dupin's face was pinched with annoyance. "It makes little sense to me. Perhaps it's a quiet place to steal in and out of the tunnels at night."

We reached the cemetery gates.

"And now?" I asked Dupin.

"I must see if Valdemar has arranged a similar torment for me." He took a deep breath and exhaled. "It might be better if you took a carriage back to the apartment, for my task now is to make my way to the morgue. You have endured enough today."

His kind words made me all the more determined not to fall prey to Reynolds's ghoulish theatricals.

"I will come with you. Of course."

A trace of a grateful smile appeared on Dupin's lips and he nodded.

We crossed Pont Neuf and the carriage rattled along quai des Orfèvres for a short distance before slowing to a stop behind a number of other vehicles.

"It's best if we walk from here," Dupin announced and exited the carriage. He paid the coachman, then he and I continued along the road that overlooked the Seine in the direction of Notre-Dame, which crouched dramatically at the other end of Île de la Cité. Before long we came to a grim-looking building that was surrounded by a crowd of well-dressed people—men, women and children—most of whom were in high spirits and cheerfully heading toward or away from the building. Another group was gathered near the wall that looked out over the river and was observing some activity on the water.

"What is this, Dupin? Some entertainment?"

"For many," he said. There was a line of people waiting to enter the building, which I realized was our destination, and Dupin was immediately impatient. "Wait here," he instructed when we joined the line, and he strode off to the entrance, where a boy in uniform—blue trousers with a white stripe down the leg, a deep red jacket and a soft red hat—lounged against the wall. After Dupin spoke to him, the boy scurried into the building and returned moments later. He nodded to Dupin, who signaled me to join him. "Brace yourself, Poe," he said when I reached him and we walked inside.

I nearly turned back round again. Our stroll through the ossuary had been macabre enough, but this was hideous. We were in a sort of enclosed courtyard; large viewing windows with metal grilles ran round the perimeter and behind them were tables where the recently dead were displayed for anyone to gawp at. A number of the bodies had been ravaged by the waters of the Seine or time itself, and I struggled to keep the contents of my stomach in place, then felt overly sensitive when I observed a boy and a girl, both no more than ten years old, press their faces up to a grille and stare hard at the corpses. I joined Dupin, who stood in the center of the courtyard, scrutinizing all the living people as if looking for someone. Perhaps Valdemar.

"I take it you are well known here."

"Well enough. I told the service boy I was here under instruction from the prefect of police, and the morgue-keeper allowed us immediate entry." Dupin nodded at a middle-aged man smoking a meerschaum who wore the same uniform as the boy outside. "The dead are brought here daily, often by barge on the river—you saw the spectators at the wall overlooking the Seine. If a person is missing, relatives and friends are encouraged to come here to look for the body—as we are now doing. The dead are kept here for three days then sent for dissection."

"So it is important not to delay if someone goes missing."

"Precisely. If Madame Morel is here, we'll know she has been murdered. If she is not, we can only hope that she still lives."

We joined the line of people shuffling along slowly, peering through the metal grilles at the corpses on display as if admiring paintings at an art exhibition. The bodies were lying on inclined marble tables, their heads resting on a copper pillow so the faces were visible. They were unclothed but for a small screen of metal to hide their private parts, and the clothing they were found in hung from a hook on the wall behind them.

"This building was once a butcher shop." Dupin indicated the hooks. "The garments are hung with the bodies to assist with identification. If a body has been in the Seine for too long it can be difficult to recognize the features."

That certainly seemed to be the case with several of the corpses we gazed at as we moved along with the crowd. Dupin breathed in sharply when we came to the body of a woman the same height and build as Madame Morel, with a face that had been mauled in a terrible way—by some hideous underwater creature, I imagined.

"Vitriol," Dupin muttered. "A horrible trick of some of our worst citizens. Thrown in the face to disfigure the victim or to prevent identification of a body." He stood for a time, staring at the unfortunate woman.

"I do not think those are Madame Morel's garments," I offered. "The lady favored somber clothing, but it's plain to see, even though the dress is ruined, that it is expensive and frivolous, made of pale pink silk and much lace."

Relief came over Dupin's face. "Yes. Of course. Certainly not a dress she would wear." He shook his head slightly as if to clear it, then he continued a brisk examination of the corpses on display and I followed after, watching those around me more than the dead, if truth be told.

"Do so many people go missing in Paris each day?" I asked Dupin.

He gave a cynical huff of laughter. "They are not looking for lost relatives or loved ones, they are merely voyeurs. It is an entertainment as you surmised previously."

I shuddered. "I'm not certain which is worse, this or the public carnival that surrounds a hanging in England."

"Monsieur Gondureau has told me that he has arrested murderers here, standing in the morgue and watching with pleasure as the spectators"—he waved at the others in the room with us—"viewed his victims. He thinks it is a common occurrence with those who make a habit of murdering others. And I believe he is correct."

"But no sign of Valdemar?" I said.

Dupin shook his head. "Now we must visit Monsieur Bayard. He keeps records of all who arrive here. He lives upstairs."

"What? You would think one would wish to escape such a place of employment."

"Many would," Dupin agreed. "Though perhaps not those most suited to such a profession."

He led me from the morgue viewing area to an apartment at the top of the building and knocked at the door. Moments later, there was a sneezing sound, then the door opened to reveal a rather round man of later middle age dressed in an expensive-looking suit and an embroidered waistcoat. He was bald, wore thick spectacles and twitched his nose like a rabbit.

"Ah, Monsieur Dupin. It is my pleasure to see you." Then the fellow stared at me quizzically. "You have a brother? I was not aware."

"This is my friend Mr. Poe visiting from America. He is my brother in spirit if not by blood."

"Interesting." Monsieur Bayard stared at my face. "Please come in. I presume you wish to view my records."

"Indeed, sir."

We followed the fellow into his apartment, which was quite large and extremely tidy. The windows revealed a spectacular view of the Seine and I immediately understood why a person might choose to live there after all.

"Here, please." Monsieur Bayard indicated the dining table chairs and we both sat down. "Coffee?" he asked as he fluidly removed a snuffbox from his waistcoat pocket, opened it and inhaled a pinch, then returned the box to its place.

"Please do not go to any trouble."

"Very well. I will get the record book." He made his way to another room and came back moments later with a large leather journal. He opened it and placed it before Dupin. "Who are you looking for?" This time Monsieur Bayard reached into his jacket pocket and removed a jeweled box, flicked it open, inhaled a pinch of snuff and returned the box.

"A woman in her early forties. Brown hair, gray eyes, pale skin. About five foot three inches and medium build. She was dressed in gray clothing: a skirt and jacket with a white linen blouse. House slippers, no shoes or socks. The lady was abducted yesterday."

"I see," Monsieur Bayard said. "I am certain no one of that description arrived here in the past day, but please do examine the records." His nose began to quiver and Monsieur Bayard removed a large handkerchief from his trouser pocket and sneezed loudly into it. "The air here." He waved his hand as if to circulate it. "I fear the miasma," he explained as he patted himself and seemed to magic another snuffbox from his clothing. He inhaled another pinch of snuff.

I found myself staring, so redirected my gaze to the ledger. The entries were very neat and detailed, including the time and date the dead person arrived at the morgue, where he or she was found, cause of death, a description of the body and details of the clothing and any other possessions. Dupin finished read-ing the entries then closed the ledger.

"Thank you for letting me read your notes, Monsieur Bayard. You were correct, of course, but might I trouble you to keep your eyes open for a lady of the description I gave? It is very important to me."

"Absolutely, my friend. I will get word to you immediately if the lady arrives."

"And I gather you are already watching for Madame Legrand for Monsieur Gondureau?"

"Yes. We have decided that she will not be put on display if she does arrive. It would cause chaos at the morgue." He shook his head.

"Very good," Dupin said. "If you would offer the same cour-tesy to Madame Morel, the lady I am seeking, I will be appreciative."

"Certainly, sir. It will be my pleasure."

Dupin and I stood up and Monsieur Bayard ushered us to the door, ingesting another pinch of snuff as we walked. I wondered how many boxes of the stuff he had secreted on his body.

"Farewell, sirs," the fellow said with an elegant bow and shut the door. As we descended the stairs, I heard another sneeze as the morgue record-keeper did his best to rid himself of the miasma that evidently polluted the air around us. I could not in truth ridicule his fears as I sensed they had foundation. When we stepped outside I expected Dupin to say something, to express his relief, but he was silent and focused on his own thoughts.

"It is a relief not to find Madame Morel in this hideous place," I said tentatively. "Or Madame Legrand." I recalled with repug-nance the two children gawping at the unfortunate persons inside the morgue and shivered.

"Yes, a great relief," Dupin said quietly. He stared straight ahead as we walked, but he hardly seemed to see the world around him. Then he looked at me and said, "But time is of the essence. Let us hope that the Great Berith's performance tonight reveals something that helps us save the two ladies and put an end to Valdemar."

19

As the day faded, the true character of Montparnasse emerged like a gaudy insect from a chrysalis. The streets were so lively, one would hardly imagine how near we were to the tombs of the Cimetière du Sud. The smell of food filled the air from restaurants selling mussels and fried potatoes, and revelers crowded around outdoor drinking stalls imbibing quantities of wine and beer. We walked past dance halls and pleasure palaces where men in theatrical suits tried to persuade us that the talented ladies employed there would not fail to entertain us.

The exterior of number twenty rue de la Gaîté gave little hint that a performance was to occur there that night. It was only the colorful and strange poster affixed to the wall by the door that suggested a theater might be inside. It offered an unsettling vision of a man in his prime dressed all in scarlet, a swirling black cape embroidered with stars and mystical symbols attached to his shoulders. He wore a top hat and a silken mask rather like a blindfold from which peered hypnotic— or perhaps deranged—green eyes. His pale skin was smooth, his hair black as coal, as were his short, pointed beard and mustache. In one gloved hand the fellow clutched what looked to be a sorcerer's staff with a small silver owl embedded at its end. It had emerald eyes as fierce and strange as those of its master. *"Le Grand Berith"* was written in a bold arc above the man and his familiar. *"Magicien"* was printed in elaborate gold letters beneath the image, and miniature leering demons clung to each Gothic-styled letter.

"A devilish magician assisted by the imps of Hell," Dupin said dryly. "Do you tremble with delicious terror, Poe?"

"I am doing my utmost to conceal that fact, my friend, though I fear the Great Berith will discern my unease." In truth I was not without trepidation after the events of the day, and undoubtedly some trap had been set. Where might a misstep on our part land us?

We entered the building and came to a sizable reception room—a low partition separated it from the seats and there were two large entrances into the theater itself, which gave a welcome sense of spaciousness, for a large crowd was gathered and it was both noisome and boisterous. The size of the audience was unexpected. I had assumed few would be aware of the show, but clearly the Great Berith was renowned in Montparnasse, both admired and feared for his strange art. Men and women with countenances that suggested they would run a sharp razor across the throat of anyone who crossed them were giddy with the prospect of witnessing firsthand the magician's supernatural powers.

"I believe most attending this performance are more familiar with la Cité than Montparnasse," Dupin murmured.

"Certainly I can imagine most here at home in the Lapin Blanc," I replied.

Then a loud voice captured my attention and I could not help but eavesdrop on a motley group standing nearby, waiting, as we were, to make their way through to the theater seats.

"I hear he magicks things from thin air," said a stout lady wearing a very ugly, very dirty yellow wig. "Not just coins and cards and handkerchiefs, but fireballs and spirits—eerie things that do his bidding."

"Perhaps he conjured up her wig," Dupin said quietly. "It is a very eerie thing."

"I had the same notion," I muttered from behind my hand, which was concealing my smile.

"And he reads minds—you cannot hide a thought from him. He sees through lies and trickery," the lady continued.

"Just as well he's not a *ficard* then," an extraordinarily ugly fellow in his fifth decade observed, using the argot term for an officer of the police. The man's face was so brutalized, perhaps by disease, that his nose was almost gone and the scars obscured whatever noteworthy features he had been born with.

"I believe we are in the company of a legendary villain called the Schoolmaster," Dupin murmured, as we all shuffled forward. "A man of some learning, apparently, but he prefers to give lessons with his fists. He escaped from the hulks and endeavored to alter his features to hide his identity, with fearsome results."

Any man that would subject himself to that much pain in order to ruin his own face seemed capable of horrifying violence.

"His appearance fits the legend. He barely looks human," I murmured, surreptitiously watching the little group.

"How do you know he's not a *ficard*?" asked a stout woman with well-muscled arms.

A swell of laughter rose up in answer.

"Well?" she asked sharply.

"The Great Berith is acquainted with the finest jewelry shops in all of Paris and knows the backstreets of la Cité better than anyone here," the Schoolmaster stated.

"And he has been known to move items from one place to the other," an old man who resembled a basset hound added.

"Items he secured for a very, *very* good price, if you understand me."

"Interesting," Dupin said in a low voice.

"Did Monsieur Gondureau never ask for your assistance regarding such thefts?" I asked quietly.

Dupin shrugged. "There are a great many thieves in Paris, especially in la Cité. Gondureau would appear completely incompetent if he asked for my help to find every stolen jewel in this city."

"Disappears into thin air," a bear-like man added. "One minute he is there and the next—" He snapped his fingers.

"Into the catacombs," Dupin murmured. "I am certain the Great Berith is Valdemar."

"We shall see, I suppose," I replied, following the group we'd been eavesdropping on as we finally filtered through into the seating area. "We are obviously meant to learn something of great importance tonight if Valdemar has invited us here."

The man known as the Schoolmaster suddenly turned and stared directly at me, as if he'd heard my words—his eyes appeared completely black and full of venom. Unnerved by the villain's look, I shifted my gaze from his.

"Shall we?" I said hurriedly to Dupin, indicating the rows of about one hundred seats before us.

"It appears we are at the very front," he said, examining the tickets.

"He wants us to see every aspect of his performance."

"And he wants to know precisely where we are," Dupin added.

As we escaped the crowd and moved toward the elegant seats, we were confronted by a girl dressed like a female acrobat in an exotic costume of purple velvet decorated with innumerable golden spangles. Her legs were encased in thick white tights, her feet in violet silken boots. The girl's curled hair was heaped upon her head and decorated with ostrich feathers.

"Tickets," she demanded, arms akimbo, fists resting lightly on her hips as if ready to employ them in an instant.

Dupin handed them to her. When she noted the seat numbers I was certain that her eyes narrowed. A false smile revealed unfortunate teeth that ruined the prettiness of her features.

"Follow me." She whirled like a soldier on parade and marched down the aisle, pivoted again and stopped dead center before the front row. "Here you are, sirs. Best seats," she said with a dramatic flourish, and grinned again as if she had just made the two chairs appear before us through some sleight of hand.

"Much appreciated," I said, whereas Dupin made no effort at any false niceties. The girl bestowed a contemptuous look upon him and marched away.

"No doubt the delightful young woman is in league with Valdemar," Dupin said as he settled into his chair. "I would not be surprised if the ostrich plumes were tipped with some kind of sharp blade, so be cautious if she reaches for one," he added.

"Do you think Valdemar will attack, given the number of witnesses?"

"Poe, look around you. This mob would gladly pay double for such an entertainment and would happily lend their services against us if told that I occasionally assist the prefect of police."

I peered back at the crowd and realized that what I had taken to be nervous observations about the criminal pastimes of the self-proclaimed magician, were truly expressions of hearty admiration. This was an audience that would fully ally itself against any representative of the force of law.

"Perhaps we should leave while we still can?" I suggested.

"I will not be affronted if you choose to do so," Dupin said. "But I must stay. Valdemar did not lure us here merely to beat us insensible or to imprison us—this is far too elaborate a contrivance for that. The Great Berith is held in high esteem by this crowd and these performances may be his way of building an army in la Cité—for as I said, that is where I believe the majority of this audience dwell or do their business. But we should be safe enough tonight. I suspect he will send his message and then disappear into thin air, as is his habit." Dupin deftly rolled the ebony shaft of his walking stick between his fingers and its cobra head spun in circles, ruby eyes flashing as light dripped onto them from the chandeliers that bloomed with crystal above us. I half-expected the golden creature to strike—to lodge its venom-spewing fangs into the first flesh that neared its maw. "But should he disappear, we will know where to find him," Dupin added with great satisfaction.

"The catacombs?"

"Precisely. There must be an entrance in this theater. You noticed the silver owl on the magical staff, or whatever that thing is meant to be, in the ridiculous advertisement pinned near the door?"

"Yes, it is certainly a peculiar staff of some sort."

"And of course you recall the carved owls at the library and Madame Morel's house?"

"Yes, certainly. They signaled entrances to the catacombs."

"I predict," Dupin said with mock gravity, "that an owl will make an appearance tonight."

"And if you are correct, sir, I will feel inspired to organize your own *Soirée Fantastique* to startle the masses with your ability to predict the future."

"Rival magicians. Valdemar would relish that."

As if in response to his words, the gas-fired chandelier above us dimmed, and the rabble milling around at the back of the theater took their seats, still talking and laughing.

"Hurry up, ladies and gents! Move along!" a male voice squealed loudly. "Sit yourselves down, the show begins!"

Dupin must have noticed me shudder, for he said, "He uses a *sifflet-pratique*—what you might call a swazzle—a device held in the mouth to create the unpleasant voice."

However the strange voice was created, the crowd was obedient to it and all quickly lowered themselves into their chairs. The stage curtain rose as if to hurry them along and twin beams of light shone on each end of the stage, revealing two puppet theaters, which were about six feet tall and five feet wide, beautifully painted, their own stages concealed by red curtains.

"Begin!" the inhuman voice commanded, and the curtains parted. Then there was a flash of light, a puff of smoke and a figure appeared in each theater—two Chinese acrobats, a male figure in one theater, a female in the other. They both began to sway gracefully to strange chiming music that filled the air. The acrobats were perhaps three feet tall and dressed in loose golden trousers and long poppy-red oriental jackets embroidered vividly with beads and sequins that sizzled in the light. The male acrobat had long mustachios and the female hid her face with a painted fan that she waved coquettishly. So elegant were their movements and so expressive their features, it was difficult to believe that the marionettes were not fully alive. From the applause of those around me, it seemed our fellow spectators were equally impressed.

The male acrobat produced two small golden hoops that he set spinning on top of his fingertips, much to the delight of the audience. Then he threw the gleaming hoops across the stage to the female, who caught each and proceeded to sling them from one hand to the other in time to the music. The male acrobat, meanwhile, conjured up three golden balls, which he began to juggle, finally lobbing each one to his fellow performer.

Without losing a beat, she threw away the hoops and deftly caught each ball, which she commenced juggling while the entranced spectators sounded their appreciation. The female acrobat then tossed the three golden balls back to her partner, but mid-flight they burst into flame with a loud pop. Smoke billowed and the lights dimmed.

"Cleverly done," I whispered to Dupin.

He nodded, but I noticed his eyes were scanning the crowd around us.

"Nimble, ain't they?" came the horrid voice. "Think what they might get up to at night in Paris where the pickings are rich."

All around us laughed.

"And if they was caught, you couldn't keep 'em locked up, could you?"

"Not likely!" someone roared from the crowd.

"The same can't be said for this poor fella," the voice shrilled and a light illuminated the marionette theater on the left of the stage. Its curtains parted to reveal a puppet imprisoned behind bars, which he commenced to hammer with a baton.

"I didn't do it!" the fellow protested in a voice as screeching and unpleasant as the invisible compere's. "It wasn't me!"

The audience roared with delighted laughter.

"And it wasn't me!" someone echoed.

"Nor me!"

"I didn't do it either, Guignol!" another rogue shouted.

The puppet was a character fondly known as Guignol in France, similar to Punchinello, but dressed in French peasant garb, wearing an expression of perpetual surprise and always armed with a baton to fight off adversaries. It seemed that he had lost the fight this time, but illogically, he had not been made to give up his weapon.

"You know what they said I did?" Guignol asked the crowd. "Can you guess?"

"Pickpocket?"

"Housebreaking?"

"Stagecoach robbery?"

"No, no and no," Guignol shouted. "They says I went about cutting ladies' skirts! Taking knives and cutting ladies' skirts across the derriere, the backside, the *arse*!"

This proclamation was met with a roar of laughter, but a chill wriggled up my spine and Dupin glanced at me, his brows knitted into a frown. It was more than obvious to both of us that Guignol was referring to the crimes committed by my grandparents in London over half a century ago, the crimes that earned them the sobriquet the "London Monster".

"Cutting ladies' skirts? Not wearing them?" a scallywag asked.

"No, my fine sire—*you* might like wearing frocks, but not Guignol. Not me. I didn't do the wearing or the cutting." He shook his baton. "This ain't a knife, is it?"

"No!" shouted the crowd.

"Yet here I am, unjustly in prison."

And his audience jeered.

"But there's proof of who really done it," Guignol said, pressing his face up to the prison bars. "Proof. Look there." Guignol pointed his baton and a light beamed on the puppet theater to the right of the stage. A female puppet, very plain of face, wearing a towering powdered wig and a pink dress in the fashion of the late eighteenth century, cut very low across her bosom, was ambling along, carrying a reticule in one hand and waving a fan with the other.

"What a lovely evening for a perambulation," she declared. "The moon is full and her beams make the city so very pretty."

Two more marionettes skulked onto the stage and loitered together near the curtain. One figure was a tall, burly male, but the other was much shorter and slight, a female disguised in the fancy suit of a dandy that matched that of her accomplice, but with a face that was painted and powdered.

"She's mine," the burly figure told the other in a stage whisper and he began to tiptoe in an exaggerated fashion toward his oblivious victim.

"Look behind you!" members of the audience shouted to the lady marionette.

"Or your pocket will be picked!" someone in the crowd cried out.

"Shhhhh!" the female in disguise hissed at the auditorium, finger to her lips, and the crowd around us laughed and stamped their feet with glee.

The lady in pink stopped and pointed at the heavens. "A shooting star! I must make a wish. A husband, wealthy and generous and kind . . ."

"Here he comes," a rogue in the audience warned. "A gentleman . . . *robber!*"

And the male scoundrel pounced. *Slash!* The reprobate cut the lady's pink skirts . . . and again! The audience voiced its outrage.

"Oh my!" screeched the victim. "Oh, my dress!" She patted her posterior. "Oh, my *fundament!*" She grasped at her skirts then fainted dead away as the audience roared with laughter and the culprit and his accomplice vanished in a puff of smoke.

Guignol banged on his prison bars with his baton and the sound reverberated, unnaturally loud, through the room.

"You see—it wasn't me! The lady and her husband committed fifty such crimes," he squealed. "But I was blamed and thrown in prison. Is that just? Is that fair?"

"No!" all around us shouted.

"Just as George Reynolds's father was imprisoned for the crimes of your grandparents," Dupin murmured, unnecessarily, for I was more than aware of the parallels between my family history and the farce being enacted on the stage.

"And they wrote about their exploits. Letters, a confession," Guignol said, as if to torment me further. "If justice were truly to be served, what would happen?"

"Madame Guillotine!" a man with a booming voice shouted. The audience took up the chant: "Madame Guillotine! Off with their heads!"

"Very well," Guignol said through the bars. And a light beamed onto a third puppet theater that seemed to materialize in the middle of the stage. Its red curtain opened to reveal a miniature guillotine, blade at the ready. "Ah, but we have a problem," Guignol said. "The monsters disappeared. Escaped, evaded capture, got away with it." And the beam of light revealed that the puppet theater to the right of the stage was empty. "But look," said Guignol. "There is someone else. The grandson of the true villains. Perhaps he should lose his head instead. What say you?"

"Lose his head! Lose his head!" all around us shouted. "Make him pay. Lose his head!"

A burly puppet appeared, pushing another puppet ahead of him, whose hands were tied behind his back. All around me gasped, but not as loudly as I, for the marionette resembled a face I knew very well, one I saw in the looking glass most days. My very own face.

"Lose his head! Lose his head!" The chant continued, and now I had a sense of what Dupin's grandparents had experienced in facing the mob before their execution. Fear scurried through me, for it was clear that George Reynolds had contrived the little play and if he were quite literally pulling the strings, what unpleasant fate had he dreamt up for Dupin and me at the hands of this mob?

"Do not react, Poe," Dupin muttered. "It is what Reynolds wants. We are not amongst friends."

He was right that I was being deliberately provoked and to react would result in nothing but trouble for us. So I sat and watched as the burly executioner roughly pushed the head of the marionette that resembled me into the lunette.

"His head, his head . . ."

"Remove his head!" shouted Guignol in his awful voice. The blade of the guillotine dropped with a sickening clang and the marionette's head flew from its body with an explosion of blood. I yelped, as did many around me, while others laughed and whistled. Then the crowd applauded vigorously.

"Justice is finally served, ladies and gentlemen. Guignol wins the day again," he proclaimed in his bizarre voice. The crowd continued to cheer and clap and stomp their feet in appreciation. I could not help but wonder how I would fare if any in the mob around me perceived that the executed manikin had been fashioned in my likeness. The stage's curtain fell and moments later the theater plunged into darkness.

20

But all was not over. Just when those around us became restless, the eerie yet beautiful notes from a violin soared through the air—someone high above us played a slow, maudlin tune that I did not recognize and it had the effect of making the audience both uneasy and attentive. There was a swish overhead that made the back of my neck tingle, and nervous cries rippled through the crowd. A beam of light pierced through the gloom, revealing the stage curtain rising up again. The puppet theaters were gone and in their place, center stage, was a large table covered with a black cloth shot through with silver thread like spider webs that caught the sun. Then a dark form plummeted from the ceiling, down to the table, landing in the circle of light.

"You see," Dupin said.

It was, as he had predicted, an owl. I hadn't truly believed that Dupin's prophecy would prove accurate, but after the threatening performance we had just witnessed, the dainty, speckled brown bird that stood quietly before us was something of a relief. And the little owl was frowning at the crowd, or so it seemed from the white tufts above its yellow eyes, which resembled eyebrows. The delighted chuckles from those sitting around me made my tense nervousness ebb.

"*Athene noctua*," Dupin whispered. "The little owl. Diurnal, territorial, often mates for life."

"And easily trained?"

"They become accustomed to humans," Dupin agreed. "Your friend Miss Loddiges would tell you that Julius Caesar's murder was heralded by the cry of this type of owl."

"And is that a message to us from Valdemar, do you think?"

"Quite possibly."

Light spilled onto the theater seats as the chandelier above us glowed again. Seconds later, a flurry of small objects soared through the air like birds disturbed into flight. There were shrieks then giggles amongst the audience as playing cards fell into the laps of a number of spectators. At that moment, an invisible orchestra played a brassy entrance tune, and with a flourish of his cape, the man we had been waiting for appeared in a new shaft of light, his scarlet suit glowing as if he were the Devil himself. He was a tall man with an imposing physique who looked precisely as he did in the poster, wearing the same black silken mask. I would have guessed him to be roughly forty years old.

"Surely he is not Valdemar," I whispered. "He looks far too young."

"It is impossible to judge his true age with that costume," Dupin responded in a low, stubborn voice. "We will know for sure after this performance, of that I am certain."

I found it difficult to believe that the man on the stage could be over eighty years old—the age that Valdemar must be—but perhaps appearing immune to the physical ravages of time was one of the illusionist's powers.

"Good evening, ladies and gentlemen," the Great Berith intoned in a rich, cultivated voice. "I am the Great Berith, mind-reader, mesmerist and expert in the magical arts." The audience applauded loudly and he bowed like a dancer. "If you have a playing card," he continued, "please hold it straight up in the air, facing away from me so I cannot possibly see what it is."

A dozen people scattered through the audience held up cards as instructed.

"Athena," he commanded. "Fetch me the queen of hearts."

The little owl immediately flew into the air, circled the room and snatched a card from the hand of a large-nosed old woman with only one eye who was seated with the Schoolmaster. It was *la Chouette*, the hideous crone we had seen in the Lapin Blanc. The owl returned it to the Great Berith, who, with an elaborate flourish, displayed the queen of hearts to the audience. Wild applause greeted his success.

"The owl is well trained," I whispered, my interest in the show calming my nerves somewhat.

"Not such a difficult task. And throwing cards is quite a standard trick," Dupin muttered with ill-grace.

"And now the queen of spades," the Great Berith instructed. The owl obligingly fetched a card from the hand of an over-rouged woman bedecked with such a quantity of glittering jewels that they could only be false. Again, it was the correct card. "The queen of diamonds and the queen of clubs," the Great Berith instructed and Athena the owl fetched each card correctly, the "diamonds" from a thick-set, sun-burnt woman who had been with the group standing near us in the reception room and the "clubs" from a rosy-cheeked girl who seemed far too dainty to be amongst such a rough-looking crowd. The audience cheered and stomped their feet at the little owl's success.

"Very good, Athena," the magician said. He clapped his gloved hands together twice and produced a live mouse, which he delivered to the owl's beak. It was quickly gobbled down, much to the delight of the spectators. The Great Berith held up the four cards in a fan, the queens facing the audience, then shuffled them into a full pack of cards with phenomenal dexterity, after which he flicked four cards from the top of the deck at the crowd. They flew up like winged creatures and fell back down into the laps of the four women who had held them previously.

"And now, my queens," the Great Berith said. "Show us your cards, for I believe I have delivered them correctly this time."

The ladies looked at their cards in disbelief, then held them up for all to see. This time the one-eyed harridan was clutching the queen of spades, the sun-burnt lady the queen of clubs, the bejeweled hussy the queen of diamonds, and the prettiest one held the queen of hearts. The audience roared again and shouted out quips that made little sense to me.

"The Great Berith wishes to impress the crowd with his knowledge of these ladies," Dupin whispered under the noise, leaning toward me. "It is obvious why the comely one received the queen of hearts and what her profession might be. One might presume that the creature with the queen of diamonds trades in paste jewelry and is probably involved in the sale of stolen gems. Your friend Herr Durand told us at the Lapin Blanc that the queen of spades—the old crone with one eye—is a murderess. This seems likely given her association with the Schoolmaster and the unease of those sitting near her. The queen of clubs—the stout, sun-burnt lady—appears to be a laborer, but perhaps is a ruffian who specializes in assault."

Dupin's theories certainly seemed possible. The Great Berith had succeeded so far in impressing those around us.

"If the Queen of Hearts would join me, please," the Great Berith said as the noise of the audience died down. Much to the amusement of those around us, the one-eyed harridan stood up and tried to make her way to the stage, but the magician lazily flicked his hand toward her and the silver-owl-tipped staff appeared in his hand, pointing directly at her. The live owl immediately took wing, swooped and dragged its talons over her greasy bonnet. She screeched and fell back into her seat beside the Schoolmaster as the audience laughed uproariously.

"Your time will come, *la Chouette*," he intoned, and she shivered, seemingly unnerved that the magician knew her nickname.

The Great Berith beckoned to the pretty girl. She coyly made her way to the stage as the owl flew back to its station on the table. When the girl was next to him, the magician swept his top hat from his head and bowed gallantly.

"Would you be so kind as to hold my hat?" he asked, pushing it into her hands.

"I'd be happy to, sir," she said in a disharmonious, high-pitched voice at odds with her physical beauty, which made the crowd chuckle at her expense.

"Now, please confirm that the hat is empty, that there is nothing whatsoever inside it."

The girl turned the hat this way and that in her hands, put it on her own head, banged it against her knee several times and said, finally, "It's empty, sir. Emptier than an empty glass of beer."

"That's mightily empty, that is," some rascal shouted and the crowd roared again.

"She is in league with the magician though they pretend otherwise," Dupin murmured.

"She does seem to know how to entertain a crowd," I agreed.

The girl held the mouth of the hat toward the Great Berith and he reached in, then immediately pulled out four gold coins, three of which he tossed with remarkable accuracy to the three queens in the audience, who managed to grab their prizes despite the efforts of their neighbors to steal the coins away. The magician threw the fourth gold coin into the air directly in front of his new assistant and it spun down as if in slow motion, disappearing into the bodice of her dress.

She squealed, the audience laughed, and the magician immediately pulled a white dove from the hat, provoking cries of delight. The owl saw the dove, and it saw the owl, and both took flight. Just when it seemed that Athena would sink her talons into the gentler bird, the Great Berith aimed his staff at it and a puff of white feathers exploded then drifted down like snow. The dove was gone and the owl returned to its table with a mournful cry.

"Now let us begin the real performance—the sorcery and the magic. All that I learned from the Devil himself!" The Great Berith swirled his cape theatrically and the crowd, in response, stamped their feet, clapped their hands and chanted, "Begin! Begin! Begin!"

The magician approached the cloth-covered table. "First, I must summon up an assistant, in addition to the Queen of Hearts here. Athena, come." The owl flew back to its master's shoulder, and as the Great Berith raised his staff and muttered incomprehensible incantations, the theater was again cast into darkness. The magician's voice grew louder and he waved the staff furiously at the table until smoke rose up from it and the smell of incense drifted through the room. The smoke then congealed into a thin stream of light and a demon manifested itself, then another, and another, and the audience around me drew breath as one. All but Dupin. He remained silent and unmoved.

"Come, minions, rise up at my command and do my bidding," the Great Berith intoned. In response, the ghost-like demons dipped and dived above the crowd and an eerie chattering and squealing filled the theater. "Do my bidding!" the magician thundered.

My heart tapped at my chest and my hands trembled—it was as if the Great Berith had opened a gateway to Hell and demons were entering our world.

"It is a magic lantern, Poe," Dupin said into my ear, over the squeals of the demons and cries of the audience. "It is hidden within what appears to be an ordinary table. Remember how Professor Renelle made it look as if birds were flying around us during his magic lantern display? It is merely smoke and mirrors."

Dupin's explanation seemed plausible when I recalled the impressive display we had viewed at the Philosophical Hall in Philadelphia during our search for Miss Loddiges. The professor had manipulated his magic lantern in such a way that it seemed as if we had been transported to a Peruvian jungle and its winged inhabitants were fluttering around us. I immediately felt quite ridiculous to fall for the Great Berith's trickery.

Dupin must have read my expression. "Fear not, Poe, it is the job of the illusionist to fool his audience, to gain their confidence. I am certain now that Valdemar is attempting to make himself the leader of this mob. He knows his audience well and is doing his best to persuade them that he has infernal powers."

"Even though the man before us appears too young to be Valdemar?" I said quietly. "He could, however, be in Valdemar's employ—his *puppet*."

"That is possible," Dupin reluctantly admitted. "But I feel in my soul it is the man himself."

"You will do my bidding!" the Great Berith thundered, throwing his arms into the air and down again. Balls of fire burst up from the table, exquisite coruscations, which had the audience murmuring half in fear, half in admiration.

"Phosphorus in water, heated. A simple trick."

If I had been there solely to witness a show of magic, Dupin's constant interruptions ruining the entertainment would have irked me, but knowing that the Great Berith—or Valdemar, if it were truly he—did not have magical powers was a relief, for his demonstration was very convincing.

The magician lowered his arms, made some signs with his hands and the demons faded away as light shimmered up around us. I guessed that the magic lantern had been stowed away inside the rigged-up table.

Moments later, the girl in the purple and gold-spangled costume appeared onstage, wheeling a cart filled with various glass flasks, instruments and other paraphernalia.

"Thank you, Martinet."

She nodded her head then left the stage in a flurry of back flips and curious dance moves, which the audience cheered.

"She can almost fly," he told the crowd.

"In and out of windows," someone quipped.

"Leaving with more than she flew in with," another added.

"Lies!" came her voice from offstage.

Dupin and I exchanged a glance, no doubt reaching the same conclusion—had it been the acrobat who "flew" into Dupin's window and attacked Madame Morel?

The Great Berith stamped his owl-tipped staff against the floor and a boom reverberated through the theater, while smoke whirled up around him.

"Alchemy," he said loudly. "Do you know what alchemy is?" he asked the Queen of Hearts.

"The Devil's work?" she replied, blue eyes wide with innocent wonder.

"Some might say so," the Great Berith leered. "For it is magic. An alchemist can transform one substance to another. Now watch carefully," he directed the crowd. "The Queen of Hearts will fill this flask with water." She did as he asked and the Great Berith took a swig from it. "You see? Nothing but water. Now place it on the table," he instructed his assistant, and again she did as he asked. "I will now add a few drops of syrup of violets." He removed a flask thus labeled from the little cart and dripped some of its contents into the water, which turned violet in color. The magician muttered incantations and waved his hands above the flask without touching it in any way, and moments later the violet-colored liquid turned crimson. The crowd marveled at his trick. He repeated the process, chanting and waving his hands—the crimson liquid in the flask magically separated into three different colors: crimson at the bottom, violet in the middle and green on top. Again, the crowd was impressed. The magician repeated the process once more and the colors reversed themselves with green at the base, violet, and red on top. Furious applause rose up around us and the Great Berith bowed to the crowd. Soon all were clapping wildly.

"Alchemy of the most basic kind," Dupin muttered.

"But he knows how to manipulate his audience. They believe he has strange powers."

The Great Berith did a number of other impressive tricks that entertained the crowd as fully as they irritated Dupin. He had the Queen of Hearts place an empty box on the floor and after he placed a dramatic spell upon it, the magician invited the strongest-looking man in the crowd to lift it up. Much to the burly fellow's chagrin, he failed.

"Iron base and a magnet," Dupin explained.

The Great Berith demonstrated that he could move objects with his mind or by waving his staff at them, which Dupin dismissed as trickery involving a Leyden jar, but the mob around us were utterly convinced that the showman onstage had unearthly magical powers, particularly after he levitated the amiable Queen of Hearts.

"And now, ladies and gentleman, for the last demonstration of my extraordinary skills," the Great Berith announced as he took a step forward, owl-tipped staff held outward, his piercing glare directed at his audience. He pivoted dramatically, as if staring into the eyes of every person before him. When his eerie gaze finally met Dupin's, a sardonic smile curled his lips. "I am the foremost mesmerist in the world, as you will witness tonight," he thundered. "I will put the Queen of Hearts into a trance if she is willing."

"Is it painful?" she asked with exaggerated fearfulness.

"Only if you resist," he replied.

"Oh, I never resist," she said coquettishly, provoking laughter from the now nervous crowd.

"I require another victim. Athena, please choose."

The little owl immediately flew into the air, circled the room, then gave the Schoolmaster's head a glancing blow with its feet. All drew breath at this choice.

"Do you dare, sir?" the Great Berith asked.

There was no doubt even to an outsider such as myself that this was a challenge.

"Interesting," Dupin murmured, finally impressed.

"I fear nothing," the Schoolmaster said and pushed his way to the stage.

"Of course not," the Great Berith said graciously.

The girl with the ostrich feathers in her hair carried out two wooden chairs and placed them center stage.

"Please, sit," the magician told his subjects.

They obliged him and he retrieved from his pocket a large red jewel on a chain; it glittered so strangely under the gaslight it seemed to be pulsing with life and emitting sparks of fire that danced along the floor and across the walls. He held the chain between two fingers and let the jewel swing back and forth.

"Watch the jewel," he instructed. "Keep your eyes on the jewel. You will hear nothing but my voice, see nothing but the jewel."

Moments later, his subjects looked heavy-eyed and unblinking and the magician began to count backward from ten. Both the Queen of Hearts and the Schoolmaster looked to be asleep.

"Open your eyes," the Great Berith demanded. Immediately, they complied, but their gazes were at infinity rather than the here and now. The magician proceeded to make them perform a variety of different activities at his command, from walking a tightrope to dancing a jig. He instructed the Queen of Hearts to slap the Schoolmaster, which brought him to tears at the magician's suggestion. This unlikely act made the audience cheer and the Great Berith smirked at the disfigured criminal's humiliation.

"Please applaud the Queen of Hearts," he finally said. And all around us stamped their feet and clapped their hands together. The Great Berith dangled the red jewel on the chain in front of the girl's eyes and said, "Watch the jewel." Her eyes immediately followed its repetitive arc. "You have given a magnificent performance, but you will remember nothing of it, unless I instruct you to. Understood?"

"Yes," the Queen of Hearts murmured.

"When I snap my fingers, you will awaken."

Again she nodded and the Great Berith clicked his fingers together in front of her face and the girl woke up with a start, or so it seemed.

"Queen of Hearts! Queen of Hearts!" the crowd chanted, and she curtsied and smiled prettily at her admirers, while Martinet came onstage, pushing a large, curtained box. The magician pulled back the curtain to reveal an empty chamber. "Time to go, my dear. Please step inside."

The Queen of Hearts obeyed and he pulled the curtain closed, then made the box spin as he chanted strange words. He tapped the box once with the staff, which sent sparks into the air, and pulled the curtain back. The chamber was empty. The crowd roared again and Dupin sighed.

"Your turn, sir," the Great Berith said to the Schoolmaster, who sat quietly on a chair, staring blankly ahead. The magician suspended the red jewel in front of the villain's face and set it swinging like a pendulum. "You will remember nothing of this evening, but that I am your master. Nothing at all but that. Do you understand?"

"Yes," the criminal muttered reluctantly.

"Do you understand?" Berith roared in his ear.

"Yes, master."

"Good. Now enter the chamber," he directed as he pocketed the gem.

"Leave him asleep," someone shouted from the back as the Schoolmaster climbed in.

The Great Berith considered this for a moment. "As you wish." He shrugged and pulled the curtain abruptly shut. He repeated the process of turning the curtained box, mumbling an incantation, tapping the box with his staff, and threw open the curtain again. All expected to applaud an empty chamber, but instead they saw a figure seated inside. It was not the Schoolmaster. Dupin emitted a strangled cry—and I suspect that I did too—for there, slumped inside the chamber, was Madame Morel, Dupin's missing housekeeper. The magician reached for her hand and said, "Onto the stage, madame."

She immediately obeyed and as she was ushered into one of the wooden chairs, it was clear that she was in a trance, or perhaps overcome by a powerful calmative. The Great Berith brought out the strange, glowing gem and set it in motion before her eyes.

"You will speak the truth, only the truth. Any question you are asked, you will answer honestly and without hesitation. Do you understand?"

The housekeeper nodded.

"I cannot hear you," the Great Berith said sharply.

"I understand," she murmured.

"Good. Now tell us your most recent occupation."

"A housekeeper."

"Where?"

"Thirty-three rue Dunôt, Faubourg Saint-Germain."

"How long have you been employed there?"

"Five weeks."

"And did your previous master dismiss you?" the magician asked, an edge of steel running through his voice.

"No," she muttered.

"You absconded?"

"Yes."

There were a few cheers from the audience, which immediately faded away when the Great Berith glowered at them.

"When did you abscond and why?" he asked.

"Five weeks ago. To help my grandson," she said, a note of rebellion in her voice.

"Your grandson," the magician said mockingly. "Is he aware that you are his grandmother? His father's mother to be precise?"

She shook her head and those around us were immediately more attentive and as intrigued as I was.

"Now why might that be?" he pondered. "Why might your own grandson not know who you truly are?" He paced in front of Dupin's housekeeper like an interrogator.

"She gave away her children!" shouted a woman from behind us.

"Or they were stolen from her," suggested another.

"She was locked up!"

"Are any of those suppositions true?" the Great Berith asked the housekeeper.

"No," she said softly.

"No, indeed. Let us try another tack. What is your birth name?"

"Sophie de Bourdeille."

A sharp hiss came from Dupin, but the magician did not slow his inquisition.

"Where were you born?"

"Near Lyon."

"On what date?"

"Twenty-sixth of August 1765."

"And that makes you how old?"

"Eighty-three," the housekeeper said.

The audience laughed at the absurdity of her claim, for she looked half that age.

"Eighty-three years old," he repeated. "When did you come to Paris?"

"When I was eighteen."

"And why was that?"

"I married my husband."

"Who is?"

"He was the Chevalier Charles Dupin."

I stared at my friend, trying to ascertain what he made of the situation—was Madame Morel in league with the Great Berith? Was she part of his show, like the Queen of Hearts? But Dupin gave nothing away. He simply kept his fierce gaze fixed on the magician.

"*Was?* Is he no longer with us?"

"No," she said quietly.

"And why is that?"

"He was executed," she replied.

"Executed! I suppose you will tell me that Monsieur Dupin was executed during the so-called Terror."

"Yes."

"I see." The Great Berith tapped the table on the stage with his staff, swirled his cape in front of it, then revealed a box that was about eighteen inches square on the tabletop. He delivered it to the housekeeper. "For you," he said. "A small gift."

All around us leaned forward in their seats to see what it might be, some laughing nervously.

"Open it," the magician commanded.

The housekeeper cautiously removed the lid and peered inside. A look of revulsion came over her face.

"Show us, please," he instructed.

Hands shaking, she reached into the box. Slowly, reluctantly, she withdrew the object and almost every person around us shrieked with horror—or tried to swallow a gasp of shock as I did. There, dangling gruesomely from Madame Morel's fingers as she gripped it by the hair, was a severed head.

"Executed, yes. Your husband lost his head, but here it is again. Does that make you happy?"

"No," she said firmly.

The Great Berith laughed. "You see?" he said to the crowd. "She cannot lie when mesmerized. For some reason, she is truly unhappy to see her husband."

The audience murmured nervously at the magician's macabre statement.

"This is a wax model," the Great Berith explained. "I paid a handsome price for it from an old friend of the lady's, a famous sculptress in wax. Madame Tussaud, she is called."

Sighs of relief bubbled up around us.

"And this husband of yours, was he your first true love?" the magician asked the housekeeper.

"Yes," she said with a faint smile.

A look of anger contorted his face. "But you were betrothed to another."

"I was," she agreed. "But I did not love him."

The magician growled: "That is not what you said at the time."

The housekeeper remained silent, clutching the ghastly head in her lap.

"When was Charles Dupin executed by the people of France?"

"Eighteenth of May 1793."

"And how did you escape the bite of Madame Guillotine?"

"You."

"Me?"

She nodded. "You sent another in my stead—she appeared to be me, but was not," she tried to explain, her own confusion clear.

"Are you saying, Madame Dupin, that I have infernal powers? That I cheated Death himself?" The magician's grin was unsettling and a deep pall of unease fell upon the room. While the notion sounded absurd, no one seemed prepared to disbelieve the man who had performed miracles all evening.

"Madame Dupin," he continued in a hushed voice that had the attention of the room. "I believe your grandson is in this theater. Would you point him out, please?"

The lady raised a trembling hand and pointed directly at Dupin, the pain on her face evident.

"One final question, madame. You said that you hoped to help your grandson. In what way?"

"I wanted to save him. From you," she said, bitter sadness strangling her voice.

"But you failed, didn't you?" the Great Berith said. "And he will die like the man who took what was mine." The magician made a peculiar gesture with his hand and Athena the owl took flight up toward the ceiling, all eyes upon her, then plummeted down, directly toward Dupin. There were screams from the crowd, followed by a loud *crack*, and a cloud of violet smoke enveloped the Great Berith and Madame Morel. Dupin managed to unleash his rapier from his walking stick and slashed at the bird, but it escaped the blade's bite and flew up to a chandelier, where it stationed itself. Dupin leapt from his seat and charged the stage.

But it was empty.

"Follow me, Poe," he shouted, then ran directly into the magical box that had spirited away the Queen of Hearts and the Schoolmaster.

There was an awful baying from the crowd, and although I instantly responded to Dupin's instruction, I feared the mob would tear me to shreds as I clambered onto the stage. As soon as I entered the box, Dupin pulled the curtain closed and lifted a concealed panel in the floor. It revealed a chamber beneath it. We climbed down and he closed the box's trapdoor, dampening the sounds of the confused and angry audience. The room in which we found ourselves was dimly illuminated by a lantern hanging from the wood-paneled wall. It held a collection of stage props and paraphernalia for the magician's show, but it seemed that we had delivered ourselves into a prison, for there were no windows and no doors—we were cornered like a hunted fox and I waited for the mob to crash through the trapdoor and tear us to pieces.

"Light these," Dupin directed as he thrust two pocket lanterns, candles and matches into my hands.

Glad for something to do, I quickly unfolded the flattened lanterns, put the candles inside and lit them. When I looked up from my task I saw that Dupin was at the furthest wall, his fingers inserted in a groove in a wood panel. And then I noticed that the dark grains on the wall formed what looked to be the shape of an owl. As Dupin pulled, a door opened. My friend held out his hand and I gave him a lantern. He immediately dashed down a set of stairs into the pitch black, and I quickly followed him into Hell itself.

21

The lantern trickled light, but truly I had only faith and hope to guide me as I ran down the staircase. I could hear Dupin's footsteps in front of me, but could not see him. When I reached the path at the end of the stairway, I held my lantern up and caught a glimpse of him still running and so chased after. Every few steps I glanced over my shoulder, expecting to see a swarm of bobbing lights, to hear the crunch of feet on gravel, for surely the mob from the theater would pursue us into this underworld.

But thankfully I saw or heard nothing until I ran another two hundred yards and almost fell over Dupin. My lantern revealed that he was standing at the junction of three tunnels.

"Poe, hold your lantern near mine," Dupin directed. "There must be a marking that will indicate where we are and, therefore, where they might have gone. Look for the sigil of Berith. I believe it will indicate which path to follow."

We moved in unison, holding our lanterns up, searching for any symbol marked onto the rock.

"Here," Dupin said at last.

There was a flash of silver and I saw the strange sigil about a foot above our heads. Dupin immediately made his way down that pathway.

"What is your plan?" I asked.

"I will free Madame Morel."

This was hardly a plan, as he well knew.

"Is it not more advisable to find out where Valdemar is holding her captive and return with Monsieur Gondureau and his
men?" I asked in as measured a voice as I could muster in the
circumstances.

"Too late." He picked up his pace and I had no choice but to
trot after him, my ears straining for any sound of pursuit, eyes
darting from one shadow to the next.

We came to another turning and Dupin scrutinized the
wall, but did not find a sigil and continued forward. We came
to three other bends in our journey through the tunnels and
turned several times, following Valdemar's trail to wherever he was keeping Madame Morel prisoner, or so Dupin
believed.

"Do you know where we are?" I asked.

"Roughly. There have been a few quarry markers. I recognized one of them."

We turned another corner and my heart near stopped as we
came face to face with a pale woman, her arms extended in
supplication. I must have gasped, for Dupin said, "*Notre Dame
sous terre*—'Our Lady underground'." Dupin held his lantern
higher, as did I, and the brightly painted chapel in which the
ghostly white statue was standing became more visible. "Put
here by the quarrymen for their protection."

"Let us hope she will protect us also," I muttered.

Dupin continued along the path he had chosen for us, but I
noticed that he glanced back at chapel and the gloom of the
tunnel behind us. Soon we came to another turning, and after
establishing that the sigil of Berith was on the wall, we followed
it to the right.

"I have the sense we are going in circles." Worse still, I was utterly disoriented and Dupin's tale of the caretaker who lost his way in the catacombs tormented me.

"We are not, I assure you. I believe I know roughly where we are."

His answer did not fill me with confidence. Moments later, there was a gleam of metal against the wall and Dupin held up his lantern to reveal an open gate.

"Interesting," he murmured, examining it more closely. "There's a lock and it appears that it can be used to seal off this passageway."

My heart galloped. "Perhaps a route to avoid."

Dupin ventured further down the tunnel then returned to me and said quietly, "There's a light up ahead." He immediately went back in and I warily followed. At first I could see nothing, but then perceived a subtle flickering.

"Do as I do," my friend instructed in a low voice.

He made his way forward, holding his lantern low so that it illuminated his feet but threw little if any light upon his face. As we walked, the passageway began to widen, but Dupin kept near to the wall. When we neared the end of the passage, a dreadful sight confronted us. Hundreds of skulls were stacked on top of each other to form a wall that reached the ceiling and was about twenty feet wide. Worse still, several of the skulls glowed eerily as if from some infernal glimmering light.

Dupin raised his finger to his lips and stood very still as if listening for something. Moments later I heard voices—angry ones—that seemed to be coming from behind the macabre wall. Dupin silently gestured that we should make our way along the left-hand side of the tunnel and I followed. There was a narrow opening between the tunnel wall and the blockade of skulls. Dupin stepped through it. Again, I crept after him. The sound of two people arguing grew more distinct. A few paces along, Dupin's lantern revealed a wooden door in the tunnel wall, just in front of us. A large gap between the door and its frame emitted a stream of light—the chamber on the other side was illuminated. Harsh words were being exchanged by whoever was inside. Dupin leaned near the doorframe to peer through the gap and spy on those in the room and I drew closer to hear what I could.

"I pay you, do I not? Quite handsomely in fact."

It took me a moment to realize that the person was speaking in English, albeit with a French accent. It sounded like the distinctive voice of the Great Berith and I clutched at Dupin's arm to stop him from charging through the door.

"You promised me. You said I would have my chance to reveal his perfidy to the crowd tonight."

I immediately froze in surprise, as the voice belonged to George Reynolds. Despite all our discussions about a possible alliance between Dupin's enemy and mine, it was still a shock to hear his voice and his intentions toward me.

"I promised nothing of the sort," the Great Berith replied. "He is required until I tell you otherwise. When I am finished with him, you will have my permission to do what you like to your enemy."

"Your permission? You seem to think yourself the emperor of France already. If you believe that the pittance you pay me means that you *own* me, you are very mistaken."

"It is hardly a pittance and you will receive a fortune in gold when I achieve my objective. But if you disobey my orders, you will receive nothing at all," the magician said in icy tones.

"I do not like being lied to," Reynolds retorted. "My assistance was conditional on your honoring our agreement." A sound of wood scraping stone and the clink of rattled glass preceded a cry of pain. "Unhand me!" Reynolds yelped.

"I set the terms, not you. Do you understand?" Berith demanded.

Reynolds gave another gasp of pain and said, "Yes."

"Very good. You will bring the charming lady to me as we arranged." Reynolds must have nodded, for Berith said to someone else in French, "See him out."

Dupin quickly stepped away from the door and gestured for me to retreat. Moments later light flooded into the tunnel as the door opened.

"Run!" Dupin muttered. I immediately took to my heels and he followed. There were shouts in French and the sound of footsteps pounding behind us. I glanced quickly over my shoulder and caught sight of two brutes charging after us. Reynolds and Berith might have been right behind them, but I did not dare look back again to see for sure. I simply ran all the harder, dashed through the gap in the wall of skulls and continued down the corridor, hoping that my lantern would stay lit. Dupin drew close behind me and said urgently, "Put your left hand to the wall and keep following it. It should take us back to an area I recognized."

We moved at speed, footsteps echoing behind us. The wall curved sharply to the left and we followed it, back past the chapel and down another tunnel.

"This way now. A bit further." Dupin took the lead, his breathing ragged, his footsteps heavy and uneven. We made a few more turns, our pursuers still audible, but fainter, and then I heard the scrape of wood on stone. Moments later Dupin pulled me through a doorway and slid the door back in place. We then proceeded down the concealed passageway, which curved to the left, and as we turned, the darkness lifted. Suddenly, we were facing a large chamber where dozens of lanterns glowed and the stench of horse manure assailed my nose. Two men wearing indigo cotton smocks, trousers and caps stepped in front of us, clutching hoes in front of them like weapons. One of the men had a wooden leg, the other was missing a hand. Dupin eyed them calmly.

"I am Monsieur Dupin here to see Madame Duresnal. We urgently need her assistance." Dupin's voice was raised enough to carry through the cavernous chamber.

"Here," a woman's voice called out. "Let him through."

The two men let us pass and Dupin hurried toward the sound of the voice, with me at his heels. As my eyes adjusted to the light in the room, I was amazed by what I saw. The chamber was lined with long, narrow mounds of dirt mixed with manure, or so it seemed from the smell. There was a group of about thirty workers in these peculiar fields, all of whom stopped what they were doing to stare at us.

"I am sorry for the intrusion, madame, but we are being pursued by Valdemar's accomplices. Is there somewhere we might hide ourselves for a time?" Dupin spoke to a plump woman of about fifty—presumably Madame Duresnal—who was dressed in the same indigo cotton costume as the other workers.

"Of course," the lady said. "Follow me." She led us into a small cave hollowed into the wall. I was surprised to see two low makeshift sofas inside, a storage chest, cooking implements and other household items neatly organized. "Please, sit," she said, indicating one of the sofas, both of which were covered with patchwork quilts and had large cushions placed against the wall. There were rag rugs on the floor and dried herbs hanging from hooks stuck into the cave roof. She put a lantern on the low table and sat opposite us.

"This is Madame Duresnal, who runs this place," Dupin said to me. "And this is my friend from America, Edgar Poe," he told her.

"It is a pleasure to make your acquaintance, sir." She smiled broadly at me. "Even if in such an unusual manner." She looked to Dupin, awaiting a clearer explanation.

Dupin took a breath and said, "My housekeeper, Madame Morel, has been abducted. By Valdemar. Suffice to say, we pursued him into the tunnels via a secret entrance at the theater on rue de la Gaîté. We heard Valdemar arguing with another man and when I peered through a crack in the door to the chamber, I saw that he also had two henchmen with him—it was too risky to confront him there. We did not manage to hide ourselves before they unexpectedly left the room and we were spotted. I believe we lost them, but I can't be certain."

Madame Duresnal did not look concerned. "Valdemar's men are unlikely to disturb us, for I'm quite certain they don't know of the doorway you came through. As for Monsieur Valdemar himself, we have something of a truce. He is supplied with all the mushrooms he needs and he leaves us alone. We have nothing he values but an occasional delicacy for his table."

Her words brought back the taste of the exquisite mushrooms Dupin had cooked for us. "Are these . . . ?" I asked him, gesturing to the fields.

Dupin smiled. "Madame Duresnal and I have our own arrangement, for I too appreciate *champignons de Paris*. It is how we met. I found them in the market and soon could eat no other mushroom. Their taste led me to believe that the mushrooms were grown in the limestone quarries. I searched for the mushroom farm in my explorations and found this." He gestured at the mushroom fields and the workers who were plucking mature fungi from the compost and putting them into sacks.

"Monsieur Dupin was lucky I was here at the time and knew of his illustrious family, for intruders risk becoming compost." She smiled warmly, but I could not be completely certain she had made a joke.

"Ingenious," I said. "Few would expect to find a mushroom farm down here."

She laughed. "That is quite a relief. As you may imagine, we prefer that people do not know we live here."

Her words took me by surprise, but as I looked around me, I saw that the small cave we were seated in was not the only one. It seemed that all of the mushroom farmers lived within the large limestone chamber as a colony, which included children and the elderly. I noticed that most if not all the men had befallen some terrible accident and were missing arms or legs or were blind.

"Soldiers?" I asked.

"Quarry men, mostly," Madame Duresnal said. "Injured working. They and their families were left with nothing. Until we thought of the mushrooms."

"It was Madame Duresnal's idea," Dupin said. "Her husband was not a quarry man, but an associate of Valdemar's."

"A criminal. There is no need to be indirect. He absconded with all I had and broke my heart. I would have put a final end to my anguish if I had not met my friends here on the streets of la Cité."

My heart went out to that noble woman. "He sounds a terrible scoundrel. You have made a better family for yourself with these fine folk," I said in hopes of comforting her.

"Except that the rogue took our son with him—that is the extent of his evil, for he has no love for the boy. He merely intended to make him a criminal too. But I am proud to say that my son refused and now we are both in hiding. Or so I hope, for I do not know for certain if he is still alive."

Dupin frowned and said softly, "I am sorry. I was unaware of your great loss. If there is any way I may assist, do not hesitate to ask."

"I appreciate your kind offer, but an old family friend—truly an angel in disguise—has commenced a search on my behalf. He is convinced that my son is still alive. Of course I dare not dream it is true until I see him before me."

It was obvious from her face that she *did* dare to dream and would be crushed if the dream proved false.

"Would your angel happen to be Herr Durand, with an accomplice called Murphy?" Dupin asked, a tinge of irritation plain in his voice.

"How did you know?" she replied with wonderment.

"The man seems to be everywhere and is fearfully reckless. Believe nothing he says until you have incontrovertible proof."

"I see." Madame Duresnal was immediately despondent and Dupin's pettiness angered me.

"Herr Durand is at times overly confident, but he seems an honest fellow and I'm sure would not intentionally give you false hope. Truly I wish you luck."

"I will survive now, no matter what the truth is of my son's fate," she rallied. "Here I have a family, a home, an income, a *life*. It is the same for everyone who is part of our colony."

"It is a bold endeavor. I admire your camaraderie, but think I would miss the sunlight and the delights of Paris," I said.

"The city is right above us, as is the sun, the moon, the weather. We can visit them whenever we like, but we have flourished down here. We have a saying: 'To be happy, stay hidden.'" She indicated the large cathedral-like chamber with limestone pillars and fields of mushrooms. "This is not a prison, it is a refuge."

"I see." And truly I did, for Madame Duresnal's colony seemed far preferable to the poorhouse, debtors' prison or begging on the streets of any city.

"I will make us some chicory to drink, then we will get you to the surface without running into Valdemar's men. Some of the most vicious criminals of la Cité are in his employ, but they confine their activities to just a few tunnels and most are frightened of the ossuary. The remains of the dead are useful for hiding passageways and storage chambers. It is amazing how often a brute of a man will run screaming when he encounters a glowing skull in the dark." Madame Duresnal grinned as she set the kettle over a small fire. She was a very canny leader and I was further impressed as I watched the mushroom farmers at work—it was an incredible operation.

"But you are none the wiser as to the location of Valdemar's hideaway down here?" Dupin asked.

Madame Duresnal shook her head. "We leave mushrooms for him outside a locked metal gate a good distance from here. It's near an exit to the outside we previously used. Valdemar sent an associate to approach me when we were transporting a crop, and a deal was struck there and then: he and his men would leave us alone and we would provide him with as many *champignons de Paris* as he desired." She smiled and added, "We hope he continues to appreciate mushrooms as much as he does, for it keeps us safe."

"Have you or your compatriots heard any rumors in the marketplace about his activities? We attended his performance as the Great Berith and were surrounded by citizens from la Cité who believe he has magical powers," Dupin said. "And that makes them all the more dangerous as an army."

Madame Duresnal shivered. "There is talk of the Great Berith all over Paris. The poor believe he can turn base metal into gold and will richly reward his followers. No doubt it is all trickery, but I worry that he will succeed in his aspirations to be emperor. And then he will destroy our lives here, intentionally or otherwise."

"He will not succeed in his ambitions," Dupin vowed. "I am closer now to knowing where he lives."

"You are?" He had not revealed that fact to me previously.

"I believe so. From what I could discern through the gap in the door, the chamber in which we just heard Reynolds and

Valdemar arguing was a laboratory. I could make out shelves of books and items an apothecary would stock, and the paraphernalia an alchemist might need. It would not surprise me if he lived either in a house above the laboratory or perhaps even in a chamber in the tunnels near it."

"In the tunnels? Valdemar? But why? I understand why Madame Duresnal and her colony would choose to live here, but Valdemar? I thought he expected nothing less than luxury."

"It would explain why I have been unable to find where he lives in Paris all these years, even with the assistance of the prefect of police and less salubrious informants."

"It is certainly possible," Madame Duresnal said. "The tunnels are vast and as you can see, one can make a comfortable enough home here. Equally, there are many houses with entrances into the tunnels."

Dupin nodded. "When I have a chance to pinpoint on my map the route we took from the theater to the laboratory, I believe I will know much more." He placed his cup on the table and rose to his feet. "Thank you for your assistance and hospitality, Madame Duresnal. I think it is time to take our leave. Have you thought of the best route for us to take?"

"Yes," she said with confidence. "Follow me."

She called for two burly men to accompany us—one had a wooden leg and the other wore an eye patch. She led us from her little dwelling and past a deep water well and bags filled with mushrooms, until we reached two large baskets hanging from heavy ropes attached to pulleys.

"This is the safest route. In you go." She gestured at the baskets, and Dupin and I stepped into them gingerly as the two mushroom workers went over to man the winches. "Fear not. We use these every day. Easiest way to get the mushrooms up and us down," she said with a reassuring smile.

"Thank you, Madame Duresnal. And should you need anything for the commune or if I can assist you in any way, please tell me," Dupin said.

"Thank you, sir. Safe journey." Madame Duresnal smiled warmly, then nodded at the two men, who began turning the handles. Our baskets slowly started to ascend from the quarry chamber up toward the night sky, which was glazed with moonlight and littered with stars.

22

The streets were eerily silent as we made our way to Dupin's apartment and once we were inside, Dupin made coffee, which we drank in the parlor without saying a word. There was a look of confusion on his face that I had never witnessed before, so deep was it, so unconcealed.

"I admit that I am unsure what to think after tonight's theater show," he finally said, echoing my own thoughts. "The only thing I feel certain about is that the Great Berith is truly Ernest Valdemar, as illogical as that might seem."

"It is entirely illogical given the disparity in their ages."

Dupin hesitated for a moment, then said, "The Great Berith, as he calls himself, recounted information that only I would know. Or someone from my immediate family, all of whom are dead. Or so I have been led to believe."

"But there must be many others who know how your grandparents died and the information he presented. The Great Berith is an illusionist. It is his job to make people believe improbable things."

Dupin immediately dismissed my comment. "What you say is correct, but I had no sense that Madame Morel was performing. Indeed, after living with her for more than a month, I

believe her incapable of playing the actress—consider how difficult she finds it to pretend niceties or to suffer what she consid-
ers foolishness."

"Perhaps she is an exceptional actress who fooled us both by
feigning her ill-temper and bad manners."

Dupin fixed his eyes on mine, his gaze intense as a cobra's.
"Do you truly believe that, Poe? Truly?"

I had to admit to myself that I did not. Madame Morel's
obstreperousness did not seem at all feigned.

"But the alternative is impossible," I said. "It is obvious that
neither she nor he is eighty years old. Unless you are suggesting
that the Great Berith is such a gifted mesmerist he created a
new past for Madame Morel?"

Dupin tilted his head to one side and narrowed his eyes as he
considered this thought. "That is a possibility. I would have
thought the Great Berith's exhibition of mesmerism to be an
utter hoax if I had not witnessed his success with the
Schoolmaster, for I am certain he was not in the mesmerist's
employ like the Queen of Hearts. And while it is conceivable
that the son or grandson or some other heir of Valdemar has
committed himself to carrying on his attempts to destroy my
family, there is another possibility."

Dupin was hesitant to offer his idea, which piqued my curiosity all the more.

"You are not going to tell me that you think Madame Morel
is truly your grandmother? That she was Valdemar's fiancée
and he saved her from the guillotine, then kept her a captive
down in the catacombs all those years? That he somehow
managed to slow the progress of time upon Madame Morel
and himself—that somewhere beneath Paris is the fountain of
youth?"

Dupin was silent for a time, then said, "No, I do not think he
slowed the progress of time, not least because Madame Morel

bears no great resemblance to my grandmother. You remember the locket ring with her portrait and you've seen her face sculpted in wax by Madame Tussaud—they do not have the same features."

I shuddered to recall the macabre display of guillotine victims Madame Tussaud had created in her exhibition halls in London, which included the decapitated heads of Dupin's grandfather and grandmother molded in wax.

"I recall the wax heads very well. The head Madame Morel clutched onstage resembled the one at Madame Tussaud's, but the lady herself bore no resemblance to the wax replica of Sophie Dupin. Considering that alone, how can she possibly be your grandmother as you insinuate?"

"Let us revisit the name 'Berith'," he said. "What can it tell us?"

"Your ancient grimoire lists Berith as a demon associated with alchemy," I recalled. "And you believe that Valdemar chose the name purposefully when selecting his stage name."

"Correct. And we know now that Valdemar has an alchemy laboratory in the catacombs—or it appears to be one," Dupin amended, as if interrogating himself. He was silent for a moment, then asked, "Do you recall the stories about the Comte de Saint-Germain?" When I did not immediately answer, he added, "The Comte de Saint-Germain never aged and lived to be well over a century old."

It came back to me. It was the sort of folkloric legend that was appealing as a tale of the uncanny, but Saint-Germain was no doubt a hoaxer who fooled the aristocracy of eighteenth-century Europe.

"But surely the Comte de Saint-Germain was a clever fraud and a charlatan," I said. "An illusionist, perhaps, like the Great Berith, with tricks that you yourself would be able to explain."

Dupin shook his head slightly. "There are certain esoteric arts that I have studied, but of course have not practiced. Some believe that Saint-Germain was an adept in those arts and others dismiss him as a charlatan. As I have not met the fellow—to my knowledge," Dupin added with a sardonic smile, "I cannot form an opinion on the matter."

"You mention 'certain' arts. Am I meant to guess which dark arts you are referring to?"

"I am not playing a guessing game with you, Poe. I hesitate as I am aware how very peculiar many would find my studies—even you, my friend. The esoteric art, if that is the best term for it, is metempsychosis." Dupin's smile was wry. "I believe you are familiar with it?"

I was very familiar with the word, as he well knew, for it was the focus of "Metzengerstein", a Gothic tale I had written purely with the intent to intrigue or terrify the reader. It was not a doctrine I gave any real credence to, but I indulged Dupin and recited a definition of the term, as I remembered it: "Metempsychosis is the belief in transmigration of the soul at death into a new body of the same or a different species. It is a tenet of a number of religions and cultures."

Dupin nodded in agreement, then after a pause said, "And what if Valdemar discovered a way to conduct metempsychosis? Of moving one's soul or 'self' into another's body so that he completely possessed that body much as a demon might possess a human host—but permanently?" Dupin's gaze was intense, his expression solemn. This was not a frivolous question.

"Are you suggesting that Valdemar tormented your grandparents, your parents and now you, but literally in a different form? And the reason he does not seem to age is that his consciousness or spirit has inhabited a new body?"

"Some believe that this is how the Comte de Saint-Germain appeared to be the same age for decades, but it is only conjecture. I have no proof at all and am aware most would find the notion pure madness." Dupin shrugged then added, "But it would explain much."

"It would indeed if such a fantastical feat were possible. Valdemar would certainly relish the thought that you believed he had conquered Death."

"It is merely a theory," Dupin said. "But let me approach it this way. Do you believe that any part of us survives after death? One's spirit perhaps?"

I felt a chill creep over me and wondered if my friend had fathomed my visitations from Sissy, that he somehow knew my wife's spirit had come back to me several times in the night.

"Like a ghost?" I said hesitantly.

Dupin considered my question for a moment. "Something like a ghost. I don't mean the trickery that we endured during that séance in London—false mediums preying on gullible ladies with messages of love from beyond the grave. I mean the true spirit of the person."

"I think it is possible," I said slowly.

Dupin waited for me to continue.

"In truth, I think I have seen Sissy," I confessed. "Though perhaps I dreamt it. I was half-asleep."

"That may make one more susceptible to seeing the spirit that has left its shell. Given what you have seen, perhaps it is not such a stretch to imagine that your wife's spirit might inhabit another body if her will were strong enough?"

It was true that I had written about such a horror in my tale "Ligeia". It was also true that I would have done anything to save my wife as I watched her life force seep away. But Dupin's macabre words unsettled me. There was something malevolent in the notion that Sissy might return in the body of another. I wanted my wife home again, but fully as herself and no other.

"Look, it matters not if I believe in the possibility of metem-psychosis," I finally said, wishing to steer the conversation back to firm ground. "What matters now is that we establish whether Madame Morel has truly been abducted against her will by Valdemar or if she is in league with him. There must be a clue of some kind in her possessions and we should search her room again."

Dupin's mood instantly changed from contemplative to defensive. "I don't know why you persist with the notion that Madame Morel has an alliance with Valdemar. It is a ridiculous thought. But have it your way. We will search her room again, despite the fact we discovered nothing previously," he added rather petulantly.

"But we were searching for her last time, or for evidence that she had absconded. We were not looking specifically for clues regarding her true identity."

"Fine. Let us examine every inch of her room." He got up from his chair and strode down the hall to Madame Morel's bedchamber. Dupin immediately began to empty the chest of drawers, piling the lady's clothing onto the bed. He made a great show of checking each drawer for concealed compart-ments and scrutinizing every item of clothing with cynical intensity. I examined the carpet bag that was stowed on top of the armoire, going so far as to separate the lining from the heavy cloth. Nothing was hidden there. Dupin emptied the armoire of clothing and I inspected the empty interior, but found nothing. Then I removed the small jewel box from the toe of the boot where it was hidden and examined the interior of the box for any markings that might give a clue. There was nothing. But a thought occurred to me.

"You told me that your grandfather kept a detailed inventory of everything of value the Dupin family owned and that is how you knew what to look for at the auction houses that were

selling stolen heirlooms." I held the open jewel box toward my
friend. "If this locket and wedding ring belonged to your grandmother, then surely they will be included in this inventory. The
locket is quite specific in style even if the wedding band is
ordinary."

A gleam appeared in Dupin's eye and he was instantly
re-energized. "Excellent idea, Poe. Come, let us have a look."
He took the jewel box from my hand and made his way at speed
to the parlor, leaving me to trot after him.

Dupin went directly to the library shelf and pulled out a
large tome, which he placed on the table in front of our
armchairs, and we sat down to admire it. It was bound with soft
black leather and embossed with the name "Dupin". The frontispiece featured a stunning illustration of the Dupin coat of
arms: a golden human foot crushing a rampant serpent with its
fangs embedded in its heel on an azure background. A striking
border like a chain enclosed the design, each link a winged
serpent, its tail gripped in its jaw.

"Magnificent, isn't it? There are four volumes with separate
inventories for jewelry, objets d'art, paintings and furniture."
Dupin turned through several pages that outlined the book's
contents, including a description of each item, the year it was
made or acquired, the jeweler and a page number. The first
illustration of a jewel in the collection took my breath away, for
not only was the jewel itself remarkable, the page looked as if
it were from an illuminated manuscript.

"You mentioned there was a detailed account of the Dupin
family property in your grandfather's will, but I'm certain you
didn't tell me it was a work of art in itself. What possessed your
grandfather to commission such a costly artifact?"

"It was begun in the sixteenth century by my forebear
Antoine Dupin, inspired by an illustrated inventory commissioned by Duke Albrecht the Fifth of Bavaria, who founded the

Bayerische Staatsbibliothek—many families of wealth were inspired to commission similar works. Each generation added to the illustrated inventory, including my grandfather, who had it bound and gave it to my grandmother as a gift. As a child, I was told the work existed but was lost when my grandparents were executed. You will not be surprised where I discovered it."

"Bibliothèque Mazarine?"

"Correct. Given the inscription to my grandmother and that the Dupin name is throughout the work, there was no argument when I demanded it."

"Inscription?"

Dupin turned the book over, opened the back cover and revealed the last illustrated page. The joyous scene depicted in riotous color took my breath away. A couple drawn to resemble Dupin's grandparents, hands clasped, heads gently touching, were seated in what might be described as an Eden. Written underneath in French was the dedication: *For my Sophie. All that is mine is yours—my heart, my mind, my soul—for eternity.*

"It is truly beautiful, Dupin. A thing to treasure."

Dupin nodded. He ran his little finger gently under the dedication, then abruptly turned the volume over and returned to the contents pages, which he rapidly scanned. "Page one hundred and four," he murmured, then leafed through until he came to the correct page. Flying doves and a cascade of scarlet roses framed an enlarged illustration of a golden band tilted in such a way that the fragment of a word was visible, etched on its interior. The ring in Dupin's fingers resembled the illustration, but it was a simple design, so that proved little. Dupin picked up the magnifying glass he had left on the table next to him and examined the interior of the ring by the light of the Argand lamp. A slight smile tilted his lips.

"Look."

He handed me the ring and the magnifying glass. There, in minuscule script, were the words: *Pour l'éternité.*

I felt unsettled by the discovery but was determined to remain the voice of reason while Dupin was fixated on fantasy. "Not an uncommon sentiment for a wedding band," I said. "Shall we see if the locket is cataloged?"

Dupin raised his brows, but returned to the contents. "'Locket, gold with diamond. Oval shaped.' Page one hundred and twelve," he read out, then immediately paged through the tome again until he came to another extraordinary illustration: a firebird, wings spread wide, held a chain in its beak from which a locket dangled—an illustration of the jewel Dupin had placed on the table before us.

"Any thoughts?" he asked, a look of triumph on his face.

I was filled with pity at Dupin's determination to believe the impossible, for I knew very well where that would lead—the pain of hope and the madness that walks with deep sorrow, with the grief of losing someone.

"I think this proves that the Great Berith is a descendant of Ernest Valdemar who wishes you ill, just as George Williams— the forger known as George Reynolds—wishes to torment me," I said quietly. "Perhaps this Valdemar the younger has mesmer- ized Madame Morel and convinced her she is your grand- mother. Or perhaps she is in league with him. I agree that the former seems the more likely scenario given the lady's charac- ter, but we cannot dismiss the second possibility, as you well know."

"Will you not open your mind to other possibilities?" His voice was filled with disappointment but I knew that to support his false hopes would assist my friend's enemy rather than him.

"I am sticking to the basic principles of ratiocination and you are letting your imagination get the better of you."

Dupin scrutinized me as if trying to determine if I truly meant what I had said.

"We shall see," he said calmly. "But now we should sleep, I think, for in just a few hours we must search for two women who may be held in the catacombs: Madame Morel and Madame Legrand. The fact that both ladies were abducted at approximately the same time must be relevant. Either one could be the 'charming lady' to whom Valdemar referred in his argument with Reynolds, although given Madame Morel's stage appearance tonight, Madame Legrand is the more likely subject—in which case she may be moved soon from wherever it is she's being held. We should therefore begin our search at the tunnel entrance near her house. Valdemar's laboratory will be heavily guarded after our intrusion, and were we to return there I am certain we would find the gate locked this time."

The thought of returning to any part of those tunnels again made my heart sink. "Perhaps it would be more fruitful to try to locate George Reynolds," I suggested. "He must know where the ladies are—Madame Legrand, at least."

Dupin nodded. "I agree. We will try again to find him after our trip to the tunnels."

Dupin's stubbornness could be exasperating and in this instance I felt it was potentially dangerous.

"As we were just pursued through the tunnels by the Great Berith's ruffians, I think it would be prudent to enlist the assistance of Herr Durand and Mr. Murphy. We have the same objective after all—to capture your mutual enemy. If we join forces, we are more apt to be successful," I said. *And more apt to stay alive*, I thought.

"Absolutely not," Dupin snapped. "I will be able to conduct a much more thorough investigation without that German swashbuckler blundering about."

"He did assist us at the Lapin Blanc."

"Until he overstepped and alerted the ogress to our interest in Valdemar, Reynolds and whatever smuggling operation Madame Legrand was involved with. He should have trodden more softly."

"Even so, we learned more than we could have done alone," I insisted.

"I doubt that," Dupin countered. "And I have no fear of confronting Valdemar or his ruffians."

"Very well," I said. "I can only hope to dream of something pleasant for a few hours before our descent into the land of shadows." Even more, I hoped Dupin might see sense by morning.

23

FRIDAY, 13 JULY 1849

If you've ever lost someone precious you will know. It's no good haggling or trying to strike a bargain, for Death will not be cheated or appeased with promises to give over your own poor gimcrack of a life. Death always wins his game. Knowing that does not make losing any easier. At first the pain deadens everything, but eventually a familiar object, a beloved scent or perhaps the fragment of a melody brings back a moment of joy and you stay within it for a time, the darkness receding inch by inch. Those moments eventually become more frequent, less tainted with sorrow—her voice bringing grace to a poem, fingers conjuring music from harp strings or piano keys, eyelashes glistening with droplets of rain or, on a warm summer day at the river, her bare feet leaving exquisite patterns in the mud. If you're lucky, those moments of sweetness will stay with you, will prevail with the insistence of sunlight, as love should. If you are lucky, recollections of those moments will bring you joy and will not cut your soul to shreds.

When I saw my wife that night, she was singing to me. It was a song she enjoyed, "The Little Turtle Dove". Her voice was clear and sweet:

"Oh, can't you see yon little turtle dove,
Sitting under the mulberry tree?
See how that she doth mourn for her true love:
And I shall mourn for thee, my dear,
And I shall mourn for thee.
Oh, fare thee well, my little turtle dove,
And fare thee well for a while;
But though I go I'll surely come again,
If I go ten thousand mile, my dear,
If I go ten thousand mile."

And as her words faded away, so did she and I was alone once more.

We made our way along the Seine, weaving through Parisians enjoying the morning sunlight and workers heading to their places of employment.

When we approached the entrance to the secret tunnel that led to Madame Legrand's house, we came upon a crowd of people.

"I presume this mob is not hoping to enter the catacombs," I said.

"Certainly not." Dupin strode toward the crowd, which parted at his stern-faced approach. I hurried after, but was forced to elbow my way through as the onlookers resumed gawping at whatever sight had captured their attention. When I finally reached Dupin, I saw that he was standing on the bank of the Seine with an officer of the police. Both were staring at the river, so I too looked at the water and, there, witnessed a macabre sight. A woman, her arms spread wide as if in benediction, was floating in the Seine next to a small rowboat. Flowers were scattered across her bosom and in her long blonde hair, which flowed around her so that she resembled her namesake all the more: Undine.

"She is dead?" I said in disbelief.

Dupin frowned at my statement of the obvious, then rolled his eyes when the police officer, a young man with a surfeit of confidence, declared: "She seems to have drowned while out rowing."

"She seems to have been *murdered*," Dupin countered. "Look at her wrist and her ankle. They are tied to the rowboat. And she is dressed in her nightgown. A lady like Madame Legrand would not venture out dressed in her nightgown and she certainly would not go rowing on the Seine—a ridiculous notion in itself—dressed in such attire."

"Did you know the lady?" the young police officer asked. "Did she have reason to take her own life? Many jump," he explained, indicating the bridge. "A bad romance, debts and the like."

Dupin shook his head impatiently. "Madame Legrand was unquestionably murdered. It is basic science. The corpse is floating, yet shows no signs of decomposition, which almost certainly indicates that she was dead before she entered the water, and that her death was recent."

The young man frowned slightly at Dupin's words. If this was the caliber of officers under Monsieur Gondureau's command, it was clear why he so often relied on Dupin when attempting to unravel the complexities of a crime.

"If Madame Legrand had drowned, her body would be at the bottom of the river," I interjected. "For her lungs would have filled with water. But if she were killed first, then put into the river, her body is more likely to float. Do you see?"

The officer eyed the buoyant corpse while Dupin stared at him as if he was a very stupid student. "Where is Monsieur Gondureau?" Dupin demanded.

"Here, here," Gondureau puffed as he hurried along the footpath toward us. "When I was told who it was in the river, I came immediately." He turned to stare at the body of Madame Legrand and sighed. "Pity." Then he turned to the young officer. "Why are you standing there? Fetch the lady to the shore."

The fellow's confidence immediately trickled away. "Yes, sir." He hurried over to a small fishing boat and had the fisherman row him and one of the other officers who had arrived with Gondureau out to the floating corpse. After some struggles to pull her into the boat without success, they towed Undine, obstreperous even in death, back to dry land. They settled her on the bank, where the crowd had grown in size. Madame Legrand's nightgown was a very fine cotton embellished with lace, but when saturated by river water it did nothing to preserve what little modesty she had once possessed, much to the pleasure of some of the bawdier onlookers.

"May I examine her?" Dupin asked Monsieur Gondureau.

"Of course. Please do." The prefect of police then turned to his officers. "Move this mob back, you imbeciles! We need space to work." He glared at his team then turned his attention back to Dupin and the victim.

Dupin's countenance remained grave and intensely focused as he circled Madame Legrand. "No blood," he observed. "May I examine the other side?"

"Turn the victim over," Gondureau ordered the young officer, who gingerly complied.

Again, Dupin scrutinized the corpse. "No visible wounds or bruising. I suspect the lady was poisoned."

"Poisoned," Gondureau echoed. "And her murderer thought to hide her body in the river, but it would not sink."

"No," Dupin corrected him. "The murderer put her in the river to make a statement to us. She was tethered to the boat."

Gondureau grimaced. "I did not notice that. Even more cold-blooded."

"True," Dupin agreed.

I could not turn my gaze from the expired Undine, who fully resembled a water sprite washed up on shore. It seemed likely that her murder was connected to her stolen letter and perpetrated by Valdemar with the assistance of my own nemesis, George Reynolds, given the letter forged in my hand that was left in her bedchamber. Furthermore, there was something peculiar about the scene of Undine's death. Certainly, it was cruel to leave the lady exposed in her nightgown, but the flowers strewn across her floating form, the blossoms still clinging to her long blonde hair—it was a purposeful and odd display that Dupin had not commented on. The tableau of Undine floating in the Seine, surrounded by flowers, conjured up a speech in my mind, and the words came unbidden to my mouth.

"'I would give you some violets, but they withered all when my father died: they say he made a good end . . .'" These lines of Shakespeare I spoke softly to myself, but Dupin heard. He looked at Undine, then returned his gaze to me.

"Ophelia's death in *Hamlet?*"

"I could not help but think of the play, of Ophelia's death scene, when I saw Madame Legrand displayed like that in the water. Perhaps I am being overly fanciful, but I wonder if that *reconstruction*," I said hesitantly, "was contrived by George Reynolds."

Dupin frowned slightly, but nodded for me to continue.

"Reynolds, scrivener turned playwright, is perhaps making reference to a play that centers on avenging one's father—and his misguided desire to take revenge on me for what happened to his own father."

Dupin considered my words carefully, then said, "What you suggest is possible, given Reynolds's actions in the past. And we know that he has been hiring out his services to Valdemar. But *this*?" Dupin indicated the dead woman on the riverbank. "Why? Madame Legrand had no real connection to you and there is little to be gained by suggesting that you murdered the lady—I refer to the forged love letter signed with your name we found in Undine's room. It is simple to prove your innocence regarding her murder. What purpose is served by killing the woman?"

"I really could not guess. To me there is little logic in the man's actions. Maybe he acted upon orders. Perhaps we should pay another visit to Madame Legrand's home," I suggested. "It may reveal something we have missed."

Dupin nodded once, then turned to the prefect of police. "Would that be feasible, Monsieur Gondureau? To go now to Madame Legrand's home and examine it again?"

"Of course," he said. "My men will take the lady to the morgue. There is no need for me to go with them."

"Excellent," Dupin said. "And I would appreciate knowing if anything is discovered regarding Madame Legrand's demise after she is examined there."

"I will personally relay everything to you," the prefect of police answered.

"Thank you. Now let us go at once to the lady's house and see what we might discover."

And we three made our way to rue de la Bûcherie.

24

I was beginning to think that Madame Legrand's servants had abandoned their positions, as no one came to the door, despite Gondureau's heavy clangs of the leonine door knocker. When the door finally opened, Monsieur Poiret was there, bleary-eyed. He slouched against the doorframe, his orange jacket unbuttoned and his white shirt stained with what must have been cognac, judging by the smell that emanated from him.

"Ah, Monsieur Gondureau. Have you found her?" the fellow asked.

"We have," the prefect of police said gravely. "Perhaps it is best if you let us inside, Monsieur Poiret."

The servant staggered away from the door and made his way down the hall and to the salon. Mademoiselle Michonneau was there, seated at a card table with a half-filled glass of cognac in front of her. Her glazed expression suggested she had imbibed the other half and probably a few glasses on top of that. I could not help but feel there was something suspicious about the two servants helping themselves to their mistress's cognac when she might return home at any moment—unless they were certain she was not returning home at all. Were they far less innocent than they pretended?

"Monsieur Gondureau! Is there news? Is she safe?" the lady's maid cried out.

"Sit, please, Mademoiselle Michonneau, Monsieur Poiret," the prefect of police instructed gently. The two servants retreated back into their chairs. "I will come straight to the point," Gondureau said. "Madame Legrand is dead. We found her body floating in the Seine."

Mademoiselle Michonneau wailed and threw her apron up over her face. Her juddering sobs were noisy and distressing. Gondureau patted her arm awkwardly, attempting consolation. I was surprised by the woman's emotion given that both servants had seemed to possess little love for their mistress when we had last interviewed them. Undine was clearly a harsh taskmaster, which rarely inspires much affection.

"Madame Legrand's demise is a terrible thing for both of us. Terrible," Monsieur Poiret said.

"Oh?" Dupin waited for an explanation.

"She has not paid us in six months. And she refused to give either of us a letter of reference. She claimed that giving us employment was charity, we were so incompetent." His eyes narrowed in memory of the lady's words. Neither I nor anyone else in the room seemed surprised by the explanation. "Her death is likely to be the ruin of us," he added, and Mademoiselle Michonneau burst into renewed sobs.

Gondureau scrutinized the servants for a moment then said, "If it proves true that Madame Legrand has failed to pay your wages, I will make certain that you are recompensed the full amount." He gave a little wave at some priceless ornaments and their faces lit up with hope or perhaps avarice. "But if any of Madame Legrand's possessions go missing—any *more* of her possessions," he growled, "you will regret it, I promise you."

Fear replaced hope on their faces and both shook their heads, denying that any notion of theft would ever enter their minds.

"Now, we must re-examine Madame Legrand's bedchamber for clues to her abductor and murderer," he announced.

Poiret jumped to his feet. "Of course, Monsieur Gondureau."

The servants led us back to Madame Legrand's rose-infested bedchamber, a place I had hoped never to subject my senses to again. Dupin opened the door, but stood stock-still at the threshold and muttered something incomprehensible. He then turned to the servants, who hovered behind him. "Explain yourselves at once."

Monsieur Poiret frowned, taking umbrage at Dupin's accusation, whereas Mademoiselle Michonneau's face twisted in fear.

"Is there something wrong?" she stammered.

"Very wrong," Dupin said to Monsieur Gondureau and me. He stepped inside the room, and when I saw Madame Legrand's chamber, I immediately understood his concern. The room had been dramatically altered in its décor.

I walked into the chamber and Monsieur Gondureau followed.

"*Mon Dieu*," he said. "This is very strange."

When Monsieur Poiret and Mademoiselle Michonneau stood on the threshold and looked at the room, their expressions suggested that the redecoration of Madame Legrand's chamber had not been their doing. Gone was the explosion of pink, the roses were pruned clean away and the cupids shooed back to heaven. The immodest portrait of Undine as Aphrodite was replaced by a tranquil painting of a country field filled with wild-flowers. The bedcovers were of blue silk, as were the curtains. The dressing table remained, but the dainty clutter of perfume bottles and powders, hair accouterments—all gone. Instead, there was a silver-backed hand-mirror with matching hairbrush and comb. Vanished were the decorative bagatelles on the mantelpiece. In their place was a small collection of books, held upright by a pair of wooden bookends painted gold.

"When did this happen?" Dupin asked the servants.

Poiret just shook his head, his mouth slack with shock.

"It is impossible!" Mademoiselle Michonneau squealed. "Madame Legrand will be very furious. My life is not worth living." She threw her apron up over her face and wailed.

"Madame Legrand is dead, you fool," Poiret growled at her and Mademoiselle Michonneau wailed all the more loudly.

"Am I to presume that you were both unaware that the décor was altered—the walls repainted, the furnishings changed, items removed and new ones installed?" Dupin waved his hands this way and that.

Monsieur Poiret shrugged, at a loss. "I do not come to Madame's bedchamber."

Dupin turned to the lady's maid. "Mademoiselle Michonneau?" he said in a harsh voice.

She slowly dragged her apron from her face, revealing suspiciously dry eyes. "I did not go to her room. There was no point if she was not there."

"And you heard no noise emanating from this chamber? Nothing?"

"No, I heard nothing."

"Do you usually sleep as soundly as the dead?" Dupin stared hard at Mademoiselle Michonneau then Monsieur Poiret, making it clear he did not believe a word of it.

"I have slept very well in Madame Legrand's absence." Monsieur Poiret took a hasty gulp from the glass he seemed to magic from the air.

"Perhaps Madame Cognac had something to do with it," I said to Dupin, nodding at the glass. "I'd wager that Undine's cellar has been severely depleted since she went missing."

"That cannot account for everything." He turned back to the two servants. "Did someone pay you to leave the house unattended? Tell the truth," he demanded.

Mademoiselle Michonneau immediately crumbled. "He said that Madame would be back soon and our positions would be secure if we did exactly as he instructed—"

"And that we would be *paid* for doing our work," Monsieur Poiret interrupted. "And paid all the wages Madame Legrand owes us."

Dupin nodded. "And what else?"

"He gave us money to go out for the day yesterday—to have lunch, supper, an entertainment. He was a very kind fellow," the maid added.

"What was this man's name?" I asked.

The two servants exchanged a surreptitious glance that both Dupin and I noticed.

"He said he was Madame Legrand's agent," Poiret offered. "That he would be taking over the management of her estate. We were pleased as she is very bad at managing it herself."

"What did he look like?" I prodded.

"Ordinary," Mademoiselle Michonneau said. "Brown hair and eyes, normal height."

"Was his name Reynolds?" I demanded. "Or Williams?"

Poiret grimaced at me. "I don't remember."

Dupin stared hard at him. "You understand that if Madame Legrand's agent promised to pay you more to keep quiet about his identity, he was lying."

"And if you lie to us, my offer to assist you with the money you are owed will be withdrawn and your new home will have bars on the window," Monsieur Gondureau said, glowering.

"It was Monsieur Reynolds!" Mademoiselle Michonneau immediately cried out. "He is English and came to Madame's salons on occasion. He told us their business relationship was highly confidential and we would be rewarded for our discretion, and also for being his eyes and ears in the household. We did not think he would hurt Madame Legrand. They seemed very friendly."

"He told us Madame Legrand would be back in a few days and that her character would be much improved," Poiret added. "He promised that our work would be much easier and we would be paid on time."

Dupin nodded as if everything they confessed made sense to him. "Monsieur Gondureau, we will need to inspect the room thoroughly. And this investigation for the police must be treated with utmost confidentiality."

"Yes, quite right." Gondureau immediately turned to the two servants and seemed to grow several inches as he struck a formidable pose, his bushy eyebrows lowered over his narrowed eyes. "You will speak to no one of this. A murder has occurred and until we find the villain who killed your mistress, you will continue to be suspects, so it is most obviously to your advantage to assist us in every way that I demand, or I will lock you up right this minute. What say you both?"

Mademoiselle Michonneau's apron flew up over her face again as she wailed.

"Of course, of course," Monsieur Poiret agreed, his face sagging with fear.

"And you will continue on with your duties here as if nothing is amiss. If Mr. Reynolds returns to the house, Mademoiselle Michonneau will immediately fetch me. Understood?"

The servants nodded, their eyes wide.

"I shall know if you fail to do as I instruct. Now leave us while we finish our work." The prefect of police pointed dramatically at the doorway and the two servants scuttled away at speed.

Monsieur Gondureau was quite the tiger when stirred. It was interesting to see that side of the normally amiable fellow and I better understood how he had risen to his position.

"Well done, my friend. It is best if there are no prying eyes while we work," Dupin said. "There must be something here that gives us a clue as to what Valdemar and Reynolds have been up to and why they were in league."

Dupin's choice of words took me by surprise. "*Were?* You think the two are no longer colluding?"

Dupin stared at me as though I was an imbecile. "Madame Legrand is dead. I do not think that was Valdemar's plan."

"And so you believe Reynolds murdered her against Valdemar's wishes?"

"I think it is possible."

Dupin had a habit of presenting his conclusions without bothering to explain how he arrived at them. This was often unsettling as it made him seem like something of a magician or mind-reader, an illusion I think he rather enjoyed. Given his presumption that my enemy, Reynolds, had murdered Undine, I was determined to press him further.

"Why do you think Valdemar would arrange to have Madame Legrand abducted? Is it something to do with her missing letter and her family's involvement with him in smuggling stolen goods?"

"That was my thinking at first, but now, seeing this . . ." Dupin waved his hand at the transformed room. "I wonder if Valdemar's plan was to install someone else in this house. Against their will," he added and stared intently at me.

My heart sank as I recalled the exhibition of mesmerism we had witnessed and the strange tale involving Madame Morel that the Great Berith had presented to the audience or, truly, to Dupin.

Monsieur Gondureau's face was the picture of confusion. "Why would Valdemar do that?"

"It is only a theory," Dupin said. "It's best if we search the room and see if we can find any evidence that suggests why Madame Legrand was murdered and by whom."

"Excellent," Monsieur Gondureau agreed. "Where shall I begin?"

"If you would look through the chest of drawers for anything of interest. And, Poe, if you would please examine the armoire," Dupin instructed.

And we set to work. It was the third time in as many days that I had been obliged to search through a lady's boudoir, which was vaguely unsettling. I opened the armoire, expecting to discover that all of Madame Legrand's clothing had disappeared, but this was not the case. It was filled with costly gowns, very different to the plain garments that Madame Morel favored. I looked at Dupin to see what he would make of this, for if I understood his "theory" about the room being prepared for a new inhabitant, then this seemed to disprove that. But he was busy searching the drawers of the dressing table. The same applied to the collection of footwear stored in the armoire—all expensive-looking and frivolous, unlike the housekeeper's. As I looked for objects concealed within the shoes, I wondered why Dupin had allocated me the task of scrutinizing the ladies' garments. Perhaps he thought I had some greater insight into the apparel of the fairer sex, given I had a wife, and perhaps he was correct. But it was a task I found unsettling and intrusive. I removed all the clothing and heaped it upon the bed, then proceeded to investigate the armoire's interior, but found nothing concealed there and no hidden compartments or panels.

Monsieur Gondureau's assignment was far easier but perhaps more disconcerting—his face was flushed pink as he riffled through the chest of drawers, which was filled with a selection of beribboned, lacy undergarments. He decanted these to the bed and just as quickly returned them to the drawers, having ascertained nothing was hidden amongst the clothes.

Dupin's quick search of the dressing-table drawers turned out little besides bars of scented soap, a bottle of perfume,

several pairs of fine leather gloves and a collection of drawing
crayons, inks and watercolors, with an unused sketching pad.
He moved on to a tall, decorative cabinet painted with roses. Its
doors were locked, but Dupin quickly remedied this with his
stickpin. The cabinet proved to be an armoire for storing valuable adornments, and the thirty drawers that swiveled out
contained an array of jeweled necklaces, bracelets and rings.
We gathered round it.

"A treasure trove," Monsieur Gondureau murmured. "I have
only seen such a quantity of jewels in a shop."

Dupin stared at the glittering display for a moment, then
removed a necklace with a diamond so large it might be worn
by a queen. He peered through the diamond, then took a book
from the mantelpiece, opened it and placed the jewel upside-
down on the print. Dupin stared at the jewel and frowned. He
then took the necklace to the window and ran the edge of the
diamond across the glass. It left a faint scratch.

"It is genuine," he announced. "And extremely valuable.
Madame Legrand wears a quantity of jewelry, but I had
expected from the overtly false jewels she is known for wearing
that this too would be a fake."

Gondureau shrugged, his eyes wide at the enormous
diamond that seemed to inhale the sunlight then release it back
into the room in a confetti of dazzling light.

"If this entire cabinet of jewels is genuine, Madame Legrand
was a very wealthy woman. That being so, would she truly hire
such lackluster servants and then refuse to pay them?" Dupin
wondered.

"I don't doubt that she was small-minded enough to cheat
those in her employ," I offered, "but if she had genuinely been
so very wealthy, I believe she would have hired a more extensive
and elegant staff."

Gondureau nodded. "I should not spread rumor, but Madame Legrand is called 'Undine' not so much for her beauty, but because she has the heart of a merciless creature of the sea. It did not surprise me to learn that she had not paid her servants." He shook his head. "It is spiteful—it matters not that the servants are incompetent, it is the principle of the thing. Further," he continued, "Madame Legrand is known for her love of her own beauty—jewels as magnificent as these would eclipse some women, but not Undine. They would only serve to make her appear more magnificent, and the lady would not deny herself that. So it is most strange that Undine was renowned for wearing extravagant false jewels if she always had these treasures in her possession."

I was impressed with Monsieur Gondureau's deduction—or perhaps "insight" was the better word for it. He had an admirable instinct for human motivation and follies.

"I agree," Dupin announced. "And therefore I question whether these jewels belong to Madame Legrand or if they were brought here when George Reynolds had this room redecorated. It is a very curious thing. Very curious."

"Shall we come back to the jewels?" I suggested. "If the room holds a better clue, perhaps it will shed light on your queries."

Dupin nodded. "Poe, if you search that part of the room—the floorboards, walls—for concealed hiding places. Monsieur Gondureau, please examine this area," he said, waving at the bed. "And I will take the fireplace." He immediately picked up the brass fire-iron that stood on the fireplace's marble plinth, crouched down on the floor and used it to prod up into the chimney. When he discovered nothing, I began my own investigations, checking for loose floorboards and hollow walls, even if I did not believe there were any to be found.

"How strange," Dupin muttered.

I turned and he handed me a book. It was a rather battered tome and an unwieldy title was printed on the cover: *Le Promenoir de M. de Montaigne qui traite de l'amour dans l'œuvre de Plutarque* by Marie de Gournay. Madame de Gournay again?

"Interesting, is it not? A book that Madame Morel would read, but certainly beyond the capacity of the flighty Undine," Dupin observed quietly. He continued perusing the volumes on the mantelpiece, flicking through each one. "Impressive," he said. "Quite the array of eighteenth-century literature."

"Do not forget that Undine considered herself quite the poet and literary scholar," I said. "It is not impossible that the books were hers."

I did not wholly believe my words and nor did Dupin from his expression. He continued his search, but failed to discover anything hidden within the books, so pushed them neatly back into place with the wooden bookend. Then a thought came to him and he picked up a bookend in each hand, using them like scales. He immediately put one of the bookends back on the mantelpiece and began to examine the one in his hand inch by inch. He then yanked at the base of the thing and it shifted slightly. He pulled once more and narrowed his eyes as a gap was revealed, from which he extracted a rolled-up piece of paper. Making no effort to hide his sense of triumph, Dupin put the bookend back in its place, unfurled the paper and read it. His face seemed to drain of color as he did so.

"Are you quite all right?" Monsieur Gondureau asked Dupin anxiously. "Perhaps you should sit down. You're as white as a boiled egg."

But Dupin remained on his feet, utterly focused on the page in his hand, scanning it at speed.

"'To Madame Sophie Dupin,'" he read out. "'The Bastille.' It is from Charles Dupin." Dupin handed the letter to me. "This is my grandfather's handwriting, without doubt," he declared.

I stared at the words on the page in my hand.

To Madame Sophie Dupin
The Bastille
17 May 1793

My dear wife,

These past four months of imprisonment were nothing compared to the pain of being separated from you. I know that you still live, as Valdemar comes to gloat ever more frequently and promises that we will be reunited side by side tomorrow as we meet Madame Guillotine. In some ways death will be a relief, as the days of hoping for a reversal and being reunited with my family have been nothing but cruel.

I have written to François so that he may always be reminded of the love we have for him and my belief that the best of us lives on in him—that he will grow to be a fine and principled man. I am certain you have written the same to him.

Your mother and sister have given me their word that they will be our son's guardians and will do all they can for him. I have given them the names of those they can call upon for financial assistance. I do not doubt their loyalty and good hearts as they are your kin. I have demanded but one promise from them: when the time is right they must tell François that the person responsible for all our grief is Ernest Valdemar.

Know, my dearest, that I would prefer to live many more years together with you and our son, but fate has decided otherwise and I will be proud to die by your side and leave this earth with you. Know too that I am calm as one always is when one's conscience is clear.

I send you all my love.

Your devoted husband,

Charles

Dupin's eyes were fixed on me as I read the letter.

"Do you think it genuine, Dupin?" I asked. It certainly looked so, but George Reynolds had proved himself to be a gifted forger and French linguist; making a hasty judgment would be folly.

"I know so," he answered. "The letter is dated the day before my grandparents' execution. It was common to allow those facing the guillotine the opportunity to write to a loved one. I believe my grandmother kept the letter, treasuring the last words she had from her husband."

"Kept the letter?" Monsieur Gondureau queried. "But your grandparents were executed together."

"She did not die," Dupin said. "My grandmother was taken from her cell before her planned execution and my grandfather died with a stranger who merely resembled his wife."

Gondureau frowned at this explanation. "But how did the letter end up in Madame Legrand's bedchamber? Hidden in her bookend?"

"It is not her bookend, Monsieur Gondureau," Dupin said. "It belongs to my grandmother, Madame Sophie Dupin. She used it to conceal this treasured missive from Valdemar because she believed he would destroy it if he found it."

"I see," Gondureau said.

But he did not. Certainly, how could he guess that my friend the Chevalier C. Auguste Dupin believed that his grandmother was still alive? And if I was following his unspoken train of thought, Dupin presumed that Valdemar had been planning to make Madame Sophie Dupin the new mistress of Undine's house—and even of Undine's very self.

25

Dupin pressed hard on the owl carving and the secret doorway near the fireplace in Madame Legrand's salon opened. Monsieur Gondureau left us at the threshold, and we descended into the dank, pitch-black tunnel that had been our intended destination earlier that morning. Our lanterns did little to ameliorate my sense that the walls might collapse at any time and imprison us forever. When we came to the sigil of Berith on the wall, we turned right.

"We will follow this route again for a time, but we will avoid the path that took us to Cimetière du Sud," Dupin said.

"With pleasure," I muttered. "I have no desire to see Reynolds's vindictive tableau again." Then a thought came to me. "If the ogress's insinuations are to be believed, Undine herself was involved in smuggling, and if that is the case, then surely she was aware of the tunnel leading from her house, but deliberately concealed that fact from you."

"Yes, I had the same thought," Dupin said. "And if it was Valdemar who stole her letter, then it's likely he used the hidden passageway to do so."

I didn't believe Valdemar himself was the thief—so elderly a criminal could not be capable of all the activities Dupin attributed to him. But rather than contradict Dupin when I knew his mind to be set, I ventured what to me seemed the more likely scenario. "Or someone in his employ. Maybe Reynolds was their go-between. Madame Legrand suspected that someone from her literary salon stole the letter and Mademoiselle Michonneau admitted that Reynolds attended them on occasion. She and Monsieur Poiret were even prepared to believe that he was their mistress's agent. George Reynolds in the guise of a famous playwright from Philadelphia meeting with Undine the *salonnière* would provide an excellent façade for any business dealings before or after her famous salons."

"Interesting," Dupin said as he lifted up his lantern to scan the tunnel. I did the same and our lights sent shadows skittering up and down the walls like startled vermin, but did little to conquer the black all around us. "Perhaps it was Reynolds who took the letter. He may even have done so to serve his own purposes rather than Valdemar's. It would give him some control over Madame Legrand, and if the letter provided evidence of Valdemar's smuggling activities, Reynolds might presume it would give him leverage over his employer."

"It's possible," I agreed. "Madame Legrand did not specify what was in the letter. She merely suggested that it gave her some sort of alibi."

"And judging by the conversation we overheard in the tunnels last night, Valdemar has agreed to release most of Reynolds's payment only once the scheme is completed. So Reynolds may have felt the need to acquire some form of insurance."

"Yes, that seems logical."

"In any case, Reynolds clearly feels that Valdemar betrayed him by denying him his chance to put you at the mercy of the mob during the theater show. Murdering Undine could simply have been retaliation." Dupin's voice echoed slightly in the tunnel, giving it a sinister cadence, and his matter-of-fact yet chilling words made me shudder to imagine that vicious mob descending upon us at the theater, eager for blood.

We continued our journey in silence for a time, Dupin using his lantern to scrutinize the walls, ceiling and floor, and me stumbling after him, the dusty air sticking to my lungs, the crunch of gravel underfoot unnaturally loud. We eventually came to a fork in the tunnel. Dupin held his lantern toward the wall and the sigil of Berith glimmered. Then light swooped up to the ceiling and Dupin said, "Poe, raise your lantern."

His voice was urgent and I immediately did as he demanded. There on the roof of the tunnel was an arrow drawn in what appeared to be charcoal. It pointed at the passageway that was not marked with the sigil.

"Possibly a quarrymen's mark, but perhaps not," Dupin murmured.

"What do you mean?"

Dupin's attention came back to me. "As I explained before, many have lost their way down here. A tunnel that appears to be constructed in a straight line might actually curve in such a way that you find yourself a large distance from where you imagined you might be. The quarrymen would sometimes draw arrows such as these to help them navigate the tunnels and keep their bearings. This strategy was also used by those who created the catacombs—precautionary lines were drawn on the ceiling with tar to guide those who went into them back out again. But this looks different," he added. "I believe it is a newer addition."

"Drawn by a smuggler? Or Madame Legrand's abductors?"

"There is only one way to know for certain." Dupin went in the direction indicated by the arrow and I followed. My heart accelerated when I found that the ceiling there was lower, the walls closer together, making the space all the more oppressive.

I tried to focus my mind firmly on our task as we journeyed along it.

"It seems quite a distance to move her, even if subdued."

"The tunnels were designed for transporting blocks of limestone from the quarries to the surface. Madame Legrand would be no more difficult to move if she were unconscious."

That was true enough. We walked some distance further and at length came to another turning. Dupin raised his lantern again and revealed another charcoal mark on the roof, pointing to the left. We moved in that direction. About twenty paces later, the tunnel veered in a sharp arc—again to the left—and as we rounded the turning, we both pulled up short as we were confronted with a wall constructed from human femurs stacked like bricks, stretching from one side of the tunnel to the other.

"How odd . . . *surprising*," Dupin muttered. "I've never found human bones used in this way such a distance from the ossuary."

I had no notion of where we were in relation to the world above us and whether finding such a construction in that location was unusual or not. As Dupin and I held our lanterns toward the wall, I noticed that the human skulls at its center formed the shape of a cross. Their mouths grimaced in our lantern light.

As Dupin examined the bones more closely, I simply held up my lantern for him and it wasn't long before my heart stopped thumping and my initial shock fizzled away. The greater shock was in realizing how normal it was beginning to seem to find human skulls and bones used as macabre bricks.

"Interesting," Dupin murmured. "Candles within the skulls. While religious services have been conducted in parts of the catacombs, I do not believe that was the case here." Dupin moved to the right side of the structure, then back to the far left. "A gap," he announced and disappeared from sight.

I quickly made my way to the same spot and caught sight of Dupin's lantern glimmering. Behind the wall was a small room, a prison really, with a pallet on the floor, a blanket, a tin cup, a jug and a chamber pot.

"Do you think Madame Legrand was kept here?"

"It appears that someone was. The candles in the skulls would provide some illumination. A captive might have been restrained or simply left here without any light."

I shuddered to think of being imprisoned by absolute darkness and it made me all the more aware of the fragility of our candle flames.

"And if Undine was imprisoned here, I do not believe it was at Valdemar's bidding," Dupin added.

"Reynolds, acting alone? To defy Valdemar?"

"Yes. I suspect Valdemar instructed Reynolds to hold Undine captive until he needed her. Reynolds was probably told to keep her in rather more salubrious circumstances than this," he said, "but in an act of defiance—and perhaps as a form of insurance, much like the letter—I think Reynolds brought the lady here. When Valdemar did not meet his demands, he murdered her, leaving her body on very public display in the Seine."

We stood for a moment in the dismal little cell. As much as I had disliked the supercilious and unkind Undine, it was dreadful to imagine any person spending his or her last hours in such a place. And then a horrifying thought came to me—was Madame Morel held captive in a similar location? I knew Dupin was wondering the same thing.

"What do we do now?" I asked. "Shall we try to find Reynolds and force him to tell us where Madame Morel is being held captive? For surely he must know."

Dupin sighed. "Paris is rather large, Poe. Where do you suggest we begin?"

"With Durand and Murphy. Please remember that Valdemar is their enemy too and they may have information we are not privy to, or they may be able to learn something from some other insalubrious residents of la Cité."

Dupin did not like this possibility, but seemed to have no better notion. "Did you take down their address?"

"Yes. It seemed prudent. Murphy resides at number seventeen rue du Temple."

"Very well," Dupin said. "Let's retrace our footsteps and find these friends of yours."

We had made our way across Pont Neuf to the Île de la Cité and intended to continue directly over to rue du Temple on the Right Bank, avoiding the Lapin Blanc and any of its habitués. But when we reached the bronze statue of King Henri IV astride his horse, a boisterous crowd of men, women and children drew our attention. Dupin and I were unable to resist looking to see what was provoking the revelry. As we approached, a portable puppet theater came into view. It was beautifully painted with a base of green, and highly decorated with flowers and two grinning, green-eyed black cats with wildly crooked tails. Above the stage was painted: *Le Théâtre des Chats Noir.* Curtains framed the stage and a puppet show was in progress.

A woman with long blonde tresses was in her bed. She looked ill, face gaunt, purple circles under her eyes, dressed in a white gown like a shroud. A tiny crown was set crookedly on her head. There was something unnaturally realistic about the puppet and its stricken expression, as though one were watching a miniature human performing onstage—and it seemed that many in the crowd around us were wholly immersed in that illusion.

"He doesn't love me," she whispered in the voice of the dying. "I should never have left my homeland!" Her sentiments seemed to capture the sympathy of the females in the crowd, who muttered in agreement.

"He's a devil," one woman declared.

"Driven one to her death and now he tortures the new wife," another agreed.

The "he" in question was a puppet slumped indolently in the armchair near the foot of her bed. It was the pale-faced fellow with dark hair and a mustache—the marionette that was beheaded before the Great Berith's performance, the marionette that was meant to be me.

Dupin's eyes met mine and I knew we were thinking the same thing. We could do nothing until the crowd was dispersed.

"Thirsty, I am thirsty, husband," the princess in the bed croaked.

Her husband rose from his armchair, the jerky movements of the puppet's limbs adding to the effect that my miniature doppelgänger was staggeringly drunk. He produced a goblet of wine, then took a vial from his jacket and tipped its contents into the goblet.

The audience hissed and shouted, "Don't drink it!"

But the withered princess did and immediately succumbed to a brutal, writhing death. The curtains closed again. The crowd continued to hiss and grumble until the curtains reopened to reveal that the figure in the bed was enshrouded with bandages, ready for the grave. Her husband was slumped back in his armchair, an opium pipe held to his mouth.

"The devil," the woman near us muttered again.

And then the bandaged figure in the bed slowly raised her hand and pointed at her husband.

"Murder," she whispered in a spectral voice. "Murder."

The crowd reacted with screeches of horror mixed with hope that something ill would happen to the devil-of-a-husband.

They were not disappointed. The enshrouded princess sat up in her bed with a hideous groan and the bandage fell from her face. But it was not the withered blonde princess returned from the dead, but rather a pale-faced, dark-eyed woman with copious amounts of curling raven-colored hair. The marionette had a blood-red mouth affixed in a gruesome smile of sharp white teeth that looked real, as if removed from a rodent and placed in the puppet's mouth.

"You have murdered us both," she rasped, pointing at the cowering man before her. "What say you of conscience grim—of the specter before you? Know that henceforward you too are dead—dead to the World, to Heaven and to Hope! For in your devious actions you have murdered your own self," she pronounced.

And the hushed crowd watched as blood stained the white shirt of the marionette fashioned to resemble me, and he collapsed to the ground, lifeless. The curtain fell closed and the crowd applauded.

"It is without doubt Reynolds behind this," I said to Dupin. "Using puppets to make a mockery of me and my work."

"It seems very unlikely that a French puppeteer playing to the rabble of Île de la Cité would borrow from your tales to make a play," Dupin agreed. "Let us just hope that no one in the crowd notices the similarity between you and the marionette—he is not a popular character."

I lowered my head to obscure my face. And then a familiar figure came hobbling through the crowd, hat in hand.

"Show your appreciation, ladies and gentlemen. Give us some coins to feed the poor ladies—revenge is sweet but it don't fill the belly." It was the limping boy who had followed us from the Lapin Blanc, the sly fellow Durand had called Tortillard. I quickly turned from him, as did Dupin, but he appeared at our elbows seconds later, his wheedling voice begging for money.

We threw coins into his hat, both carefully keeping our faces obscured from him.

"Interesting," Dupin murmured as the boy moved away. "If Reynolds is behind this puppet show, as we presume, then it appears the ogress's spy is working for him."

I wondered if Mother Ponisse was in league with Reynolds or whether young Tortillard was spying on Reynolds too and reporting back to her. Either way, I did not relish the notion of coming across the unpleasant and dangerous woman again.

"What is our strategy, then?" I asked Dupin. "Do we follow Reynolds to see where he lives, then bring Monsieur Gondureau and his men to arrest him?"

"Monsieur Gondureau might oblige, but we have no real proof Reynolds has done anything. As much as I dislike saying this, it might be best to follow Reynolds to his lodgings, then summon your friends and approach him. I suspect the two are adept at retrieving information from hostile characters and we are more likely to learn where Madame Morel is being held with their assistance."

"Very good," I said with relief. "It would be best to wait out of view until we can safely trail Reynolds."

We pretended an inordinate interest in the statue of King Henri IV and his mighty horse while waiting for my enemy and his accomplices to emerge and pack up the theater and wheel it back to wherever it was he resided. After about fifteen minutes, an elderly man pushed the rear curtain aside and came out with a girl of about fifteen. They shuttered up the theater then tipped it back onto a wagon base, with a yoke the old man stepped into. Reynolds was nowhere to be seen, nor the boy Tortillard. We followed the girl and the old man as he trudged along, pulling his wagon all the way to rue de la Juiverie, where he came to a halt before a run-down, ramshackle building. He chained the wagon wheels together so it could not be rolled away, then he and the girl carried the theater into the building. A few minutes later, the girl exited and walked briskly away.

"I do not think Reynolds is there, Poe, but the old man must know something."

"Yes, the play was undoubtedly Reynolds's work. Perhaps he saw us and slipped away."

Dupin shrugged, unconvinced. He immediately crossed the street and opened the door to the hovel as if he lived there. I followed him into the musty, ill-lit interior, which was surprisingly neat, and we climbed the groaning staircase, looking for the room that belonged to the puppeteer.

26

The place was cluttered with body parts—arms, legs, heads, hands, feet and torsos; they dangled from every inch of the walls like ghoulish ornaments, and were scattered over a large table positioned in front of the solitary window, awaiting resurrection. Some were close to life-size and others looked as if some tiny creature from a fairy tale had been dismembered. But the figure that caught my eye and held it was hanging on a stand placed on the work table, like a dead man from a gibbet. With his dark hair and mustache, gray eyes and what some would describe as a noble forehead, dressed in black with a neat white neckcloth and wearing a serious expression, one might mistakenly believe that I had posed for the miniature. And while I stared at the marionette, the puppeteer stared at me with undisguised fear. He was seated on a rickety chair near his creations on the work table, while Dupin paced the small room examining everything in it and I stood in front of him.

"You made this?" I indicated the puppet.

He nodded silently.

"Were you aware that you were creating a facsimile of me?"

The puppeteer shook his head vehemently this time.

"Who engaged you to make it?" Dupin asked.

"The Great Berith. For his show," the old man stuttered. "I make the puppets. And make them move. That is all. He pays me well. I am old," the fellow said plaintively.

I looked at the small room and all it contained—there was little there beyond the fellow's marionette pieces, the tools of his trade, his work table and a tiny cot in the corner of the room. The puppeteer did not seem to be lying and his gaze was filled with fear each time he looked at me, as if I were some demon summoned from the puppet itself.

"The show we saw this afternoon, who wrote it?" I asked. "I'm assuming you did not?"

The old man shook his head again. "It was the Scrivener—that is what he calls himself. He writes the stories and tells me what the puppets should look like—or draws them," he added, nodding at the figure of me. "He finds me when the Great Berith needs me or my puppets. Sometimes he brings them alive with me."

"Such as last night, during the Great Berith's performance at the theater on rue de la Gaîté?" Dupin asked.

"Yes, sir."

"And did the Scrivener tell you to give the performance on Pont Neuf today?"

The old man looked stricken. "No. He doesn't know. Please do not tell him, I beg you. The people like my two ladies and their story. It pays for my supper." Three female marionettes were also resting on his work table: the healthy version of Lady Rowena, her wraith and the raven-haired Ligeia.

"Do you mean to say that you are forbidden to perform the little play we saw today without the permission of the Great Berith, as he calls himself?" Dupin asked.

The old man shrugged. "I do not know if he cares. It is the Scrivener. He has forbidden it. He says no one will pay to see the play in a theater if they have seen it already on the street."

The old man rubbed at his face wearily. "But sometimes I must. Truly I must."

I felt outraged by Reynolds's presumption—the thief accuses the old man of stealing?

"It is hardly surprising, Poe," Dupin responded to my unspoken complaint. He reached into his pocket and retrieved several gold coins. "Take these," he instructed the old man, whose eyes immediately widened in astonishment as he looked at the gold Dupin had pressed into his palm. "Tell no one who gave them to you," Dupin added sternly. "And if you show us where the Scrivener lives, I will give you the same amount again."

The old man stared at Dupin like he was the Devil or a magician with powers to rival those of the Great Berith. He made no move to clasp his fingers over the coins as most might.

"I will tell no one," the old man whispered. "I swear. But I cannot take you to the Scrivener, for I do not know where he lives. He always comes here. I am sorry," he added anxiously.

Dupin nodded. "I thought that would be the case," he said to me. "We will have to find him ourselves."

"Then we are no closer to locating the wretch than we were this morning," I grumbled.

"I am sorry," the old man said again.

Dupin bowed slightly to him. "Your puppets are exceptional, sir. They are a testament to your skill as an artist. We have no grudge against you. It is your employers who have wronged us, so fear not."

"So long as you keep your word," I added.

"I will. I swear I will," the old man said to me. "And thank you, sir." The old man smiled tentatively at Dupin. "This is my family now," he said, indicating the small figures that surrounded him. "The rest are gone but for my sister's granddaughter, who helps with the puppets when she can. If they cannot perform,

this"—he waved his hand at the walls covered in his creations—
"becomes our tomb and nothing more."

"I understand," Dupin said.

"Good luck, sir," I added, feeling rather ashamed at my lack
of grace with the puppeteer. I turned and made my way to the
door, as did Dupin.

"I saw him in the Lapin Blanc one night," the old man called
out tentatively. We both immediately turned to face him. "He is
not a regular customer. It was . . . peculiar."

"Go on," Dupin instructed.

"I was there for my supper and he came up from the wine
cellar with the tavern-keeper."

"He knows Mother Ponisse?" Dupin asked.

The old man shrugged. "All know her. She is a fearsome creature but her harlequins are heavenly."

Dupin's nose wrinkled slightly but he said, "Was the Scrivener
there for his supper or was he discussing something with the
ogress?"

"He did not eat," the puppeteer said. "They spoke but I did
not hear what they had to say."

"And did the Scrivener leave by the door or did he return to
the cellar?" Dupin asked.

The old man thought for a moment and he frowned, puzzled.
"The cellar," he said. "He went back down into the cellar and
did not come out again while I was there."

Dupin dipped into his pocket and brought out another gold
coin. "Thank you very much, sir," he said, giving it to him. "Buy
yourself a good supper, somewhere far away from the Lapin
Blanc—far away from anywhere in the Île de la Cité." He smiled
slightly at the old man, who nodded mutely, mesmerized by the
gold on his palm.

27

The haze of smoke from our meerschaums gave form to our downcast silence as we sat in Dupin's parlor. We had gleaned disappointingly little of use regarding the whereabouts of George Reynolds or the ever-elusive Ernest Valdemar, and were therefore no closer to finding Madame Morel. Dupin had lost all interest in enlisting Durand and Murphy's assistance after our meeting with the puppeteer, insisting it was a waste of our time and he preferred to think in the quiet of his apartment. His lethargy and pallor concerned me and I wondered if, in truth, he wished to get home as he was feeling unwell.

"Dupin, you look as if you haven't slept in days," I said, putting down my pipe. "Can I get you something? Tea or some food or Froissart's elixir, perhaps?"

My friend shook his head impatiently, but before he could speak a loud rapping startled us both. Dupin looked at his timepiece.

"Eight o'clock. Unusual."

I followed him to the hall. Dupin peered through the spy hole he had drilled in the door, then immediately opened it. A

man of sixty years or more, quite fat, with a melancholy countenance and heavy features, stood there. He wore a workman's
indigo-blue cotton trousers and shirt and was clutching a folded
piece of paper in front of him.

"Monsieur Pipelet. Is something wrong?"

"No, sir. There is a letter. Very important I was told." He
handed over the paper, which was of parchment and fixed shut
with a black wax seal with a rosette of red ribbons caught
beneath it.

"Thank you. Most kind."

The old man shuffled away and Dupin closed and bolted the
door. "The building's caretaker," he explained. "And the invitation has arrived at last."

"Invitation?"

Dupin tilted his head and gave me a quizzical look. "It is the
thirteenth of July, Poe. While all know *when* the event will be,
no one knows *where* until the invitations are released, normally
a day or two before the fourteenth of July."

And then I understood. "Another *Bal des Victimes*?"

"Naturally. Valdemar's little game. Or so I can only presume.
Those who organize the balls are known only to each other. The
invitations are sent out anonymously to aristocrats descended
from Madame Guillotine's victims and the ball is organized by
someone who is paid extremely well by the host or hosts, as was
the case with Madame Tussaud."

"And she did not know the true identity of her employer," I
said.

"Correct," Dupin said. "I have received an invitation every
year since my eighteenth birthday, as is my birthright," he said,
his voice laced with sarcasm. "But since my misadventure in
London, normally I send my regrets. Or would if there were an
address to send them to," he added with a bitter smile.

"But you will not decline the invitation this time?"

"Of course not. We will repeat our previous masquerade, with you playing my brother again. I have all we require to dress for the event."

"Where is it to be held? Somewhere quite extravagant, I expect," I said, remembering the pageant held at Madame Tussaud's exhibition halls in London.

"At a thirteenth-century *maison de santé* south of the Cimetière du Sud."

"Cimetière du Sud? Where Reynolds sent us to visit the tomb he made for me?"

"It is a quiet spot with large gardens, secluded enough to conduct such an event. Probably there is nothing more to it than that."

His response was not convincing.

"A ball for victims of the Terror in an institution for the sick near a cemetery. What a charming location. Quite apropos somehow."

Dupin suppressed a smile at my mordant response. "It is said to be a most charming location, actually, for the gardens are quite lovely. And there are numerous quarry tunnels in the area," he added slyly.

"Ah, you think the event might be held underground? Better still."

Dupin laughed. "It is only a guess, for, as I said, I can only presume Valdemar is organizing this particular victims' ball given his efforts to ensure we were both in Paris for the event. But fear not. You are far more acquainted with what lies beneath the city than most who will attend."

"That provides little comfort. And who will be stalking us there—the elderly Monsieur Ernest Valdemar, the illusionist who calls himself the Great Berith, or both?"

"Both, for they are one and the same," Dupin said with a shrug. "But we will be searching for the magician, the man who holds Madame Morel against her will."

I sighed. "Given the nature of the event, we must hope there's little chance that the Great Berith will have his supporters from la Cité with him."

"Unlikely indeed. But truly you do not have to attend," Dupin said in a more serious tone. "In fact, it might be better if I go alone."

That I could not allow. How many times had I echoed his dictum, *Amicis semper fidelis*? To cower in his apartment while my truly faithful friend confronted his enemy alone would be reprehensible.

"I will attend with you, Dupin. Someone must ensure that you think with your head and not your heart, or both you and Madame Morel will be lost."

Dupin scowled. "On my word, Valdemar will fall this time."

"I'm sure he will—after Madame Morel is safe. For if you end his life first, you risk never finding where she is held captive."

"You underestimate me, Poe."

"Not at all," I said, my response as ambiguous as his.

Dupin looked to the heavens, then poured himself more cognac.

"To change the subject, of which I am utterly weary, something has been bothering me about the forged letter you received urging you to come to my assistance in Paris. It specifically requested that you bring the letters from your grandparents with you, did it not?"

"Yes, it did. I assumed at the time that you had learned something new about either my grandparents or my nemesis."

"I can't think of any reason for Valdemar to want the letters, but I imagine Reynolds might like to have them back—useful for blackmail or to destroy a reputation. And the obvious victim would be you."

That had not occurred to me. I had half-forgotten that I'd brought the letters with me.

"Reynolds originally delivered them to you so you would learn all that your grandparents had done. He enjoyed tormenting you with them. His wife persuaded him to put his desire for revenge aside and he did so until her murder. In the meantime you have established a name for yourself through your writing, a reputation you must cherish. George Reynolds the playwright had his work performed in many places in America, but perhaps it is fair to say that his wife, the actress, was the main reason people attended his plays?"

"Very true. She somehow rose above his dreadful scribblings."

"Then it is possible that Reynolds envies your accolades and likely that he would enjoy the chance to tarnish that reputation."

"He would try, given the opportunity."

"If the letters your grandparents wrote were made public, he might succeed in his goal. While it is obvious that you are not responsible for the crimes your grandparents committed, many may believe you tainted by them if told so in a persuasive manner."

I had feared precisely that if my wife had ever read the contents of the letters—that her love for me might diminish if she learned that my grandparents were criminals. It hadn't occurred to me that my public reputation would be tarnished as well—or perhaps the first possibility tormented me more than the second.

"To prevent that, I suggest you destroy the letters," Dupin concluded. "To my mind, it is odd that you have not done so already. Who will safeguard them if something happens to you? Or what might happen if they are stolen?"

"Any thief would need to know who Henry and Elizabeth Arnold were, which is unlikely."

"But Reynolds does."

I hadn't feared those possibilities as Reynolds himself had delivered the letters to me, but Dupin's words made the scenario come alive. Any person with a grievance against me—a few literary dilettantes, perhaps, who did not much care for my honest opinion of their work—might pounce upon the chance to discredit me. *Edgar Poe, grandson of criminals: what's bred in the bone will come out in the flesh.* I had considered destroying the letters many times, but something had always held me back. They were amongst the few things I possessed that gave me a sense of who my family were, the family I was born to and lost as an infant. But the story the letters held was not one that filled me with pride.

"Shall I burn them here?" I asked at last, indicating the fireplace.

Dupin nodded. "If you wish. Or in your room. It is your choice." He rose to his feet, bowed slightly. "I will retire. Today's events were enervating and we will need our wits about us tomorrow night. Sleep well."

"And you."

Dupin left the room, but I sat alone for a time, as his offhand reply had shifted my attention from my dubious legacy. While to most Dupin would not appear very changed, I sensed an alteration in him—a dissipation of the coiled energy he had possessed, a slowing of his reflexes, a diminishment of his very self. And yet he would not confide anything substantial to me about his health and I did not know if he was still consuming the *elixir vitae* Dr. Froissart had prepared for him without Madame Morel to lace his food or drink with it. Then a thought came to me—was Dupin's peculiar fondness for the irascible Madame Morel rooted in a reliance on her that was far beyond

her unremarkable housekeeping skills? Dupin had refused to
reveal what condition was impairing his health, but I had
observed a few similarities with Sissy's early decline. Did he fear
that he might become housebound and unable to care for
himself? He had found companionship with Madame Morel
and had lost it again—did that make his future seem all the
more uncertain?

Shame took hold of me, for my dislike of the lady had
blinded me to my friend's plight. Dupin had spent his life solving mysteries and attempting to right the wrongs done to his
family. And yet his life of study and of service—for that truly is
what it was—might end in his apartment with no one to mark
its passing, his scholarship and many accomplishments forgotten, all that he had achieved erased as if he had never existed at
all. I was filled with remorse. If I had entertained doubts about
the foolhardy mission we would be undertaking in hopes of
finding Madame Morel, those were cast away like a rogue's
promises. I would help my friend to find the lady, just as he had
always come to my aid without hesitation.

I made my way to my room and took the mahogany box out
of my trunk. It was time to ensure that the life I had forged for
myself would not be overshadowed by my grandparents'
crimes. I opened the box's secret panel and took out the confes-
sionary letters. The first mistake I made was in opening one.
"My dear Henry," it began. My heart leapt to my throat as I
began to read my grandmother's words—it was as if she were
speaking to me, telling me all she had endured. How could I
turn her voice to ash? But another voice spoke to me, the voice
of reason. I knelt down at the fireplace, struck a match and held
the letter to the flame. It leapt up to receive the delicate page,
embracing it in an orange glow, transforming it to a curling
black wave of ash as it lay in the grate. I took a final glance at
my grandfather's exuberant penmanship and his dishonest

words, then held a match to that too and watched the flames consume the paper until it dissolved into nothingness. My heart grew heavier as I burned letter after letter, my poisoned legacy, and watched as the charred paper whirled and danced, the words of love, perfidy, bitterness and retribution mingling together into a heap of silvery dust.

28

SATURDAY, 14 JULY 1849

Perfume snaked through the night air, intoxicating and cloying as the scent of death, accompanied by a haunting voice raised in a song without words. We were amongst a crowd of masked revelers, walking toward an open door set within a high stone wall. Dupin and I were dressed exactly the same: black jackets, white shirts open at the neck, black silk masks that hid our eyes and matching *chevalières* of gold, set with a lapis lazuli intaglio engraved with the Dupin coat of arms. We carried paperwork that proved we had the right, as descendants of Madame Guillotine's victims, to attend the *Bal des Victimes*: a certificate confirming the executions of his grandparents Madame Sophie Dupin and the Chevalier Charles Dupin, and identity papers for C. Auguste Dupin and François Dupin, his twin. Dupin's papers were genuine and mine were forged by him.

When we passed through its arch, we were transported into another world, magical, sublime. It was a vast, walled night garden filled with pale flowers and foliage that shimmered in the light cast off by the quarter moon above us. It was exquisitely arranged and enhanced by pale moths of various sizes sailing amongst the blooms. The walls were covered with night jasmine, moonflowers and honeysuckle, and white roses cascaded over arches that were placed to direct the eye to a flower bed or to frame a bench. Casablanca lilies, gardenias and tuberose scented the air, along with night gladiolus and flowering tobacco. Hydrangeas with snowball-like flowers, white hibiscus and silver sage were artfully planted amongst them. It seemed that great care had been taken to coerce the flowers to bloom simultaneously. The source of the music was revealed to be a girl wearing a white-feathered dress and standing in a large bird cage. Her voice was heart-rending and beautiful.

"The girl from the Lapin Blanc," Dupin whispered.

And I saw that it was true—she had been transformed into an ethereal angel by the dress and the garden's strange light. But the main attraction was at the garden's very center, surrounded by an ornate fence.

"*Selenicereus grandiflorus*," Dupin said. "I believe we are in for a show."

It was a peculiar-looking plant, about fifteen feet high with sprawling tangled stems gathered around a support that was shaped in such a way that the plant had grown into an almost human form. It had a large bud near its top that gave the appearance of a head.

And Dupin was not wrong. The Great Berith seemed to materialize from a puff of luminescent smoke and walked through an arch of roses to the plant's enclosure as though he was the celebrated victor of some important battle. His silken black mask was in place, his magical staff was in hand. He was dressed in a black suit with a blood-red waistcoat embroidered with skulls.

"Good evening, fellow revelers. I have been asked to welcome you all to this year's *Bal des Victimes*. Feel proud, for you were invited because of who you are—your heritage, your importance to France."

This pronouncement was met with applause and Dupin sighed.

"As some of you may know, I am the Great Berith, magician, seer, alchemist. I foresee a magnificent future for France, and I am determined to ensure that destiny is met. Do me the honor of supporting my quest."

Again, his words were applauded and the Great Berith gave a theatrical bow.

"I trust you will enjoy the revelries tonight and that you will eat, drink and make merry as if there were no tomorrow—that is my one wish for you all tonight. And in the weeks to follow, I hope you will join me in bringing France back to her former glory." The assembled clapped their hands together again but the Great Berith raised his staff until silence fell. "If you will allow me, let us begin the evening with one small display of magic. Here we have the rare and special plant, the night-blooming cereus, the Queen of the Night. This lady blooms but once a year and when she chooses—how like a woman." He chuckled in a ghastly manner that set my teeth on edge. "But in honor of this ball, in honor of France, she will bloom tonight under my instruction."

There were murmurs from those who had some understanding of the nature of the plant. The Great Berith took that moment to rap his staff upon the metal fence that surrounded the Queen of the Night. There was a burst of blue and silver sparks, with more smoke that swirled around us.

"Behold," the Great Berith said.

The flower bud that had been tightly closed had opened and was blooming at an accelerated, unnatural rate, long petals unfurling, star-like blossoms exhaling the scent of vanilla and orange. I was as fascinated as the rest of the crowd—it mattered not if one knew that the plant flowered but once a year, on a date determined by its own whims: the speed and manner of the blossoming was a strange magic.

"How?" I murmured to Dupin.

"It is but a trick," he muttered, but did not offer an explanation of how it was done.

When the flower had finished opening up, all around us applauded once more, and the thing shivered on its stem as if it had understood that it was being admired. There was something ominous and *cognizant* about its movements.

"I am pleased that you enjoyed the display," the Great Berith said. "For you see, when I direct my will at achieving a result, even to the point of controlling the spirit of Nature, I succeed in my task. Now, please enter the real Paris and enjoy all that it offers you." He pointed his owl-topped staff at a doorway set into the wall facing the one by which we had entered. The crowd swarmed toward it and we were swept along with them. And the Great Berith disappeared.

The *Bal des Victimes* that Dupin and I had attended at Madame Tussaud's exhibition halls had been an elaborate event, with extraordinary entertainments, food and wine. I presumed the same would apply this evening, but perhaps in a slightly different form.

The revelers we followed were dressed in the same manner, the women in white gowns with a scooped, low back, worn with red ribbons at the throat where the blade of the guillotine would have delivered the fatal blow and crossing diagonally over the back like trails of blood. Many of the ladies wore their hair cut short at the back—*coiffure à la victime*—a style purportedly worn by those who awaited execution as it would facilitate the passage of the guillotine blade through the neck. The men were dressed to reflect the affiliation of the relative killed by Madame Guillotine.

As we entered a gloomy and unwelcoming vestibule, I saw several attendants conducting inspections of each guest's papers proving they had the right to attend, and noticed our

fellow revelers greet each other *à la victime*—a graceful movement of the head to simulate the placing of the condemned
person's head upon the guillotine. My forged paperwork passed
scrutiny and I was not interrogated about my identity, which
was a relief. Guests left their weapons in the vestibule as
requested, except for Dupin, who pretended an injured leg and
hobbled inside, leaning heavily on his cobra-headed walking
stick with its concealed rapier.

Just as we began to make our way with the crowd toward a
staircase that led to wherever the ball was being held, I caught
sight of two fellows wearing black silk masks that covered their
eyes and dressed in the foppish attire of *Incroyables*, with tight
green jackets, extravagant cravats, wide trousers and large hats.
Both were carrying wooden walking sticks, which they were
refusing to relinquish.

"Look," I murmured. "Durand and Murphy, badly disguised."

"Very badly," Dupin agreed. "Murphy looks much too
uncomfortable in his costume and it is a fundamental error to
insist on keeping their sticks when they have no trouble walking.
Now their paperwork will be scrutinized more thoroughly."

Dupin's prediction was realized and moments later the two
men were rudely escorted oustide, Durand's protests falling on
deaf ears.

"I thought the ball was a secret event—how did Durand find
out about it, I wonder."

"Little remains secret for long in Paris when one has enough
money to pay for information. Look." Dupin pointed at the
owls that were stationed on either side of the entrance that led
to the tunnels.

"The secrets you could tell," I murmured as I stepped past
them and descended into the void, following Dupin and the *tap-
tap-tap* of his walking stick. It seemed that we walked through
utter blackness for an eternity, but then a shimmering gold

began to play across the spectral walls. Eventually the tunnel opened to a wide chamber, and as each person entered it, he or she gasped in awe. The display before us was breathtaking in a most ghastly way, for one entire wall was composed of skulls, each of which had a burning candle inside of it. Concealed violinists played a melancholic air while an ensemble of dancers, all dressed in white gowns with red ribbons and wearing masks that looked like skulls, whirled and moved their arms gracefully, weaving in formation through the crowd like a troupe of the dead. Men dressed entirely in black and wearing the same masks ushered us forward until we reached a strange and wonderful lake that glowed blue and was scattered with floating candles. A fleet of gondolas captained by sinister ferrymen awaited to carry us to the other side.

"Ah, we shall be ferried across the River Styx to the Kingdom of the Dead," Dupin intoned. "A metaphor both costly and unoriginal."

"But striking. And the water looks . . . supernatural. Is it an illusion of some kind?"

Dupin shrugged slightly and stepped into a gondola. I carefully followed him—it would not be difficult to lose each other in amongst the crowd of guests. When we were underway, Dupin trailed his fingers through the limpid water and his hand shimmered with an unearthly light.

"I believe it is lit from underneath. There is a sea cave in Capri where the water has the same appearance, caused by sunlight passing through an underwater cavity and illuminating the pool, so that it glows even in the cavern."

"But night has fallen, it cannot be the same effect."

Dupin shrugged. "We are meant to believe it is a kind of infernal magic, but of course there is some other explanation."

Dupin did not offer any theory, however, and certainly the other passengers in our gondola were half-delighted and half-frightened by the extraordinary water. When we reached the other side of the lake, I saw that it was shaped rather like a bowl filled with water, its steep bank rising up into a wall with a cleft through it. We clambered from the gondola and followed those who had arrived before us through the passageway in the wall. The tunnel itself was exceedingly dark, but short, and the chamber on the other side was lit by an enormous chandelier with twisting arms of glass that dangled crystals, the light from its candles making the pale walls shimmer like ice. This appeared to be the ballroom, as a small orchestra played and dancers whirled across the floor.

"How will we find him here, Dupin? It seems an impossible task. We should have pursued him after his performance."

"No, there were too many others there and all were far too alert. It is better to ensnare him when he is alone and his guests are distracted by the spectacle or the wine. I suspect Valdemar will put on another miraculous performance as the Great Berith, particularly if he wishes to persuade more supporters."

"And what is our plan if we do find him?"

Dupin tapped his walking stick on the ground. I remembered his failed attempt to skewer his nemesis during the ball at Madame Tussaud's and did not feel reassured by his silence.

"You suspect he is keeping Madame Morel down here somewhere. Do you hope to locate her tonight?" I asked, trying a different tactic.

"Naturally. I believe Valdemar will attempt to use her in another performance to display his infernal powers," he said, sarcasm sharpening the last two words. "And the performance will not begin until we are in attendance, I am certain of it. Come, this way." He indicated a door cut in the limestone that led to another chamber.

When we stepped inside, we found ourselves in a circular room. Its walls were of human bones pressed into mortar, arranged in intricate patterns: skulls encircled by femurs, like ghastly haloes; human hands arranged to resemble flowers; vertebrae fashioned into crosses and spirals. Against this aesthetically wondrous yet utterly ghoulish backdrop were tables heaped with a variety of foods, which the guests were transferring to their plates, seemingly unintimidated by their surroundings.

"Look there, Poe." Dupin pointed at the farthest wall, and I saw that bones had been affixed to the wall to spell out the words: *Théâtre des Morts*. Revelers were gathered in that "Theater of the Dead" near a trio of glass coffins, and when we joined them we saw a silken rope with a "pull" sign beside it. A masked fellow complied. The glass tops on the three coffins immediately swung open, and the trio of skeletons, elaborately decorated with jewels, sat up. The eyes glittered blue, the teeth and rib cage were overlaid with gems, rings were attached to the fingers. Every bit of bone sparkled with precious stones. They were beautiful and eerie and looked as if they might step out from their glass enclosures. Those around us drew in their breath in wonder or fear or both. One woman fainted dead away.

"A clockwork mechanism that makes them move, nothing more," Dupin announced loudly, which seemed to reassure some of our fellow spectators. "The bones of saints and the work of nuns," Dupin said to me. "It is a tradition in some places to decorate religious relics in such a way."

"The nuns who decorated these ones had a good deal of time for such meditative work. It is both nightmarish and beautiful."

Dupin nodded slightly. "Another of Valdemar's tricks to win followers through fear." He moved on, glancing briefly at the other clockwork displays. The spinning figure of a ballet dancer metamorphosed from young girl to skeleton and back again.

The grim reaper sprang from a clock like a cuckoo. A mechanical artist picked up his stylus whenever someone sat on the stool in front of him. He appeared to study the sitter and draw their likeness, but each portrait proved to be a skull, captioned with the words "*Memento mori*". I was compelled to examine each clockwork figure, they were so superbly made yet peculiar in design. I turned to make a comment to Dupin, but he had already moved on and was standing near the doorway to another chamber, in front of another display. I quickly joined him.

There before us was the marionette that resembled me. Or, in fact, its larger twin, for it was about three feet tall. Furthermore, it had no strings and seemed able to stand upright with the aid of the Malacca cane gripped in its right hand. Next to it was another figure, identical in size, which looked to be Dupin's doppelgänger in miniature. It was dressed as he normally was and carried a cobra-topped walking stick.

"An uncanny likeness of you," I said. "And these both look to be the work of the puppeteer, but I did not see them in his workshop."

"Because they were already delivered to the man who commissioned them," Dupin observed, his voice sharp with irritation. "Something the old man neglected to tell us."

"What is the purpose of this display, do you think?"

Dupin studied the two puppets that stood on a platform. "No strings, no puppeteer. Ah, there is a button here. Stand back." Dupin retreated too, then extended his walking stick and pushed it. The two figures immediately whirred into life. Dupin's twin reached to unsheathe the blade concealed in his cobra-headed walking stick and I expected the manikin to thrust it toward us, but before it could do so, the puppet resembling me quickly extracted a rapier from the Malacca cane and, with a fluid movement, pivoted and thrust the blade through the other puppet's chest, who crumpled to the ground as if dead.

I gasped, as did Dupin, though he tried his best to hide it. The puppet then withdrew his rapier from the chest of his victim, who resurrected himself, and both retreated back to their original places as if nothing had happened.

"How macabre," I muttered, completely unnerved by what I had witnessed and the viciousness with which the puppet made to resemble me had so casually stabbed the replica of Dupin. I felt almost as if I had truly betrayed my dearest friend. "If the point of this display is to provoke and unsettle us, then it has succeeded admirably with me."

"It is unsettling. I do hope you have no secret desire to murder me," Dupin said with a saturnine smile. His words broke the spell of the automaton as he had intended.

"I have not, though you do provoke me terribly at times," I replied. "But what is the purpose of this piece of theater? For surely it is designed specifically for our dubious pleasure. To make us feel threatened or perhaps to sow discord between us?"

"Both those things, but I believe there is more to it than that." Dupin took a candle from a wall sconce and held it to the base of the automaton. Words were etched into the wooden plinth:

Pestis eram vivus—moriens tua mors ero.

"'Living, I was your plague. Dying, I shall be your death.'" My heart sank as I murmured the words, for I had used them as an epigraph for my tale "Metzengerstein". When I turned my gaze back to Dupin, I knew that he also recognized the inscription.

"As I suspected, Valdemar could not resist a little game at our expense. First, let us consider your tale. It focuses on the intense enmity between the Berlifitzing and Metzengerstein families."

"Which you believe parallels the animosity between the Dupin and the Valdemar families?"

Dupin shrugged. "That is relevant, but more importantly, when Wilhelm Berlifitzing dies in a fire set by the young Baron Metzengerstein, his soul enters the body of his red horse—rather like the red horse associated with the Great Berith," Dupin noted. "The young Baron Metzengerstein then literally rides himself to death—his nemesis Berlifitzing takes his revenge while in the form of the red horse." Dupin paused for a moment, then said with a bit too much self-satisfied drama, "Metempsychosis."

"Naturally, I am familiar with my own tale. There is nothing in it that directly relates to this automaton, however," I said, gesturing at the two figures. "If one of the figures were riding a horse, perhaps. The quotation could be read as a threat, of course, but I fail to see how associating the quotation with this automaton does anything other than stir up a disagreement between us."

Dupin stared at the automaton for a moment, then raised his walking stick and pushed the button again. The figures sprang into action, the puppet resembling me skewering the figure of Dupin with his blade.

Dupin shook his head again slightly and sighed. "I believe there is more to it than that, but I cannot tell you precisely what just yet." Dupin bowed slightly and gestured toward the next area. "Let's leave your duplicitous double behind and see what other amusements Valdemar has concocted."

He walked to the next tunnel entrance, beautifully decorated with garlands of white lilies. I followed him into the passageway, which was just wide enough for two people to walk side by side. It was dimly lit by candles situated in alcoves close to the low ceiling. The funereal scent of lilies trailed after us. When we neared the end of the tunnel, a ghostly girl welcomed us, holding out a basket filled with pomanders—each person was invited to take one. They were quite lovely things, the size of an apple and encircled by immortelles, small wreaths of artificial blossoms constructed from wire that was threaded with white beads. We marched forward with the rest of the crowd and at the end of the tunnel there was a curtain through which we had to pass before entering a glorious room glowing with phosphorescence—not a candle in sight. It was wonderful to look at, but a noxious odor pervaded the chamber.

"Extraordinary," Dupin muttered, gazing at the domed ceiling, which was intricately painted to evoke the constellations and shimmered as mysteriously as the stars. He turned in a circle, head tilted up, and looked all around him. I did the same, as did many of those around us, but just as many took sniffs at their pomander, which smelled strongly of lilies—a remedy for the stench. "I believe the paint is made from dead fish, thus the glow and the smell."

"Dead fish?"

"Yes. As they decay they emit a feeble light. Miners sometimes use dead fish rather than lanterns to illuminate a chamber. The smell is repugnant, but it is safer than a candle flame if there might be combustible gases."

"It is a terrible smell, but an ingenious solution," I said, pressing the pomander of immortelles to my nose.

I sensed that Dupin's attention was diverted and turned my head to see a young girl, dressed in white, approaching him. She was holding something toward him—a gold ring perhaps. Dupin immediately strode to meet her.

I was about to follow when I was consumed with a terrible sense of dread, and a chill descended upon me, which seemed to take on a physical presence.

"Do not . . ." A whisper in my ear.

I hesitated, breathed in the pomander more deeply, trying to dispel the terrible odor and clear my head with the fragrance of the lilies.

The sound of footsteps padding behind me made me whirl round—what I saw was not of this world. Crackling blue flames danced over the walls then slowly coalesced into a ghastly figure, a woman blazing with unearthly fire. It resembled Sissy in the most horrible way, as if she were returned from the grave. Very faint and very far away, a voice: *"Go back. Go back . . ."* The words echoed until the dreadful vision dissipated.

The room swelled with heat and the stench of fish became unbearable. I was overwhelmed with dizziness and pressed the pomander to my nose again while looking for any sign of Dupin, but he had vanished. Then, to my left, a woman collapsed in a faint. Then another reveler fell, and another. And, finally, I too was enfolded in a smothering blanket of lilies.

29

A thick scent, Arabian in nature: night jasmine, frankincense, musk and myrrh . . . then the metallic stink of asafetida, like a stiletto hidden under a velvet cloak. The darkness dissipated, and I saw a long wall shelf crowded with shimmering candles, a haze of incense drifting from strange vessels placed amongst them. Painted on the Prussian-blue wall above the shelf was an enormous, diabolical owl, beak agape to shriek its unearthly cry, wings spread wide as if rising up from the flames and smoke. Grinning human skulls were stacked like bricks on either side of the peculiar fresco.

My eyes were bleary and my head throbbed as if I'd been on a spree for days. I could not feel my limbs at all. As my vision cleared, I saw that I was shackled to a large barber's chair—my arms, my legs, my body secured with thick leather belts. Directly in front of me was what looked to be a twin of the chair that imprisoned me, upholstered in leather and mounted on a solid metal base so that it could pivot, with two sturdy armrests and a footrest.

To the right of the owl fresco was a closed chamber door. When I looked to my left, my labored breath caught in my throat, for there was a man working at a table where immense flasks and flagons were arranged before him. There was a library filled with treasure books and shelves cluttered with jars of infernal substances, as if gathered by the Devil's own apothecary. I recalled Dupin's description of the laboratory he had glimpsed when eavesdropping on the argument between Reynolds and the Great Berith and wondered if that was where I was being held.

The man, whose back was turned to me, was heating a vessel over a low flame. I must have emitted a moan of pain, for he turned to gaze at me and there was a look of pure cruelty on his face. I cried out again, this time with terror. The fear coursing through me brought me more quickly awake.

"Ah, you have rejoined the living." He spoke in English—his voice was mellifluous, his tone mocking. A leer contorted his harmonious yet unsettling features. He looked to be about forty-five years of age and was of medium height, slim but with the build of a sportsman; his hair, pointed beard and mustache were black; and his hypnotic eyes were an unearthly green. It was the first time I had seen him without his mask. "I am Ernest Valdemar," he said. "Better known now as the Great Berith— you have, of course, seen my show." His sardonic leer widened and he dipped into a graceful bow.

"Yes, you're quite the illusionist," I replied, trying to regain some semblance of composure. "Most convincing." I tried to wriggle my fingers but saw only a slight twitch. My legs still did not shift at all. Whatever he had dosed me with was potent.

"It is more than illusion, Mr. Poe. It is an unexplainable power, it is supernatural—demonic some might say."

I thought back to the Great Berith's performance and how Dupin had an explanation for every one of his tricks. And I half-remembered what my friend had tried to tell me when he showed me the grimoire and the image of the demon Berith from whom the magician took his name—the demon that rode a red horse and had the power to turn all metals into gold. A demon that spoke in a clear, subtle voice and only told the truth when asked a direct question. Certainly, the man I was facing, who called himself by that demon's name, was a liar. Might something be gained by engaging him with questions? Time, perhaps, if not the truth? Time that might help me find a way to escape or allow Dupin to locate me, assuming my friend was still alive and at liberty? I breathed in deeply and did my best to muster a sense of calm.

"Do you call yourself Berith because you have the ability to transform base metal into gold?" I nodded at the laboratory where he had been working.

The illusionist laughed. "Very good, Mr. Poe. You have an awareness of the esoteric arts. And in a manner of speaking, you are correct." He scrutinized me intently; it was as if his eyes were razor-sharp blades on my flesh. If I was to escape murder, I needed to keep my wits about me.

"You are obviously a very wealthy man. Have you found the philosopher's stone?"

"Yes. You have seen it."

"The philosopher's stone? When?"

"During my performance."

There had been no displays of transforming objects into gold, but before I could speak, he took a red jewel from his waistcoat pocket, the gem suspended from a chain that sparkled as if an unearthly fire were within it, the one he had used to hypnotize the Schoolmaster, the Queen of Hearts and Madame Morel. As I gazed upon it, this time from scarcely a yard away, it glittered so strangely that it seemed to have a tiny figure dancing within it, like a djinn imprisoned in a bottle or a captured faery. Or, perhaps—*a homunculus*? Impossible. Such a thing could not exist. The vibrant jewel that swayed before my eyes with what appeared to be a tiny creature moving within it—unquestionably an illusion. Merely another trick, like the demons that appeared in the theater, projected from a magic lantern.

"It is an unusual jewel, very beautiful," I said as calmly as I could.

"And powerful. It has many properties: turning base metal to gold or silver, common crystals into jewels, rejuvenating dead plants. Shall I show you?" Berith asked cordially.

"Please."

He immediately made his way back to his work table and I tried to flex my hands, to shift my feet. The sensation of pins and needles pricking my extremities made me breathe in sharply and Berith looked up.

"It is no good, sir. The paralysis will last for another hour, perhaps more. Now watch carefully." Berith took a large glass jar from one of the shelves and placed it on the table. It was filled with dried roses, the heads lopped from the stems but still intact. "Quite dead. The petals dried and brown. No scent. Would you care to inspect them, Mr. Poe?"

"That will not be necessary."

"Good, good." He smiled. "I am placing six of the dried roses on a sieve, which I will now suspend over this flask containing ground-up *lapis philosophorum* mixed into a special oil I have created." He attached the handle of the flat sieve to an upright stand and adjusted its height to his liking, tilting it slightly so that the dead roses were plainly visible to me in my prison-chair. "And now I will add another candle to heat the flask vigorously so that more steam is produced." This he did, and moments later I thought I could discern a strange haze rising up from the flask, like a roiling storm cloud at sunset, twisting with purples and golds and pinks. "It begins," Berith said, his satisfaction plain. "Do you see?"

I did. The heart of each rose turned black, as if a dollop of ink had been thrown into it, and then it spread outward to the very edges, as if the frail, dusty petals were putrefying. Moments later there came another change—white bubbled up from the center of each flower and spread to the petals in the same manner, and six inky roses now looked as if they had been covered entirely by a perfect layer of crystallized snow.

I glanced at the illusionist and found he was watching me as acutely as I had been watching the roses. "It is not complete," he said.

A yellow cast came to the pure white flowers, which deepened to citrine, and I was filled with wonder, expecting the flowers to change to pure gold. But instead the color deepened further and further still until the petals were a luxuriant red and the air richly scented with attar of roses—for surely the magician had found a way to perfume the air with that oil? And with some trick of the light had given the dried flowers the appearance of freshly cut blooms?

It seemed he read my mind, for Berith gathered the roses in his hands and carried them over to me. He held them right near my face so that I could scrutinize every petal and breathe in the aroma. The scent was undeniably from the flowers and the petals were fresh. All I had witnessed suggested sorcery, but I knew that the magician had managed, through some sleight of hand, to utterly fool my senses again.

"Most impressive," I said with as much composure as I could muster.

He raised his brows. "Impressive? That does not do it justice. *Extraordinary*, perhaps. Or *wondrous*. Most would say that you have witnessed a miracle, Mr. Poe. The rejuvenation of dead matter." He let the roses fall onto my lap and returned to his work table. "And soon you will witness—indeed, *participate* in—a greater miracle."

He busied himself with decanting the fluid containing the ground philosopher's stone into a very large glass alchemy vessel of about three feet high with a rounded base that was a foot in diameter. The thin neck was at least two feet long, and attached to opposite sides of the glass base were a pair of flexible black stalks that resembled a creeping vine with a cupped flower shape at each end. Berith placed the contraption on a wooden trolley and wheeled it over, situating it in between my chair and its twin. He locked its wheels into place with his foot.

"The miracle you are about to participate in is metempsychosis."

My heart fluttered painfully at that word. My end was about to arrive at the hands of the madman who stood before me.

"Fear not, Mr. Poe. I am not going to murder you. Far from it. I will pull you back from the brink of death with the elixir. You witnessed yourself its immense powers. And then your vital essence—your soul if you like—will be rehoused in this." He indicated his own body with a flourish.

I looked from the man before me to all the strange things in his laboratory, the chair I was imprisoned in, the equipment he had set up. My tormenter truly seemed to think that he could cheat Death and send a person's soul or spirit or *self* into a new body. I remembered Dupin's dismissal of the conjurer's tricks at the theater, but also his surprising willingness to believe that metempsychosis was possible, that the man before me had achieved through the science—or perhaps magic—of alchemy what most would deem a miracle. And even if the Great Berith, the man Dupin believed was in truth Ernest Valdemar, was able to send my vital essence into his body without killing me, it was certainly not something I wanted to happen. Whatever the truth was, I needed to delay his gruesome experiment for as long as I could, in hopes the paralytic he has given me might wear off.

I willed myself to be as calm as Dupin would be if he were in my situation. I knew for certain that the man before me was a showman and enamored with his own intellect. If I managed to keep him pontificating about his discoveries and about himself, perhaps I would achieve my goal. And perhaps if I asked questions, the man who'd named himself after the demon Berith would answer truthfully.

"Am I correct in understanding that somehow my soul—my consciousness—will animate your body and vice versa?" I asked.

"Precisely."

"And if your experiment fails, we will both be dead?"

"Have faith, Mr. Poe. I have successfully completed the process several times. My first success in accomplishing metempsychosis was with animals many years ago, when I was betrothed to Sophie de Bourdeille—you've made the lady's acquaintance," he said with a mocking smile. "And since then I have perfected my methodology with human subjects, including Sophie de Bourdeille and myself." Again, he indicated his own form with a theatrical sweep of his arms.

"You were betrothed to Sophie de Bourdeille? The woman I know as Madame Morel? You did not directly state that in your performance. Does she help you in your work?"

He shook his head in annoyance. "She failed to understand the importance of what I was devoting my time to and abandoned me for Charles Dupin. She brought disgrace onto my family, but my revenge was complete."

"How so?"

"You were at my theater performance and should recall that Charles Dupin was executed."

"And Sophie Dupin with him?"

"No. As you heard from the lady herself, another woman was executed in her place through the use of metempsychosis.

Guards were well paid so that I might undertake the experiment, as was the woman who agreed to participate. The experiment succeeded and Madame Sophie Dupin was returned to her cell, or so it appeared. In truth, she was in another form and safely with me when the time came for Madame Dupin to meet with Madame Guillotine."

"Did the other woman know that Madame Dupin was facing execution?"

"A small detail I omitted." Berith waved his elegant hand in the air as if shooing a persistent fly. "Her performance on the way to the guillotine was amusing, though. All thought her mad when she protested that she was an innocent, a woman forced to beg on the streets, that she was not Madame Dupin. Only Charles Dupin fathomed the truth, but he said nothing, for he was happy that Sophie escaped death."

"Was she happy too?" I asked.

He laughed. "Quite the philosopher, Mr. Poe. She should, of course, be happy. She is alive and wants for nothing. Now we will proceed."

My efforts to slow down my tormenter's plans were not as effective as I had hoped they might be. He picked up one of the cupped objects connected to the tubing, covered my mouth and nose with it, then tied it around the back of my head. I could not resist in any way. "Now, Mr. Poe, through mesmerism and alchemy I will perform an exchange of our souls—the magnetic fluid that runs through you will be drawn into this vessel, as will the magnetic fluid that courses through me, and when I activate the machine, our respective forces will flow into their new home. Understood?"

I wondered if the cloud of mist inside the vessel was a gas that would poison me when it emanated from the tube. And then, as the mist whirled, I saw something else. Before my eyes was the tiny dancing creature, the homunculus inside the red jewel. It was swinging back and forth and I could not resist tracking it with my gaze.

"You will not feel any pain. When the elixir enters into your body, your essence will slowly withdraw and enter the vessel. You will not resist as your soul moves through the other tube and into what is now my body. And when the transference is complete, you will not dare speak of what has happened, for no one will believe you. Do you understand? You are rendered mute on the subject."

The red jewel moved back and forth. Berith made several motions with his hand in front of my face. He put on the other mask, attached the jewel to the top of the glass vessel and sat down. The jewel was suspended in a direct line with both our gazes, and as I watched the tiny dancing figure, I felt cool, damp air seep up through my nose then curl down my throat like thick fog. A creeping cold inched over me and my eyelids began to flutter shut, despite my efforts to keep them open. Soon all I could see was the tiny creature dancing before my eyes, a leering imp with sharp gnashing teeth.

Darkness splashed over me. I struggled to rise up through it, but it was as if I were caught in a powerful current. And as I slipped down, my eyes were still held by the jewel—but suddenly it changed. It was not the demonic imp captured within it: I saw with astonishment that it was my wife, standing calmly, gazing at me with a smile on her lips. The further down I sank, the larger she seemed to be until her dear face was before mine and her hand stroked my cheek.

And then I was gasping for breath and found that the peculiar mask had been pulled from my face. My eyes flew open and as my vision began to return, I saw a blurred flash and heard the terrible sound of metal piercing flesh. Berith's mouth gaped open wider and wider still, and I watched in horror as blood roared from his chest where the rapier had pierced it. And then his body seemed to collapse in upon itself, dissolving into a putrid, swirling black ooze, while his shriek of rage reverberated through the eerie chamber.

30

SUNDAY, 15 JULY 1849

When I opened my eyes again, I met the concerned gaze of an angel hovering above me in a deep blue sky filled with stars as shiny as new coins. It took more than a few minutes for me to ascertain that the angel was one of a circling host, painted so realistically that I could almost feel their wings raising up a breeze, or so it seemed to my befuddled mind. I was lying in a bed, one I did not recognize, and had no notion of where I was or how I had arrived there.

"Welcome back, Monsieur Poe."

I jumped at the voice and turned my head to see Madame Morel seated on a chair next to me.

"The same to you, madame." I did my best to keep my voice calm, for I had no way of telling if Madame Morel was friend or foe. Was I confined in this strange place with her as my guard? Was she in league with the man who called himself the Great Berith, a man who must surely be Valdemar's puppet? And was his hideous demise merely a hallucination, brought on by whatever drug he had forced me to breathe?

"I will call for Auguste." Madame Morel tugged at a bell pull and I was immediately filled with relief. "And tea, I think." She then tugged twice at the pull, folded her hands in her lap and stared at me. Despite her pitiless gaze, the mention of Dupin's name reassured me.

"Is he dead? Or did I dream it?"

"Dead," she said with undisguised satisfaction.

"Where are we? I have no recollection of this room."

"It is my bedchamber. Auguste and I brought you here." She smiled slightly. "It was not easy."

I struggled into a sitting position and looked more carefully around me. The walls were curved and of stone, but were painted blue like the sky of the fresco above us. Candles gleamed from niches cut into the walls and a large candelabra with a dozen glimmering tapers was situated on a fireplace mantelpiece. I found I was still dressed in the garments I had worn to the ball, except for my jacket, which was hanging on the back of another wooden chair.

"We thought it best to disturb you as little as possible," Madame Morel said upon observing my confusion. "You had a great shock, but we are safe now."

"I am glad you were not injured by that madman."

"Thank you. Obviously, I am glad also."

"Poe! You are with us again." Dupin materialized from the gloom and strode over to me, looking innervated, his gaze overly intense. "And sitting up—excellent. Are you able to feel all your extremities or does the numbness persist?" I wriggled my fingers and Dupin nodded. "Very good. I will have to examine what Valdemar had in his laboratory to ascertain what was in the paralytic, but given your improvement, I do not believe there will be any lasting damage."

A rattling noise curtailed his words and moments later a young girl emerged from the same concealed doorway, wheeling a tea trolley. The girl, ebony-haired and pale, seemed familiar, but I could not recall why. She carefully poured out three cups of tea from a silver pot.

I must have been staring, for Dupin asked, "Do you recognize the young lady, Poe?"

She gazed at me solemnly, her eyes large and dark. And then I knew where I had seen her before.

"She was in the glowing chamber and approached you. And before I knew it, you were gone."

"Here, drink. It will do you good." Madame Morel pushed a cup toward me.

I tried to take the beverage, but my hands began to tremble and the porcelain teacup rattled unbearably against the saucer. Madame Morel held the cup as I drank the tea, which was liberally laced with sugar. She immediately refilled it, and the tremor in my hands subsided enough for me to manage myself.

"Thank you, Madeleine," Madame Morel said to the girl. "Please tell your mother that we will have supper at six o'clock."

"Yes, madame." The girl curtsied and left the room.

"That is in two hours, Monsieur Poe," Madame Morel added helpfully.

I had thought it to be early morning, but it seemed that I had been asleep for well over twelve hours. We drank tea in silence for a time, a rather uncomfortable experience as both Dupin and Madame Morel stared at me, scrutinizing my every movement.

"Do you recall what happened?" Dupin asked.

"Perhaps . . . though I suspect it was an opium nightmare. Certainly I was drugged with something."

"Tell us what you remember," Dupin encouraged me. "Just before you saw Madeleine."

Strange images of the previous night immediately filled my mind. "We saw the display with the two puppets that resembled us. The figure representing me plunged a rapier through the heart of your double."

Dupin nodded. "Yes, go on."

"Then we walked down a passageway to the room that glowed and smelled horribly of decomposing fish. I began to feel strange and thought it was the stench. I saw the girl approach, as I've said. And you followed her."

"Show him why," Dupin instructed Madame Morel.

She held her left hand toward me. A golden *chevalière* set with a lapis lazuli intaglio engraved with the Dupin insignia encircled her little finger. "Until now, I have only dared to wear it near to my heart, hidden in a small pouch pinned to my dress. I gave the ring to Madeleine—she was hired by Ernest to be my servant. I instructed her to wait in the glowing chamber until she saw two men of similar countenances, one with a cobra-headed walking stick. She was to show Auguste the ring and bid him to follow her. I thought you would go with Auguste." Madame Morel gave me a look that suggested I was an incredible dolt for not having done so.

"I believe Mr. Poe is feeling a good deal better," Dupin said, "for he looks very cross with your presumption."

"I would have followed if I had seen the ring," I snapped. "You charged off without a word to me."

"It is done now." Dupin shrugged. "I too presumed you would follow. But I am sorry I did not look to see if you were behind me."

The apology surprised me but Dupin's actions did not. He was single-minded in the pursuit of anything to do with his family.

"But why did I and all around me fall unconscious, yet you did not?" I asked.

"It was the immortelle pomanders. The glowing room had a purpose. The stench of decaying fish encouraged all who stayed in the room to hold the pomanders to their noses as the lilies provided relief against the terrible odor, but they also contained a powerful sedative that you breathed in. When you collapsed, Valdemar's men brought you to the alchemy chamber."

I remembered that everyone around me had lifted the pomanders to their noses and soon after collapsed. "How did you find me, given you were taken to Madame Morel?"

"Ernest could not resist divulging his plan, knowing it would cause me pain," Madame Morel explained. "But he did not count on Madeleine's loyalty to me. She brought Auguste here and he released me."

"Then she guided me to the alchemy laboratory and obviously we arrived at precisely the right moment."

"Thank you, madame," I said. "It seems I owe my life to you too."

She shrugged. "You are Auguste's friend."

"And Berith is truly dead? What I witnessed was . . . inconceivable," I muttered.

"Valdemar—the man you knew as Berith—is absolutely dead, for I pierced his heart with my blade and, as you witnessed, he dissolved into base matter. Nothing can bring him back," Dupin added with immense satisfaction.

I shuddered, picturing the gruesome scene again. "I was certain it was an illusion, that he escaped."

Dupin shook his head. "Justice has at last been done. At last."

"Thank you, Auguste," Madame Morel said softly. "You bring valor to the Dupin name. I am very proud."

"It is an honor, Madame Morel." Dupin nodded his head to her as one might to a queen, but she reacted with an injured expression. "Madame *Dupin*," he corrected, then softly added, "Grandmother." His face was imbued with happiness, an unnatural expression for my saturnine friend. "It will take me time to readjust."

"Of course," the lady said.

Madame *Dupin*? How absurd that sounded, for I still could
not lay my doubts to rest—all the spectacles engineered by the
illusionist had not convinced me that metempsychosis was truly
possible. There was no absolute proof that we were not the
victims of a grand hoax. But, equally, all along there had been
something honest about Madame Morel's concern for Dupin
and her apparent efforts to protect him. She genuinely acted as
if they were family. I found myself in a state of complete
confusion.

"And now, Poe, we must find a way to make an end to *your*
nemesis," Dupin announced. "Madame Dupin has confirmed
many of our deductions—that Reynolds was in the hire of
Valdemar, forging documents and acting as his emissary in various unscrupulous enterprises, including her own abduction."

"He was very well paid," Madame Morel said. "But Monsieur
Reynolds wanted more. He demanded to be allowed to reveal
your story at the theater after the puppet show. He believes that
your grandparents were responsible for his father's unjust
imprisonment and alleges you were responsible for the death of
his wife." She raised her brows and scrutinized me for a
moment, as if trying to fathom whether his assertions were
true. "He wished to destroy your reputation onstage in front of
an audience and hoped the mob would take action against you.
Given his claims, it is very likely you would have been
murdered," she added matter-of-factly.

"I believe that," I said. "But why did Valdemar break his
promise to Reynolds?" I'd meant to say "Berith", but such was
my confusion.

Dupin stared at me, his gaze intense. "Do you feel well
enough to walk a short distance?"

"Yes, I think so."

"Good. You will understand it all more easily if you can see
what I have seen," Dupin said eagerly. He helped me to my feet

and ushered me across the room to the door. It was concealed behind a partial wall and as we passed through I saw a metal gate open to the side: the room was also a prison. "This way," he said.

Dupin and Madame Morel linked their arms through mine and guided me down a passageway lit by torches affixed to the walls. I had the sense I was in a medieval castle and was being led to an even more secure dungeon. But after a walk with a number of twists and turns that Dupin navigated with supreme confidence, we arrived at the same door Dupin and I had discovered after the Great Berith's show. He unlocked it using a set of keys and pulled the heavy door toward us. And there was the strange laboratory where I had thought I was going to die. Dupin walked in and surveyed the room with huge satisfaction.

"Magnificent, isn't it? Valdemar spared no expense. The equipment. The chemicals and ingredients. And the books— rarer than you can imagine." He indicated a library that was next to what looked like an apothecary's shop.

I stared at the demonic owl that hovered on the blue wall as if preparing to attack and the ghoulish partitions constructed of skulls. What kind of person could work in a laboratory like this day after day?

"I'm sure there are many treasures here, no doubt stolen, but truly I'll be glad to escape this chamber of horrors," I said.

"I am afraid that I agree with you." Madame Morel glanced apologetically at Dupin. "Subterranea has been my prison for too long."

"There is no denying that Valdemar was quite brilliant." Dupin opened a drawer in the alchemy table and retrieved a pouch. From it he pulled out the red jewel, which radiated with unnatural light. "To create this, even with the most ancient esoteric tomes, is highly impressive." He then indicated the two chairs with restraints and the masks, the flask that had contained some potion—the place where I had nearly met my death. "And of course you remember this?"

I nodded slowly, but my attention was drawn back to his hand. Dupin held the red jewel in front of my eyes as a mesmerist might and my gaze was captured by its unearthly, scintillating gleam, and in between flashes of ruby light I thought I saw that dancing imp.

"It is an uncanny thing," I murmured.

"And a powerful thing. Imagine if I had not interrupted Valdemar's experiment. If he took you to the point of death with the philosopher's stone elixir and then transferred his soul into your body and vice versa. What would be the outcome?"

"I would be poisoned. I would be *dead*."

Dupin made an exasperated expression. "You are being stubborn. There are more things in heaven and earth, my dear Poe, than are dreamt of in your philosophy."

"Most do not have the imagination to grasp what Ernest achieved," Madame Morel said. "It is not his fault."

If the lady's intent was to annoy me into playing Dupin's game, she achieved her goal.

"If the illusionist's fantasy could ever possibly have succeeded, then presumably he would have pretended to be me and got up to all kinds of trickery with you. And if I had inhabited, so to speak, Berith's body and approached you, it is likely you would have murdered me before I could persuade you that I was . . . *me*."

"Precisely. If Valdemar were in your form and, for example, pulled a rapier from his Malacca cane and thrust it through my heart, my last thoughts would be that my truest friend had taken my life." He paused for a moment, as if visualizing the scene that had been enacted by the two automated puppets. "It would be a most terrible revenge."

Madame Morel patted his arm and gave me an aggrieved look. I had to admit to myself that such a vile scheme seemed in keeping with what I had been told of Valdemar's vengeful character.

"But you thwarted Berith's plans," I said, "whether they were feasible or not. And it seems we need fear him no more. But Reynolds wishes to destroy me, and as far as we are aware, he is still somewhere in Paris. It seems he is unafraid of the tunnels and knows how to navigate them to some extent. And we know he has been in this laboratory before as we heard him arguing with Berith in here."

Dupin immediately reverted to his more logical self. "Quite right, Poe. We will stay down here again tonight, but don't worry, you will be safe. You need more time to recover from your ordeal and I wish to continue looking through Valdemar's papers—I am certain there is information there that will lead us to Reynolds, it just may take some time to find it as the devil was involved in numerous schemes. But I give you my word, we will solve the problem of your enemy once and for all." He looked to Madame Morel. "Is all secure?"

"The north, south and east gates are locked," she said. "We must do the west gate."

"Very good. I believe I have mastered the layout of the apartments, but it is best if we go together."

"Of course," Madame Morel said.

"We will be moving back toward the chambers where the *Bal des Victimes* was held. Perhaps you would prefer to wait here, Poe? You will be able to bar yourself in."

The demonic owl glared down at me and the ghoulish skulls shimmered and grinned. "I will come with you," I said.

31

We closed and locked the door on the strange laboratory with its exotic ingredients, precious tomes and diabolical contraption, then made our way, with the aid of three brightly burning torches, into the tunnel that I had evidently been transported through the previous night.

"It is something of a maze," Dupin said. "But there is a system of symbols that Valdemar put in place, and once learned, it is simple to navigate without losing one's way."

Torchlight skittered through the tunnel, occasionally illuminating some ghastly human fragment set into the wall—a skeletal hand, a foot, a femur. After a time, I realized that these fragments were pointing out the route that we were following. When we came to a display of bones that resembled a strange altar, Dupin halted and inserted a key into a hidden lock then pushed open the concealed door.

"Look."

An opulent chamber was revealed, its walls swathed in silks, a Persian carpet on the floor and a canopied bed in pride of place.

"You will sleep here tonight. There are a number of other chambers: a sitting room, dining area, kitchen, bathing room—quite extraordinary."

"He had years to construct it," Madame Morel observed. "And vast resources. Ernest paid handsomely those who served him well. And murdered anyone disloyal," she added.

Dupin pulled the door closed and we continued on toward the mysterious gate that I did not recall seeing. Soon a familiar stench crept into the air. We circled a large stone column and saw a doorway into a chamber that still glimmered with eerie light.

"It is wondrous," Dupin observed. "Concocting such spectacles was one of Valdemar's greater skills."

"Truly a magician," I agreed. "Or perhaps sorcerer is the better term if one believes his illusions."

Dupin shook his head at me. "Many scientists have been denounced as sorcerers. Eventually they are vindicated."

"But surely Berith will never merit vindication."

"That is not what he meant," Madame Morel countered. "There is no doubting Ernest's genius, it was his character that was irrevocably flawed."

Madame Morel was always exceedingly quick to defend Dupin and while she projected an insurmountable reserve— rather like Dupin—I once again sensed a genuine affection for him, and was therefore finding it increasingly difficult to believe she could ever wish my friend harm.

We made our way through the glowing chamber and into the room where the automatons had been, but it was completely empty. One would hardly know that anything had occurred there the previous night.

Madame Morel answered my unspoken question. "The recompense for setting up the ball and clearing it away was that the workers were permitted to take all the uneaten food, any wine that was left and all the decorations. There will be feasts courtesy of last night's ball for at least a week and the more enterprising amongst them will make quite a profit in the marketplace."

"Who do you suppose took the clockworks, the puppeteer who made them or Reynolds?" I asked.

"The puppeteer, I imagine, who would be glad to make further use of them," Dupin replied. "I should be surprised if Reynolds had come back after murdering Madame Legrand. He would not have received a warm welcome."

"He must have hoped to witness your reaction to the clockwork figures, though," Madame Morel said.

"Whether he found some way to be here or not," Dupin murmured, "Reynolds won't be aware of the outcome of Valdemar's experiment. I wonder if we might use that to our advantage."

His musings were interrupted by a loud bang that made us all jump, followed by boisterous voices. Dupin's rapier was out in an instant and he placed himself in front of Madame Morel and me.

"I see light," came a voice, and moments later, Herr Durand followed his words, with a disgruntled-looking Murphy hard at his heels, each with a pistol in one hand and a torch in the other. "Oh, hello," Durand said, with a smile. "We were expecting someone else entirely."

"I hope so," Dupin said calmly.

"Apologies, madame," Durand said, holstering his pistol in his boot. "We did not wish to frighten you."

"You did not," she said.

It was only then that he—and I—noticed that Madame Morel had a small gun leveled at Durand.

"I see," he said with raised brows. "Well, I am glad of that. But I am less glad that we have not had the pleasure of your acquaintance and you feel the need to protect yourself. I am Rodolph Durand and this is Walter Murphy. We have met your companions several times."

"It is true," Dupin said to Madame Morel as he resheathed his rapier. She lowered her gun, but did not put it away. "These are the gentlemen Dr. Froissart told us about—the Duke of Gerolstein, who goes under an alias while in Paris, and is on a mission to act as the friend and protector of all worthy people who are unhappy." Dupin's tone made it sound as if Durand had committed some crime. Durand frowned but did not retaliate to the implied criticism.

"We understand you are assisting Madame Duresnal in finding her son," I said, attempting to remove some tension from the atmosphere.

"You know the lady?" Durand said with surprise.

"Admirable woman," Murphy added.

"I met her recently at her colony in the tunnels. Dupin is acquainted with her and knows her mushrooms very well."

"Ah, the mushrooms. Delicious." Durand kissed his fingertips. "Yes, we were assisting Madame Duresnal, and I am pleased to have located her son, who is in good health. I have organized a small farm for her to run outside Paris so that she and her son remain safe."

"I see," Dupin said.

"The mushroom farm will continue, fear not, sir," Durand added with a smile. "Now my task is to bring Valdemar to justice. We understand that he has a hideaway in the tunnels?"

"He is dead," Dupin announced.

"Dead?" Durand looked stricken.

"Shouldn't you be pleased with the news of the villain's demise?" Dupin asked.

"We wished to interrogate Valdemar," Murphy interjected. "We were told he had information about Rodolph's daughter, who died under suspicious circumstances twelve years ago."

"And you believe Valdemar might have had a hand in her murder?" Dupin asked.

"In truth, we wish to ascertain if my daughter is truly dead or if there is a chance she is still alive," Durand admitted.

"How can you be unsure if your daughter has died or not?" I asked.

"A damning question you are correct to ask," Durand said. "And it sheds a very poor light on me."

Dupin gave a small sigh of irritation at the fellow's somewhat showy self-abnegation, whereas Madame Morel nodded with agreement.

"It is a complicated tale," Murphy said. "Suffice to say, Rodolph made many poor decisions in his youth, one of which was to be tricked into marriage by an unscrupulous and ambitious woman when he was still an innocent. His father had the marriage annulled, which provoked an unfortunate rage in Rodolph."

"I drew a sword on my own father—there is no way to sugarcoat it," Durand said bitterly. "And I went into exile and have tried, through helping others, to expiate my sin. But I neglected my own child."

"It isn't quite like that," Murphy countered. "The woman who seduced Rodolph was banished by his father and went back to England, where she gave birth to their daughter. Not long after, she married Count MacGregor and Rodolph attempted to get custody of his daughter, but Lady MacGregor refused to let him see the girl."

"When she turned four years old," Durand continued, "her mother—"

"Who had absolutely no interest in the girl except as a pawn," Murphy interjected.

"Her mother sent her to France with two guardians to care for her until she was of school age. She advanced them a very large sum I had sent as a nest egg for little Amelie, but I was told our previously healthy daughter died just a few months after joining those guardians. No satisfactory reason was given for her cause of death."

"And what happened to her body?" Dupin asked.

"It was sent to her mother in Scotland."

"Who thought nothing amiss?"

"Correct."

"As I said, Lady MacGregor has no interest in anyone but herself, including little Amelie, hence sending her away," Murphy added.

"So you never met your daughter?" Madame Morel asked Durand.

"No. But that does not mean I would hesitate to do all in my power to find her—or to seek justice if she was harmed in any way."

Madame Morel nodded her approval.

"We have been in search of her guardians ever since," Durand said, "but they disappear into the insalubrious nooks and crannies of la Cité like ghosts. I presumed they absconded through fear of what the loss of my daughter might unleash in me."

"And how does all this relate to Valdemar?" Dupin asked with more than a touch of impatience.

"We were recently informed by a man in his employ that Monsieur Ernest Valdemar had information regarding my daughter's whereabouts and would supply me with that information in exchange for a certain property in the principality of Gerolstein," Durand explained.

"A type of blackmail," Dupin observed. "When did this happen and why would you give any credibility to such a promise?"

"The day after we arrived in le Havre. The ninth of July," Durand said, reaching into his pocket.

"I was certain someone on the *Independence* was spying on us," Murphy grumbled. "And at the port. It's not the first time we've been followed, despite our efforts to remain incognito," he added.

I had my doubts that the flamboyant Durand ever remained unnoticed for long, despite Murphy's best endeavors.

Durand withdrew a small packet of documents from his coat. "This is what I received from Valdemar."

He revealed a portrait of a young girl. It was charming, a very good pastel drawing of a child of perhaps four years of age, with delicate features, a noble forehead, large eyes the color of bluebells and auburn ringlets. She wore a necklace of coral-pink beads. Attached to it with a seal of wax was a lock of auburn hair.

"It is my daughter, a portrait completed in France just before her health failed."

"Or before she was abducted and falsely registered as dead," Murphy said grimly.

"What is this portrait meant to prove?" I asked.

"I have had its duplicate in my possession for twelve years. Her mother sent it to me with Amelie's death certificate, which I have here." He unfurled the document and showed it to Dupin. "I do not know how or why Valdemar would have a copy of the portrait unless he was somehow responsible for my daughter's fate, one way or the other."

Even by torchlight, it was obvious that Dupin was assessing Durand's tale for clues. "Abduction, theft, and blackmail are certainly crimes Valdemar has committed in the past," he offered. "You state that generous funds were advanced to cover your daughter's expenses for several years. Was any of the money returned to you? Or to Amelie's mother?"

"The money is not the issue," Durand said with an injured air.

Dupin shrugged. "The money was given for a purpose and that purpose died with your daughter. The unused funds should have been returned to you. If your daughter's guardians disappeared with a considerable sum of money, then it supports the notion that they were culpable for her death or disappearance."

"A person of good character would offer to return the funds," I said.

Murphy nodded in agreement. "The money was not returned to Rodolph or Lady MacGregor—she complained bitterly about that."

"May I see the portrait again, please?" Dupin asked. He examined it carefully, then handed the drawing to Madame Morel. "Have you seen it before?"

"No. And I was not aware of any plan on Ernest's part to acquire a property in Gerolstein," she added. "But I wanted nothing to do with his various treacheries."

Dupin nodded, then turned back to Durand. "Your daughter would be about sixteen years old?"

"Last week she would have turned that age," Durand replied.

"I suspect the death certificate is a forgery, based on the actions of her guardians and Valdemar's attempts to extort a property from you. I think there is a chance that your daughter is still alive, though living in conditions that will not please you."

I was surprised by Dupin's declaration, but Durand and Murphy were nonplussed.

"I hope you are not jesting with me, sir," Durand said in a low and dangerous voice.

"He rarely jests and never in circumstances like this," I said, then turned to Dupin. "You have a theory about where Herr Durand's daughter might be?"

"It is merely a supposition, but I believe the girl may be hidden in plain sight at a place you know very well."

Durand narrowed his eyes and shook his head in bafflement. "The Lapin Blanc," Dupin announced.

I quickly understood where Dupin's train of thought was leading. The German, however, remained slack-jawed and silent, which seemed to please Dupin greatly.

"I repeat, it is only a supposition, but a number of things make me think you should investigate the possibility further. First, let us examine the drawing." Dupin held it up. "Consider your daughter's auburn ringlets, her distinctive large blue eyes, the shape of her face." He indicated each on the drawing. "Now let us recall the auburn-haired songstress, the frail girl under the thumb of Mother Ponisse. Her features are remarkably similar."

It was obvious that Durand and Murphy were thinking back to our visit to the Lapin Blanc, trying to remember the girl's features.

"And there is the necklace," Dupin continued, indicating the strand of coral beads depicted in the drawing. "A gift you sent to the child?"

Durand nodded, his astonishment clear. "Yes. How did you know?"

Dupin shrugged. "The girl's mother hoped to manipulate you through your daughter. The inclusion of the necklace in the portrait was to remind you of your connection."

"The songstress in the Lapin Blanc wore the same coral necklace," I said, recollecting the way her fingers nervously touched the beads. "It is close around her throat now that she has grown."

"Quite right, Poe. And did you notice that the girl hastily disappeared when *la Chouette* entered the Lapin Blanc? With a look of pure terror on her face?"

"I noticed she had left, but did not see her reaction to the villainess," I admitted.

"You think *la Chouette* was involved in Amelie's abduction?" Murphy asked.

Dupin shrugged. "It is not impossible given the creature's associates and reputation. It would be wise to find the girl before she does and discover for certain if the songstress of the Lapin Blanc is indeed your daughter risen from the dead."

"Thank you, sir. I almost dare to believe . . ." Durand's words died away, so extreme were his emotions. He took a moment to compose himself then bowed deeply. "Should you—or Mr. Poe or Madame—ever need anything, do not hesitate to call upon me."

"Indeed," Murphy added. "It has been a stroke of luck meeting you in this hellish place." He too bowed.

Dupin's patience came to an end. "May I suggest that you immediately retrace your footsteps and make your way to Île de la Cité before word spreads that you are searching for the girl." My friend did not elaborate how that might possibly happen, but Durand did not think to question him.

The two swashbucklers that fate had thrown into my path charged off in search of the songbird of Île de la Cité. We followed their trail until we came to the western gate and Dupin locked it to keep the empire of the dead safe against any more intruders. Or that is what we hoped.

32

Rubens, Rembrandt, da Vinci and Dürer. Vermeer, Velázquez and de la Tour—their works and other masterpieces covered the walls of what might be called the reception room in that subterranean mansion. Each painting was magnificent, but the display was disconcerting, like a museum gallery with no logic to its display. Furthermore, the room was crowded with elaborate furniture, rich carpets and objets d'art. The effect left one oversatiated by unremitting opulence. This was the room of a man who wanted to show the world how wealthy and powerful he was. And yet, who would ever see his underground palace but him and a few others who were there by force rather than choice?

"It is . . . exuberant," I offered.

"It is hideous. Pretentious and lacking in grace. Each item in the room is masterly—the paintings, the furniture, even the carpets—but to crowd such disparate works of art all into one space, only a madman would consider it," Dupin said cheerfully.

Madame Morel nodded in agreement. She was settled back on a chaise longue that might have belonged to a sultaness, sipping at a glass of cognac. Like me, she seemed to find it difficult to keep her eyes open, but Dupin was animated with nervous energy, his eyes overly bright, his face covered in a damp sheen. He was exultant but did not look well.

"I will alter all that," he announced, gesturing at the room. "I will impose a sense of true harmony upon the place."

"You will stay here?" I asked. "In this *tomb*?"

"It is hardly that, though my grandmother agrees with your assessment. She will take up residence in Undine's house. She prefers it to the tomb, and as you will remember, Valdemar began preparations for her move there."

Madame Morel saw the confusion on my face, for she said, "That is why you found my things in Madame Legrand's bedchamber. I was to live in her house, in her *form*, but as a prisoner. Ernest claimed that it was to make me happy, to prove he still loved me, but if that is love…" She shrugged expressively. "I would have ended my life long ago if it weren't for Auguste."

"And I must presume that is why Valdemar did not murder me, when he undoubtedly had many opportunities to do so," Dupin said. "My existence gave my grandmother a reason to continue."

Madame Morel nodded. "It's true."

"Were you in Paris, in these rooms all this time?" I truly did not know what to make of Madame Morel or her impossible tale, despite my sense that she had some true connection to Dupin.

"No. For many years I lived away from Paris. Ernest feared that I might encounter someone who knew me who would not think me mad if I told them my story. A quite irrational fear, wasn't it, Monsieur Poe?" She gave a wry smile. "It is in part why Ernest accumulated properties in various places. Moving from residence to residence made it more difficult for his enemies to hunt him down and he accrued many enemies. It also gave me something of a life. If we were in Rome or Berlin or London, for example, I was permitted to go to museums, to cafés, to shops and markets—always with a chaperone. I could buy books, attend concerts, walk through a park—I could *breathe*. But if I ever displeased him or if he was traveling, I was locked in the house. All I could do was wait and watch."

"As Valdemar's ambitions grew—his notion to make himself emperor of France—the danger grew to me and others who pursued him for such a long time," Dupin continued. "He had constructed the apartments and laboratory years previously during his smuggling operation, but only brought my grand-mother to live here two summers ago. She believed that this was part of a strategy to bring about my demise."

"As Ernest plotted how he might achieve his political ambi-tions, and as he, in the role of the Great Berith, gathered a following through his magic and mesmerism, I prepared to attempt my escape, carefully observing all I could about the apartments and finding any excuse to explore the tunnels up to the gates that secure this fortress."

"How did you abscond from what you rightly call a fortress? It seems the perfect prison." My own journeys through the tunnels under Dupin's guidance made it difficult for me to believe the lady would easily find her way to the world above, particularly if Berith had been watching her as intently as she claimed.

"I managed to steal the ingredients for a soporific from the laboratory, took Ernest's keys, money, a very small bag, and found my way out. I knew to follow the symbols of Berith and had made a secret study of the quarry markers, but feared even so I would lose my way and die in the tunnels."

"And she arrived on my doorstep asking for a position, claim-ing to be a beleaguered relative," Dupin said.

"You would have thought me a madwoman if I'd told you the truth." Madame Morel smiled fondly at Dupin. "You have witnessed Ernest's talents onstage," she said to me. "It was not trickery. Through mesmerism he made me believe that something dreadful would happen if I revealed anything about this place, about his true identity or mine."

My mind was swimming from the strange tale she wove and I tried to steer the conversation back to more practical realms.

"Dupin, you say that you will remain here and Madame Morel will move into Undine's apartments. But how? She was a very well-known woman—you can't simply usurp her home."

"Ernest purchased Undine's house almost a year ago as she had driven herself into debt. Or perhaps, in truth, he forced her into that position," Madame Morel said. "He permitted her to live there at no monetary cost, but of course Ernest's intent was to take everything from her."

"Obviously Valdemar was going to use Madame Legrand to do an exchange—to transfer my grandmother's spirit-essence into Madame Legrand's body and vice versa. But Reynolds murdered Undine—ruining Valdemar's plans for the transference."

"Madame Legrand's body would be of no use to Ernest after her demise," Madame Morel explained. "His elixir rejuvenated dead plants, but he had not been successful in bringing human corpses back to life, though he claimed it possible."

It is one thing to write a tale in which the uncanny disrupts the ordinary world, it is quite another when one experiences the unexplainable. When Madame Morel talked about her life with the mysterious Valdemar, a man I had heard much about over the years but had only seen in effigy form almost a decade previously, I had the sense she was speaking the truth. I hadn't much cared for Dupin's housekeeper when I first met her such a short time ago, but could not deny that she seemed fiercely protective of him, and she expressed a certain affection toward him, perhaps in a similar way to

Dupin's own reserved expression of friendship. And she knew enough about Sophie Dupin to convince my friend the great ratiocinator that she was truly his grandmother. I almost felt persuaded too . . . But here again was their insistence on Valdemar's mastery of metempsychosis, their shared belief that Valdemar and the Great Berith were one and the same. I could easily believe that he was a younger relation or accomplice, or even, after all the incredible things I had witnessed him perform, that he had somehow created the illusion that he was half his age, but that Valdemar was actually inhabiting the body of someone else?

I did not know if Dupin's enemy was still alive and we were all part of a final Grand Guignol show with Valdemar as puppetmaster or if I had actually witnessed his death, as Dupin and Madam Morel believed. I felt dizzy and more than a little confused.

"Monsieur Poe, are you all right?" Madame Morel's words startled me from my reverie and I found that she was gazing at me with concern.

"I am not sure what to think about anything," I said.

She rose to her feet. "I will wish you goodnight and hope you will feel fully recovered in the morning." She stared at me, and her gray eyes seemed to look directly into my soul. Then she turned to Dupin. "And please, you must rest, Auguste. All of this has depleted you more than you care to admit, even to yourself. I fear you will drive yourself to your death and all we have suffered will be in vain."

"I am fine. I will rest. Fear not."

But neither she nor I believed him. Madame Morel raised her hands slightly then let them drop back to her sides as if the air itself were too weighty. And she abruptly left the room.

Dupin poured us each another measure of cognac. I stared at the amber liquid as I swirled it around the glass.

"It was not easy, what you saw, what you experienced. It would be a shock to both the body and mind," he said quietly.

"I cannot fathom whether what I witnessed actually happened or if it was a vision conjured up from the drug he gave me."

I could still picture Berith's death perfectly, for it was the stuff of nightmares—the dissolving of his flesh and bones to putrid fat and grease, the final horrible flow of black ooze.

"It was not a hallucination. After I pierced his heart with my blade, Valdemar's body dissolved into a black gelatinous substance. I believe the unnatural extension of his life caused him to undergo the accelerated decomposition that you witnessed. I captured some of the essence in a glass bottle and sealed it shut. I will show it to you in the alchemy laboratory as proof if you wish."

I shrugged my shoulders. If what I had witnessed was real, his explanation was as plausible as any.

"As for Madame Morel, when you first queried my decision to employ her as a housekeeper, I told you that I had done so as she informed me that she was related to my father. I tested her knowledge of the Dupin family in numerous ways—historical facts regarding our forebears, the names of my antecedents, information about family heirlooms I recovered from the catacombs. It would be inconceivable for any imposter to have such detailed and correct information—utterly inconceivable. In truth, she knew things that I did not, which were substantiated by my subsequent research. And beyond all that, she is *familiar* to me—she reminds me of my father, perhaps not in the surface of her looks, but her mannerisms, her gestures, certain expressions. She could not know such details to feign them." Dupin paused for a moment, then said, "I am, as you know, a man of logic and deductive reasoning who demands evidence when attempting to unravel a mystery or solve a crime. But I am also a man of science and scholarship and I know that there are many things that seem impossible and strange based on the facts as we currently perceive them and that often new knowledge turns the impossible into possible and makes the strange less threatening."

A vision of Sissy flared in my mind and I considered how, in my heart, I believed that she—her spirit—had somehow torn the forged letter into four pieces, that she had tried to warn me of danger. I wondered if my sense that one might return from death in hopes of protecting a loved one was any less incredible than Dupin's belief that Madame Morel was in truth Madame Dupin, his grandmother, merely in another form.

"I have long struggled, as you know, to put an end to Valdemar. Perhaps it has been too much the focus of my life," Dupin added softly. "There is something I must tell you—and ask of you," he continued in a low, calm voice. "You know that I am not well. You observed my decline when you first arrived, yet politely did not comment. You spoke with Dr. Froissart after he came to attend to me and you are aware that I take his *elixir vitae*—which I do purely to humor Froissart and to comfort Madame Morel." He closed his eyes, breathed in deeply, then out again before returning his gaze to mine. "While I may seem relatively well, Poe, the truth is that I am dying."

His declaration was made without emotion, and despite the fact that I had intuited what he had proclaimed, his words shook me.

"Angina pectoris," he said, waving at the left side of his chest. "It may be an organic affliction, Froissart tells me, caused by damage to an artery so the heart is overpowered with blood accumulated in its cavities. He also offers a less scientific theory based on the writings of Napoleon's physician, Jean Nicolas Corvisart, which seeks to connect psyche and soma. Froissart thinks the anxious passions of men, as he puts it, cause physical defects of the heart, and the elixirs he concocts are meant to counter this. I am certain they do nothing at all. Worse still, Froissart will not venture a prognosis regarding how much time might be left to me." Dupin offered a wry smile. "He has merely told me that I might feel a terrible ache in my chest and simply fall down dead."

I do not know what I had suspected Dupin's ailment to be. I had tried to get Froissart to reveal Dupin's secret, but in truth I did not try very hard and nor did I directly confront my friend. And it was not from politeness as Dupin presumed. It was because I was afraid. To give a name to his illness and be told there was no remedy was to give that insidious thing power by murdering hope. And I knew also, in my own battered heart, that my friend abhorred commiserations and would not generously receive any that I might offer.

"I am glad you have confided in me and it is difficult to express how sorry I am. Please know that I want to assist in any way I can and hope you trust me enough to let me try."

"Thank you, Poe. Truly." Dupin's expression was solemn.

"And I beg you to continue with Dr. Froissart's elixirs. There may be no proof that they will cure you, but if there is any possibility, then you must keep taking them." Before Dupin could protest, I added: "If a doctor half as learned as Dr. Froissart had attended to Sissy and offered elixirs to treat her illness or mitigate her pain, I would have used them all."

Dupin nodded once. "I understand." He paused for a moment, then ventured: "You confided that your wife's apparition has visited you several times since her untimely death and that her presence provided you with some comfort."

"On several occasions I felt she was with me, yes, and that was a comfort, though I cannot honestly say whether the spirit of my wife was with me or the vision was merely a manifestation of my hopes."

Dupin nodded again, steepled his hands together, pressed them to his forehead, then asked, "Where is it said that our spirit, our soul, must die? Or that it does die? Perhaps it is temporarily homeless. What if the body is simply a shell that may be shed like that of a crustacean that has outgrown its home? What if a new home were provided for it?" Dupin flung his hands open and then clasped them again, as if capturing ideas from the ether. Then he looked directly at me. "There is plenty of the philosopher's stone solution left, and I have studied alchemy and metempsychosis long enough to grasp how the transfer would work."

I frowned at Dupin's words, hoping that I was misunderstanding them.

"Madame Morel knows a strong, healthy fellow who is willing to undergo a transfer in order to better the life of his family. And before you ask, it is not my grandmother's suggestion that I pursue this course of action. It is fully my idea. In fact, she advises against it."

"Then you must listen to her. If she herself has undergone metempsychosis as you believe, then she must know its dangers and fear you will fail—that you will die."

"As I have just explained," Dupin said quietly, "I *will* die and possibly soon unless I find a way to save myself. There is nothing for me to lose in trying and everything to gain."

There was little I could say to counter that, given his prognosis and the fact that he believed Ernest Valdemar had discovered a way to cheat death by transporting himself into another body.

"If metempsychosis were possible," I said, changing tack, "surely it is an abomination, for it goes against the laws of Nature."

"Why? If man has the intelligence to find his spirit a new vessel when the old one begins to wear out, then what is wrong with that?" Dupin stared at me.

"Do not forget that Berith or Valdemar, or whoever he was, attempted to transfer himself into my body, utterly against my will. Is it ethical to exchange your body with its weak heart for the other fellow's healthy body?"

"He is aware of my ill health. And he will profit greatly from the exchange, for he owes money to people who will not hesitate to murder him or his family. Instead he will be able to pay his debts and they will move into my apartment, and everything there, aside from some family treasures, will become theirs to enjoy. I will take over Valdemar's residence."

"A devil's pact," I muttered.

"Not at all," Dupin replied. "His family's life will be much improved and possibly he will recover with Dr. Froissart's elixirs, as you yourself suggested is possible."

My appeals to his intellect had failed and silence—oppressive and fragile—conquered us for a time.

"It seems I cannot dissuade you," I finally said.

"No," Dupin agreed. "But I need your assistance. I can do the mechanics of the operation myself, but I wish to know when I emerge if my memories are fully intact, for I am nothing without my mind, without my memory. You know me better than anyone, Poe. I would trust no other."

I drained my glass of cognac, then said carefully, calmly and in a voice designed to end our argument, "I will not go to that infernal laboratory with you, and I most certainly will not watch as you kill yourself and murder a poor unfortunate. You ask too much, Dupin." I started to stand up, but Dupin grasped my wrist tightly and fixed me in his intense gaze.

"I will go through with my plan whether you are there or not, but I ask as a friend that you help me." His grip on my wrist intensified and he continued in a low voice: "For if I fail, as you believe I will, I would be grateful if you would ensure that I am laid to final rest in my family's tomb." He released my hand and dropped his gaze, his eyes fixed on some invisible thing upon the table. "I fear that if the experiment fails, Valdemar's laboratory will become my crypt and then truly he will have won, for it is impossible that I could ever be more alone than that," he murmured.

Dupin's words filled the air until it assumed the weight of water and pressed down on us both. I was enraged by his foolhardy stubbornness and yet my heart ached at his words. If Sissy were there at that very moment, she would instinctively know exactly what to say and do and all would be well, but I could not find her spirit in that place and could not think of a single argument or consolation. When the silence finally became utterly unbearable, I said in a voice that was cracked and imperfect, trembling like the last leaf on the branch as winter creeps in: "*Amicis semper fidelis.*"

"Thank you," my friend replied softly.

I could think of nothing else to say. Perhaps those words were enough.

33

TUESDAY, 17 JULY 1849

The clink of cutlery on china rang out like a discordant piece of music played by an orchestra whose members were pained by each clanking note. We had returned to number thirty-three rue Dunôt to breakfast with the fellow who had agreed to be Dupin's partner—or perhaps victim—in his experiment. Despite myself, I was half-amused by Dupin's choice of a subject, for he was approximately twenty-five years of age, with pleasing Italian looks—curling ebony hair, large hazel eyes, full lips—he might have stepped from a Caravaggio painting. He was roughly Dupin's height, but far more muscular in form. Monsieur Pier Judici was a stove-fitter with a large family who lived in the rue Saint-Lazare amongst a community of Italians from Domo d'Ossola. He struggled to put enough food on the table and had borrowed heavily from ruthless moneylenders. His wife had been recruited to cook for Madame Morel and their daughter Madeleine was Madame's personal servant. Dupin had offered to give Judici his apartment on rue Dunôt along with a small fortune to participate in a daring experiment and the desperate fellow had agreed. As the impoverished stove-fitter wolfed down his breakfast, he said nothing, but his eyes darted around the room, taking in all the details.

"The furniture will stay?" he finally asked.

"Yes," Dupin said. "And a selection of linens, the kitchen items."

For two days Madame Morel had organized the removal of Dupin's books, writing desk, paintings, objets d'art and coat of arms along with some clothing and other personal effects. The strange chambers Dupin was moving into had all the expensive furniture, necessities and luxuries anyone might desire.

Monsieur Judici nodded. "And the costs? All will be paid even if the exchange is not a success? I must be certain my family is safe."

"Yes, they will be met. Madame Morel will see to that. And fear not, the exchange will be a success."

The young man nodded again, satisfied, but I was not. Dupin's foolhardy venture was bound to fail, leaving him either disappointed or dead. Furthermore, I still could not rid myself fully of my suspicions toward Madame Morel. She might yet prove to be an imposter who had found the perfect way to acquire Dupin's apartment and wealth with his own permission. The only way my doubts would ever be laid to rest was by witnessing metempsychosis with my own eyes: the very thing I was desperate for my friend not to attempt, as I feared it would end him.

Monsieur Judici put down his cutlery just seconds before Madame Morel entered the room. "It is time. His family will be here in two hours."

"Very good," Dupin said, as we stood up. "You will ensure they are settled in?"

She nodded.

"You are not coming with us?" I asked suspiciously.

She shook her head silently and showed Monsieur Judici out to the hall.

I was about to follow when Dupin took me by the arm. "I told you before, she does not want me to undertake the transferral. She seems to trust Froissart's elixirs more than my ability to master Valdemar's experiment." His face expressed how ridiculous he found that notion. "But it is my decision. And Monsieur Judici's. We will proceed."

We took a carriage to Cimetière du Sud and I watched as Monsieur Judici's air of calm diminished steadily as we entered the tomb and descended into the catacombs. When we walked into the alchemy chamber with the skull decorations and the fierce owl on the wall, his courage disappeared completely, or so it seemed by the trembling of his lower lip that he tried to hide with a shaking hand. His eyes darted nervously this way and that, taking in all the accouterments from Valdemar's failed metempsychosis attempt. He stared with unconcealed fear at the large glass alchemy vessel with its strange masks on the trolley between the two leather chairs. The mist that had been inside the peculiar vessel had transformed back into a blue shimmering liquid and had the look of some beautiful poison.

"Poe, would you light the candles while I prepare? And you, Monsieur Judici, please sit." Dupin indicated the leather chair I had been imprisoned in.

I did as Dupin asked, creating a sulfur fug by lighting all the candles I could see. When the room was a-glow, Dupin consulted a book Valdemar had left on the alchemy table and looked strangely confident, whereas the young man, his likely victim, seemed ever more fearful, particularly when Dupin said: "Bar the door, please, Poe."

I did as he asked while Dupin lit a candle under the alchemy flask that held the mixture containing the philosopher's stone. When it was to his satisfaction, he retrieved the red jewel from his pocket and hung it on the alchemy vessel just as Berith had done. He took his seat facing Monsieur Judici.

"Poe, if you would fasten us both in. It is important," he told the young fellow, "that the masks remain on until the transfer is complete or the experiment will be compromised."

"And we will die?" Judici said fearfully.

"There is a possibility as I explained before," Dupin said. "So let us ensure that all goes smoothly." He strapped his left arm to the chair and looked at me expectantly. I hesitated, then reluctantly fastened the other. "Would you help Monsieur Judici, Poe? And when I say, put the masks on us both."

His words made my stomach roil. Dupin had maneuvered things so that I had no choice but to participate in an experiment I was fully opposed to.

"You are not obliged to go through with this," I said in a low voice to Dupin. "Monsieur Judici will understand."

Dupin fixed me with a fierce glare. "I will not change my mind and nor will he. If you would prefer to leave, very well. Unstrap me and I will manage alone, as Valdemar did."

Of course, he would. When Dupin decided on something, he rarely changed his mind. Normally his decisions were made logically, using his formidable intellect. In this instance, he was driven by hope that a madman's claims might be true. But I could not leave him—*them*—to die alone in the catacombs. So I strapped in Monsieur Judici as instructed.

Dupin's glare softened and he nodded once in thanks, then said: "Monsieur Judici, please stare at the red jewel here. Nothing else. Only the red jewel. Focus on its center."

The fellow did as Dupin instructed and his face changed from fear to wonderment.

"There is a figure," he said. "It is moving. It is *dancing*."

"Yes. Keep watching it. Soon, you will see nothing but the dancing figure. I will count to ten and when I finish you will be in a trance. Then Mr. Poe will put the mask on you and turn this valve here to let the elixir flow. Do you agree?"

"Yes," he said softly.

And Dupin began to count, his voice soothing and soporific, the red jewel with its dancing figure captivating. My own lids began to flutter shut.

"Ten, nine, eight . . ."

Dupin's firm voice had the effect of jolting me awake, whereas Judici's gaze was still utterly fixed on the jewel. My friend nodded to me and I put the mask over the young man's face and then over Dupin's, hoping that I was not sending my friend and the desperate fellow to their deaths. I checked the glass vessel as instructed—there was the same roiling cloud inside it, tinted with blues and purple, pinks and gold, so I turned the valve and the fog oozed into the tubing. Both breathed in and out deeply, their chests rising up and falling back down ever more quickly until each twitched and shivered in a horrible way as their eyes bulged and blinked furiously. It was hideous to watch, wondering, heart trembling, if I should intervene. When the last wisps of fog curled up through the glass and into the tubing, each heaved a sigh and their bodies relaxed, their eyes closed and their heads lolled forward. I blew out the candles that warmed the vessel, closed my eyes and muttered an improvised prayer. After what seemed an eternity, I heard a rustling and my eyes flew open—and my gaze met Monsieur Judici's. Dupin did not move and I could discern no breathing. My heart dropped in my chest.

"Unstrap my arms, please," Monsieur Judici said, breaking the spell.

I immediately did so, and he stood up and tentatively stretched.

"It feels . . . strange," he said. "It's almost as if I need to *think* to move my hand before it does so and to *will* my legs to move before I walk." He took several cautious steps toward Dupin, leaned over and studied Dupin's face, then waved his palm in front of it. "He breathes."

I quickly joined him by Dupin's side and patted my friend's cheek gently. "Dupin, wake up. Can you hear me?"

Moments later his eyes fluttered open and a look of confusion filled his face. I unstrapped his arms and he slowly stood up with great effort.

"It worked?" he asked, his voice quavering with disbelief.

"Yes, it seems so," Judici said.

The two men examined their hands, their bodies, then each walked tentatively around the room, like some newborn creature learning how its legs worked. Then they scrutinized each other with wonderment.

"How do you feel?" Judici asked Dupin.

"Exhausted. Everything is heavy and stiff." He gently shook his hands.

Judici nodded. "Do you remember what happened before you woke up in the chair?"

Dupin nodded slightly, but his expression was of disbelief. "We had breakfast at the apartment, then we took a carriage to the cemetery. And then we came here." It was odd to see the normally confident Dupin struggle for words. "Monsieur Poe helped strap us into the chairs and put on the masks. There was a very cold sensation throughout my body and I must have fallen asleep. When I woke up, I was . . . changed."

"Yes, that is correct," Judici said. "Tell me about yourself and your family—who you were *before*," he added, gesturing at his own body.

"My wife is called Véronique. We have been married for ten years. My children are Emile, Madeleine, Victurien, Armande, Marie and Pierre. My mother-in-law is Béatrix. I am a stove-fitter by trade."

"You remember everything about your past life?" Judici asked and Dupin nodded. Or it looked like Dupin, but there was something different in his gestures, his mannerisms. His tangible sense of fear.

"And now let us discuss your new identity," Judici said to the man who looked like Dupin. "There is one important thing I ask of you and your family: always use your new name."

The fellow nodded. "François Dupin." He examined the fronts and backs of his hands with wonder, then peered at the gold *chevalière*, set with a lapis lazuli intaglio engraved with the Dupin coat of arms.

"Where do you live and why are you there?"

"Apartment thirty-three rue Dunôt, Faubourg Saint-Germain," he recited. "I am François Dupin, brother of Auguste Dupin, who has gone to Budapest for his studies. I do not know when he will return."

"Very good." Monsieur Judici smiled. "Madame Morel will ensure that you have all you need for the next few days. Now let us guide you to your new home."

In a strange reversal of our journey to the alchemy laboratory, the jovial Italian and I led a nervous Dupin through the tunnels and thence in a carriage to thirty-three rue Dunôt, and all the while I had the peculiar sense that I was captive in some waking dream, even to the point where we waved Dupin farewell.

After we made our way back to the underground compound, Monsieur Judici led the way to the reception room that was crowded with valuable paintings. The fellow had not been to that room before, but certainly Dupin had. We settled ourselves into armchairs.

"Are you amazed, Poe? You were quite certain the experiment would be a failure."

"It is truly you?" I asked hesitantly. "Do you remember everything . . . that makes you—"

"The Chevalier C. Auguste Dupin? I believe I do. I am the son of François and Eleanor Dupin and the grandson of Charles and Sophie Dupin. Before they married, Sophie de Bourdeille was betrothed to Ernest Valdemar. And when she left him for my grandfather, Valdemar swore he would destroy the Dupin family." He raised his eyebrows and looked at me in that challenging way that Dupin had. "Am I correct?"

"Yes. Yes, you are correct."

"But this information is not difficult to find out and could be taught to Monsieur Judici the stove-fitter." He paused to think, gazing in apparent wonder at his hands, his legs, his body. "Let me see. Perhaps this will convince you," he continued. "When we were in London together in July 1840, we tried on several occasions to meet the writer Charles Dickens, but instead we regrettably made the acquaintance of his irascible pet raven. And when I visited you, your delightful wife Virginia and your practical mother-in-law in Philadelphia five years ago, we met a number of peculiar characters, including Mrs. Mermaid and a young lockpick called Billy Sweeney."

These were indeed facts that no one but Dupin could readily recite. A shiver crawled my spine, for as much as everything about his character and manner was utterly *Dupin*, the exterior was not. The comely young man of toil with his jolly face and stocky frame was my friend's polar opposite in form, and I struggled mightily with the reality I found myself in.

"*Amicis semper fidelis*," the fellow said with a smile. "Always faithful to my friends. It was your promise to me before the experiment and has always been my promise to you." He turned slowly, examining the dizzying array of paintings that filled the walls. "Valdemar built a kingdom beneath Paris, it is undeniable." He faced me again and said, "But at last the serpent is crushed." His eyes narrowed in satisfaction as he smiled.

And I felt completely certain that the man before me was Dupin, merely in a different form—or else that all reason had finally abandoned me.

34

WEDNESDAY, 18 JULY 1849

Our lantern lights soared and dipped and wheeled through the darkness, but revealed nothing except the ghostly walls pressing in around us. We were making our way back to the theater on rue de la Gaîté as Dupin had announced the previous evening that he had a notion Reynolds might be hiding there:

"I suspect he was allowed to stay in the apartment above the theater, with the promise from Valdemar that the entire building would be his once he helped Valdemar to destroy me," Dupin had explained.

"Valdemar owns the theater?"

"Yes, according to papers I found in his study. It would be quite a prize, wouldn't it, for a playwright to have his own theater?"

"Of course. Reynolds could have all his dreadful theatricals performed and it would not matter if the seats were empty."

Dupin had laughed, an oddly merry sound, utterly unlike any expression of mirth my friend used to make. "It occurred to me that Reynolds might be living there when I thought about the bride in the casket and the plaque predicting your demise in the mausoleum, for the theater is very close to the Cimetière du Sud. Reynolds would have been able to move between the two locations via the tunnels at any hour, making it far simpler to arrange that terrible surprise for you."

"Without anyone noticing," I added.

Dupin's suggestion made sense. But would he still be there after what had happened with Undine? Dupin seemed to think that it was possible, given the speed at which rumors of Valdemar's demise and the Great Berith's disappearance were likely to spread.

And so now, before the rising of the sun, we were making our way through the tunnels once again, hoping to surprise my enemy in his bed at the apartment above the theater on rue de la Gaîté and deliver him to Monsieur Gondureau.

"Poe, look." Dupin held his lantern directly in front of himself and a stairway made of wood. "We've arrived. Come."

He climbed the stairs with all the energy of a man who had just entered the third decade of his life and I followed. At the top, he pushed open a door and we were back in the concealed chamber under the stage of the theater. It seemed as if we had been in that oppressive space months previously rather than mere days ago. Dupin located the trapdoor, cautiously pushed it upward and peered through the gap.

"Empty." He heaved the trapdoor completely up and climbed out. I followed. We stood on the stage where the Great Berith had fascinated the mob, but faced rows of empty seats. "Let us proceed cautiously," Dupin said rather unnecessarily.

We made our way quietly to the back of the theater, where he had decided the staircase must be. He was proved right and we silently climbed the stairs until we came to the upper floor. Dupin picked the lock and eased the door open. We tiptoed in, lanterns held low.

The apartment was certainly lived in, well furnished, and there were paintings on the walls. Dupin led the way toward where the bedroom was likely to be. When we reached the end of the hallway, he eased open the door and peered in, then turned to me and shook his head. I quietly retreated and tried another door. Inside was a study, but that was empty also. The back of my neck prickled and I turned—my heart juddered at the sight of a man creeping down the hall toward me, for at first I was certain it was Reynolds. But it proved to be my friend, incognito. Or that is how I tried to make my mind accept Dupin's new form. He shrugged and led the way back to the sitting room, checked the curtains, cupboards, everywhere a person might hide, but it seemed that Reynolds was not there.

Dupin turned on the gaslights and we searched again. There were signs that Reynolds had lived there—framed posters on the walls of plays his wife had been in, some of which were written by him. There was some clothing in the wardrobe that might have been his, books, a writing desk with paper, ink, pens. But Reynolds himself was gone.

Dupin held up a folded piece of paper. "It is addressed to you."

I joined him at the dining table where the note had been left and opened it.

20 rue de la Gaîté, Montparnasse
14 July 1849

Dear Mr. Poe,

If you receive this letter, then you have survived the Victim's Ball and perhaps your friend Dupin has made an end to that dissembler who calls himself the Great Berith. I hope so. If you have died, then I will deeply regret your passing, as the final act of our little play will be unsatisfying to me. I pray that is not the case.

I must now leave Paris as Berith or his employer, Valdemar, will murder me for poor Undine's fate. I intend to return to the country that established my reputation and begin again. And I will find you. My arrival will be unexpected and you will understand your fate too late to alter it. And then at last your debt to me and my family will be erased.

I remain respectfully yours,
George Rhynwick Reynolds

I handed the letter to Dupin, who quickly read it.

"I am sorry, Poe," he said. "I hoped we would finally conclude things with Reynolds here."

I nodded, but realized that I had not dared to believe that the earnest young man before me would bring an end to my enemy when the inscrutable Dupin could not.

When we returned to the underground chambers, Madame Morel—or Madame Dupin as she now expected to be called—was instructing the girl Madeleine and Madeleine's mother what to pack for her move to Undine's house and what to leave behind. But she stopped her tasks to stare or perhaps marvel at Dupin.

"How do you feel?" she asked.

"Aggrieved. Poe's enemy abandoned his lair. He is gone—back to America."

Madame Morel shrugged slightly. "Good riddance. He knew too much and was a danger to us."

"It is Poe I'm concerned about."

Madame shrugged again. "From what you have told me, Monsieur Reynolds has not managed in almost a decade to truly put Monsieur Poe's life in danger. Instead he has merely tormented him. We must hope that this incompetence

continues." She bestowed a smile on me. "Dinner will be at six
o'clock. I will see you both then." And with that Madame
Morel dismissed us and returned to her packing, while Dupin
and I retreated to the sitting room with its array of paintings.
Dupin poured us each a glass of cognac and collapsed into an
armchair.

"I should have fathomed where Reynolds was sooner," he
complained.

"It matters not. The letter is merely a threat designed to
unnerve me. Indeed, he doesn't know if I am dead or alive."

Dupin contemplated this for a moment, then said, "Why not
preserve his ignorance on that matter? Stay here in Paris. Stay
here—then you will be completely safe."

"Here? In this opulent dungeon?"

Dupin laughed. "Yes, of course. As you know, I have given
my apartment to Monsieur Judici. This is to be my home now.
The space is vacant and is ingeniously constructed. It is
furnished, there is room for both of us and our possessions, it
has an enviable library—to which I will add my own collection—and a laboratory. And it will cost nothing. Why not?"

Why not? Because those decadent chambers were located in
the catacombs, with the discarded bones of all the dead congre-
gated there. Because it would be living underground like a
burrowing creature, a corpse or Hades himself. Why *not*? Most
would avoid such a place with every fiber of their being, but not
Dupin. If any doubt had lingered within me regarding whether
I'd been duped with some incredible hoax and that the metempsychosis was all a sham, my reservations would have been
erased. My friend, who enjoyed nothing more than wandering
Paris at night like some nocturnal creature, only he might relish
the thought of living in a city beneath the city of his birth—of
living in the empire of the dead.

"And of course we will never want for anything." He indicated the treasures in the room. "It is incredible that Valdemar amassed so much plunder."

"Will you try to return it?"

Dupin shook his head. "That is impossible. If I should happen to discover that anything in these rooms had sentimental value to some person, it will be returned to them, but will I waste my time trying to locate the original owners? No."

"You will continue Valdemar's practice of auctioning his plunder?"

"The trifles, yes. There is quite a collection of jewels, most of limited historical value. I will find a way for the Louvre to procure the important paintings."

"And will you continue Valdemar's studies?"

Dupin looked at me as if I had said something insufferably stupid.

"Of course! If a man of Valdemar's intellect managed to create the philosopher's stone and discover how to put the principles of metempsychosis into action, consider what I might be able to achieve?"

Dupin was never one to pretend his talents or intellect were any less than they were, but it was odd to hear his frank comments delivered in such a different voice and form.

"What would you hope to achieve?" I asked. "It appears that the experiment worked. Your memory and intellect seem unimpaired from what I can gather."

"I agree with the second part of your statement," Dupin said, and smiled. "As to what I hope to achieve—you will remember that my grandmother spoke of Valdemar's attempts to bring dead creatures back to life. She said that once death had occurred, once the spirit had been fully severed from the body, Valdemar could not reanimate the body. But what if that were achievable?"

His question brought the most ghoulish images to my mind. "You don't mean to play resurrection man with the corpses from the morgue? It is unspeakable, Dupin."

I expected him either to argue or reassure me, but he did neither. Instead he looked at me intensely and said, "Do you see the possibilities of metempsychosis now? If there was a chance to bring your wife back from death, to rehouse her spirit in a new form, would you not leap at it?"

"What? No. As much as I miss her, it would be . . . *wrong*."

"Would it? Your wife died when very young—'before her time' is how many would describe it. What would be wrong in giving her the chance to live into her old age? With you? Surely an intelligent and gracious woman such as your wife had more to offer the world?"

Obviously she did, but the notion of bringing her back from death filled me with horror and I simply could not speak.

"It is not an alien notion to you, Poe." Dupin stared at me with a gentle smile, his young, handsome face at odds with his intense, knowing gaze. "Stay in Paris—stay here. Write. Help me with my work." His voice was persuasive, his eyes mesmerizing—it was as if he knew all the tricks of the magician he had finally conquered and was trying them on me.

But a movement and a breeze captured my attention. Or perhaps it was a voice. And I shifted my gaze to the doorway and saw my wife Virginia standing there. She beckoned to me once, then called out my name so that it echoed through the chamber.

And I ran. Away from my friend—or perhaps a stranger who seemed to have the knowledge and the spirit of Dupin. I truly did not know. As I ran down the oppressive corridors built from pale limestone, I would catch a glimpse of Sissy just ahead, moving swiftly, leading the way.

Words came into my head: *Do not look back. Do not.*

For I believed that if I did, either she or I would be lost in the empire of the dead forever.

At last I reached the stone staircase and made my way up, looking for blue sky, our treasured garden in the spring, the hummingbird pair whirring and darting, and my wife.

35

SUNDAY, 7 OCTOBER 1849

She does not leave me, the little tortoiseshell. She sits where I can see her, as if on guard, tail curled around herself. Detritus whirls in hypnotic circles and dust sprays into my eyes, which fall open and closed. Rain patters around me, but splintering light fills my head with sparks and jumbles my thoughts. Only the cool of the cobblestones against my cheek diminishes the pain. Shoes, rustling skirts, the tap of walking sticks . . . but no one seems to see me here, disgraced, my arm—I think it is mine—flung before me on the ground, wrapped in a coat sleeve that I do not recognize, the cuffs worn and dirty. I am ashamed.

Later, a murmuring near my ear, words I cannot quite discern, then hands on my arms and feet, and I'm lifted like a sack of flour and lugged, awkwardly, into some pleasantly shaded place. I try to speak, to explain what I remember, but a violent nausea overtakes me and my words are lost. Finally, I slip into blessed slumber.

My disgrace is not yet complete. When I come to again, a council is being held above me, blurred faces staring down, voices I know. No effort is made to conceal their contempt for

my lack of temperance, for having drunk myself into a stupor—
and this from my friend Joseph Snodgrass, and my uncle, Henry
Herring. Again, I am roughly collected up, put into a carriage
and taken to the hospital. Relief. At last, they will see what truly
ails me. They will see.

But I am fully wrong.

The strange clothes I have somehow acquired are removed
and taken away. A damp cloth sponges away the filth from the
street and another is left on my brow to take away the
heat. The fresh sheets are a calmative and I dip into sleep, but
there is a knot of memories inside my head that I cannot
untangle.

*A man staggers, his clothes ruined, drenched through with salted
water from his own body. He rubs at his eyes and smacks his parched
lips.*

I can feel his pain in my own head, the pit of my stomach,
the fire consuming my skin.

*When he tries to speak, his tongue protrudes uselessly from his
mouth, swollen and red, and his eyes glitter strangely, black and
utterly empty. His breath is ragged. The words do not come.*

Just as I cannot answer those gathered around me, whose
faces are impossible to make out. They are wondering how I
ended up lying in the street and argue about what is wrong with
me. Yesterday they had thought me overwhelmed by drink,
today they are not so certain. Watch and wait. Nothing more
we can do.

The sheets are cool, the room is dark. I should perhaps allow
my mind to sink into the heaviness of sleep, but I fear that if I
do, I will not swim back up into wakefulness. And I feel that
the tangled knot is loosening, that when I separate out each
strand, I will remember what—and who—brought me to this
place.

From a distance, a voice: "A visitor for Mr. Poe."

My vision is blurred and I cannot discern the details of the face that peers down at me.

"How pleasant to see you again." The voice is hard and arrogant. I know it, but cannot put a name to it. "I swore that I would even the scales, that the wrongs your family inflicted upon mine would be redressed."

The face looking down on me moves in and out of focus. It is a cruel face and familiar.

"You have written that a wrong is unredressed when retribution overtakes its redresser, and that it is equally unredressed when the avenger fails to make himself felt as such to him who has done the wrong. I am confident that I, as avenger, have satisfied both your tenets of justice, for you have long known my aim but no other person living will grasp that your life was cut short with purpose."

The name, I cannot remember the name of the man who has long tormented me and who does so still.

"I fear you do not recall how your family's crimes were redressed. I will tell you. We were at Gunner's Hall. You'd had a drink and I had another delivered to you—a dwale, wine fortified with belladonna. There is an elegance in that if we consider the actions of your grandmother."

A woman tips the contents of a cobalt blue bottle into a flask of water. A man gulps it back. It's night. The pair walk together and she supports him across the sands that border the sea. And then she walks away alone.

"Your grandmother ensured that my father was imprisoned for her crimes, then silenced your grandfather so the truth would not see her hanged. She escaped retribution, but you have not. Goodbye, Mr. Poe. Our business is finally done. *In pace requiescat.*"

And the heavy presence leaning above me fades away, the tormenting voice stops at last. The truth roars over me like a fierce wave, the sort that knocks you down, half drowns you. I was not overcome by my intemperance. I do not have some fever or other natural ailment. I have, most assuredly, been poisoned. And the culprit's face appears before me, clearly this time, as if he has returned to my bedside to revel in his handiwork. George Rhynwick Williams, the man who now calls himself George Reynolds, has finally murdered me.

When Dr. Snodgrass returns, I try to speak the name of the man who ended me.

"Reynolds," I tell him. "It was Reynolds."

He either cannot hear me or the words that tumble out make no sense to him. But Dupin must be told the truth, that I have not willfully taken myself to an early grave, but have been ushered there by the enemy he knows so well. Dupin will seek justice.

"Reynolds," I say again as loudly as I can. I repeat it over and over. "*Nemo me impune lacessit*—you must tell Dupin. It was Reynolds."

But to those all around me, my words are the babbling of a man who has lost his reason. Nothing more.

I come awake. I do not know how much time has passed. The little tortoiseshell cat is walking on my bed with delicate footsteps until she reaches my shoulder, and she stops to stare down at me with her peridot eyes. Then she curls up against my chest and purrs, her hum snaking through me, and I am comforted.

The stars have long since vanished and the birds begin their celebratory singing as morning prepares to breathe light into the darkness. Then, somewhere very far away, I hear her joining them in song.

"Virginia?"

Her beautiful voice rises up around me and dissolves the pain that has been my constant companion since my arrival in this place.

"Sissy?"

At last she arrives, barely perceptible in the shadows, then increasingly tangible. She glides to my bed and looks down at me and I am filled with joy. Her face, her beautiful face—I once believed I had memorized every aspect of it, but to see it now, close enough to touch, love pierces through me, fresh and fatal.

I have regrets, many more than I care to recall. I have perhaps made more enemies than friends, have produced no son or daughter to grieve my passing or to remember me fondly. I leave behind only my sister, who scarcely knows me, and my dear mother-in-law, who will struggle without me. Both things fill me with sadness. My legacy is ink on paper, words scratched out, fictions turned to memories contrived from a restless mind. These too perhaps will be forgotten, vanquished by time as must be our fate.

I feel myself falling, as if into seawater, sinking down as the green-blue closes overhead and pulls the very breath from me. And then I see her again. She stands at the side of my bed, whole and healthy and beautiful. She is so calm and perfect. My racing heart stills and my breath, which has raged against my chest like a moth throwing itself against the window glass, slows and calms until it is perfectly quiet. My wife reaches out her hand to me and I fold it into mine.

"My darling," I say. "I have waited much too long."

Her fingers stroke my brow and the fever lodged there dissipates like mist under sunlight.

"And I have missed you more than words can possibly say."

"I am glad," I tell her. "But I am sorry too."

She leans to kiss me, then gently pulls me to my feet. "Come. Let us go home."

She walks back into the shadow and I follow.

ACKNOWLEDGMENTS

Many thanks, as always, to my very wonderful agent Oli Munson. Thanks also to Florence Rees and the entire fantastic team at A.M. Heath.

I'm very grateful to my editor, the lovely Jenny Parrott, and to Paul Nash, Margot Weale, Thanhmai Bui-Van, Harriet Wade, Anne Bihan, Charlotte Norman, and all at Point Blank/ Oneworld Publications.

It was a delight to work again with the incredible Helen Szirtes, such an eagle-eyed, creative and patient copyeditor. Huge thanks to my writer/reader friends: Alice Bowen, Shauna Gilligan, Sally Griffiths, Andrew Middleton. And cheers, Alice, for wandering Paris with me and to Frances Clarke, Jeanine Hurley, Mandy Steele and John Hoare—you are life-savers!

Thanks also Darren Hill, friends and family for all the support. Much appreciated.